A 2021 Vivian Award ⬚⬚⬚ ⬚⬚⬚
in the romance indust⬚ ⬚⬚⬚⬚
stylish and sensational ⬚⬚⬚⬚
emotionally epic tales ⬚⬚⬚⬚⬚⬚
by reality's paintbrush. ⬚⬚⬚⬚⬚⬚⬚ ⬚⬚⬚
unapologetically bold, c⬚⬚⬚⬚⬚⬚ven stories.
Her novels feature diverse ensemble casts who
are confident in their right to appear on the page.
Contact her at dot.cards/laquette.

Maya Blake's hopes of becoming a writer were
born when she picked up her first romance at
thirteen. Little did she know her dream would come
true! Does she still pinch herself every now and
then to make sure it's not a dream? Yes, she does!
Feel free to pinch her, too, via X, Facebook or
Goodreads! Happy reading!

ROYALLY HIS

LaQUETTE

MAYA BLAKE

MILLS & BOON

First published in Great Britain 2025
by Mills & Boon, an imprint of HarperCollins*Publishers* Ltd,
1 London Bridge Street, London, SE1 9GF

www.harpercollins.co.uk

HarperCollins*Publishers*, Macken House, 39/40 Mayor Street Upper,
Dublin 1, D01 C9W8, Ireland

ISBN: 978-0-263-34488-2

11/25

MIX
Paper | Supporting
responsible forestry
FSC™ C007454

This book contains FSC™ certified paper
and other controlled sources to ensure responsible forest management.

For more information visit www.harpercollins.co.uk/green.

Printed and Bound in the UK using 100% Renewable Electricity
at CPI Group (UK) Ltd, Croydon, CR0 4YY

THE KING'S PREGNANCY PROPOSITION

LaQuette

MILLS & BOON

To my sister, Ebony. We may not be twins, but it's reassuring to know there's someone in the world who don't play about me.

CHAPTER ONE

"ALÉX, I'M NOT quite sure what you hope to gain by dragging this out. You're a king. You have a responsibility to marry and produce an heir. We both know I'm the best choice for a consort. I've always been the best choice for a consort. Why are you dragging your feet?"

King Aléxandros of Obsidian Island internally cringed as he listened to the words coming out of Lady Katia's mouth. It wasn't as though Aléx hadn't heard these things from his late parents and his royal advisors seemingly since birth. He'd been reared in the expectation that he would fulfill this particular duty since he drew his first breath.

Aléx had also been taught the skill of keeping one's feelings from public view. Yet when Lady Katia slid an unwanted hand on his thigh, his outrage at being touched so intimately without his permission seeped out through the taut muscles of his face. His quick hand pried her claws from his person and placed them atop the elaborate gold-and-black marble bar they were seated at.

"Lady Katia, you forget your place. As a member of the Obsidian Court, the privilege of speaking to me with such familiarity hasn't been given to you. Please address me as is proper, King Aléxandros, Your Majesty, or Sire."

Aléx watched as Lady Katia's thin, classic features pulled tightly into sharp lines at his reprisal. She was part of the Obsidian aristocracy. A woman who had been bred to believe she and her ilk were better than people who didn't have aristocratic blood in their veins. The only people who were better were royals, which was why she'd been campaigning through various methods to situate herself as the perfect consort for the unmarried king. She and every other single woman at court made no secret of their desire to be his queen. As a result, Aléx never dated or slept with anyone at court, not since the first and only time ended so horribly.

Not since he'd lost everything.

Never again.

Lesson learned, Aléx was extremely selective of the women he chose to bed. They could have nothing to do with royal or aristocratic life, and most importantly, they couldn't expect more than physical release.

Yes, he had a duty to marry and procreate, and he would eventually fulfill that duty. But until he was sure he'd found someone he could trust, someone who would stand by him and choose him and the family they created over everything and everyone else, including the crown, he would remain single. His past demanded that he accept nothing less. And since Katia's only goal was the clout and wealth associated with being the king's consort, there was no way in hell he'd ever choose her as his wife.

He knew she'd never want to hear that. This standoff they were currently engaged in was proof of that. Being turned away so blatantly wouldn't sit well with a woman like her. The stiff shoulders and pointed stare she leveled at him after his reprisal confirmed every instinct he had about Katia. At all costs, he needed to keep her away from him.

"Your Majesty?"

A sultry voice that he barely recognized filled his senses,

pulling his gaze from the cold ice of Katia's blue gaze to a rich warmth the color of dark cognac drawing him in.

"I'm sorry to interrupt, but you told me to find you here for our meeting. Are you still available?"

Aléx took in the beauty before him. Reigna Devereaux, the CEO of Gemini Queens Cosmetics. She was a regular attendee at Obsidian Island's annual Commerce Gala. But never in all their interactions had she ever caught his notice so completely.

Her dark hair was braided into an intricate pattern that spoke to her heritage as an African American woman, putting her cultural pride on display for all to see. Her lips were covered in a matte red lipstick that artfully highlighted a mouth that made him wonder how it compared to the sweet berries that grew in the wild forested soil of his land.

He stood to his full height of six feet two inches, noticing that even in her impossibly high heels, she barely reached the middle of his chest. Tiny though she might have been, there was confidence in the way she stood in those slinky, strappy heels and the one-shouldered bodycon red cocktail dress that caressed her ample, plus-sized curves.

That self-assurance called to him, and he had to fight his natural urge to get closer to her, to lean into her and take in every glorious inch she possessed.

"Absolutely," he replied, noting the spark of mischief that flashed in the woman's eyes. "I've been looking forward to speaking to you all evening."

With his eyes still locked on to Reigna's, Aléx said, "Please excuse me, Lady Katia. I must attend to a most urgent matter."

Before Katia could reply, he extended his arm to Reigna, waiting for her to wrap her hand around his bicep. When she did, his body tensed, but not in revulsion as it had with

Katia. This was excitement mixed with a healthy dose of satisfaction of knowing what her touch felt like, even through the fine threads of his tailor-made tuxedo jacket.

"Shall we, Ms. Devereaux?"

He lifted a brow, waiting for her response, delighting at the devious curl of her lips and the devilish grin that resulted.

"Certainly, Your Majesty."

Katia completely forgotten, Aléx moved away from the bar and through the grand ballroom of the largest luxury hotel in his country.

"Would you mind following me to my suite? I'm afraid if we remain in any of the public areas of the hotel, all eyes will remain on us. I promise you will be perfectly safe."

She conceded with a nod to Aléx as two large men converged and fell in step at a comfortable distance behind them. She smiled up at him with that same mischievous grin.

"Oh, dear King Aléxandros, I know I'll be perfectly safe in your suite. You know just as well as I that starting an international incident with a Devereaux wouldn't be good for you or your country."

He couldn't help the genuine chuckle that rumbled in his chest and out of his throat. There was that poise he'd seen in her stance when she'd interrupted his tense exchange with Katia. Up close, with no distractions between them, it was even more brilliant than before.

His guards were positioned all throughout the building, so Aléx had no fear of her apparent bodyguards pulling up their rear.

He directed her toward the private elevator to the penthouse and noticed that two other men joined two of his own at the doors.

"It appears your security team is just as thorough as mine.

I wouldn't be surprised if your men are already in place when we exit the elevator as well."

"Of course they are," she replied. "You don't get to be a woman as successful as me by not taking your safety seriously, even in the presence of kings."

The elevator reached the penthouse floor. The doors opened following a soft ding, and just as he'd surmised, in the corridor there were extra security members he assumed were part of her team, standing side by side with his own.

He didn't know how she'd managed to get clearance to do this, but there was something enticing about the fact that she wielded enough command to thwart a king if she chose to.

Possessing so much power himself meant Aléx always had to be mindful of the positions he put people in, making sure he wasn't taking advantage of the immediate dynamic that came when you were the ruler of a nation dealing with a common person.

Reigna stepped into his suite and sat in an armchair in the living room before he'd even offered her a seat, crossing one thick, enticing leg over the other while offering him a captivating smile. It was a power move; he was certain of that. Reigna Devereaux didn't ask for permission. She simply did what she wanted because she was always in control.

Reigna Devereaux was not a common person. How he'd missed that fact in all their polite exchanges over the years, he didn't know. But tonight, more than anything or anyone else, Aléx understood that this woman was both temptation and a threat tied together in a sexy bow.

"Considering we've said less than a handful of words to one another over the years, how did you know I would welcome your little ruse to get me away from Lady Katia, Ms. Devereaux?"

Regina Devereaux relaxed a little in her chair. Hearing him use her surname meant she wouldn't have to keep reminding herself to answer when he called her by her twin sister's name, Reigna.

She'd agreed to represent Gemini Queens by pretending to be Reigna at this fancy gala while the real Reigna was playing the part of the dutiful new queen of Nyeusi. Yes, Reigna and her husband, Jasiri, were the newly installed king and queen of Nyeusi. Jasiri's ascension to the throne was an unexpected event devised to save the kingdom from his power-hungry uncle. With the Nyeusian monarchy so unstable, Reigna had begged Regina not just to take her place, but to pretend to be her at this gala.

According to Reigna, Aléxandros was a staunch stick-in-the-mud who demanded the heads of the top-selling foreign companies in his country meet once a year at this gala. It was essentially a way for the king to put faces to the people Obsidian Island did business with. It seemed a bit micromanage-y for Regina's tastes. However, with as much revenue as Gemini Queens garnered from this particular business relationship, Regina had given in to her sister and agreed to cosplay as Reigna the way no other person in the world could.

Her sister was the one who loved the limelight and exuded confidence in social settings. Regina was self-possessed, but usually in numbers and scientific formulas and equations. Dealing with people was an altogether different matter. But when she'd seen that woman pushing herself uninvited into the king's space, something protective in her flashed hot, forcing Regina into action.

"I'm a woman in corporate America; I can spot uninvited and inappropriate attention and action a mile away. Even with your cool facade, you seemed tense. That was especially true when your speaking companion touched you. I figured I'd do for you what's been done for me dozens of times when I found myself in similar situations, where cursing fools out or smacking fire out of them would cause me and my business more harm than good."

The king mouthed *smacking fire out of them* as if he were testing the weight and meaning of the phrase, and Regina couldn't help but chuckle. This man was a king. He'd probably never encountered such language, figurative or otherwise, in his rarified circles.

Regina gave herself a mental shake at the word *rarified*. She was part of a billionaire family; she too moved in rarified circles. But the Devereauxs had kept their feet, and their sensibilities, firmly planted in Brooklyn, meaning it wasn't every day they were seated in the private company of actual royalty.

Reigna was going to owe her big-time for this particular game of twin swap.

Not only was being the face of Gemini Queens far outside her skill set, but this king with his thick midnight-black hair and Caribbean-blue eyes was seriously messing with her John Stamos fixation.

For anyone who hadn't noticed, John Stamos was fine long before he was Uncle Jesse on *Full House*. Although it was before her time, she'd found a couple of clips of him on *General Hospital* playing the character Blackie Parrish on YouTube. Yes, he was fine even back then too.

King Aléxandros was, for lack of a better word, HAWT!

Yes, HAWT.

His level of sexy, with his rippled muscles peeking through the expertly crafted tuxedo, coupled with that distinguished yet powerful gentleman affect he was giving off, could not be contained or explained in the simple three-lettered spelling of the word. It needed an extra letter, an alternate spelling, and exaggerated pronunciation just to scratch the surface of how attractive and enigmatic this man was. Attractive enough that while she'd faithfully worshipped at John Stamos's altar of fine, the king was making her seriously think of switching her allegiance from the Hollywood heartthrob to this revered monarch.

"Ms. Devereaux." The king's rich voice broke through her thoughts, bringing her attention directly to his face. His jaw was strong and clean-shaven, and along with his overall countenance, just exuded authority. "As a king, people scurry to attend to my commands or what they think I want. Very few people look beyond the crown to consider what I might need."

The lines around his face softened as he unbuttoned his jacket and sat on the ottoman directly in front of her. The cool scent of his cologne tickled her senses, forcing her to fight the powerful urge to shove her nose in his neck and fill her lungs to their capacity with the smell of him.

"Thank you for looking beyond the crown and seeing the man in need."

He was sharing his vulnerability with her, and that fact made desire twist a knot in her gut. A man who held might at his fingertips but still managed to understand and express his own vulnerability? She was sure it had to be stronger than any controlled substance on the planet.

She'd never been tempted once in her life to indulge in substance abuse. But everything she'd seen from this man tonight, especially now when he was laying his guard down, it made her want to crawl into his lap and wrap her arms around those broad shoulders she was certain were holding the weight of the world.

"I know what it's like for people to not see you, to never

allow you to be your authentic and individual self. I'm just glad I happened to see what was going on. No one should be touched without their consent. You being a king or a man shouldn't mean you're excluded from that expectation."

A flash of fire in his eyes called to the twin flame burning in her gut. After she'd just told this man no one should touch him without his consent, all she wanted to do was touch him—hell, taste him, if he'd allow it.

God, why must I have home training and be so principled? Why can't I be like that thirsty heifer downstairs and just take what I want?

She closed her eyes and answered her own question.

Because you're not gross, Regina. You actually care about other human beings.

That fact hadn't meant she'd always been treated with the same care and respect she gave to others. She didn't play games, at least not usually, and that seemed to be a major turnoff to the men that crossed her path. If she was interested in something long-term, she didn't try to trick men into being with her. When you grew up living in someone else's shadow, appearing invisible to others was a fate worse than death. So she made a habit of saying exactly what she meant. At least then, potential suitors would jump ship early, and she wouldn't have to go through the heartache and hurt of falling for someone who didn't want what she wanted and didn't see the value in her.

"Ms. Devereaux."

The king's voice pulled her out of her head and made her focus on him. That same fire was still there burning between them, no matter how she fought to douse it.

"Please know that you can absolutely reply no to this question, and there will be no reprisals for your company and the business you do on Obsidian Island."

Intrigued, she nodded, wondering what the king would say next.

"Would you be amenable to me kissing you?"

The woman with home training should've said no. The accomplished businesswoman and scientist should've said no. But when she opened her mouth, the only thing that toppled out was, "Hell yes."

A satisfied smile curled his lips as he reached for her, pulling her into his lap and locking his mouth to hers.

She went willingly, and matched his enthusiasm, opening for him with the slightest pressure of his tongue against her bottom lip.

His fingers threaded into her braids, making the sensitive flesh there tingle. Her resulting moan was rewarded with his hand tightening on her thigh, holding her securely against him.

He was a king, a man who was polished and refined to shine like new money. But he kissed like a street brawler. His movements fierce, lacking the poised control and elegance his station in life demanded. He was consuming her with that kiss, and simultaneously remaking her one cell at a time. She would be forever changed after this, and judging from the way her nipples hardened and her sex throbbed, she was perfectly okay with that as long as he kept doing what he was doing.

God, please let him keep doing what he's doing.

As if he'd heard her thoughts, Aléxandros tore his mouth away from hers, leaving them both panting. There was a slightly feral look in his gaze that did nothing to quench the heat and the need for this man building inside her.

He opened his mouth to speak, but she preempted him, holding up her hands.

"Just in case you want to ask me if it's okay to invade

my personal space even further, and God willing, in much more detail, just know I am one hundred percent amenable to whatever you have in mind."

He closed his eyes as he pulled her closer to him, the hard swell of his flesh pressing against her thigh and letting her see for herself she wasn't the only one affected by their unexpected chemistry.

He pressed his forehead to hers and groaned as if he ached for something, anything to satisfy whatever this was building between them.

"From the moment you captured my notice, I knew two things, Ms. Devereaux."

She pulled away, locking into his gaze as he continued to speak.

"One, you are the most alluring woman I've ever seen, and two, you're dangerous."

CHAPTER TWO

SHE GATHERED WHAT little of her senses remained and whispered, "Does that mean you'd like me to leave?"

He shoved his hand under her knees and his other arm around her waist just before he stood with her cradled against him like she was a real-life Disney princess.

"The only place I want you is in my bed. If you don't want that too, I need to know now."

She circled her arms around his neck, pressing her breasts into the hard wall of him.

"One hundred percent amenable. Isn't that what I said?"

She hadn't been kidding when she'd said it. She was ready for anything and everything this king wanted to do to her.

If she were thinking with her brain, she'd acknowledge how bad an idea sleeping with this man was. He was a whole king, a man with unbelievable power who, if he chose to, could use that power to make her life a living hell. Not to mention, one-night stands with men connected in tangible ways to her business made this uncharacteristic "to hell with it" attitude she was currently sporting problematic and unwise. That rational thought was trying to gain some traction by tugging at the back of her mind. But then he looked at her, and rational thought left the building with no plans on returning anytime soon.

His eyes narrowed, intensifying the fire burning in them.

She thought he was going to speak again, possibly be the one to exercise some good sense in this situation, because she certainly wasn't capable of that in this moment. Instead, he took long steps out of the room, walking through an opened door that led to one of the largest hotel bedrooms she'd ever seen. This suite really was made for a king.

He kicked the door closed, and the next thing she knew, she was standing—well, barely standing, considering how her legs felt like limp noodles suddenly—on the prettiest pair of strappy platform heels she owned.

He yanked off his tie and jacket and began undoing the diamond cuff links at his wrist. She thought he'd walk away and put them in a secure place. She was wrong. He pulled them off and discarded them on the foot bench like they were knockoffs being sold by a street vendor in Brooklyn.

His shirt was gone next, and when his smooth, tanned skin came into view, without thought she stepped closer to him, touching his skin reverently.

"It really should be illegal for you to be this fine and feel this good at the same time."

"Flattery will get you everything you want, Ms. Devereaux. But first, I need a bit of what I want."

His large hands covered her shoulders and turned her away from him.

Slowly, painfully so, his fingers found her zipper. He was so exacting and punishing with his slowness, she was convinced she could feel every tooth of her zipper release until it reached its end in the middle of her back.

As deliberate as he was with unzipping her dress, he was as driven to shove it down her body and expose her to him.

The hunger in his gaze was palpable. She could feel it sweep across her sensitive flesh as if he'd reached out and touched her. He was damn near salivating, which was another plus in the tally she was keeping on him. He was powerful, yet not afraid to show vulnerability, and by the way he was sizing her up and walking her backward to his bed, he liked thick girls too.

Okay, Mr. King!

Regina and her twin had always been plus-sized. A fact they were both fine with. They loved their bodies and killed it at the fashion game, proving repeatedly that fluffy was indeed fabulous.

Just because Regina loved her body and knew she was everything a man could want or desire, it didn't mean she hadn't run into men who didn't see her value. She didn't waste time, effort, or thought on those men.

If the king had shown anything but uncontrollable desire when he'd taken off her clothes, she would've walked out of this room in her bra, panties and heels while telling him to kiss her round ass as she left.

Fortunately for them both, Aléxandros seemed enthralled and utterly captivated by her curves.

As soon as she was spread out against the expensive linens, Aléxandros lost whatever restraint he had. He was out of his pants and silk boxers in what seemed like an instant, proudly displaying the length and girth of what by anyone's standards was an impressive erection.

She leaned up to grab for it, and he pushed her greedy hand away.

"Soon, but not yet. You can't present such a fine selection to a man and not expect him to feast."

That was the only warning she had before he kissed his way down her body, stopping to pull the cups of her strapless bra down to take one and then the other pert nipple in his mouth.

He hovered over her soft stomach, allowing his hands and

lips to worship her there too. And then he finally, with the deliberate patience of a man intending to savor his meal, removed her lace panties, taking a moment to inhale her essence as if it was the most wonderful thing he'd ever encountered.

The first stroke of his fingers against the delicate flesh of her mound made her tremble to her core. Why was the feel of him against her flesh so familiar, as if her body had prior experience with this king?

He opened her to him, gathering her waiting arousal and spreading it over the tender flesh with his gentle touch. Pleasure uncoiled at her core, drawing a needy moan from her.

"Yes," he moaned in reply as he slipped one and then two digits inside her. "I want to hear you moan pretty for me. Just like that."

His words drew another deep moan from her, and she had to wonder how he could sound so proper and filthy at the same time. To be clear, she wasn't complaining about it. She just never thought the two would seamlessly blend so well.

The flick of his tongue against her swollen nub suppressed the air in her lungs while rendering her completely under his spell.

His coordinated assault with his mouth and his fingers had her hips bucking as she tried to get closer yet pull away from the unimaginable pleasure he gave to her.

He placed a firm hand across her waist, keeping her right where he wanted her.

"No, running, Treasure. Not until I get to feel you break apart on my tongue."

"For a king," she choked out through the waves of pleasure crashing over her, "your mouth is so damn nasty."

She could feel his smile burgeon against her mound, and she couldn't decide if it was disturbing or damn sexy that he was literally smiling against her clit.

"Oh, Treasure, if you think my mouth is filthy, just wait until you experience my sex."

He licked and sucked her flesh while sliding his fingers in and out of her, grazing against the knot of nerves, forcing her to the edge of release even if she wasn't ready to be there.

"Your Majesty, I'm…"

He pulled his mouth away from her, hovering over her as the intensity of his stare bore down on her. His eyes were searing with fire and filled with what looked like righteous anger.

"While it takes a certain amount hubris to don the crown, I am not so full of myself that I want my lovers to refer to me using a courtesy title. Hear me and hear me well. The only name I want to hear crossing your lips when my face is buried in your sex is Aléx."

He added another finger to the two already inside her, creating a glorious stretch that had her clamping down on his digits.

"To you, especially when we are like this—" he used his thumb to circle her clit, dragging another hungry moan from her "—I am always Aléx."

The hunger in his gaze was too raw. She tried to close her eyes and shield herself from him. She was so close, if he moved his fingers just the right way, she'd reach her peak.

"Look at me when I'm speaking to you."

He removed his fingers, lightly slapping them against her swollen clit. The sensation was surprisingly erotic, ramping up her arousal, but keeping her from coming at the same time.

She opened her eyes, finding a wicked gleam in his eyes.

"Oh, God," she mewled. That got her another slap against her clit, leaving her body strung so tightly with pleasure she was worried something in her might snap.

"No, not God." He swatted her nub again, but this time he followed that with a soothing strum of his fingertips against the sensitive flesh. "Aléx."

She nodded, quite frankly, because she couldn't find the focus to speak. Her climax was hovering over her just out of reach, and her entire body was aching for it. The truth was, she'd give this man anything he wanted, call him whatever he wanted if he'd let her orgasm right now.

It wasn't lost on her that he was certain of this information himself. Even if she hadn't come to that conclusion on her own, the diabolical gleam of satisfaction swimming in his gaze disabused her of any notion that Aléx wasn't completely aware of the power he held over her right now.

He slammed his mouth against hers, spreading her arousal between their lips, allowing her to taste herself on him.

"Whose fingers are you going to ride to completion?"

"Yours." The word was barely loud enough for him to hear if his face hadn't been so close to hers.

"Who is going to bury himself inside you and take you as rough as you can stand it?"

"Y-you," she stammered. "It's…you."

His fingers were playing her like a skilled musician's, knowing almost instinctively which note would complement the arrangement he was composing.

"And what…is…my…name?"

Her body, and mind for that matter, were no longer under her control. She ached for release, and this man was the key to that. If she weren't naked with her legs spread wide without the slightest bit of shame, she'd tell the good king about himself. But right now, the only thing she wanted, needed, was to come, and she wasn't going to jeopardize that for a silly thing like her pride.

"Aléx…your name is… Aléx."

"Such a good girl deserves a reward."

He slid down her body again, resuming his position between her legs, latching on to her nub and suckling as if the secret elixir of life could be drawn from it. With a twist of his wrist, her body bowed as her orgasm crested, pulling her muscles taut, forcing her to clamp down on his fingers with abandon.

When her body finally relaxed, she fell limp, throwing her arm over her eyes as she tried to come to grips with the fact that a king she'd met for the first time in her life had given her the best orgasm she'd ever had.

"Oh no, Treasure." In the distance, she could hear the familiar sound of a wrapper being torn. "There's no rest for the weary. That was just an opening salvo."

His weight returning to the bed pulled her gaze to him in time to see the angry purple dome of his hardened length. His arousal had gone from impressive to mouthwatering, with its bulging red veins denoting just how much he wanted to be inside her.

Apparently, his filthy mouth had done more than just aid in her climax. It had amped up his need to what looked like an almost painful level.

She watched him slide the condom down over his length. He stalked over, leaning down and kissing her softly before he asked, "Are you still with me?"

He was sexy and thoughtful, checking in to make sure she was still all right with this.

This man cannot be real.

He started to pull away when she closed her hand over his length, stroking him from root to tip and reveling in the full-body shudder that she could feel passing through him.

"Yes, Aléx." She made a point of saying his name, feeling the raw heat of his need emanating from his body. "I'm more than ready for whatever you plan to dish out."

He parted her thighs, seating himself at her entrance, slowly pushing himself in.

Despite her eagerness for him after already experiencing such a fantastic orgasm, there was a definite sting as her body stretched to accommodate him.

Aléx placed a gentle kiss on her temple as he softly whispered, "Shhh, Treasure. That's right. Be a good girl and take all of me."

She moaned, eagerly accepting him into her body.

Why this man's words and voice made her brain shut off and her body respond with such unapologetic acquiescence, she didn't know. What she did know was that when he finally bottomed out inside her and lightly raked his thumb against her clit, pleasure exploded inside her. Once again, she'd lost control of her body and willingly, enthusiastically ceded that control to him. He began to thrust in and out of her while she was still amid her climax, driving her higher, prolonging it until she was nearly ready to cry.

Throughout their passionate encounter, he kept pushing her beyond her limits, making her crave the way his powerful strokes pushed her closer to and through such earth-shattering climaxes that she was weak, and yet so needy for more.

There had never been anyone who knew her so well that it was almost as if they could reach inside her and pull her secret wants and needs from her and be so certain how to answer them. It was almost like he knew her. Like he saw her…the real her.

She held on to the bed posts for dear life, and Aléx buried himself in her over and over from behind until she was spilling over into bliss again.

"Aléx," she cried out.

The sound of his name crossing her lips as both a plea and a prayer made him deepen his strokes, fusing them together in body and spirit.

"Say it again." He ground the words out through what sounded like his clenched jaw. Her face was buried in the plush pillow, so she couldn't swear to it.

"Aléx!" she screamed as she succumbed to the orgasm locking her muscles in place.

At the sound of her yelling his name, his grip on her hips tightened, his rhythm faltered, and he buried himself inside her one last time until his climax took hold of him. She could feel the throbbing pulse of his release as he emptied himself into the condom. When he collapsed against her, blanketing her with his strong form, she felt more cared for, more content, more herself, than she could remember in her recent years.

This was absolute heaven. As far as she was concerned, nothing could ruin this perfect moment.

Aléx rolled to his back, quickly disposing of the condom before pulling her into his arms.

And then the universe showed her why she should never tempt it to show her just how terrible it could be. Aléx said, "Good, God, Reigna. How could I have gone all these years of seeing you at this gala, never knowing how fantastically we would fit together?"

Just like that, per usual where Regina was concerned, her sister Reigna had been hoisted into the spotlight, and Regina's place was in the background, if visible at all. This was the best sex of her life, and her lover thought she was her twin sister. Even in the most unlikely circumstances, Regina had ended up in her sister's shadow yet again.

CHAPTER THREE

Four months later...

ALÉX STARTED HIS day the same way he had every day for the last four months. He sat up in bed, fighting the urge to reach for the body he knew wouldn't be there. The same body he'd cursed at each new sunrise and ravaged in his dreams each night.

Once he'd forced himself to forget about how tantalizing those vivid dreams were and intentionally ignored how his body tightened at the memories he couldn't seem to let go, he made quick work of showering in ice-cold water.

"Damn it."

Aléx slammed his hand against the hard tile of the shower stall. He was fairly certain it was the finest marble on the market he was slamming his ringed hand against, and here he was treating it like it was a cheap piece of plastic that could be scratched without thought and replaced without much effort or cost.

This was not like him.

No matter that Aléx had grown up in opulent wealth. He'd always known that his lifestyle was a gift for his service, and he should never take it for granted. Yet since that night four months ago, he'd been holding on to his focus and his discipline with every ounce of his being, all because he couldn't forget her.

This also wasn't like him.

Aléx didn't pine over women. He used them for mutual pleasure, and when both parties were satisfied, he went back to his life of duty and service without a care. He wasn't cruel to women. He simply made sure he only ever slept with women who knew there would be no more beyond their mutual physical satisfaction.

As his mind began to replay that night for the millionth time, he ran a harsh hand through his wet hair, trying to figure out what was so special about this particular woman. She had him so desperate to taste her that he'd forgotten to give her his practiced "we only have tonight" speech that proceeded any sexual encounter he had with a partner.

A derisive laugh climbed up from his chest, spilling through his lips and echoing in the marble-and-glass stall. The joke was on him. He hadn't needed to give Reigna Devereaux that speech because she was gone as soon as he'd fallen into a sound sleep. And the next time he'd heard of her, he was receiving a royal wedding invitation announcing her as the Nyeusian king's bride.

How's that for turning the tables?

He should've been relieved that Reigna hadn't had designs on him. The fact that she'd so quickly married someone else should've made his year. Too bad the ugly mark of jealousy that clawed at him from the inside hadn't received the memo. As a result, he was still obsessing over her four months later.

Still disgusted with himself for being unable to shake whatever this thing inside him was that kept him fixated on the woman, he dressed and headed to breakfast in his office. Finding his plate waiting for him and the global news playing on the television reminded him what he was here to do.

He was here to take care of his people, not obsess over a single sexual encounter that happened four months ago.

He was just about to drink the piping hot black brew in his cup when he heard the news anchor say, "When a concrete princess from Brooklyn becomes the real-life queen of an exotic island paradise, you get a fairy tale come true. Viewers, please welcome one of Brooklyn's most famous daughters. She's formerly known as Reigna Devereaux of the Devereaux Inc. ilk. Now she is known as Her Majesty, Queen Reigna of Nyeusi. Oh, and her husband, King Jasiri, is joining her too."

Aléx's fist closed around the delicate china, and he had to force every muscle in his hand to relax so he wouldn't shatter the thing in his palm.

He thanked every deity he could remember for the foresight to put the cup on a level surface, because the sight of her on the television left him boneless, unable to move or do anything but watch her on the screen.

She wore a cocktail-length A-line dress with its high waist accented by a large belt. She was breathtaking, her full cheeks high as she greeted the anchor with a smile and an enthusiastic handshake. Seeing her form again made him lean toward the television, giving it and her his entire attention.

The camera angle widened, giving the viewing audience a full-body shot, and the floor beneath him might as well have opened and swallowed him. She was beyond royal. She was celestial in vibrant purple, gold, and black colors. They were woven into a beautiful African print, and the gold lioness broach on her collar highlighted her strength, grace and poise as she continued to walk across the stage.

He was losing himself in the way those colors complemented her beautiful, deep brown skin, producing a soft and inviting glow around her that called to him so strongly he nearly stood from his chair. But then a hint of something familiar plucked at the back of his mind until he realized why she wore those colors. They were the national colors of Nyeusi.

Jasiri's land.

Her husband's kingdom.

Had Aléx known Reigna and Jasiri had a past? Yes. According to the headlines, they'd been broken up for at least two years when she'd found her way into Aléx's bed. Reigna was a free agent, and her choosing to go back to her ex after a night with Aléx shouldn't have bothered him one bit. Irrationality aside, receiving their wedding invitation had pulled out a jealous possessiveness Aléx hadn't known himself capable of, and he'd been fighting it every day of the last four months.

Regret and anger mixed in his gut, creating a toxic concoction that was probably going to give him an ulcer if he didn't get the rage spreading through his system under control. And there, just as his vision began to cloud with red, he saw Jasiri's hand touch hers, guiding her to the sofa where the hosts of the news show sat.

How had he missed the man? The answer to that was simple. Reigna. She was all he'd seen or focused on since he'd heard her name announced.

The host went on to fawn over Reigna. Even though Jasiri was at her side, it was clear Reigna was the star of the show. Honestly, it was fitting. No one compared to the sultry, strong and caring woman who'd set his body on fire.

Aléx tried to focus on just her, to ignore Jasiri's presence, but he couldn't. Because slowly he began to see that Reigna wasn't a separate entity. She was with Jasiri. Not just married to him, connected to him.

Aléx could see the way she glanced up to Jasiri, the way she sought his hand or his arm whenever more than a few moments passed without the couple touching. It was there for anyone looking to see. She adored her husband.

He waited for the jealousy he'd been harboring since he'd declined the invitation to their Nyeusian royal wedding to flash hot in his blood. But as he watched their exchanges, he understood they were truly in love.

Whatever the thing was that had had Aléx in such an unbreakable hold for these last four months, it didn't so much as simmer within him. It wasn't just quiet. It was gone.

He pulled his eyes away from the screen, trying to focus on his own thoughts. Reigna was in love with Jasiri. As much as he wanted to be angry about that, as much as he couldn't stand that Jasiri had one-upped him, Aléx couldn't begrudge the two the obvious connection they shared.

He was just ready to change the channel literally and figuratively when Reigna said, "We're happy to announce we're expecting our first child." She placed a loving hand against the bottom of her stomach, display a slight bump that had been concealed by the silhouette of her dress. "I'm four months along."

Cold spilled down Aléx's spine as he did the mental math in his head. It had been four months since the night they'd shared. Four months since he'd lost himself inside her.

Yes, he'd worn a condom. But he knew from personal experience that condoms didn't always work.

There was a crack in the door he'd kept soundly shut around his heart. He took in a noisy breath that was equal parts pain and joy. Could this be his baby? Could he be a father again?

And as he watched Jasiri place a possessive hand on Reigna's stomach, that anger he'd thought he'd lost came roaring back to life like a powerful flood slamming against his chest, making it almost impossible to breathe.

"So help me, Reigna," he growled through clenched teeth. "If you'd stoop low enough to try to pass my baby off as Jasiri's, you'd better prepare yourself for a battle. Because I'm coming, and I'm bringing hell with me."

* * *

Aléx stood in front of the floor-to-ceiling window that made up the fourth wall in the conference room of Gemini Queens, Reigna's cosmetics company. He'd had few direct dealings with her with respect to commerce. He had people to handle the dirty details of business. There was no reason for him to have muddied the waters in that respect.

His pulse beat loudly in his ears as he waited for Reigna to join him for what she believed was a matter of her company's business dealings with his country.

They had business to deal with, certainly. But it didn't have a damn thing to do with commerce.

"Your Majesty, thank you so much for stopping by to speak with me while we're both in town."

He turned around, bracing himself for seeing her in person after their last time together. Unbridled anger raced through his vessels like poison when he thought of what she might have done. But he also feared the tangible chemistry that had put them in this situation to begin with might be there too.

When he laid eyes on her in a fitted knee-length dress, her bump just beginning to show and all her curves on display, attraction never made an appearance.

He shook his head, not understanding what was going on inside him. He'd obsessed over this woman for months. Now, except for the notion that she might be the mother of his child, there was nothing there between them.

She smiled and offered her hand to him. He didn't take it. He was so busy trying to figure out what the hell was going on, touching her seemed unwise.

"Reigna, let us dispense with the niceties of royals meeting. I think you know why I'm here, and things will work out best for everyone involved if you're honest with me."

"I'm not sure what you're referring to, King Aléxandros."

That was the second time she'd called him by his title, and it stirred something in him as he remembered her spread out beneath him, wild with pleasure as he forbade her from calling him anything other than his name.

It was on the tip of his tongue to correct her. But as he looked at her, the pull of fire and need that had been there before wasn't now.

"Then I'll be blunt." She lifted her eyes in anticipation of Aléxandros's next words. "Am I the father of the baby you're carrying, and are you attempting to pass it off as your husband's?"

Her jaw dropped, and her brown eyes turned to steel as she gazed at him. She took a step back and moved her hand to her wrist, where her smartwatch rested elegantly against her skin. He grabbed her arm, preventing her from touching what he was certain was some kind of security alarm.

"Uh-uh, Queen Reigna. I've got one of those too. Let's say we settle this before you bring in the cavalry. Is it possible I'm the father of the child you're carrying?"

She snatched her arm from him, anger burning in her gaze as she put distance between them.

"Who the hell do you think you are, asking me something like that?"

His jaw tightened, making him worry that he might crack the bones there as he pried it open to speak.

"I'm the man you begged to pleasure you exactly four months ago. So I'll ask again. Am I the father of your child?"

Something sparked in her eyes that he couldn't quite make out. She tilted her head, staring at him as if she was understanding something he wasn't privy to.

"King Aléxandros, considering my husband is a dark-skinned Black man and you're of European descent, I think it would be pretty stupid of me to try to pass your baby off as Jasiri's. This is not your baby."

Her gaze was steady and her voice calm. Everything about the way she stared at him painted her as the picture of poise and virtue. Everything in her countenance said she was telling him the truth. But the familiar darkness he'd fought so hard to bury in his past wouldn't let this small kernel of hope die.

Not again...not this time.

"Forgive me if I don't take the word of the woman who went from one king's bed to another with such apparent ease."

She folded her arms as she leaned to one side, jutting out one hip.

"I'm not going to be too many more liars and whores, no matter how prettily you dress up your words. I've answered your question. Now get out, before I cause an international incident and throw you out on your ass."

He knew he was out of line with his insinuations, but the need to know wouldn't let him curb his tongue.

"This won't be the last you've heard from me, Queen Reigna. If I must sic my lawyers on you and your king to establish paternity, I have no problems with the inevitable scandal that will follow. I don't think your newly installed king can say the same."

With that, he took his leave. Reigna Devereaux might have Jasiri wrapped around her finger, but she didn't hold any power over Aléx...not anymore. If he had to fight for his child, he would. Never again would someone take a child from him without him battling tooth and nail with blood and bone. If Reigna's child was his, he'd go to hell and back to claim it.

CHAPTER FOUR

"HEIFER, DID YOU sleep with King Aléxandros when you were at the commerce gala on Obsidian Island?"

Regina pulled the phone away from her ear to look at the screen as if her sister could see the shock on her face.

"Ahhh, yeah. I did. How do you know about that?"

Regina and her twin sister Reigna were close, but not so close that Regina would share the details of her sex life with her. Especially when she was too embarrassed because her sex partner thought he'd been screwing the popular twin instead of her.

"Because he ambushed me in the Gemini Queens' conference room, demanding to know if the baby I'm carrying is his. I cannot believe you let this happen."

Reigna's voice jumped across the phone line, delivering a metaphorical slap upside the head that Regina nearly physically tried to dodge.

"Listen, you were the one who asked me to pretend to be you at that stupid gala in the first place."

Regina knew it was a silly argument. She sounded like she'd barely made it out of elementary school instead of having a whole Ph.D.

"Regina." The hard way her sister called her name made a chill spill down Regina's spine. By all accounts, she was the serious twin, and Reigna was the fun one. When Reigna got serious, things were bad...really bad.

"Regina," her sister said again. "I didn't tell you to sleep with that man while pretending to be me. He's threatening lawyers. Nyeusi cannot afford a scandal. There cannot be even a sliver of doubt that I'm carrying the next rightful monarch of the House of Adebesi. You'd better fix this and do it fast. I found out where he's staying. I'm texting you the address now. Get up off your ass and make this right."

Her messenger app dinged, alerting her to the new text from her sister. Before she could pull the phone from her face to look at it, she heard the click of the line ending the call. Damn, if her sister hung up on her without saying goodbye, then Reigna was pissed off.

Her sister was right. It was time for Regina to grow a backbone and come clean with Aléx. She'd hoped the Atlantic Ocean would've been wide enough that she'd never have to see him again and deal with this. Just like always, her luck was trash, and yet again, the universe was denying her what she wanted.

Four months ago, she'd wanted to stay snuggled up with Aléx in his hotel room. That man had delivered the best sex of her life, and walking away from that while her body still ached from all the things he'd done to her was the hardest thing she'd ever had to do. She might've stayed if Aléx hadn't called Regina by her sister's name, pulling her back into reality, where she knew that moment could never be extended into more. How could it be? He thought he'd slept with her identical twin. There was no way she could explain the twin swap thing to him and have him meet her with anything but rejection.

That's what she'd told herself for the first couple of months, that he'd never understand. Once Reigna and Jasiri's marriage became public, there was too much at stake for her to attempt to reach out to Aléx. The Nyeusian monarchy couldn't afford the scandal, and the Nyeusian people would suffer for Regina's selfishness. She couldn't allow that to happen, so she did the only thing she could do: she swallowed her wants and buried herself in her work to forget.

There was only one problem.

She hadn't forgotten.

Aléx's large steps ate up the plush carpet as he headed toward the door. Reigna had finally come to her senses, and she'd come to address the predicament they found themselves in. He was relieved she hadn't attempted to ignore him. If she was here, maybe, just maybe, she was willing to work this out amicably so they could come together and do what was best for the child.

If that's your child.

He pushed his thoughts away, back into the recesses of his mind. He couldn't handle that prospect. Not after the small sliver of hope had pierced his heart and made him want what he'd lost so long ago.

He shook his head and straightened his shoulders, stepping into his king's persona.

"Queen Reigna," he began as he opened the door. "It seems once again we find ourselves in my hotel—"

Aléx's jaw dropped as he looked at the woman before him. She had the same build, the same face as the woman he'd spoken to earlier today. But with her cropped T-shirt exposing her soft stomach, he knew this was not the woman he'd crossed swords with earlier today.

"Oh my God, you're not her."

The woman shook her head as she stepped past him and into the room. She waited for him to close the door behind him. Once he had, she gave him a shaky smile.

"Hello, Your Majesty… I'm Regina Devereaux, Reigna's

identical twin sister, and the woman you slept with four months ago."

The shock of her words turned his blood to ice, hardening him from the inside out, making it impossible for him to speak.

A twin?

She was a twin?

His mouth hung open in disbelief as his eyes poured over her, looking for a sign that this was some sort of joke.

The same dark eyes he'd connected with when she'd swooped in to rescue him from unwanted female attention stared back at him. Even now they were filled with compassion and concern for him.

That spark of worry he saw floating in her gaze scraped across his soul, igniting a blaze of anger that threatened to overcome him.

He fisted his hands at his sides as if he were physically trying to wrestle his rising anger under his control. He was a king. Control was kind of his thing. Losing it could mean the difference between life and death and between the success and failure of his nation, his people. He had to keep his head on straight.

"What type of game are you and your sister playing at?"

His jaw clicked with each word. He was certain it would ache later, considering how tightly he was clenching his teeth. He tightened the muscles there even more, knowing it was either deal with a sore jaw or put his fist through the wall of a hotel he didn't own in a country he didn't rule.

She stepped closer to him. He was sure she could see the fury humming off him in waves, but she kept walking until she was directly in front of him, as if she welcomed his anger, accepted it. He reasoned either she had no sense of self-preservation, or she was out of her mind. His anger was at a raging boil now; he was certain he could rip her to shreds with his bare hands.

Then the soft scent of roses and vanilla filled his senses, acting like a soothing balm, dousing his rage even though he wanted nothing more than to pour gasoline on it.

"Your Majesty."

"Aléx!" He bellowed. "To you, I am always Aléx. Don't make me repeat myself."

He didn't know why her use of his courtesy title raised his hackles so much. People used it repeatedly throughout any given day when addressing him. And yet it sounded so wrong crossing those full lips. Lips he'd tasted, lips he'd devoured, and heaven help him, even in his anger, he wanted to devour again.

"Aléx… I… I didn't mean to deceive you."

"You sure about that, Treasure? Because I've spent the last four months thinking I slept with your sister and not you. If that's not deception, I don't know what is."

He expected her to cower at his words. That's what most people did when they earned his displeasure. But not this woman. She stood bold before him, owning the disdain he was so generously dishing out.

She held his gaze, as true and as strong as it had been that night four months ago. Again, it soothed him, making him want to forget even when he needed to remember.

"I never intended to say more than hello and goodbye to anyone that night. Reigna and Jasiri were secretly married in a civil ceremony at the Nyeusian embassy here in America, and she was off in Nyeusi helping Jasiri secure his throne. That's the only reason I was there in the first place."

His eyes narrowed into slits as he watched her try to make sense out of the nonsensical.

"What does any of this have to do with you crawling

into my bed and letting me think I was sleeping with your sister?"

To her credit, she didn't falter. Her gaze remained steady on him, and he couldn't help but be impressed by whatever it was that was driving her to face him and his wrath.

"Reigna's absence would've been noticed at an event of that social and business magnitude. The press would've begun digging, and Jasiri's Uncle Pili would've thwarted their plans and possibly stolen the throne away from Jasiri. Besides that, it would've been bad for Gemini Queens if the face of the company didn't turn up. I was only supposed to show my face, smile and mingle. But when I saw that woman pawing at you, I knew I had to do something."

Her forthrightness threw him. How could she be so calm as she recounted her wrongdoing?

"I wasn't expecting to end up in your bed, Aléx. It all just sort of happened. One minute we were talking, and the next we were all over each other."

They certainly had been. He could still feel the heat of her burning flesh against his, still feel the need that vibrated through her body every time he touched her.

She was so close to him, his fingers ached to touch her. Although he knew he couldn't give in to that desire, it still spread through his veins like an opiate, making every ounce of his being crave her from the first and only taste he'd had of her.

He turned, spotting the desk behind them. He leaned over it, pressing his knuckles into its cool wood surface. He hoped the bite of the wood against his flesh would sober that temptation. The discomfort was supposed to keep him focused instead of making him want to reach out and possess her the same way he had four months ago.

"I was trying to protect my sister, Aléx. That night with you was an unexpected gift I had no way of anticipating."

He chuckled at her use of the word *gift*. He straightened as the heat of his anger began to swell again.

"Funny how I'd thought of it that way too until I thought you were trying to pass my baby off as Jasiri's."

Yes, this…this rage, this searing, ugly thing that made him want to lash out, *that* he could hold on to. He turned and closed the distance between them again.

"Until you walked into this room obviously not pregnant, tore open a familiar hole in my—"

He clasped his jaw shut, refusing to let the rest of that sentence find its way into the ether. That was his alone. He wouldn't share it with anyone else. Not now. Not ever.

The fire flashing in Aléx's eyes turned from fury to pain. Sharp pain that seemed to stab at something vital inside him, robbing him of breath. Fear for him, not of him, pushed her forward, making her grip his forearm.

"Aléx, are you okay?"

He didn't respond; he simply stared at his arm where they were joined as if it was some mystical puzzle he was trying to complete or unlock.

What the hell was going on? He was a king, for goodness' sake. If she'd broken him with this little twin swap stunt, Reigna was going to kill her. Having this king drop dead of shock because of something she did would haunt Regina for the rest of her life. She had to fix this.

"Aléx, please," she begged frantically. "What is it? What can I do?"

A dark focus crystalized in his eyes as he shifted his arm until he shook her hand free and clasped her wrist in his painful grip.

He pulled her so close that her body was flush against his. She could feel the hard drum of his heart pounding through his chest. She wanted to flatten her hand against it, try to soothe him until she could see reason slip into his expression again. But he kept her to him, keeping her wrist in his unyielding grip so she could do nothing but stand there looking up into his fiery blue gaze.

It should've frightened her. It should've had every one of her danger bells going off in her head. But fear wasn't what she was feeling. No, deep in the pit of her belly, desire flickered from a small spark to a full-on inferno. There was no fear. There was only need. The same need that had found her in his bed, beneath him, begging for every filthy thing he'd done for her, to her. She melted against him, hanging on to every sliver of emotion she saw play across his face.

Beneath the obvious anger, there was that same need she felt burning through her system. The flush running just beneath his skin was the same as the night he'd taken her to unimaginable heights in his bed. Yes, she was here for another round of that, even if it was because he was so furious with her that devouring her was the only way he could temper his anger.

Too needy to be patient, she licked her dry lips and opened her mouth to speak.

"What can I do, Aléx?"

His lips turned up at the corners, giving his classically handsome features a sinister twist.

"You can start by making up for the little trick you played on me by marrying me and giving me the child you owe me."

Well damn. Of all the things she'd expected—no— wanted to hear from him, it sure as hell wasn't that.

CHAPTER FIVE

"Say what now?"

He watched confusion clear out the lust he'd previously seen in her eyes.

She'd wanted him. He was certain of it, because the same ache that had her licking her full lips had his heart racing inside his chest. But then the ache that had threatened to swallow him whole four months ago tried to crawl its way out of the dank grave he'd buried it in. Instead of leaning into need, he'd lashed out by saying the most unhinged thing he could think of.

But now that he'd said it, he wouldn't take it back.

"You owe me a child, and in order for me to have a child, I must be married due to legitimacy laws concerning the line of succession. That means you're going to marry me and give me what I'm owed."

"What you're owed? You seriously think I owe you a baby because you jumped to conclusions about my sister's pregnancy?"

She was right. He had jumped to conclusions. That didn't matter as far as he was concerned. He would not take fault in this. Not one single iota of it.

"The bill's come due for the little game you and your sister played. I've come to collect, and you have to give me what I'm owed."

As the last syllable of his sentence left his mouth, her left brow rose as she pointed her forefinger at her chest.

"I don't have to do anything but stay Black and die."

Her words short-circuited his brain, disrupting the anger and lust that had clouded his senses since she'd walked into his hotel room announcing that he'd slept with the wrong twin.

He tilted his head, taking her in. Her round hip was jutted out to one side, and her face, usually bright with sass and snark, was pulled into tight lines. All the softness her curves held was now replaced with stern rigidness that let him know Regina Devereaux was no pushover.

Everything in her stance said she was going to fight him on this. That was okay. He was a king. He was used to waging war to get what he wanted. Regina Devereaux would fall prey to his will the way everyone else did.

On its face, his request was obviously ludicrous. Even he wasn't so far gone in this moment that he couldn't see that. Unfortunately, the empty hole in his heart that had been sitting there for five years had shrunk enough for him to notice when there was a chance that he was going to become a father. God help him, after feeling hope for the first time in too many years, he couldn't simply walk away from it just because this was all some cruel twist of fate.

He was a king. He made his own fate. He would be a father again. Making that happen depended on his ability to convince this woman he wasn't as unbalanced as he sounded.

"I have absolutely no idea what that means." He shook his head and stepped toward her. "What I do know is that I want a child, and you're going to give me one."

"People in hell want ice water, but they're still hot and thirsty. I'm not giving you a damn thing. Not even the time of day. Goodbye, King Aléxandros."

She turned toward the door, and he stepped in front of her, halting her forward motion.

"We're not done yet."

"We absolutely are done. You cannot force someone to marry you and have a child with you. Just because you're a king doesn't mean you can just command people to do whatever you want."

He shrugged. "Actually, it kind of does."

That comment took some of the steam out of her stance. He knew he'd made a chink in her armor when he saw one side of her mouth begrudgingly lift into a small smile.

"You are so insufferable. Is that also part of being a king?"

He nodded, taking another cautious step to her. When she didn't bolt, he ushered her over to the large sofa in the center of the room and bade her to take a seat next to him.

"What kind of man goes around demanding a woman marry him and give him a baby? You know nothing about me. Why would you want to tie yourself to me like that? We don't love each other. How could you consider marrying someone you don't know if you like, let alone love?"

He sat down, extending his arm against the back of the couch and crossing his legs. As he relaxed, so did she. He liked that she took her cues from him. Her willingness to follow his lead had gifted him unimaginable pleasure. If he could only convince her to follow his desires in this matter, maybe he could find something else. Peace.

"Regina, this would be a marriage of convenience, not love. Love is messy and unstable, and when it goes bad, it can poison everything. It can be weaponized, and when it strikes a blow, it can kill you as dead as any bullet."

If anyone understood that, it would be him. What happened five years ago had taught him a very slow and painful lesson about love. It nearly killed him, and his resuscitation from it hadn't left him unscarred or unchanged.

"As the king, my number one concern is to simultaneously uphold the monarchy while serving my citizens. Choosing a consort comes down to a few things. Trust, the willingness to provide support to the sovereign, and compatibility in the ways that are important to each party."

"You said trust is a must." Her words were quick and sharp as if she were trying to get them all out at once. "Knowing that the only reason we're in this mess now is because I lied to you, how on earth can you trust me enough to be such an important part of your life?"

He waited to see if she was going to say more and found her rapt attention zeroed in on him, waiting for an answer to her question. If she was waiting that intently, he had to hope that somewhere deep down, she was considering his proposal.

"Yes, you lied. But before that, you interjected yourself into a situation to help a man who was a total stranger to you. That tells me you're strong and compassionate. Those are two qualities that aren't necessarily in abundance when it comes to wealthy people. Your actions, much more than your words, tell me I can trust you to do what's right when necessary. It was also proof that you'd be willing to support me as I support the nation. Lastly, if Reigna is the face of your company, I know that you're the brilliant sister who works science like it's magic in her lab. That's a beautiful mix of qualities that I couldn't buy with all the money and power at my disposal."

Her shoulders sank as she leaned into the cushions. Her gaze was still furtive as it flitted across him. But she was at least listening to him.

"Aléx, this makes not one bit of sense. Why would you

even consider marrying and having a child with a complete stranger?"

"As I said before, I'm a king, Regina. My duty is to produce an heir so that the line of succession can continue. That heir must be legitimate, so marriage is also my duty. There's no one in my circle that I trust enough to contemplate having a child with. As I'm sure your sister can tell you, the royal court can be a pit of vipers waiting for an opportunity to strike. And I'm thirty-seven."

"Hey," she interrupted him. "That's only three years older than me. You say that like thirty-seven is ancient."

Her offense was noted by the wrinkling of her nose, making him chuckle. "In my world, that *is* ancient for a sitting king to be without an heir. If I must have a child, I'd like it to be with someone who at least understands what kindness and compassion are."

She closed her eyes as if she were trying to conceal something from him. He had no right to it. He had no right to her. But the selfish king in him wanted all her secrets. In his world, secrets were power. With Regina, though, he didn't want to use them against her. He simply wanted to unburden her of whatever darkness her thoughts were cloaking her in.

"Is it that you don't want children?"

She shook her head, looking away in the distance before bringing her gaze back to him.

"I'm the twin who planned her imaginary wedding and how many imaginary kids she and her imaginary husband would have. I even named all three of them. Reigna wanted nothing to do with a future family and children. Fate's funny like that. It gives the very thing you've always ached for to people who never wanted it."

Was that resentment? Did she envy her sister's life?

The thought of Regina pining for something she couldn't

have tightened an invisible knot in his chest. In his bed, he'd given her everything she desired. And as he watched her push down this apparent desire of hers, he ached to give her this too.

He hardly knew her. Until today, he hadn't even known her real name. Yet when her soft, sad eyes met his, he was certain she'd shared the important parts of herself when they'd met in his country.

"We can make our own fate, Regina. All it would take is you saying yes, and we can make it happen together."

Her mouth opened slightly, and he could see the yes taking shape on her lips when a shrill ringing sound disturbed the moment.

Regina shook her head, pulling her phone from her pocket. "This is my sister. I've gotta go."

She stood up, quickly hurrying toward the door.

"What about my proposition, Regina?"

"What about it? It's the most absurd thing anyone has ever said to me. No, I will not marry you and have your baby. This isn't some sort of rom-com where two quirky strangers agree to something this ridiculous and it all works out. Life doesn't work that way. My life doesn't work that way."

She yanked the door open and ran into the hallway, leaving him to watch her retreat to safety.

As he watched the elevator doors close, he smiled.

"You can run, Regina…for now."

Regina went directly home from Aléx's hotel. She knew she should've gone back to her sister's, but she was too raw to do it. Aléx's proposal, on its face, was unthinkable. There was no way she could agree to marry this man and have his child. He was a king. This wasn't how monarchies worked, was it? Wasn't there some sort of vetting process when it came to becoming a monarch's intended? It couldn't be as simple as a handshake and a deal. Could it?

She shook her head as she stepped off the elevator and walked to the door of her penthouse apartment. Her brain was firing on all cylinders as it tried to make sense of Aléx's proposal. No matter how she tried, there was no sense to be made, and so she did the next best thing. She dropped her things on the front table, grabbed her iPad Pro off the charging dock she'd left it on this morning, and sat down in her armchair with all the fluffy pillows a scientist could want.

Calm began to settle in her mind and in her bones as she twirled the Apple Pencil now in her hand. She drew a tightly coiled strand of African American hair, attaching notes on the opposite side of the image on what Black hair needs to thrive.

Moisture retention
Gentle yet effective cleansing
Deep conditioning with effective detangling
Styling products that provide moisture but don't weigh the hair down
Styling products that decrease frizz, provide hold, and prevent dryness and breakage
Gentle fragrance

She continued jotting notes down, getting lost in her work, trying her best to ignore the ache that had flared up inside her since Aléx made his offer. Having a family had always been a priority for Regina. It was probably selfish, considering how terrible her parents were at loving Regina and her sister. What made her confident she wouldn't ruin a child the way her parents had almost ruined her?

A different ache in her chest blossomed as the warmth of love and the bitterness of grief commingled like never-ending vines. Ace Devereaux, her great-uncle, the man who had taught both Regina and Reigna what it felt like to be loved. That man had swept in and filled those two affection-starved little girls with so much love, at times they'd thought they might burst from it. That abundance of love was what lit the fire inside her to love her future children that way. Her ultimate dream had been to have a child while Ace was still with them, allow him to see how powerful his love had been. That hadn't been in God's plan, however. He'd called Ace home six months earlier.

Losing Ace had ripped a hole in her soul. And since he'd been gone, that ache for a family of her own had begun to resurface. Once Reigna had announced her pregnancy, the thought wouldn't turn her loose.

She took a breath, forcing her thoughts back onto the work in front of her. Life didn't give her what she wanted. It never had; there was no reason to think if she reached for what she wanted now, it would finally come true.

Defeated, she laid the tablet down on the coffee table next to her and pulled her phone from her pocket to call her sister. Better to get this over with now or her sister would more than likely wake her up at the ass crack of dawn for a follow-up on her conversation with Aléx.

"How did it go?"

No hello or greeting of any kind: her sister just got straight to the point. It was a clear sign that she'd reached her limit when it came to patience. Regina couldn't blame her. It wasn't every day that one twin's poor judgment could lead to actual war between two countries.

"I told him the truth. He wasn't happy about it, but he

accepted it. He now knows there's no possible way that he fathered your baby."

Her sister was quiet as she took in Regina's words, as if she were letting the relief bleed through her. Her problems were over now. Too bad Regina couldn't say the same.

"He's an obnoxious ass. Did he say or do anything to you that's gonna make me want to pop him in his mouth the next time I see him?"

Regina took comfort in knowing her sister would still defend her, even though it was Regina's fault they'd ended up in this mess to begin with.

"Like I said, he was upset. But he wasn't mean."

"That bastard is always mean. Every time I attended one of his galas, he pretty much just scowled the entire time, barely sparing a kind word for any of the vendors that bring revenue to his country." Reigna's words scraped against Regina's nerves, and she couldn't tell why. It wasn't like she and Aléx were besties. But somehow, she still felt the need to defend him.

"Not to me," Regina offered. "He's always been genuine and kind to me."

"If you say so," Reigna huffed. "Just know I don't believe you."

Her sister's dismissive tone continued to rub something raw inside Regina.

"If he were being mean, would he ask to keep seeing me?"

That wasn't exactly what he'd asked. But there was no way she was telling Reigna the real request Aléx had made of her.

"And you told him to go to hell, right?"

Irritation swelled up inside Regina, instantly putting her on the defensive.

"Why would I say no without even considering his request? He's handsome, charismatic, and a whole-ass king who is good in bed. Why would I dismiss him?"

"Regina." The way her sister said her name had Regina perched at the edge of her seat, ready to pounce, even though she was in the apartment alone. It was condescending to say the least. The expectation that Regina would do whatever Reigna had said, simply because the older twin had said it, made her eye twitch. Even worse than that, Regina usually did give in. Not because she felt she had to, but because she knew Reigna needed to feel like she was protecting her sister. It was a remnant of being ignored by their parents. In every situation, Reigna always had to center herself to feel seen.

Usually, Regina went along to get along. Tonight, that wasn't happening.

"What exactly are you trying to say, Reigna?"

"I'm saying," her sister began, "the man only wanted you because he thought you were me. Why on earth would you want to see him, knowing that?"

Anger swept through Regina, making her hand tighten against her iPhone. She squeezed it so hard she'd be surprised if there wasn't a crack across the screen by the time this conversation was done.

"So, you're the only twin that can pull a king? Is that what you're saying? Because there's no way a man as fine and refined as Aléx could possibly want your slacking twin, right?"

"Regina." Reigna's voice was soft, filled with concern, and that pissed her off even more. She knew her sister wasn't saying this to be cruel. She truly believed she was trying to spare her feelings. "That's not what I meant. Aléx couldn't lick your Jimmy Choos. I just don't like the idea that he could be using you to fulfill some sort of sick twin fantasy he has in his head. That's why I think it best you stay away from him."

Knowing her sister was concerned for her didn't subdue Regina's anger. Instead, it blazed as if she'd thrown gasoline on it.

"Well," Regina spat out. "It's a good thing I'm just as grown as you, and I don't need you to make decisions for me. Whether I decide to continue seeing Aléx or not is on me. So if I'm just the knockoff he's using to warm his bed, I guess that's on me too."

She ended the call and was about to throw her phone on the table when she saw the number from her doorman's station flash across the screen.

"Ms. Devereaux."

"Yes?" Her voice was sharp. She could hear his surprised intake of breath on the other end of the phone, and she mentally reprimanded herself. Poor Mr. Aires didn't deserve her taking out her anger with her sister out on him. Realizing her mistake, she took a breath and tried again. "What can I do for you, Mr. Aires?"

"Ma'am, there's a gentleman down here by the name of Aléx. He's got a bit of an entourage. Is it okay if I let him up?"

Of course, the subject of her argument with her sister would show up. Because that's just how life worked for her. When things were bad, life could always find a way to make things worse for Regina. Tempted to say no, she imagined the headlines in tomorrow's gossip rags. "*Concrete Princess Shuts Out King Charming.* Read page two for details."

Deciding she didn't need that kind of headache, she said, "Let him up, Mr. Aires."

CHAPTER SIX

ALÉX TAPPED LIGHTLY on the apartment door, slightly perturbed that she hadn't been standing there waiting to welcome him. She'd given her permission for him to be let in. Why play this game? There was only one reason: she was trying to exert her dominance in this situation. Too bad for her that domination had nothing to do with this situation. Outside of when they were in bed, he wanted a partner more than anything else. If they were going to make this happen, it had to be as a unit.

He might hold all the political power as king of Obsidian Island. However, for the kingdom to thrive, it took a concerted effort from the monarch and their consort to keep the country running. She had to understand that.

When he heard the door opening, he braced himself to tell her exactly that. Unfortunately, that thought flew out of his head once he saw her face.

Tight lines were etched into her forehead, her jaw, and her mouth. When he looked into her red eyes, they were brimming with unshed tears. Every fiber of his being stretched taut, demanding he pull her into his arms and protect her from whatever had her so upset. Even if that whatever was him.

He moved to step inside her door when one of his security men laid a cautionary hand on his forearm.

"Your Majesty. We need to check the perimeter before you walk inside."

He leveled his gaze at Hugo, the head of his security team. He was a burly man, whose bulk had come in handy in protecting Aléx in one or two unsavory jams he'd found himself in. But tonight, Aléx didn't have time for protocol. Something was wrong with Regina, and she would never tell him what it was with his security team treating her like a potential threat to him in her own home.

Hugo gave an understanding nod and dropped his hand from Aléx's forearm. With the restraint gone, Aléx stepped inside. Before she could ask if his men were coming in, he closed the door and cupped her jaw gently.

The feel of her skin beneath his again transported him back to their one night together four months ago. A resulting fire flickered in his belly, but he refused to acknowledge it because this wasn't the time. Something was wrong, and he needed to know what it was. How could he fix it if he didn't know what she was facing?

"Treasure, what's wrong?"

She tried to shake her head, but he slipped his hand down, placing firm fingers against the back of her neck to keep her eyes focused on him.

"Don't lie to me, Regina. What has you so upset?"

She swallowed, closed her eyes, and took a steadying breath before she set her glassy eyes on him. The shimmer of her unshed tears made the rich brown of her irises sparkle.

"It's silly," she muttered. "I just had a fight with my sister. She's none too pleased with this situation I've created."

He scanned her eyes again, trying to get to the bottom of this. Regina's strong countenance was gone. Instead, hurt vibrated through her, from her inability to hold his gaze to the way she held herself with protective arms. The twins hadn't just argued. Whatever Reigna said had hurt Regina to the point that she was shaken, worn.

He dropped his hand from her neck and removed his suit jacket, tossing it on the long sofa behind him. He rolled up the sleeves of his white button-down shirt and reached for her hand.

"Where's your bedroom?"

Regina raised a questioning brow, making the corner of his mouth lift in amusement.

"Not for that, Regina. Whenever I was emotionally wrought as a child, my mother used to run me a bath and let me soak until all the tension of my harried feelings washed away with the water. Then she'd tuck me in and lie next to me until I was ready to talk. It's a practice I still use to this day. Whenever being king is too much, I take a soak, then go lie down to gain perspective on my thoughts and feelings. I'd like to do that for you…if you'd allow me to."

She studied him. Whatever she was looking for in his expression, she must have found it, because her lips curved into a soft smile before she said, "Down the hallway, last door on the right."

He gave her hand a reassuring squeeze before he followed her directions.

He didn't take time to appreciate the decor or even notice where anything was. Once she pointed him in the direction of her en suite bathroom, he set about his task.

He gave the room a brief glance before he spotted the large black hot tub with several decorative glass containers of different bath salts. He skimmed their labels until he found the lavender he was looking for.

When the tub was ready, he walked out of the bathroom in time to see her exit what appeared to be her walk-in closet in a red silk robe that fell to her mid-thigh. His body instantly tightened at the thought of what that robe was barely covering.

When she headed toward the bathroom, he cautioned himself not to look as she passed, because he knew what would happen the moment he saw that rich dark skin of the back of her thigh.

He was an admitted fool, however. Just as she passed him, his gaze dropped, and his cock went from twitching to semihard.

He pulled his gaze away just as she closed the door behind her, and thank goodness she had. If he'd listened to his body, he'd have followed her into that bath.

Giving himself a mental reprimand for not having better control over his body's reaction to her, he sat down on the foot bench of her king-size bed.

Think of financial reports, security council meeting minutes, lobbyist pitches, anything to get your body under control.

Eventually, the thought of dry reports calmed his body down, and he was able to make himself presentable.

When he looked up again, Regina was coming out of the bathroom. Now she was wearing a black camisole set with tiny silk shorts that instantly did away with all the hard mental work he'd done to make himself soft.

"So, what now?"

He was tempted to answer her question by lifting her up so that her thick legs wrapped around his waist, and he could devour her mouth while walking them to her rather large and convenient bed. Ultimately, he ignored his hardening length's demands and stood. He quickly pulled the linens back, taking her hand and pulling her to the bed.

He meant to step aside and bid her good-night, but she

scooted to the other side of the bed, leaving space for him as her eyes, soft with sleep, silently pleaded for him to join her.

You are such a glutton for punishment.

He was, but how could he be expected to deny her anything she wanted when she begged so prettily it literally unlocked something in him that made him fulfill her wishes, even if he didn't intend to?

God help him if she ever learned she had that kind of power over him. It could signal all kinds of dangers for him. Ignoring the warning bells in his head, he removed one wing tip shoe and then the other before crawling into the bed beside her.

He pulled her back to him, her ass notching perfectly into his lap as he engulfed her in his arms, completely spooning her.

A relieved sigh escaped her lips. He could hear the emotional fatigue.

He placed a kiss on the top of her head and tightened his hold as he said, "Sleep."

She chucked. "How am I supposed to sleep with that thing poking me in the backside?"

He tightened his embrace again, adjusting his head so that he was smiling against the shell of her ear.

"It's a rather inconvenient consequence of being this close to you. Whenever you're near, my body seems to have a mind of its own, and you're the only thing it wants to focus on."

He felt her go stiff in his arms. Had he gone too far? Had he made her uncomfortable? He turned her, forcing her to face him. He was learning that Regina was good at hiding what she felt, except for when her eyes were on him. It was the only time she allowed him to break through her defenses.

"What's wrong?"

She tried to drop her gaze again, and he placed a firm finger under her chin to force her to look at him.

"This thing where you hide from me, it stops now. I can't fix things if you don't tell me what's going on."

His brain tried to make him consider why he felt so compelled to fix anything for a woman he barely knew. A woman who had deceived him. That was an internal battle for another day. Right now, he needed her to open to him.

"Was it like that with my sister too?"

He wanted to rage and ask her how she could possibly think that after the time they shared together. But again, there was that soft pleading in her eyes that was as effective as a gut punch in lowering his defenses and getting him to give her whatever she needed and wanted in that moment.

"Despite that fact that I believed you to be your sister, you are the only woman I've ever had such a visceral response to. My interactions with your sister have only ever been business-related. We've never had any personal conversations. Beyond what your company could do for my country's economy, I had zero interest in her."

He caressed her cheek, letting his thumb slide against the soft skin there while desire prickled at every inch of him.

"I need you to hear me and hear me well, Regina. This isn't an attempt to mock your sister or dismiss her beauty and presence in any way. But when I met with your sister earlier today, I couldn't figure out for the life of me why there was absolutely no attraction to her. Nothing about her remotely appealed to me. The only emotion she invoked was anger because I thought she was lying to me."

He took her hand, sliding it down his clothed form until her delicate fingers were cupping him through his pants.

"This is all for you. It was that night, and it is now."

The sadness in her retreated, and he had to wonder how

long this had been plaguing her. Was she always in her sister's shadow? Was that why she didn't seem to think she compared with Reigna? Had some other man made her feel less than in comparison to her twin?

"I know it's childish. Especially considering I'm the one who let you think you were sleeping with my sister in the first place. But it mattered."

He nodded. "If it bothers you, if it upsets you, then it matters to me too. Is this what you and your sister were fighting about?"

Again, she tried to shift her gaze from his. "What did I say about hiding from me, Regina?"

Her eyes instantly snapped up to his, and the gift of her acquiescence burned through his veins like lava, scoring grooves into him and reshaping the landscape of his need.

"Yes. She thinks you might have some sort of twin kink and warned me away from you to protect me."

That might have been the gist of the conversation, yet everything in him believed that was the sanitized version of what Reigna had said. Instinctively he knew that if Reigna had spoken those exact words, Regina wouldn't have been as hurt as she was. If he ever got the chance, he'd make the new queen know exactly what he thought about her reckless mouth when it came to her sister.

Not that he had any right to engage Reigna on Regina's behalf, but that was beside the point. He wouldn't allow anyone to push Regina into a shell of self-doubt again.

"Is this what it's going to be like if I agree to marry you and have your child? Are you always going to come to my rescue?"

"Whether you choose to marry me or not, have my child or not, I will always come when you need me."

The strength of his words comforted her and surprised

him. He had no logical reason to make such assertions to her. But every instinct he had was to protect Regina. Even though she'd lied to him and that lie had put them all in a difficult position, it didn't matter. What mattered was when he saw need in her eyes, no matter whether it was sexual or emotional, he had the Pavlovian response to don his armor and protect her like the gallant kings of old.

CHAPTER SEVEN

REGINA SLOWLY CLIMBED out of the hold sleep had her in. She stretched, then remembered how she'd fallen asleep last night. She turned, hoping to find the king still lying beside her, but knowing somehow before her fingers found the cold sheets where he'd lain that he was gone.

A small ache that wasn't quite regret filled her chest as she thought about what had happened last night. He'd come to talk about his proposal. That was the only logical reason he'd shown up at her door. And yet when he'd seen her, he'd focused all his energy, all his words, on making her feel better.

She pulled herself up, swinging her legs out of the bed, and started her day with a quick shower. She threw on a pair of cream high-waisted slacks, a matching fitted crop top that fell just above her belt, and her favorite pair of Louboutins. A quick glance in the mirror at her size-sixteen form confirmed what she'd always known: fashionable and fabulous didn't have a dress size.

Intending to make a last stop in the kitchen for a cup of coffee before she headed to her lab, she ran into a solid wall of flesh. Before she could lose her balance, she felt a strong arm circle her waist, pulling her up against said wall.

She looked up to find amused blue eyes looking down at her with a matching grin to boot.

"Good morning, Treasure. How did you sleep?"

Being this close to him, she could smell the faint sweet and spicy tones of his cologne luring her to lean in and bury her nose in his chest. This chest had been pressed hard against her back as he cradled her while she slept.

Thinking over everything Aléx had said and done caused her to soften against him. Her sister had made him out to be a calculating monster. Considering he was a king, she was pretty sure that was a professional skill he had to expertly wield when necessary. The way he talked about duty and protecting his people, she was certain he didn't walk around pinching babies and kicking puppies all day either.

He was nothing like Reigna had made him out to be. How could he be when both times she was in his arms, he'd done everything to keep her safe and give her what she needed?

A spark of something warm and soothing spread through her as she thought about how he cared for her. It almost reminded her of how looked-after Ace always made her feel.

Safe.

Secure.

Protected.

Wanted.

It was that last one that was doing something to her, that made her pull back and steady herself on her own two feet. When you grew up with toxic parents who didn't hide the fact that you were a nuisance, no matter how great your life became, there was always this inkling buried deep inside your cells that needed to be wanted.

"Since I didn't even notice you slip out of the bed, you know I slept well. What are you still doing here? I thought you would've been back on your throne making royal decrees and such."

The amusement in his eyes was contagious, making her lips draw into a full grin in response.

"You Americans really do have a fantastical imagination when it comes to what a working monarch actually does."

She lifted a shoulder before stepping around him and leaning against the counter in the middle of the room.

"All we've got to go on are Disney movies and *The Crown*. What do you expect?"

She made quick work of making a single-serve cup of coffee, but kept her eyes focused on the machine so she wouldn't have to be mesmerized by the sight of him.

"What I mean to say is that I can't imagine you have a whole lot of time for leisure. Why are you still here, letting me take up all your time?"

"I'm right where I want to be."

He was standing next to her in one stride, his more than six feet of solid, broad body making her look up at him in her stiletto heels.

"Do you feel better? Are you still upset by what your sister said to you?"

She gave herself a mental shake, not wanting to think about those dark parts of her that Reigna's words had hollowed out. Unknowingly triggering the internal murkiness she fought to keep at bay. Aléx's care had wiped the stains of those parts away, and she wanted them to remain locked out.

Regina had spent so much time playing understudy to Reigna's main character that she'd somehow become supporting cast in her own life too. As much as she wanted to blame her sister for her emotional mess, Regina couldn't. She'd allowed Reigna to take the lead because it made her sister feel secure. But now that Reigna was married and living in another country and Regina was left alone, she regretted not showing up more for herself in the past.

When she was with Aléx, she didn't feel invisible. He saw her. What she wouldn't give to feel seen like that always.

Isn't that what the king is offering you, a life where you're wanted, always? A life where you're seen?

As if on cue, he came to stand behind her, putting his strong hands on her shoulders and giving them a light squeeze.

"Are you all right?" His rich tenor wrapped around her, making her feel as cozy as his arms had the night before.

"I'm fine. It must have had something to do with the lavender bath and the human teddy bear I got to snuggle up with in my sleep."

"Excuse me, Treasure. I'll have you know that I am a big scary king, not a teddy bear."

There was little bite to his voice. He wasn't taking himself seriously at all, and somehow that made him all the more attractive to her.

"Thank you for what you did last night." She finally turned around and sought out his gaze. "I realize that I completely derailed the reason for your visit with my B.S."

His gaze fell on her hard, singed with heat, and not the good kind of heat either.

"According to my sister," he began, "I can present as cold at times." There was quiet again, and she realized there was some heft to not only what he'd said, but how he'd said it. His voice deep, yet reserved, as if he were trying to sift for the truth in his own words.

"I'm sure your sister knows you much better than I. By my measure, apart from when I told you who I really was, you've only ever been kind to me."

"Perhaps I should keep you around, since you think I'm so wonderful."

"Was that a not-so-subtle hint at your proposal?"

Her quip gifted her a deep rumble of laughter that made her smile even harder. Bringing him back to this playful side felt like the biggest accomplishment she'd ever achieved.

"Since you brought it up, have you given it more thought?"

Except for when she was telling him about her fight with her sister, she hadn't thought of anything else. It was ridiculous. It made no sense at all. The problem was, after the care he'd given her last night, she'd wanted more of it. Would he give her more if she said yes? Was that even a risk she could take?

"Regina." His words drew her out of her own head and lulled her into the wonderful warm place where she felt comfortable and safe. "Despite how short a time we've known each other, we make sense. You know it. You've felt it just like I have."

He ran a light hand down her arm, letting his fingers caress her flesh gently. Felt it? She'd done more than feel it. The connection between them had haunted her for four months with relentless repetition. In her lab, out shopping, on the subway, in a cab, thoughts of him and them had burned themselves on the walls of her mind, turning her every which way but loose.

The physical connection had been immediate and undeniable between them. Last night, however, had made her want more than the physical, and that was why this was so scary. She wanted more of him, more of them together, more of the feeling she had when he'd cared for her so intentionally.

"Aléx, I do feel our connection. I just don't know that it's enough to carry on a successful marriage. When I dreamed of marriage, I dreamed of love, of a man who would always put me first. I've literally spent my life playing second fiddle to someone else. What happens if we get married, and you finally find the love of your life? Do I become an afterthought? Will I be pushed aside to make way for her? Is my only purpose going to be to give you a child? What happens once I've fulfilled that?"

"Regina—"

"No," she interrupted him. "These are real concerns, Aléx. I don't want to be stuck in a marriage where I'm invisible."

"You wouldn't be." He edged those words in, but she continued as if she hadn't heard him, because she needed to get all her worries out of her head.

"You've already told me that love won't be a factor. What assurances do I have that I won't just be the toy you pull out to show the rest of the world just how great you are and then behind the scenes, you barely interact with me? You not falling in sloppy love with me, I can handle. You pushing me to the periphery of your life and acting as if I don't matter, like I'm invisible and unimportant to you, I don't think I could live like that. I don't want my child growing up that way, believing people are disposable once they've fulfilled their designated purpose."

She tapped her acrylic nails against the white marble of the counter, hoping she didn't sound as desperate to him as she did to herself. He was probably regretting ever asking her at this point.

She was a strong and capable person. She didn't wallow in her feelings like this. Yet something inside her just couldn't let this go. Her insecurity about her position in people's lives had always been her Achilles' heel. It helped her discern how much effort and energy she gave to people. More importantly, it helped her decide how much of her heart to give.

"Regina." His voice had softened, smoothing out the rugged edges of her emotions. "As a king, I cannot be led by my emotions. As a man, love has seemed to do more harm than good. It's more often used as a weapon than a curative."

She couldn't rightly argue with him there. By all accounts, her parents were a love match. It was having children that destroyed their relationship. Perhaps if she approached it from the opposite way, maybe it might make for a better outcome.

She took a mental breath, berating herself.

This isn't an experiment. You can't science your way into a happy marriage, Regina.

"Love may not be part of our marriage, but care, concern, kindness, and consideration will be. I will take care of you every way I know how. There will never be another woman who comes before you. As my queen, it will be your right to expect that I put you first. As my wife, it will be my utter privilege to give you my devotion in mind, action and body. I promise you, Treasure, you will never doubt where you stand with me."

Her heart thumped harder in her chest. For a man who didn't believe in love, his words certainly painted the opposite picture. Because to her, everything he said made her want to fall hard for him.

"The only thing I need to know is," he continued, "...are you willing to offer me the same?"

This man and his charming and tender words were going to be the end of her. She absolutely knew it. How could she not want to run straight off the proverbial cliff just for a chance at a taste of what he was offering? She might never have been in love, but everything he offered her sounded like heaven to her weary soul.

"This marriage will be real, Regina. Whether or not you decide to continue our physical relationship beyond conception is immaterial. Our bond and our fate will be sealed. This is forever. Can you handle that?"

She was primed to agree, even though the tiny voice in her head kept asking her if she'd be able to live without love. Would it be so bad? Would she miss what she'd never had? No man had connected with her in a way that made her think a future was possible…before now. And then it suddenly occurred to her, there was something else they hadn't discussed that she had to get straight before she signed up for this.

"I can," she murmured, her mind still pulling out her metaphorical shield to protect her if what she said next made this conversation go left.

"Are we agreed, then?" His voice had so much hope that it was beginning to stir her own. But first, they had to get this all hammered out.

"No, we're not. Not yet. Aléx?"

"Yes, Treasure?"

Every time he used that pet name, some of the cold iciness she often tried to guard the delicate parts of her with melted a little more. But she couldn't get lost in how this man was making her feel. She had to ask the tough questions.

"I'm a Black woman."

"I'm aware." His answer was matter-of-fact, like race didn't matter.

She took a deep breath and pressed forward. "How are your people, your court, your family and friends going to react to you making me your queen? I've seen how Europeans like to tussle about their monarchies. I'm not trying to end up in a situation where I'm running from Obsidian Island with my children in tow because folks can't accept a Black woman as their queen."

When he was quiet and the silence stretched long beyond her patience, she spoke again.

"And if you tell me you don't see color, I'll twist your lips into a knot."

He chuckled, which was slightly comforting. If she'd seen disdain, disinterest or cluelessness in his eyes, her fight-or-flight response would have been humming in the background. Instead, she'd be out the door and getting into her car instead of standing here waiting on his next words.

She'd moved in corporate America for a good portion of her life. In those rarified circles, white people often tried to pretend they lived in a post-racial world. Her experience as a curvy Black woman from Brooklyn said otherwise. She couldn't go into this blind without knowing what she was facing.

"Obsidian Island isn't in Europe. It's in North America. We lie somewhere in the middle between Nova Scotia in Canada and Bermuda."

She rolled her eyes at his geography lesson. "Sir, you have a Greek name and look like John Stamos is your daddy. Are you really trying to argue that you don't have some European blood in your veins?"

She folded her arms, waiting for an answer, because they both knew she was right. "I wouldn't try to argue your point," he responded. "I couldn't. My mother was a direct descendant of the deposed royalty in Greece."

She went to turn away from him, and Aléx wrapped gentle fingers around her wrist, stroking the soft skin there in a silent plea for her to stay.

"I would never ignore your concerns regarding this matter. Race is very much still an issue, even on a small island nation like Obsidian Island. What I will tell you is that I will not tolerate any disrespect, outright or otherwise, at your expense. Not that this should allay your fears, but you won't be the first Black queen or monarch on the throne."

That made her cock an eyebrow, positive that the disbelief on her face was as visible as a neon sign. He was right that history didn't mean things would be a bed of roses. It simply meant she wouldn't be the first. Being the first in these situations always sucked.

"Really?" she asked.

She pulled out a chair at her eat-in counter, and he took the one immediately next to her, crowding her space and her senses.

"Yes, really," he replied in earnest. "I'll have to show you the Hall of Kings and Queens when you come back with me."

She hadn't missed that *when* in the sentence either. Listening to him, she couldn't decide if it was confidence or conceit that had him believing her leaving with him was an inevitability.

"We share the same land mass with Nyeusi, much like Haiti and the Dominican Republic. Since a good bit of the land that connects us is submerged below sea level, this makes travel between the two nations by boat and helicopter relatively easy. Now that we've built a bridge, traveling by car is possible too." He brought her back to the conversation. "Our peoples, including royals, have migrated back and forth as well as married throughout the centuries. Of course that doesn't magically make race relations better."

She couldn't call what his candidness made her feel relief. More like appreciation that he'd heard her concerns and hadn't tried to gaslight her into believing this wasn't an issue she should be bringing up. Glad to have that over with, she tried to bring some levity into the situation.

"Wow, King Aléxandros. It almost sounds like you're

signing on to be my hero, defending my honor like you've described. Does that mean you'd send people to the dungeons for me, wage war for me?"

"No." His voice was sharp and clear as he placed a finger under her chin, making her gaze fasten onto his. "It means I'd raze the ground they stood on for you. I'm not attempting to be your hero, Regina. Heroes don't exist. I'm trying to be your husband. I'm trying to show you that you'll never have to fight alone ever again."

That startled her. The idea of getting to lay down her weapons because someone else would protect her affected her on a level so deep, she could feel its impact running through her blood and bone. Black women in America didn't get to rest. They had to be three times better than anyone else to get marginally ahead. They were expected to be the mules of society, carrying all its burdens and nurturing everyone else except their families and loved ones. What he was offering her…felt like a balm to her soul.

Discomfort twisted in the bottom of her belly as reality screamed at her with a metaphorical bullhorn to make sure she heard it. She did, and recognized it for what it was, doubt. She still doubted him. Not that she believed he was lying, because his conviction came through in the steel of his voice. It was that history, both her personal history and the history of her people, that taught her to make people show and prove when it came to garnering her trust.

"Regina." He whispered her name, letting the sound pin her right where she sat. "Ultimately it comes down to this: Do you think you can trust me? If you can, I believe we can give each other everything we want."

Hearing his words was like being submerged in an ice river during a blizzard, shocking her system.

"Aléx, we're not each getting everything we want."

"All right then, what else is missing?"

Love, that's what's missing. Love.

The words were on the tip of her tongue, but she couldn't bring herself to say them. After Ace had rescued her and her sister from their terrible parents, she'd promised herself she'd never beg for love again, never believe blindly. And she never would.

"You're asking for marriage and a child, and devoted companionship. I need something more than that."

There wasn't a single second of hesitation in his voice. "Name it and it's yours."

"I need you to provide the seed capital and a fully stocked and staffed laboratory so I can create the Black hair care line I want to start."

This wasn't about being mercenary or transactional. This was about him taking on as much risk as her. In her estimation, the phrase "put your money where your mouth is" was an unassailable truth. If this all went to hell, at least she knew she'd walk away with something, even if she wound up losing her heart.

She didn't need his money or resources for this. She could pull the funds from her own accounts. She could find investors right here in the States. Her family owned a venture capital company, for goodness' sake. The money was literally at her fingertips. But if she chose any of those options, her sister would know. And if Reigna knew, she'd find a way to name all the logical reasons Regina was making a bad decision. Damn her logical brain. Regina's penchant for reason over emotion would force her to give in to her sister.

That could not happen again. Regina needed this. If she couldn't have the love she wanted, perhaps the child and the business of her heart would more than make up for it.

"Agreed," Aléx replied. "Now I just need to know when you want to get married."

"How soon can you get us back to Obsidian Island?"

And just like that, they were entering into an agreement to get married and have a kid. Panic should have been assailing her, should have had her clawing at her own throat to get air. Strangely, there was no panic, only rightness. Which meant one of two things. She was either in need of a mental competency exam, or maybe, just maybe, her instincts were forcing her to do what her mind and heart could never conceive of. Maybe, with Aléx's help, she could actually reach for her dreams and step out of her sister's shadow.

CHAPTER EIGHT

ALÉX TAPPED HIS finger against the arm of the plush leather chair of his plane. He looked around the large cabin, trying to distract himself, trying to pretend he wasn't worried that Regina would come to her senses and realize she could do so much better than a man who could never love her.

Love had gutted him, carved a cavernous hole in his chest that left him unable to hold something so precious. He'd tried it. Had given it everything he had, and when life cruelly snatched it away, he'd barely been able to survive. Thank God his father was still around then to fill in the gaps as his regent, and his sister had taken on as many of Aléx's duties as she could. Together they had borne the weight of the crown when he could hardly find a reason to get out of bed, to breathe, to live.

His chest tightened with long-buried memories that tried to climb out of the pit he'd thrown them in, making him physically shudder as he beat them back into the darkness. He would not go back there. He couldn't. Not again, not ever. He could never be that weak, broken and useless again.

"Your Majesty."

The sound of his personal secretary's voice using his courtesy title pulled him from his morose thoughts and forced him to step into the role he was literally born to play.

King Aléxandros of Obsidian Island. That man was strong and could endure anything.

"Ms. Devereaux's car is pulling up to the tarmac," Michael continued. "Would you like me to have her brought directly on board when she arrives?"

If she were anyone else, he would have been more than fine with that. The problem was, Regina never was anyone else. Even when he thought she was her sister, she was so different from anyone else he'd ever met, including the actual Reigna Devereaux.

"No, I'll bring her on myself."

He stood to his full height, squaring his shoulders and straightening his spine. His strides were long, eating up the path through the cabin, down the steps and to the tarmac. He arrived in time to see his security team opening the back door of the black limousine he'd sent for her.

Forever the charming king, he offered her a waiting hand and was gifted with a wide grin that lit up her face. It rocked him, forcing him to plant his feet so that they both didn't tip over when she placed a foot outside the car and stood on the skinniest pair of red stilettos he'd ever seen. Those shoes made electricity thrum through him, making him want to forget they stood in the open for all to see.

The sound of staffers pulling her luggage out of the car made him keep a tight leash on the desire her mere presence was stoking in him. It was a damn inconvenient time for his body to wrestle against his control.

He took a breath before taking in the full view of her. Regina was a beautiful woman in any circumstance. She'd been breathtaking in that cocktail dress when he'd met her. Today she was stunning in a fitted silk tee with cap sleeves paired with black high-waisted tailored pants that stopped just under her bust. She had business casual down to a science, and instead of making him want to crunch numbers, it made him want to peel every stitch of clothing she wore away from what he knew was the plush body of a voluptuous goddess with the softest skin he'd ever touched.

"Your Majesty." She greeted him with a teasing smirk that toyed with his self-control the way sweet cakes and candy tempted the most mischievous child. She was daring him to reprimand her about her calling him by his title.

It grated on everything inside him to hear her call him anything but what he called himself in his head. Aléxandros was the king. Aléx was the man. And more than anything, he wanted—no, needed—this woman to see him as a man. The king was what he did. The man was who he was.

"I hope Obsidian Island is ready for me, because Brooklyn is about to be in the house."

He placed her hand in the curve of his bent arm and leaned down to place a chaste kiss on her cheek.

"I don't think anyone on Obsidian Island is ready for you, Regina, least of all me. But I somehow think we'll all be the better for being graced by your presence."

Again, she blessed him with that big, beautiful smile, and all he wanted to do was tug her into his side and give her reason after reason to keep smiling at him with the same exuberance she was nearly blinding him with right now.

He remembered the last time he'd been this affected by a smile. Memories of a tall, slender woman with sandy brown hair and curious brown eyes looking back at him assailed him. The image was so sharp and so clear, he had to clutch the armrest to keep from reaching for her. As soon as the image came, it was gone, snatched away from him like she had been in real life.

Pain and regret traveled like bile from his gut, burning its way up his throat. When would his suffering stop? When would he be rid of this regret and guilt that always reminded him he wasn't worthy of love?

"Aléx, are you okay?"

He blinked away his thoughts and, through sheer muscle memory, used all his public speaking training to turn on his kingly charm and assuage the worry he saw building in Regina's pinched expression.

"I'm fine, Treasure. I'm simply cataloging the things I need to set in motion once we touch down."

She turned her head to get a glance around the cabin. "I'm sure this plush plane has Wi-Fi capabilities. You don't have to entertain me."

He pulled her hand into his and pressed his lips to the tops of her fingers. Her hands were soft and warm, inviting him to take the peace she unknowingly offered him. He'd felt it the night they'd met. He'd felt safe and cared for, and worthy in her presence. The last four months without her had left him short-tempered with chaos knocking around inside him.

All that rage and noise quieted once he'd learned the woman who'd had such an impact on him that neither his body nor his mind could forget her wasn't married to another king. He could have this again; all he had to do was keep her happy and show her his world wasn't something to fear, and he would protect her from any and all threats.

"I couldn't be better, Treasure. I'm just anxious to get you back home and make you my queen. The future we will have will be brilliant. You'll never want to leave."

"I think you're right. I don't ever want to leave this place."

Regina stood slack-jawed as she took in the ocean view from the balcony in his private chamber. He'd purposely chosen this side of the palace so he'd wake up to seeing the sun kissing the sea, and the water making the island's black sand sparkle like a flawless onyx.

"I've never seen black sand before."

The glimmer of excitement in her eyes made him proud. Obsidian Island was part of him, after all. Knowing that she saw the same beauty in his homeland made his chest fill with pride.

"It's very rare." He pointed out the coastline. "That's certainly part of its charm."

"I'm sure there's so many more charming things about it than the sand. Tell me about its history."

He closed his hand around hers, gently directing her away from the balcony, through his quarters and downstairs. Regina could hardly keep up as she took in their surroundings. Impossibly high ceilings, Roman pillars, and antique furniture and fabrics that were as old as the nation itself grabbed her interest with ease. She hardly noticed they'd arrived at their destination until he released her hand and opened the set of thirty-foot double doors that partitioned the room off from the rest of the palace.

"This is the Hall of Kings and Queens. It's the place where we honor the rulers of old, paying homage to their lives and their legacies."

They stopped by a large glass statue of a woman dressed in regal attire with her scepter clutched tightly between her hands.

"She is breathtaking. Who is she?"

He could feel the sad smile curving his lips. "Queen Carisse. She was my mother. Her reign lasted thirty years. She died eight years ago."

"And your father?"

"Six years later." He cleared his throat, trying to keep the dull ache of loss at bay. He'd adored both his parents, and being without them still made him feel unbalanced, like he wasn't quite himself.

"He, my sister, Eliana and I had our weekly family dinner. We reminisced about old times when it was still the four of us. He was happy, but tired, so he went to bed and went silently in his sleep."

"I'm so sorry, Aléx. I can see you still feel their loss."

"She was loud and boisterous and took up so much space in the room and life, and he was quiet and insightful. Together they were an unstoppable pair. It would be impossible not to feel their loss. They were amazing parents. But as monarch and consort, there aren't very many who can match their greatness. They passed on an incredible legacy to me and my sister."

She peered up at him, carefully assessing him as she spoke. "This legacy thing really is important to you, isn't it? You wanting an heir isn't just an act of ego?"

He leaned down and ran his finger over the gold plate at the base of his mother's statue. Sometimes, if he stared long enough at the statue at just the right angle, he swore he could almost see her form overlaid over the mold.

"Make no mistake, I do want a child. My desire aside, however, it really is my job. Securing the monarchy isn't just about wanting to enjoy royal trappings. We come from a line of people who have dedicated their lives in service to this land and its people. Fulfilling all those duties in the best way I can is my sole focus as king."

"Your people are lucky to have you."

"No, I'm lucky to serve them."

He took her hand and moved her further into the room, stopping to share interesting facts about his home and its history until they stopped in front of a large oil painting of a man with the same Mediterranean features Aléx bore and a darker-skinned woman with a large, tightly coiled Afro that stood as proud as the crown on her head.

"This is King Nikos. He was my fourth great-grandfather. The beautiful woman beside him is my fourth great-grandmother, Queen Nairobi, princess of Nyeusi, third daughter of King Amir of the House of Adebesi."

He could see her doing the calculations in her head, watching the intense concentration on her face as her mind took in all the factors and came to the inevitable conclusion.

"You and Jasiri share an ancestor?"

"We share three, in fact." When she opened her mouth to speak, he held up his hand. "All in different generations and different centuries. Queen Nairobi is our closest shared relative."

"Was your family here when Nyeusi was formed? Were your people part of The Trade?"

A chill ran down his spine as she stared directly at him, silently demanding his answer.

By her use of "The Trade," he knew she was referring to the Transatlantic Slave Trade. Nyeusi had become a nation when enslaved people from the 1741 New York Slave Conspiracy were wrongfully accused of sabotaging military bases and were sentenced to enslavement in the Caribbean or death in the colonies. Those brave souls overpowered their captors and were saved when they found themselves on an uninhabited island where they could live out the rest of their lives free.

"No, we weren't." His voice rang out strong in the room, echoing off the various monuments to his ancestors as if they were answering with him in unison.

"Some of those men who'd attempted to enslave Nyeusi's ancestors washed up on our shores. Our people took them in, unaware of who they were. We offered them food and shelter until Obsidians realized they were slavers. When they finally revealed themselves to be in search of an alliance in their unholy cause, we took them back to Nyeusi and turned them over for justice at the hands of those they'd wronged. From that moment, Obsidian Island and Nyeusi have been allies. We still are, even if I think their king is an arrogant tool."

"Hey, that's your cousin and my brother-in-law. Don't talk about him like that."

"He is my very distant cousin, this is true. We grew up together. Our parents were very close, and we were too."

"Were? Are you not close now?"

Aléx stepped closer to the painting of Queen Nairobi. With her uncompromising beauty and countenance, she made a fierce queen. Although they shared no blood, he could see the same qualities in Regina.

Refocusing on her question, he answered her. "Jasiri was raised very differently from me. His parents encouraged him going out into the world and experiencing life as a man and not an heir to a throne. It made him a bit wild and careless at times. I was raised to only focus on duty, to forget the self. Carelessness isn't something I easily give in to."

He wanted so badly to finish that sentence, to tell her of the one time he had been careless, and the consequences that unfolded as a result. Consequences he was still paying for to this day with a piece of his soul. Instead, he took the coward's way out and let quietness fill the room as thoughts of Jasiri filled his mind.

They had been fast friends as children. Jasiri had always brought a lightheartedness to Aléx's world he'd missed dearly when they began to grow apart.

You mean, when you distanced yourself from him, right?

That was the truth. He had pulled away once he'd learned

that Jasiri would be allowed to live in America as a Nyeusian ambassador after he'd completed university. When Aléx had finished university, he'd been summoned home to take on more royal responsibilities so that when he ascended to the throne, he would already be familiar with the process and the protocol of ruling.

Instead of being man enough to own his jealousy, he'd removed himself from Jasiri's life until the two men rarely spoke. Aléx isolated himself until he was left with nothing but his work and his immediate family.

That same sort of pettiness had cost him everything that mattered to him. When his ex, Farah, had left him, he'd slowly pulled away from her too. If he'd just had the courage to step outside her rejection of him, things might have worked out very differently, and he wouldn't have a blood debt marking his soul.

He would not make that same mistake with Regina. He would keep her close no matter what.

She slid her hand into his palm, and he sheltered it there. More and more he was finding he always wanted to shelter her. When he'd found her upset in her apartment, something ugly and possessive had churned inside him. His automatic response was to make sure she was okay and protect her from anyone who would dare hurt her, including her twin sister.

He'd question himself later about why that was. In this moment, like last night, he just wanted her to feel cared for, supported. From what little he'd gleaned about her relationship with her sister, he got the distinct impression that Regina's needs and wants were never brought to the center.

"Thank you for sharing that with me. It's an interesting bit of history I would never have garnered anywhere else in the world."

"Not even Nyeusi?" He knew that Nyeusi was rich with cultural reverence for the blood they'd shed to ensure their freedom.

"I've not really spent much time on Nyeusi. My sister's been married for less than six months. They're still in the honeymoon phase. The last thing they need is me underfoot."

He looked down at her, squeezing her hand to get her to meet his eye. "Do you always do that?" When she narrowed her gaze to silently ask him what he meant, he continued, "Do you always shrink yourself for your sister? Is that what she demands of you?"

Fire flashed in her eyes as she stared at him with sharp intention. "My sister loves me. You've known me for two days, basically. You don't get to pass judgment on her or me."

"You can deflect all you want, Treasure." He held her attention with his steadfast gaze. "I'm not going to let this drop. Does Reigna demand this kind of allegiance from you?"

He cupped her chin, forcing her to keep her eyes on him. He was learning that Regina was a fighter, and she would more than likely keep fighting if she thought it would get her out of explaining.

"I'm not going anywhere, Treasure. Tell me the truth."

The fight in her eyes retreated. She was slowly letting down her guard for him. It was a gift he would always handle with reverence.

"I don't want you to think Reigna is purposely malicious to me. She's not. My sister loves me, and I love her. In her head, I'm the little sister she needs to take care of, fuss over and protect. She doesn't want me to be small. She just doesn't want me to grow. Growing would mean I wouldn't need her."

"And you let her believe you do?" Although it was phrased as a question, he very much meant it as a statement.

"Yes," she replied as she stepped away from him, walking through the room and stopping to take in each display. This was classic avoidance behavior. But he wasn't about to let her get away with it.

When she was a few paces away from him, as if his proximity somehow made it hard to shape her thoughts, she said, "It's my way of taking care of her."

Understanding dawned. She wasn't weak. She simply allowed her sister to believe that.

He laid gentle hands on her shoulders and leaned down with his lips touching the shell of her ear. It was intimate, her scent almost intoxicating. But this wasn't about physicality. This was about his uncontrollable need to care for the woman who'd cared for him.

"Be careful, Treasure. If you keep shrinking yourself, eventually you'll disappear. And that will just never do. You will be a queen in two days. The queens of Obsidian Island are just as fierce as its kings, if not more so. Court is not for the faint of heart. You'll have to show them you can't be run over."

He saw the defiant spark in her eyes slightly letting loose the woman who had given and received pleasure like she was made explicitly for him. That was the woman he wanted to rule at his side. That was the woman who would be the mother of his children.

"I'm not worried, Treasure. I know you've got some teeth to you. I've felt them at work."

CHAPTER NINE

REGINA'S HEAD WAS SPINNING. She rested in her bed, trying to catch her breath while she could, because tomorrow was the day. Tomorrow, she would marry Aléx and become queen of Obsidian Island. How was this even her life?

Aléx had asked her if she wanted the big fancy wedding every queen was supposed to crave. She'd declined immediately. It seemed out of place when she knew she wasn't getting the whole deal. Those kinds of weddings were for people who were sloppy in love. That was not who she and Aléx were.

To expedite matters, she'd opted for a small ceremony in Aléx's drawing room with just them and Aléx's sister, Eliana. He'd informed her that they would eventually have a large observance that included her official coronation. For now, however, he would give her the small occasion, allowing her time to adjust to royal life before he presented her officially to the world.

An ache settled in her heart as she thought of both of Reigna's weddings. In both the civil and formal ceremonies, Regina had been right by Reigna's side. Despite the hurt her sister had heaped on her, Regina still wanted her here. Still wanted her support. Still wanted her love.

Her cell phone rang at that exact moment, and she didn't even have to look at the screen to know who it was. Regina didn't know if it was because they were twins or because they were just so close that they always seemed to sense when the other needed them.

Regina grabbed the phone, accepted the call and put the phone to her ear.

"What's wrong with my sister?"

That question, formed in her sister's sultry voice, was almost her undoing. It was the question they'd asked each other from the time since they'd learned to talk whenever they knew the other was hurting.

Before Regina could answer, Reigna spoke again. "Regina, I'm sorry that I hurt you. I was out of line, and I didn't mean any of it. I've tried to give you space to process. But no one in the office has seen you in two days, and I'm afraid something has happened to you. Please tell me what's going on."

Quiet tears streamed down Regina's cheeks. Keeping this secret from her sister was tying her in knots.

Her decision to keep what she and Aléx were planning a secret was selfish on so many levels. She'd done it partly to spite Reigna. Mostly, though, it was because she knew if she told Reigna the truth, her sister would go into protective mode. Regina would have to deal with Reigna's emotions instead of figuring out if Aléx's offer was the right thing for her.

"I'm fine, Reigna. I promise. I haven't been in the office because I've been spending some time with Aléx on Obsidian Island."

She heard Reigna's intake of breath and started speaking again before Reigna could interrupt.

"And if you start up again about Aléx not wanting me, I promise I will hang up and turn my phone off."

"You really like this man, don't you?"

If it were only as simple as liking him. She wouldn't go as far as to say she was in love with Aléx, but there was this underlying connection between them that she couldn't easily walk away from.

"I do."

"You sure he's dealt with the mistaken identity thing? Being queen means I have a plane at my disposal. I can be over there before you can say, 'Your Majesty.'"

Regina couldn't help the bubble of laughter climbing up her throat.

"I know you can. But I promise, everything with Aléx is going great."

"Okay?" Her sister's inquisitive but playful tone traveled through the line as clearly as if she were seated right beside Regina. "Tell me how good?"

Regina swallowed the lump in her throat, hoping she didn't end up regretting this. She knew even if she did, she loved her sister. She just wasn't built to lie to her no matter how much she didn't want to deal with her big-sister bullshit.

"If I tell you this, you have to promise me that you trust me, and you know I wouldn't do anything stupid."

"Regina." Reigna's skeptical huff made Regina smile.

"Promise. I really need my sister right now, and it sucks that I can't share some really incredible news with you because you think I'm naive when it comes to people."

The line was quiet. Regina could envision her sister biting her tongue until it bled to keep from antagonizing the younger twin.

"Regina, I won't lie to you. I do think you're naive when it comes to interpersonal interactions with people. Staying locked up in your lab all the time, you just haven't had as much practice. But you're the smartest person I know, and I do trust you. I just worry about you so much. You're my little sister, and if someone is messing with you, they gotta fight me first."

The image of her sister squared up in her royal regalia with her baby bump poking out made her howl with laughter.

"Chile, you are four months pregnant. The only thing you fighting right now is buttoned jeans."

Reigna reciprocated with an equally loud howl of laughter before she said, "Girl, you ain't ever lied. If it ain't elastic, I ain't wearing it. I'm over here giving the royal seamstress a fit because she's had to modify all my fancy clothes with elastic waists. Apparently, *elastic* is like a curse word in the palace."

Their laughter quieted before Reigna began to speak again. "Stop stalling. Tell me this good news. I promise, whatever it is, I'll be supportive if it means as much to you as it seems to."

There was the sister she loved. The sister who had always been there for her through all the rough times they'd suffered when they lived with their parents. This was the sister she could share everything with.

"Tomorrow… Aléx and I are getting married. You're not going to be the only queen in the family."

Regina waited for her sister to blow her top, to start yelling and telling her she didn't have the sense God gave a goat. It wasn't like she hadn't been saying the same thing to herself since she'd agreed to Aléx's proposal.

"He came to see me the morning after you and I fought," Reigna said.

That got Regina's attention.

"He did? What did he want?"

Reigna was quiet again, as if she were contemplating how to convey her next thought. Reigna wasn't necessarily known for her calm. If you angered her, she would pop off in an instant. But as CEO of Gemini Queens, she'd learned to temper her anger when she needed to. Considering Reigna had gone radio silent after their fight, she knew her sister was doing everything in her power to curb her tongue. Regina couldn't love Reigna more for that in this moment.

"Ostensibly," Reigna began, "he came to apologize to me for accusing me of hiding his child from him."

The hair at the back of Regina's neck prickled, waiting for Reigna to drop the proverbial other shoe.

"He was sincere in his apology, but he also came for another reason."

"For goodness' sake, Reigna, spit it out. What did he want?"

Reigna chuckled at Regina's impatience. Usually, it was Reigna who was snapping at Regina to get to the point. This was just more proof that this man was changing things in her life, possibly even changing her.

"He came to tell me to back off where you're concerned. He told me you were upset, and you felt like I didn't believe in you. He told me that my meddling made you doubt yourself, and he demanded I mind how I spoke to you and stay out of your relationship with him, because he wasn't going anywhere."

Panic settled in her bones. Those were fighting words if she'd ever heard them. Regina took a breath, letting calm spread throughout her being. Since Aléx was still in possession of all his faculties and his limbs, Regina was certain this heart-to-heart couldn't have gone too terribly. Again, Reigna was the firecracker in the family. That was especially true when she was angry. And Reigna being told about herself where her twin sister was concerned was a sure-fire way to piss that woman off.

"Considering he's still walking under his own power, I'm assuming you didn't try to commit regicide at this meeting." That got Regina a loud bark of laughter that broke the tension.

"Oh, I contemplated it." Reigna's huff was halfway between serious and "girl, you know I'm just teasing." "I told him I don't play about my sister. I also told him if he hurt you, he wouldn't have to worry about Jasiri's wrath. His pales in comparison when it comes to how I protect who and what's mine."

"Is that all you said?" Regina knew her sister, and this recitation of what had to be a heated exchange between Aléx and Reigna was all too polite as far as Regina was concerned.

"I told him, when it came to him hurting my sister, and I quote, 'Please don't fuck around and find out… Your Majesty.'"

Regina howled. Not that she condoned threatening people. However, since she'd made a similar threat to Jasiri regarding Reigna, Regina didn't exactly have room to throw stones.

"If I told you that I wasn't mad at what he dared to say to me, I'd be lying," Reigna continued. "But it needed to be said. I hadn't taken the time to really see that I was undermining you and not protecting you. For that, I'm rightly convicted and so terribly sorry. I owed you better, and your king made me see that."

Regina marveled at the turn of the conversation. She'd expected this chat to have gone in an entirely different direction. But this was Aléx changing everything for her with great ease, apparently.

"Regina, if he was willing to fight me over a woman he'd just reconnected with after four months of no contact, he must really care about you. As much as I didn't like his tone, I couldn't be mad at him for protecting my sister better than I ever had. And please understand," Reigna added quickly, "that is the only reason I didn't lose my ever-loving mind and snap his neck."

The line went quiet again as Regina processed everything her sister had said. What Aléx had done was brave, exceptionally ill-advised, but still brave nonetheless. Apparently, he'd truly meant it when he'd said he would put her first in all things.

"Are you happy, sister?"

Regina thought about Reigna's question, and deep down, she knew the answer. Even if it didn't make a lick of logical sense.

"Yes, sister, I am."

"Then that's all that matters to me. I want to be there. I want to stand up for you the way you stood up for me. Will you let me?"

Her eyes watered, and her heart swelled. Her sister was coming through for her, and damn if it didn't have Regina all weepy and emotional. She was the logical twin, damn it. Why couldn't she keep her eyes dry in her interactions with her sister as of late?

I wonder if sympathetic pregnancy emotions are a thing in twins? This had to be because of Reigna's pregnancy. It couldn't possibly have anything to do with her.

She'd have to look that up later and see if there was any science behind it. But right now, the only thing she managed was saying, "I wouldn't have it any other way."

The ceremony had been quick and quiet, and now their very small gathering of close family was moving about, enjoying wedding cake and champagne. Regina was utterly alluring in her white two-piece pantsuit accented by a matching corset. Her curves were on display, and he wanted to peel that suit off her, but these people were still in the room, extinguishing any hope he had of consummating his marriage in this moment.

"I recognize that look."

Aléx looked to his side to see Jasiri, his distant cousin and the current king of Nyeusi.

"And what look is that, Your Majesty?"

Jasiri leaned his broad body against the wall where Aléx stood, jostling him with an elbow nudge.

"The look that says you want everyone out because you can't take your eyes off your bride."

Jasiri wasn't wrong. He rarely was. That was probably the most annoying thing about the man. That and his effortless carefree air that always made Aléx want to shake him.

"You would know. From the rumors, you didn't leave Reigna's side through all three of your receptions or your coronation on your wedding day."

Jasiri nodded as he placed a forkful of cake in his mouth. "Exactly. And while you have that same hunger in your eyes, I have to wonder why you aren't plastered against your wife. I smell a marriage of convenience."

Aléx's entire body stiffened at Jasiri's words. Aléx wasn't ashamed of why he'd married Regina. But he wouldn't have anyone taking a cheap shot at her. Not even his royal cousin.

"This coming from the man who married his ex-girlfriend to be eligible to ascend to the throne. I don't think you have any room to throw stones."

Jasiri set his plate down, drawing himself up so that his back was to the room as he spoke so no one else could hear.

"I adore my wife, and by extension, my sister-in-love."

"Sister-in-love?"

Jasiri's exasperated sigh made Aléx want to smile. Good. He wasn't the only one annoyed with this conversation, then.

"It's how Reigna refers to in-laws. She says it's not the law that makes them family, but love. I love her sister," Jasiri continued. "I'm as protective of her as I am of my wife. Don't screw her over, Aléxandros, or you'll have to deal with me. Everyone knows you're not over—"

Aléx held up his hand, silencing Jasiri immediately. "Finish that sentence and you might not make it back to your throne in one piece…*cousin*."

The two men stared at each other. Both large with broad bodies, capable of matching each other's strength and rage.

"What happened to you, Aléx, was unthinkable. Nevertheless, I don't want Regina to live in someone else's shadow. Does she even know what happened?"

Aléx dipped his head, feeling the weight of his shame hit him. "No, she doesn't."

Jasiri clapped a hand on Aléx's shoulder. It was firm… yet it was supportive, as if he were really concerned for his cousin four or five times removed.

"Take it from someone whose secrets nearly cost him the love of an incredible woman. Don't hide your past from her. Let her help you with it. Because if you hurt her, Reigna will cut your balls off. And after she's done, you'll have to deal with me."

Jasiri's threat about Reigna made him shiver. He'd seen what a cutthroat businesswoman she was. After their tense conversation about her treatment of Regina, he'd had no doubt she'd slice him into tiny pieces if he hurt her sister. Neither of them had anything to worry about. Love might not be the basis of their marriage, but care and concern were.

"I'd rather cut off my own arm before I hurt her. She's special to me, Jasiri."

"Because she bears the same face as her sister?"

Anger simmered beneath Aléx's cool facade. The insinuation pissed him off, quite frankly. However, considering how their connection began, he couldn't rightly blame Jasiri either.

"I might not have known her real name when I met her, but trust me, she's the only sister I wanted then or now. Let's leave it at that before either of us says something we regret."

"Good," Jasiri said as a pleased smile set across his lips.

He was just about to step away when Aléx called after him.

"Jasiri, let that be the last time you insinuate my wife plays second to your wife, or any other woman, for that matter. If you do it again, I'll consider that an act of war and govern myself accordingly."

Jasiri's smile widened even further, showing every one of his perfect teeth. "That's exactly what a king and husband should do when someone insults his wife. You scorch the goddamn earth to protect her and her dignity at all costs. As long as you do that for Regina, you'll never hear a word from me."

The twins caught sight of the two of them and made their way to each of them respectively. Regina slid into Aléx's embrace instinctively as he pulled her into his side. This was where she belonged. It didn't matter that they weren't in love or hadn't come together in the traditional sense. She was his wife, and as he'd told Jasiri, he'd never let anyone hurt her.

Are you including yourself in that?

He closed his eyes and breathed in her sweet scent, trying to ignore the voice in his head. He could do this. He could protect and care for someone again. He would do it, no matter how much his fear tried to tell him otherwise.

"Are you ready to retire, Treasure?"

She looked up at him with queries in her eyes, questions she wanted to ask. But the soft kiss he placed on her lips prevented her from verbalizing them.

Tonight would be about them and not the ghosts of his past. If only for tonight, he would be free of his pain and give everything he had to Queen Regina. The woman who had quite literally turned his world upside down.

CHAPTER TEN

REGINA STOOD ON the balcony of the cottage they'd be spending their wedding night in. According to Aléx, this was the place where every Obsidian monarch spent their first night with their spouse. She'd tried to tell him they didn't have to bother, but he'd insisted. She was his queen, and she would be treated as such.

Regina tried to settle the dull ache in her chest as she thought about the situation she'd willingly put herself in. She had no right to be sad. This marriage was a business deal, not a love affair. Of course she would spend her wedding night alone. It wasn't a real wedding, and this wasn't a real marriage.

Outside the legality of it all, she and Aléx, for all intents and purposes, were roommates and business partners.

You agreed to that. No need to be upset about it now.

To lift her mood, she'd put on a silk robe and camisole set that stopped at the middle of her thick thighs. Regina loved the way lingerie felt against her skin. It was silky, caressing her softly, and putting her curves on display at the same time. Every night, whether she slept alone or not, she put something soft and silky on her skin to love on herself.

Tonight, she needed to love on herself more than she ever had.

Standing on the balcony and watching the waves ebb

and flow slowly against the rocks calmed the fears trying to claw their way through her system. She looked down at the square diamond sitting on a bed of small round white diamonds and the infinity diamond ring Aléx had placed on her finger today.

Her body warmed with his thoughtfulness and generosity. She hadn't expected something like this, marveling at it as the moonlight twinkled in its facets. She'd told him it was too much, and he'd replied that it wasn't enough.

This man was so sweet to her it was killing her. How was she not supposed to fall for him when he did and said sweet things like that?

I don't know how you're gonna manage, but you bet'not fall for that man. He doesn't want love, remember? He only wants a baby and companionship.

Before she could ruminate harder on her intrusive thoughts, a knock at the bedroom door drew her attention.

Aléx walked in wearing nothing but his silk pajama bottoms, and her mouth went dry with want.

Miles of tanned skin and hard muscle filled her vision, and the memory of what that flesh felt like entangled with hers instantly brought heat up her chest, neck and face.

"There you are." He padded lightly across the carpeted floor, his steps surprisingly quiet as he did. "I thought I'd misplaced my wife when I couldn't find her in our bedroom."

"Our?" Her brain tried to grasp what he was saying, but she couldn't quite get it to work properly while he was standing in front of her, tempting her to run to him and throw herself at him.

She shook her head, willing her mouth to work. "I didn't think you'd want to sleep in the same bed."

He tilted his head, silently asking her to elaborate.

"We hadn't discussed sleeping arrangements."

He stepped closer to her, cupping her cheek and letting his thumb slide gently across the flesh there.

"Is it not customary for married people to share a bed in America?"

"No, it's just that we aren't the typical couple, Aléx. I didn't think you'd want me in your bed until we were actively trying to conceive."

He tilted her head back, making sure her eyes were on him and nothing else.

"Were we trying to conceive when I first asked you to join me in my bed?"

She tried to shake her head, but his fingers were buried in her hair, preventing her from moving. As his nails lightly scraped against her scalp, she said, "No, we weren't."

"Then you should know that I expect you to sleep by my side. Are you okay with that?"

It was an impossibility to her how this man managed to be so dominant and controlling and yet still insist on her agency at the same time. It was the only reason she wasn't concerned by Aléx's domineering ways. She knew if she wanted to, she could say no, and Aléx would respect her choice. Did she want to? Hell no.

"Yes." Her voice was husky and nearly unrecognizable to her own ears. How could this man reprimand her and turn her on at the same time? There was something deeply wrong with her that she was this into his BS.

"Are you okay with everything that happened the last time you were in my bed happening again, right now?"

His hand had slid free of her hair, and now his strong fingers were curling around her neck, his thumb sliding against the pulse point at its base. Her heart was beating a loud tattoo in her chest, and she was certain he could feel every beat with his thumb positioned there.

"I'm waiting for an answer, Treasure."

"I'm not ovulating yet. We wouldn't conceive tonight."

He pulled her into him. The hard planes of his broad body fit easily into her soft curves. His length was hard and thick against her belly, and she had to fight herself not to drop to her knees right then and try to swallow him whole.

"My reaction to you wasn't about wanting to conceive then or now, Regina. I simply want you. I've been haunted by our one night together for four unrelenting months. I need to feel you under me again. I need to know it and you weren't a figment of my imagination. Will you let me have you tonight?"

Fire flickered inside her belly from a small spark to the growing inferno she could hardly contain. Did she want him? Did she want him to have her? Hell-to-the-absolute-yes.

"I'm yours anytime, anywhere you want me."

To the novice ear, she was certain she sounded thirsty and pathetic, begging for a man's attention. What they'd need to understand to even remotely comprehend the unfolding scene is that Aléx was no ordinary man.

It wasn't just his body, although Lord knew that was enough. His tanned bare chest, strong and supple with its defined muscles, didn't just represent a hot body to bring her pleasure. It represented a safe place to let go and come undone.

She'd come undone that night in his hotel room; she'd allowed him to erase every care and worry she had and just simply focus on him, to exist in the pleasure he supplied.

"Careful, Treasure." His voice was deep and rich like aged bourbon, intoxicating as it drew her in. "I might just take you up on that."

Regina slid her hands up his arms and down his pecs,

loving his warm skin underneath hers. She'd been nearly consumed by that heat all those months ago. There was no way in hell she was missing out on it now. If Aléx was offering to let her bathe in that fire again, to let her forget everything, including the fact that this would be all he could ever give her, she would allow him whatever access to her body he wanted.

"I wholeheartedly expect you to."

There was no warning. Like a lion, he was ferocious and fast, lifting her until her legs were around his hips and his lips were on hers. He drank from her, taking all she had to give and still demanding more.

When she broke away from the kiss to drag air into her burning lungs, she noticed they were no longer in the previous bedroom. They were in his…correction, theirs. She'd stayed in that other bedroom because she hadn't wanted to assume anything between them. Aléx had been clear about love not factoring into their relationship. She'd agreed that it wouldn't be a problem. She was simply here to get the things she wanted: a baby and her hair care line. Couldn't this intimacy be one of those things too?

He answered the question rolling around in her head when he loosened his grip on her and allowed her to slide down his taut body until her feet touched the plush carpeting on the floor. With skilled hands, he slipped one spaghetti strap of her camisole down and then the other.

"The night I came to your apartment, and you walked out of your bathroom wearing a similar set, I had to fight myself not to touch you. You were hurting, and me groping you wasn't what you needed. God, but how I wanted to. That image has been replaying in my head on a constant loop."

He let the silk camisole fall until it puddled around her feet on the floor, stepping behind her before placing searing lips against the base of her neck. It was a simple touch, but instant flames engulfed her as her lust consumed her. He pulled away, forcing a desperate moan from her. She lifted an arm, burying her fingers into his thick, dark strands as she attempted to drag his mouth back to where she wanted it.

"The last time we were together, everything was hot and furious, Regina."

"Are you complaining?"

He was pressed against her back now, and she could feel the soft rumble of a sexy chuckle rolling through his chest.

"Not in the least. Except that I wished I'd had more time to explore every inch of your body. I intend to make up for that now."

He pulled the silk shorts of the set down, slowly setting her skin on fire with each touch. Once she stepped out of them, he stood and cupped her heavy breasts from behind, rolling his thumbs over the sensitive flesh of her nipples. Her body tingled at his touch, need blossoming inside her that every place his fingers grazed, no matter how lightly, made her ache.

He used one hand to pull her face to his, kissing her deeply, his tongue tangling with hers as his free hand slipped between her thighs. She would've gasped if she could, but his kiss was so powerful, so thorough, it seemed to capture her breath, leaving her air-hungry as his fingers found her folds.

Carefully he slid his fingers between them, finding the slick evidence of her arousal, and he moaned so deeply she could feel it reverberate through her body, causing her sex to throb, aching for more.

More of his touch, more of him, more of the need he was stoking in her.

"How could you ever believe I wouldn't want you like this every chance afforded me?"

He slowly stroked her clit, his fingers moving in rhythm with the cadence of his words. Her hips began to swerve to the rhythm he was creating, chasing the pleasure his fingers so expertly gave to her. She was so close, right there on the precipice of release. She just needed...needed...

He slipped a finger inside her. The sensation ratcheted up her desire, causing delicious tension to pull at her muscles, making her sex flex around him. He added another finger, and the stretch was so perfect, adding the last spark she was seeking to ignite the climax that had been just out of reach from the moment he touched her.

His strong arm closed around her waist, keeping her upright as she rode his fingers to completion.

"There's my good girl. You have no idea how much I've missed her, how much I've wanted to see her break apart for me."

Slowly, her cognitive abilities returned through the haze of post-climax bliss.

"Is that all you wanted, to see her come on your fingers?"

He hissed between his teeth as if she'd struck a raw nerve. Point one for her. He might be a king with an obedience kink in the bedroom, but that didn't mean she couldn't drag him to lose his ever-present control.

He turned her in his arms, bringing them face-to-face. His eyes were dark and sinister, like she'd cut the last restraint he had. Good. That let her know she wasn't in this alone. This hunger that burned so bright in her blood, seeping into her flesh and taking control of her mind, wasn't just her affliction to bear alone.

"No," he growled through clenched teeth. "It isn't even the tip of what I've wanted."

He took her hand, leading her up the three steps that led to the platform of the bed. His gaze was fierce and hungry, a predator with his long-desired prey in his sights. "On your knees."

There wasn't a second of hesitation in her response. Her body instantly acquiesced to his command. Her brain didn't have time to think about it. The only thing she could do was give in.

He quickly dispensed with his pajama bottoms, his length springing free. Thick and red with protruding veins that wrapped around it like tangled vines, it slapped against his stomach. He leaned down, taking her chin between his thumb and his forefinger.

"I want that smart mouth of yours wrapped around my cock now."

Again, not the slightest bit of hesitation. As soon as he sat on the edge of the bed, spreading his legs to make room for her as he gave himself one long stroke from his domed cap to his base, she was in position, ready to receive him.

She wrapped her fingers around his base, testing its girth to see if he was as thick as her memory had portrayed or if it was just her imagination. She had not been wrong. He was thick and hard, and so ready for her that her mouth watered.

One lick from his sac to his tip and she was rewarded with a heavy groan. His satisfaction evident, she swirled her tongue around his cap, dragging her tongue through the salty pearl of precum waiting for her.

She took him into her mouth, groaning at their mutual satisfaction. Their bodies were in tune; even four months hadn't been enough to make either of them forget how to please the other.

His hips moved involuntarily, joining the rhythm she'd set every time he slid in and out of her mouth. With each stroke, Aléx spoke through his tight jaw, praising her for the way she pleasured him.

"Don't stop."

"God, your mouth feels incredible."

"I could fuck your mouth all night."

She'd be perfectly fine with that if it kept him impossibly hard with his entire body taut with clenched muscles. She looked up at him, seeing his imminent destruction in the fire in his eyes. It was the only encouragement she needed to keep going, until she winked at him, drawing his fire.

"Shit." He sat up, placing strong hands under her arms and pulling her onto the bed. Before she could get her bearings, she was pinned beneath him with him wedged between her thighs and her hands clasped above her head by his. He slammed his mouth on top of hers, punishing her insolence with the firm press of his lips as he devoured her, licking inside her mouth, sharing their comingled flavors.

He tore his mouth from hers once he'd drunk his fill. His chest heaved as he tried to regulate his breathing enough to speak.

"Do you want me to use a condom?" He must've seen her intended response written in the pinched skin of her brow. "And God help me, if you tell me one more time we can't conceive tonight, I'm going to turn you over and spank your naked ass until you learn to never speak that phrase to me again when we're in bed. I want you, Regina. I want to feel you with no barriers. If you're uncomfortable with that, I will wear a condom."

She could feel her arousal sliding down her leg, and she had to wonder whether it was his threat of a spanking or his stated desire for her that made her so wet. Whichever it was, she was certain of only one thing. She needed him inside her right now.

She tugged her wrist free of his hand, sliding it between them, guiding his cock to her entrance.

"No barriers," she whispered.

The last bit of his control disintegrated into nothingness as he slammed into her. There was no finesse. There were no seductive moves to draw out their pleasure. It was as if her consent drove him beyond reason. The only thing she could do was wrap her legs around his hips and hold on for the ride.

Her muscles clenched around him as each stroke pushed her closer and closer to the incredible gratification only he could give her.

"Aléx, Aléx, Aléx." His name became a litany, a psalm, a sacred hymn that expressed everything she was feeling, everything she couldn't explain, everything she didn't allow herself to think even for a second.

Her climax crashed over her. She buried her nails in his shoulders, trying to find purchase until it ebbed. But he would have none of it. He kept stroking inside her with such power and intent that another climax dragged her under its powerful waves. She couldn't breathe. She didn't need to. All she needed was Aléx and the incredible way he made her body do his bidding.

"Mine," he growled as he continued to glide in and out of her. "You're mine, Regina. Mine."

His body stiffened as he slammed into her one last time before his orgasm took hold of him. She could feel him pulsing inside her, marking her inside and out.

As they settled and he gathered her into his arms, intertwining her limbs with his, the little piece of herself she'd lost when he'd called her sister's name that first time clicked right back into place. If she was his, then he was hers too.

CHAPTER ELEVEN

REGINA TURNED TOWARD the furnace that seemed to surround her with heat, feeling familiar muscle, skin and sinew. They'd been married for three weeks now. He'd been true to his word, making sure they slept together, as in a euphemism for sex, and slept together, as in actually sleeping together every night.

"Good morning, my queen. Are you going to sleep all day, or should we go out and explore the grounds? I'm afraid I've been a terrible husband by keeping you naked and in bed almost every moment of the day."

"Trust me," she murmured through the haze of sleep and building lust. "A sistah ain't mad at you."

"I guess I should take that as a compliment, then." He pulled her into him, dropping her leg around his and notching himself between her thighs.

"Oh, it definitely was meant as one."

"You tempt me beyond reason, my queen. We do need to get up, however. I'm afraid we must hold court next week. That means this week, we have to get ourselves and the house in order. The world will not stop just because we've found undeniable pleasure in each other's arms."

She groaned loudly as she buried her face in his chest. "Boo to the world. It sucks."

"It does indeed, Your Majesty."

She peered up at him, finding the easy humor in his eyes. This was the man she'd met that night nearly five months ago. She'd never thought she'd see him again. That was especially true after she'd admitted the truth of her identity to him. But somehow, fate had managed to bring him back into her life, and Regina was enjoying every bit of it and him.

"It feels so weird every time you address me by that title."

With his elbow bent, he held his head up as his penetrating gaze seemed to look through her.

"Weird? Those titles are rightfully yours. You are the queen of Obsidian Island."

That was certainly true. The moment she'd said "I do" and signed the marriage license, all rights hereunto were bestowed upon her. Now if she walked into a room, everyone stopped and bowed or curtsied.

The first time this had happened, she'd stood quietly in awe watching for nearly a full two minutes. Aléx had to whisper in her ear that they would remain in that position until she gave them leave. She'd felt so bad. She couldn't imagine how uncomfortable it was to hold that position for so long simply because she hadn't a clue about her role.

"Aléx, I don't know how to be a queen. And the truth is, I don't want to be one in name only. If I'm going to be here, I'd like to learn your customs and your history, learn about your people and your land. I'll be teaching our children everything I can about Black American history. I want to be able to teach them Obsidian history, and why what their father does matters, too. I want to be the partner you need and the queen that they need. Show me how to be that."

His eyes widened, and his mouth was slightly slack as he stared at her. "I hadn't really thought you'd be interested in any of that."

"My lab won't be ready for another week. Am I supposed

to sit around eating bonbons while you do all the decreeing and knighting that I'm sure will take up your whole day?"

The rumble of his laughter sent tremors throughout the bed. Seeing Aléx this way, with his dark hair mussed and his skin flushed from all they'd done in this very bed throughout the night, this unguarded version of him, tugged at her heart.

"You Americans." He shook his head. "Where do you get all these wild notions about what being a monarch actually entails?"

She poked him in the chest with a playful finger. "I told you before, we've got Disney princess movies and *The Crown*. Oh." She snapped her finger and continued. "We've got *Game of Thrones* too. With those poor examples, what do you expect?"

That earned her another laugh, and she took joy in her reward. Aléxandros the king made for a striking picture. Aléx the man, however, was breathtaking in his exuberance.

"All right." He sat up, jumping out of the bed and pulling her by the legs until she was at the edge of the bed. "If my queen wants to be a queen, then I'm going to send you to someone who was trained by the best queen of all."

"Who was the best queen?"

"My mother. And she taught my sister, Eliana, everything she knew."

Regina closed her eyes, trying to remedy the slight fatigue she felt behind them. This always happened whenever she studied something too long. Whether it was looking through microscopes, reading chemical formulas, or—as she was doing now—reading all the materials Eliana had given her to bone up on Obsidian civics, her eyes were the first part of her body to give up the fight when she concentrated too hard.

"You look like you need a break."

Regina looked up to see a smiling Eliana sitting down next to her on the plush chaise in what she'd come to learn was the drawing room. To her, it looked like a big and fancy living room. She figured being royal was so fancy that even her billionaire status meant she was so out of her depth she couldn't tell the difference between the two.

Eliana, princess of Obsidian Island and current heir to the throne should anything happen to Aléx. She was tall, slender, with a full face of flawless makeup and long, dark hair falling in waves down her shoulders. The woman's beauty and poise were indisputable facts. She looked like she'd stepped right out of *Ms. Royalty* magazine to grace the peasants with her presence.

In a smart two-piece double-breasted suit, she more closely resembled someone who was running a Fortune 500 company and less like someone who could quite possibly end up inheriting a country if Regina didn't produce the heir her husband so desperately wanted.

"Do you think you've prepared enough for your introduction to court tonight?"

Regina had tried to forget all about that. It wasn't that she was afraid of being around people. She just couldn't put on airs to save her life. It's why her sister was the face of Gemini Queens, and she worked behind the scenes doing her part to make the company a success in her own way.

"Thanks to you, I think I have all the houses and families down, as well as the different titles for the royals and the aristocrats. Whether I'll end up making myself look like a fool is another matter altogether."

What Reigna offered Jasiri as someone who was well-versed in networking and socializing with the goal of furthering an agenda, Regina would never be able to provide for Aléx. Where Reigna was suave, Regina was blunt. And the first time someone said something that remotely rubbed Regina the wrong way, she was way more likely to curse them out than her cultured twin. Not that Reigna wasn't famous for gathering folks too. She was just a great deal more elegant about it, when she needed to be, than Regina.

"Are you regretting asking to learn what it means to be an Obsidian queen yet?"

Eliana's trimmed brow was lifted into a perfect arch. If it weren't for the teasing smile on her face, Regina would think the woman was taking sadistic joy in her discomfort.

"No," Regina countered. "I'm enjoying learning about your history and its connection to Nyeusi. It's sort of awesome that sister nations now have sister queens."

Eliana's smile broadened. "I hadn't thought about it like that. But you're correct, it is pretty awesome."

"You're sure you aren't bothered by that fact?"

Confusion turned her sea-blue eyes into a darker cobalt as she stared at Regina.

"Why wouldn't I be thrilled about that?"

"Well," Regina began, "if your brother hadn't married me, you'd be the next queen."

Eliana raised a manicured finger, shaking it slightly. "That's only if my brother never married or sired any legitimate heirs. And even if those two things were true, he'd have to precede me in death. Also, you're assuming I want the job."

Regina scanned the woman's face to see if she could discern any artifice. She could find none. The woman was serious. Eliana leaned in, placing a hand on top of Regina's.

"I love my country, but I have never wanted to be its monarch for any reason. I'd sooner give it to Jasiri than take it on myself."

"Jasiri can inherit the throne here?"

"One of the weird things about royal blood is that most royals in the world share some kind of consanguineous connection. In Europe, most royals are related through Queen Victoria. For Obsidian Island and Nyeusi, it's Queen Nairobi."

Regina nodded along as she made the connections in her head. "Jasiri once mentioned the consanguinity part." She opened one of the books she'd been reading and found Queen Nairobi's picture and pointed at it. "Your brother said she was a Nyeusian princess."

"Not just any Nyeusian princess," Eliana clarified. "She was the daughter of a Nyeusian king, which meant her descendants are part of the line of succession in both Obsidian Island and Nyeusi. If the royal line was wiped out on Obsidian Island, Jasiri would have a legitimate claim to the throne. The same is true for my brother and any heirs you and he produce. You could give birth to a future monarch who could claim both thrones."

She took a big, exaggerated breath as if relaying that information had tired her out. "But thanks to you, I will be pushed to the back of the line of succession once you and my brother procreate. On that count alone, you are now my official favorite person in the world. I like fun and chaos too much to want to be the monarch of this country."

Eliana's excitement about Regina's place and purpose concerning the line of succession lightened her heart while simultaneously scaring her to death. What would happen if she couldn't give Aléx, and by extension the nation, an heir?

She could feel panic trying to close its grip around her throat, but she refused to allow it. The best way to combat the unknown was to create a plan using as much viable and pertinent data as one could find. She couldn't science her way into getting her husband to love her. But she could damn sure science her way into giving him the child they both wanted.

"Are you all right, Regina? If I've broken you with all this talk of lines of succession and babies, my brother is sure to punish me by assigning me some dreadfully boring task like listening to a presentation from the minister of agriculture."

That pulled Regina out of battle plan mode and made her laugh until she could feel wetness in her eyes.

"I'm fine. I just need a little help from someone who enjoys fun and chaos and is probably good at getting things in and out of the palace without anyone knowing, especially not the king."

Eliana clapped her hands together, rubbing them in a conspiratorial way that let Regina know her sister-in-law was all in.

"I am your faithful servant, my queen. What does Her Majesty require?"

"I need a bunch of ovulation kits. If your brother and I are gonna make sure you never have to become queen, I need to use science and technology to figure out the optimal time to do that. I just don't want everyone knowing and adding extra pressure on me and, by extension, your brother."

The sharp planes of Eliana's face softened with compassion. Regina figured if anyone understood what living under scrutiny was like, it had to be an actual princess.

"You'll have them in your hands by tomorrow."

Regina had never considered what it might be like to have another sister. She and Reigna were literally two halves of one whole, a built-in second self who would always hold you down no matter what. This woman was showing her that non-twin sisters were valuable too, even if they didn't share any DNA with you.

CHAPTER TWELVE

REGINA STARED AT the negative ovulation test with disbelief. She'd been tracking her ovulation for nearly a week and with no success. Her ovaries had decided to forgo her usual cycle and refused to release an egg.

Since her first period, everything about her cycle had been textbook. A twenty-eight-day cycle starting off with three days of light menstruation. That meant two weeks later, she should've been releasing an egg. It was now three weeks after her cycle and still, every single test she'd taken had said no.

Stress.

This had to be about the stress of becoming queen. Aléx had done all he could to make this transition smooth for her. Her presentation to court had been an informal (for royalty anyway) event in the throne room where only high-ranking members of court were present. He'd also set up an interview with the two of them to introduce her to his people in lieu of an exhausting media tour and in-person events. Still, the added pressure must be getting to her if her cycle was this off.

Disposing of the test in the private bathroom of her new office at her lab, she decided she wouldn't stand there obsessing about this. She'd put in a call to her ob-gyn back in the States. Hell, she'd fly back if the doctor advised an examination. She needed to figure this thing out one way or the other.

It made no sense to involve Aléx until she had facts to help her understand what was going on. Until then, she had this beautiful new lab her husband had built for her from the ground up. She'd lose herself in experiments to calm herself down and keep herself focused.

She worked for hours, formulating, testing, reformulating and retesting relentlessly. She didn't stop until she started to feel hot.

"Damn, working under these lights must be getting to me."

She pulled off her lab coat before grabbing more of the polyethylene glycol to get this next trial underway.

She continued to work until the building ache in the back of her head began pounding, and she had to reach for a nearby stool to sit down.

Just as she sat, her phone rang. The sight of Aléx's name on the screen made her smile through the throbbing.

"Good evening, Treasure. I was under the impression that my queen would be having dinner with me tonight."

"Of course I am. I still have another hour before I need to leave."

His reprimanding tsk put her on notice.

"You should've left an hour ago if we were going to dine at home."

"That can't—" She looked down at her watch face to see that Aléx was telling the truth. She had missed dinner. That's probably why her damn head was hurting her so bad. "I'm so sorry, Aléx. I got caught up in the lab."

"I guess it's good your sister told me you tend to work so long that you often forget to eat or drink. According to her, it's not uncommon for you to become hypoglycemic when you get caught up in whatever you're working on."

The click of her lab door drew her attention away from the phone. She found Aléx walking through it, holding a large paper bag in his hand.

"You really are amazing. My head is killing me, and I'm feeling a bit dizzy. Whatever you've got in there had better have a decent amount of carbs."

"Will chef's garlic butter pasta, that you love so much, do?"

If her head wasn't pounding, she would have squealed in response. "Absolutely will. Let's just take it in my office. We're breaking all sorts of regulatory statutes by bringing food into the lab."

She stood up, and he held the door for her. When she made to take her first step, her vision began to swim. She glanced up to meet Aléx's eyes and found his face sharp and tight with panic.

"Regina?"

It was the last thing she heard before everything went black.

Aléx was king of all he surveyed. His word was law, and his will was absolute, and yet none of that mattered in this moment. That absolute power he had was rendered useless as his wife lay in the hospital ward of the palace.

Her beautiful rich brown skin looked slightly ashen against the stark white sheets of the hospital bed in the center of the room. She had an IV in her right arm and a blood pressure cuff on her left. There were electrodes underneath the hospital gown she wore with wires protruding out of the collar.

The beeps of the medical equipment joined together like the notes of an orchestra. Only this time, any change or movement in their music could mean a detriment to his wife's health.

He moved from the corner where he was hovering, needing to be closer to her, to touch her, to remind himself that she was still here, still with him.

Nothing in life had terrified him more than seeing her collapse in front of him, her head bouncing slightly off the hard tile of the laboratory floor.

He'd activated the panic alarm on his phone, and within seconds, security was in the room, assessing the situation and calling for help as he'd gotten down on the floor and cradled Regina's limp form into his arms.

Now he slipped her hand into his, startled by how cold it still was. Worry began to assail him again, so he pressed the button for the nursing station in the next room.

The doctor treating her entered. Some, just some, of Aléx's building anger subsided.

"She's been in this bed for hours. What the devil is wrong with her?"

Before the doctor could speak, he heard Regina moan. Her face was scrunched up like she was in pain, and every protective bone in his body wanted to comfort her. They hadn't sent anyone to the block in nearly a century, but if this doctor didn't fix what was ailing Aléx's wife, he was going to lose his head before morning.

"Can you stop barking, your kingship? My head is killing me."

"Treasure?"

She cracked one eye open, and relief bled through him, making his legs feel wobbly. He sat down in the chair next to her bed, never letting her hand go as he used the other to bring the chair closer to her bed.

"Are you okay? You scared the hell out of me when you passed out like that."

She groaned again. "I passed out? I guess that will teach me to let my blood sugar get that low again."

"Your Majesty, I'm afraid it wasn't your blood sugar that caused you to faint."

Regina finally opened her other eye and followed the sound of the doctor's voice until she was staring at him.

"What's wrong with me, then?"

"The ventilation system went out in your lab." The doctor opened the chart in his hand, grabbing his reading glasses from his lab coat. "The emergency technicians found an opened container of polyethylene glycol on your working station. We think the poor ventilation and chemical exposure may have contributed to your fainting."

"No wonder it was starting to get hot in there." Regina rubbed the side of her head, presumably trying to give herself some relief while she spoke. "I was so focused on what I was doing, I didn't realize. I thought it was the overhead lights at my workstation."

"As I said," the doctor continued, "we think the conditions and the chemical exposure contributed to your fainting, but we don't think it was the cause."

For the first time since she'd woken up, Aléx pulled his eyes from Regina's frail form and looked at the doctor.

"Then what the hell is wrong with her? Go ahead and spit it out, man."

There was a small, cautious smile on the man's lips, and Aléx was two seconds from calling in the palace guards and having the doctor thrown in a dungeon. How dare he find amusement of any kind in his wife's ailing condition?

"Your Majesties, the queen is pregnant."

"The queen is what?" Regina said as she sat up in her bed, grabbing her head the moment she did. "That can't be so. I had my menses as normal. It's been more than three weeks since then, and every time I've used an ovulation kit, it's said I'm not ovulating. How can I be pregnant without ovulating?"

The doctor walked closer to the bed, placing a gentle hand on Regina's shoulder, adding just enough pressure until she took the hint and lay down. He then pressed a button on the side of the bed, raising Regina's head up.

"You probably mistook implantation bleeding for your menses. The reason the ovulation tests were negative—"

"Is that I was already pregnant. Damn, I guess I'm proof that educated fools do exist. How could I be this stupid?"

The doctor chuckled. "Not stupid. Just not looking at the right signs. It happens more times than you'd think. I'll leave the two of you alone so you can talk amongst yourselves. May I be the first to congratulate you both on the coming heir."

Aléx finally found his voice as the shock of the doctor's news wore off, and he finally met his wife's gaze. His heart was pounding with excitement and worry, and if he admitted it to himself, he was all kinds of nauseous too.

"We're going to have a baby."

The words rushed out in an almost disbelieving huff. His chest was tight from the growing ball of joy swelling so quickly that it was pressing against all his vital organs. If dying of happiness was a possibility, Aléx was certain he might be nearing the end. It was a childish game Regina and her sister had played that brought them here. A twin swap gone wrong had brought joy bursting back into his life like he'd never imagined possible. For the first time in five years, Aléx was going to be a father again.

He glanced over at his wife. Her eyes were filled with tears, and she was looking at him as if he was the strongest, most capable person she'd ever met in her life. When she looked at him like that…goodness, it was more than pride, it was healing, slowly chasing away the darkness that had plagued him for so long.

He wanted to be the man she saw with his whole being. He wanted to be unscared, unafraid, and free to face his past without fear of drowning in it again.

The urge to tell her what she made him feel and what this news truly meant to him clawed at his insides. She was his wife. She should know what he'd been through and why this child was such a gift to him.

He could hear Jasiri encouraging him in his head to tell Regina the truth. Even in Aléx's imagination, his fellow king was just as bold and insistent.

Aléx took a deep breath, preparing to follow Jasiri's advice, trying to convince himself that he was stronger than his past, when the memory of what he'd become when he'd let his grief consume him flooded his mind. Weak, empty, and unfit to take care of himself, let alone an entire nation. Aléx's pain had shredded him into tiny pieces, some of which he'd never recovered.

All Regina saw was the strong man she believed she'd married. He couldn't help wondering what would happen if he shared his truth with his wife. Would she still look at him the same?

Too afraid of losing her favor and too selfish to give up how she made him feel, Aléx decided now wasn't the right time, if there ever was such a thing. Until he could be sure he wouldn't revert to the broken man he was in the midst of his grief, he'd keep his truth locked behind closed doors.

CHAPTER THIRTEEN

ALÉX SAT STRAIGHT up in bed from a deep sleep. His heartbeat thudded in his ears as his lungs gasped for air.

"Mmm, Aléx…what's wrong?"

The sound of Regina's groggy voice coming from the other side of the bed was like a slap across the face. It provided just enough control, just enough clarity for him to pull himself together.

He leaned down to her, placing his hand lightly at the base of her stomach. At sixteen weeks, she wasn't quite showing yet, but he could feel the slight firmness the small swell of their child caused. It was an ever-present reminder that this was real, and he would in fact be a father soon.

He placed a ghost of a kiss on her cheek and whispered, "Nothing, I just need to use the restroom. Go back to sleep."

She covered his hand with hers, its warmth battling with the cold chill his nightmare had left him with. He wanted to stay there, to curl around her and hold on to her and their child until the rays of the morning sun broke through the blinds and started him on his day.

He couldn't, though. Not like this. His heart was still racing, and he was barely keeping his respiration at an even level. Regina would know something was wrong. He refused to burden her with this. Her job was to grow their baby. His was to protect them at all costs. He would not fail that mission.

He slipped out of bed and into the en suite bathroom, closing and locking the door behind him, then turning on the faucet at full stream to drown out the loud pulls of air he was trying to tug into his lungs.

It had happened again. The dream had found him and had nearly strangled him in his sleep. The first time it happened had been after her eight-week doctor's visit where the first sonogram was done. The sound of their baby's heart pounding so strong through the exam room had nearly brought Aléx to his knees with joy.

They'd gone back to the palace and spent the rest of the day in bed. His heart was too full to speak, so he'd shown her his appreciation with every touch, stroke and pleasure he knew how to give to express to her how happy he was to share this with her.

That night, the first dream had come. The crash of water slamming down on a vessel, screams from the crew and passengers. Another punishing wave hitting, tipping the vessel over on its side until it capsized and was dragged beneath the waves into the abyss.

He knew that memory was real. He'd watched those very events happen. But the sound of the small voice saying, "Daddy, save us," was very much a new development. And the worst of it was that the faces of that "us" changed from blond hair, blue eyes and tanned skin to a million nearly invisible dark braids with deep, reddish-brown skin and the deepest brown eyes that had captivated his soul.

It wasn't Regina. It wasn't the child you share with her. They are safe. They are still here.

Paternal anxiety was the name for what he was suffering from. It was when an expectant father had recurring fears about his wife and baby dying in childbirth. It was rather common, especially in expectant fathers who'd experienced a loss.

He washed his face in the sink, hoping the hot water would soothe his nerves. When he caught sight of his reflection, he saw a frightened man with haunted eyes.

He came out of the bathroom, taking a quick glance at Regina in their bed. The rhythmic rise and fall of her chest made a fraction of his fear subside. Satisfied that she and the baby were okay, he grabbed his robe and headed for the only place his scattered mind would let him go.

He walked down the still corridor to the door at the end of the hall. He tried his best not to twist the knob open. He knew there was nothing but pain behind that door. That's why he'd locked it away from him and the rest of the world for the last five years.

Save for the one person tasked with cleaning this room, no one stepped inside it but Aléx. His father had known about it, along with his sister. His house staff knew about it too. There was no way to keep such a thing from spreading among the staff. But they'd all been warned that if they spoke of it in the open, they'd be let go immediately.

While they all knew about the room, with the exception of his father and sister, they'd only known that an old friend with a young child was coming to stay, and Aléx had wanted the visitor and the child to feel at home. Since the existence of the room, Charlie's true connection to him, and what the room held captive behind its doors hadn't shown up in the gossip rags in the last five years, Aléx was inclined to believe the staff didn't know who Charlie was, and they'd taken his threat about losing their jobs for speaking out of turn seriously.

Unable to stop himself, he placed his thumbprint on the

scanning panel above the knob, the resulting audible click letting him know the door was unlocked.

Aléx, you are pathologically masochistic.

He stepped inside, the motion light flickering on to show him what he'd known would be there. It was exactly the same as the day he'd closed it.

A platform bed covered in expensive pink frill. A ridiculous number of pink-and-white pillows filling up the top half of the bed.

An antique white rocker settled in one corner of the room. Matching furniture with the same accents and design strategically positioned throughout the room. This included a custom-made vanity whose mirror, surrounded by white painted iron, spelled out "Charlie" in elegant cursive letters.

He'd had this room commissioned the day he'd found out he was a father. He'd taken great joy and care in creating it. Happy fantasies of reading to his little girl in that rocker and tucking her into bed at night had danced through his head with every swatch of fabric he'd selected and every fixture he'd commissioned. When it was finally complete, he'd never been prouder of any other project he'd ever undertaken.

He hadn't known that Charlie wouldn't live to see her perfect princess room. He'd never suspected that one week after its completion, it would go from the surprise he'd hoped to give to his daughter to a mausoleum to house his pain.

His eyes continued to scan the room until he found the picture that had haunted him for years. Sent to him from Farah's phone, Charlie and her mother smiled brightly for the selfie as they boarded the boat he'd sent for them. He'd known from their last conversation that Farah was deeply angered by his commands and threats. But even in her anger, she'd found a way to share in Charlie's excitement at being on a boat for the first time and had thought enough of him to share that moment with him. What none of them had known in that simple moment of joy is that the boat would send his ex-lover and their child to their deaths.

"Save us, Daddy."

"I couldn't, dear one. I couldn't."

His shaky fingers grasped the framed picture, and he pulled it to his chest, hoping its nearness would slow his heart and comfort him in some way. Unsurprisingly, there was no comfort in sight. How could there be when he knew his failure to protect them was the reason they weren't with him today?

He placed the frame back on its perch atop the dresser and stared at it as if he were talking directly to the people smiling back at him.

"I promise you, I won't let anything happen to them."

Regina stepped outside their bedroom just in time to see Aléx exiting a room at the far end of the hall. His shoulders were drooping as he walked with his head slightly bent, like he was too exhausted to lift it.

Concern drew her in his direction. Aléx was a tall man, well over six feet, and his broad, muscular body made it impossible for him to not take up most of the space when he walked into a room. As he pinched the bridge of his nose, he seemed so small and frail; she worried he might just shrink until he disappeared into the plush carpeted floor.

"What happened?"

His head snapped up at the sound of her voice. For a moment, she could see what looked like sadness floating in his gaze, but by the time she was standing in front of him, his royal mask had dropped into place, and she could see she was no longer standing before her husband. Now, here stood Aléxandros, the king of Obsidian Island.

"Nothing. I needed to check on something for work."

"And it was so urgent that you needed to leave our bed and handle it at two in the morning?"

He walked around her, heading back toward their bedroom as if he expected her to follow without question. That wasn't happening. Something wasn't passing the smell test.

"I'm a king, Regina. I don't work a normal nine-to-five. When duty calls, it doesn't matter how late or early it is."

She stopped walking, crossing her arms as she planted her feet. "And you had to go to an unused bedroom to do kingly work, why?"

"It isn't unused," he snapped at her, the sharpness of his tone sliding across her raw skin like a blade.

Her spine straightened, and the tight set of her jaw must have conveyed he'd crossed a line, because he raised both hands before saying, "It's a secure storage closet for important files. Trust me, it's just dusty remnants from the past. Nothing you need to worry yourself about."

He closed the gap between them, returning to her and taking her hand. He brought it to his lips and kissed it, looking at her through his impossibly long, dark lashes that spread out into an elegant fan above his cheeks.

"Come, Treasure. It wouldn't do for the queen not to get her sleep. You're growing the future ruler of a nation. You need as much rest as you can get."

Something niggling at the back of her mind insisted she press him. The king, however, was a skilled strategist. When he passed those same lips across hers, she forgot exactly what she was thinking about.

He pulled her against him, deepening the kiss as his tongue pressed until he was licking inside her mouth, stroking her into a frenzy where the only thing she could think was, "More. Please, more."

"Come, Treasure." He laced his fingers through hers and gently guided her toward their room. "Perhaps we both need to burn off this extra energy so we might grasp the few hours of darkness left for sleeping."

She knew she shouldn't. Whatever was happening with Aléx, it had nothing to do with work. Of that she was certain. But letting him stoke her fire until she thought she might explode seemed so much more important in this moment. She'd find out what was going on later in the day. Tonight, she was going to give herself to her husband for as long as he wanted.

CHAPTER FOURTEEN

REGINA BURST INTO Aléx's office. Always in tune with her, he stood up behind his desk.

"What's wrong? Is it the baby?"

"Yes and no," she answered. "At least, it's not our baby."

She held her hand to her abdomen. It had formed into a full baby bump and not the cute little thing at the bottom of her stomach. She had to wear maternity clothes now since their little one had decided to make its presence known.

"Reigna's in labor!" She practically squealed the words. "I need to get to Nyeusi immediately. Can you call for the ferry?"

"You're not getting on a boat, Regina. You're five months pregnant."

She could feel her brows pinch as confusion settled in the deep V between them.

"As far as I know, there's no travel ban on five-months-pregnant women on ferries."

He pressed his hands flat against his desk. "I don't want you on the damn ferry."

The sharpness of his tone cut through her. Aléx didn't make a habit of raising his voice. As a king, he believed wholeheartedly that being ill-tempered could compromise his ability to serve his people. Which was why she couldn't figure out for the life of her just who this man was and just who the hell he thought he was talking to.

"I'm not one of your subjects. Don't talk to me like that. My sister is having her baby, and I'm not missing it. Either you find me a way off this island, or I will. Either way, I'm not missing this."

He blinked, took a breath and allowed some of the tension in his body to bleed out.

"I apologize. I was out of line. I'm just concerned for your safety."

She shook her head.

"Regina, be reasonable."

She folded her arms and tilted her head as she stared at him.

"I know you didn't just fix your lips to insinuate this baby—" she pointed to her bump "—is making me irrational?"

The sharp cut of her eyes must've been enough to convey he was taking his life in his own hands, because he straightened and held his hands up.

"I'm simply saying I just don't feel safe with you on the ferry. I'm an expectant father. Forgive me for being worried about you and our child."

She took in the tight lines around his eyes and mouth. He *was* scared.

What the hell for?

She stepped closer to him, walking around his desk and taking his hand in hers, placing it on the top of her belly.

"We are fine. I understand you're overprotective of us. But I have to get to my sister. It's either the boat or the helicopter. I thought you'd say hell no to the helicopter, so I assumed the ferry would be acceptable. I need to get to my sister now, and I'm going to make that happen however I must."

He nodded, dropping his head in both contrition and agreement.

"The helicopter will be ready to take us in fifteen minutes."

She gave him a cautious smile as she attempted to step away. He pulled her into him, surrounding her in his warmth as he wrapped his big body around hers.

"You and this baby are everything to me, Regina. Everything. Forgive me for crossing the line."

She slipped her arms around his waist, sensing that he needed her strength in this moment. Something was going on with him. Something that had been happening since she'd seen him coming out of that room. There was no proof of a correlation there. But she was determined to find out if there was. First, however, she needed to get to her sister's side. Everything else would have to wait until later.

"Look at Auntie's baby."

Aléx watched his wife holding the new Nyeusian heir. Princess Shadae, daughter of Queen Reigna and King Jasiri of the House of Adebesi, was a beautiful cherub with a head full of dark curls, and she had his wife completely wrapped around her finger.

Regina radiated with joy that shone through the room like a floodlight. The sight of her holding that baby made him ache for the moment she'd do the same with their child in another four months.

Jasiri walked over to Regina, holding his hands out as Regina leaned down to get one last snuggle from the princess.

Jasiri was well over six feet, like Aléx, and just as broad as him too. The sight of this hulking man cradling his daughter like a fragile piece of glass soothed something in Aléx. The ache that had dogged him for five years was still there. But in this moment, its tentacles didn't squeeze him with the same strength they regularly did.

"Cousin, would you like to hold her?"

His head told him to say no. He shouldn't intrude on this wonderful moment with the new princess.

"It is customary for the monarch of Obsidian Island to bless the Nyeusian heir apparent on the day of their birth and vice versa. Your mother did it for me, and my father did it for you. You wouldn't rob my daughter of experiencing that honor, would you?"

Aléx looked into Jasiri's eyes and saw hope and the cunning of a king. It was true, this was a custom shared between their people since the birth of King Nikos and Queen Nairobi's firstborn. King Amir traveled from Nyeusi to bless the new heir. When the next Nyeusian king had a child, the Obsidian king paid the same honor in return.

Jasiri was doing this on purpose, to pull Aléx out of the hell he'd lived in for five years. The arrogant bastard knew Aléx would never be able to refuse him this request.

Jasiri placed the tiny bundle in Aléx's arms and stepped back once he was sure his daughter was secure in Aléx's grasp.

"Did you forget your standard?"

Aléx couldn't take his eyes off the tiny human he was holding, not even to answer her father.

"No," he said, as the baby made reflexive sounds. "It's in my satchel. It occurred to me you might not want me to do the ceremony considering we haven't been close for a while. However, I brought it anyway figuring it was safer to have it and not need it than to need it and not have it."

Baby Shadae squiggled like a bowl of gelatin until Aléx

repositioned her, placing her head in the crook of his arm and hugging her to his body.

When he looked up, Jasiri had removed the large flag with the Obsidian royal crest on it. He handed it to him, waiting in earnest for Aléx to begin.

Aléx glanced back down at the baby as she burrowed like a cat until she found her sweet spot in his arms. Without even realizing it, Aléx was smiling as his insides softened.

Is this what children did? Did they sand down your rough edges until they were smooth to the touch and were no longer a danger to you or anyone else? He hadn't been around enough children to know if that were true. Not even the child he'd fathered.

Before he could allow his painful past to encroach on this moment with this sweet child Jasiri had entrusted him with, he wrapped the standard haphazardly around the babe before he took a deep breath.

He glanced up at his wife, her eyes glazed over in reverence as if she were imagining him holding their baby in the future. His throat felt tight with emotion, because he couldn't help but imagine that himself.

"Princess Shadae, daughter of Queen Reigna, issue of the great King Jasiri, standard bearer of the House of Adebesi, heir apparent, and crown princess of the Nyeusian throne."

He slowly swiped a reverent thumb across the child's head before he spoke again.

"May you possess the wisdom of all your ancestors so that you will rule with forethought and foresight."

He flattened his hand on the babe's chest, the rapid tattoo cinching his heart with an imaginary thread that seemed to be connecting them.

"May your heart be filled with compassion and kindness, so that you will rule with grace and benevolence."

He plucked a tightened fist from beneath the standard and gently opened Shadae's hand with his thumb.

"May your hands be as open and strong as your heart so that you may carry and comfort your people and your nation through the sorrows life will inevitably bring."

Shadae chose that moment to kick her leg free of her blanket as if she'd come into this world knowing what her role was. He took the tiny foot into his large hand, marveling at how delicate it was.

"May your feet be strong and sturdy, so that you may stand as a beacon to your people in times of light and darkness."

He readjusted her blanket so that her foot was covered and she wouldn't get cold. He looked up at Jasiri, his cousin nodding as he watched Aléx honor his daughter. There was pride in his eyes, and abounding love. Maybe it was wishful thinking, but Aléx dared to think just a little of that love Jasiri was exuding was for Aléx himself.

Aléx knew he didn't deserve it. He didn't deserve the loyalty Jasiri showed in keeping his secret from Reigna, and therefore Regina, either. That didn't stop him from wanting to be part of Jasiri's inner circle. Perhaps the birth of this little one was a means to let Aléx's walls down so he could embrace this man again.

His heart full, he lifted the baby to him. Leaning down, he placed a feathery kiss on her forehead.

"To Princess Shadae of the House of Adebesi, may your reign be long and may your legacy live on forever."

Jasiri motioned to the sisters, and they each joined him in repeating after Aléx in unison.

"May your reign be long, and may your legacy live on forever."

The new princess opened her eyes for the first time and

looked up into Aléx's face, giving him a reflexive smile. From all the books he'd read, Aléx knew logically that she wasn't intentionally smiling at him. And yet it still made his heart soar.

He walked over to Reigna's bedside and handed her the baby. Before he could step away, she squeezed his hand to garner his attention.

"Thank you for honoring my daughter."

"It was my pleasure, dear queen."

He stepped back to where his wife sat with the wet remnants of her tears on her cheeks. She motioned for him to lean down for a kiss. Their lips lightly pressed together before he tried to stand up, but her firm hand on his shoulder kept him in place.

"Aléx," she whispered. "You're going to be a great father."

From his wife's mouth to God's ear. After holding that precious babe in his arms, every fiber of his being wanted her words to be exceedingly true.

CHAPTER FIFTEEN

"YOUR MAJESTY?"

Aléx turned his head toward his secretary, who was sitting before him, attempting to review his schedule for the day. This was something that happened every day he sat in his office, and yet he couldn't seem to focus on anything the secretary said.

"I'm sorry, Michael. Could you repeat that, please?"

His focus had been shot to hell since he'd held Princess Shadae in his arms a week ago. He and Regina had spent two days on Nyeusi, celebrating the newborn with her parents and grandparents. It was two days of bliss, where Aléx hadn't been dogged by the constant ache in his soul that seemed to be a permanent reality of his life.

"The Queen's Ball is quickly approaching, and I haven't yet received any notice from the queen or the princess regarding themes and guest lists. The invitations must go out in the next ten days if we expect donors to attend."

Confusion settled over him. How could this be? The annual charity ball, given in his mother's honor to supplement the education ministry's ability to keep postsecondary school free on Obsidian Island, was one of the royal family's most important events of the year. Without it, so many scholars who didn't have the benefit of wealthy parents would be left behind. His mother believed that the best minds, regardless of who they were and what tax bracket they were in, should have access to quality education. Obsidian Island would only thrive if its thinkers were diverse and brought different ideas and experiences to help address their nation's problems.

How had he let this happen?

He knew the answer to that. He'd been so preoccupied with thoughts of the new baby, her smell, the warmth growing inside him when he held her, and how happy it made him seeing Jasiri in his new role.

That last part was what surprised him most. Aléx had never questioned the distance between him and Jasiri, only accepted that it was there and moved on with his life. But now, Jasiri seemed to be trying to breach the chasm that had existed between them for nearly two decades.

"Michael, in light of the queen's condition and her still learning about all things Obsidian, please contact the princess. I wish for her to partner with my wife to make this year a phenomenal one in both attendance and donations."

Michael nodded quickly before standing, bowing again before he took his leave.

As soon as his office door closed, Aléx's mind fell back to his distant cousin and the new heir. Before he could stop himself, he dialed Jasiri's number, hoping he'd answer and not send his call to voicemail like Aléx had done to his over the years.

"Good morning, Cousin. How fares the king of Obsidian Island on this beautiful day?"

Jasiri's jubilant tone drew a genuine smile from Aléx, one he was certain Jasiri would be surprised by if he had witnessed such a thing.

"Spoken like a man who is deliriously happy with his new daughter."

Jasiri chuckled. His deep, rich voice sounded lighter than Aléx had ever heard it.

"You are right on both accounts. I am deliriously happy with my new daughter. I'm also just plain delirious because the princess has mixed up her days and nights, and Reigna and I aren't thrilled at the idea of bringing in a nanny."

"You're forgoing a nanny?" That wasn't something he'd ever heard of in royal circles. His parents had certainly raised him, but there was no way they'd been able to keep him and his sister underfoot while his mom was queen of a nation.

"Not exclusively, no. We just want to have these first six weeks or so with Shadae until we feel we've all bonded more completely."

Jasiri's words resounded in his heart and head. It sounded absolutely terrifying doing all the preliminary work of taking care of a newborn yourself. As much as fear seemed a reasonable response, the thought of hoarding that initial time with his wife and their child sounded like heaven. Could they do it? Would Regina want it? Would their child be the better for it?

"Jasiri, aside from the new-father euphoria, you're all doing well, aren't you?"

There was a pause, and Aléx wondered if he'd gone out of bounds by asking something so personal. They weren't close. Perhaps he didn't have the right to an answer.

"We're doing well. It is difficult, especially with so little sleep, but I wouldn't trade it for anything. My daughter is everything that is good in the world. You'll see what I mean when your child is born shortly. Everything seems irrelevant but the well-being of that precious life you've been charged with caring for. If you're half the man you believe yourself to be, you'll do everything within your power to ensure your baby has the best you can offer. I do it for my little one, and I have no doubt you'll do it for yours when they arrive."

There it was again, that same tension of hope and fear mixed together that had him wondering if he wanted to cry or laugh or both.

With his throat tight, he managed to say, "Thank you, Jasiri," leaving the silent *I don't deserve your generosity* off the end.

"Now that I'm king…" Jasiri seemed to change the subject without any transition to what this new train of thought might be. "I can see just how important it is for the sovereign to rule from a place of joy and reverence. I think you know what I'm talking about."

Aléx knew exactly what Jasiri was referring to. He'd started out his reign that way. Even though his ascension had meant the loss of his beloved mother, he'd found a peace and appreciation that he could do as his mother had trained him and take care of their people in the wake of the loss of their queen.

But a handful of years later, that peace, that joy, had changed into something darker and more elusive. It was only his sense of loyalty to his mother, that understanding that he could not fail her, that made him climb out of his abyss and be a king to the people his mother loved.

"Aléx, just know I'm here." The weight of Jasiri's words sat on his chest like an immovable boulder, making him work for each scrap of air he managed to suck into his lungs. "When you're ready to tear down this damned wall between us, when you're ready to let me be there, I'll be bulldozing it from the other side."

"Jasiri, I—"

"No excuses or explanations. We are blood. In Nyeusi,

that means something. I know it means something on Obsidian Island too."

His tongue was heavy, and Aléx's awkward ineptitude when it came to letting people get close to him made him retreat into his usual snark.

"Our bloodlines aren't as intricately tied as you'd make it seem. We both know if we hadn't married identical twins, any children we had could've been the next Obsidian/Nyeusian pairing in our combined royal lineages."

Instead of cursing Aléx as he no doubt deserved, Jasiri laughed loud and full.

"Aw, you can try to be mean to me, but it won't work. I've missed you all these years. I could definitely use the wisdom of a man whose governance over the last eight years has been aspirational. But more than that, I want my friend back."

"You sure about that?" Aléx's question might have been delivered with the hint of sarcasm he always seemed to exude when he was talking to Jasiri. "I was the one who distanced myself, first out of sheer jealousy, and later out of shame."

"Jealousy," Jasiri repeated, as if Aléx's statement was an impossibility. "What could you have possibly envied me? We grew up the exact same. Two boys groomed from birth to lead their nations."

"Except your father let you be a boy and then a man. You were raised to believe being king was only part of who you are. I was raised to understand it was an identity that I couldn't escape. That's what I envied, your ability to be you. Outside of being king, I'm not really certain who I am."

Aléx stopped a minute, trying to consider if he should share his vulnerability with anyone. It was always a risk for a king to let down his guard in front of anyone. Doing so could be weaponized against him if he chose the wrong confidant.

"I thought I was beginning to figure that out when I learned about Charlie. But just like that, she, and any inkling of who I thought I could be, vanished."

Aléx closed his fist around the edge of his strong oak desk, waiting for his insides to shatter the way they did the last time he'd tried to vocalize what that loss had felt like. After more than a beat, it didn't come. Instead, there was a sliver of relief that seemed to break through the concrete slab that barricaded his feelings.

"You're not just a king, Aléx." Jasiri's words eased into his consciousness as if the man were dealing with a scared animal. "You are a good man, even if you're a bit obstinate at times. If you weren't a good man, there's no way Regina would've chosen you as her husband and the father of her future children. Your wife is, quite frankly, scary smart. There's no way she didn't calculate a million and one different outcomes before she agreed to marry you. In all her calculations, she concluded you were the one she wanted. The question is, when are you going to start believing that she made a good choice?"

He had certainly made a good choice. His wife was so patient with him, even when he was acting like a right bastard. Regina was turning out to be the source of peace and joy in his life. Maybe he could start to be the same for her.

"You said the first reason you'd distanced yourself from me was jealousy, and the second shame. How does shame factor into all of this?"

If admitting he was jealous of Jasiri's allowed freedom was difficult, admitting his deep shame felt nearly impossible to Aléx. His habit of hiding himself from the world was still there, but somehow it didn't seem to have as strong of a grip on him as it usually did.

"The night they died," Aléx began slowly, "you saw me at my worst. I was broken and destroyed. My pride probably would've recovered if I'd been able to deal with their deaths in a healthy way. But the fact that I had a mental breakdown that had to be covered up by my father and sister made me feel less than. I was the king who had been strictly trained to put the crown first and never let my feelings impact my ability to rule. I thought poorly of you for the freedoms you indulged in. I thought you were the lesser king. But then my mind collapsed in on itself, and I could hardly breathe on my own, let alone rule. How could I face you knowing you saw me like that?"

Jasiri was so quiet, Aléx had to look at the screen of his phone to make sure the call wasn't disconnected. He heard the loud sound of Jasiri taking in a breath before the man spoke again.

"You were my friend. No matter the fact that we hadn't spoken in years at that point, it was my greatest honor that you chose to let yourself go in my presence. You did that because you knew I would understand and that I would protect you no matter what. There was no reason then or now for you to fear being vulnerable in front of me. Just as back then, all I want is to be there for you, Aléx. I didn't want you to suffer alone. You chose that for yourself."

The truth of Jasiri's words smacked Aléx in the middle of the chest like a wrecking ball. They hollowed him out, making him look down for the pieces of his soul the force had fractured. Aléx was the reason for his own isolation. How could he have missed that all these years?

"Aléx, you decided to be alone. You don't have to make that same choice now. You don't have to do this work by yourself. Let your wife be your soft place to land as you put the past behind you. Tell her, Aléx, before it's too late. Don't let her find out from anyone else why you're so lost and afraid and why you especially need her in this moment. She's having your child. She deserves to know the truth."

There was no disputing what Jasiri was saying. He did need to tell her. He just didn't know if he could. Would there be anything left of him if he bared his soul to her? Could he relive that nightmare again? The truth was, he just didn't know. The even greater truth was, he was afraid to find out.

CHAPTER SIXTEEN

REGINA LOOKED AT the door at the end of the corridor, wondering if today was the day. Aléx had left the island for business, and she knew there was no time like the present to do what she'd been aching to do.

She stepped into the corridor, looking back over her shoulder before she headed in the direction of that locked room her husband absconded to when he thought she was sleeping.

She moved quickly, getting to the door and looking for cameras, although Aléx had assured her there were no cameras in the living spaces; they were instead only trained on the entrances so their privacy would never be intruded upon.

Boy, did she hope that was true. If it wasn't, she anticipated having a lot of explaining to do later.

There was some sort of unholy control this room had over Aléx, and Regina intended to find out exactly what it was. When Aléx was with her he was attentive and kind. But every time he came back to their bed after visiting the room, she could feel the tension bubbling off him. He was scaring her. But also, he was messing with her precious sleep that was already compromised by the kicking inhabitant in her womb.

She placed her hand on the knob and tried to turn it. When it didn't so much as shift, she blew out a frustrated breath.

You had to know it wasn't going to be that easy, didn't you?

She was about to try again, leaning down to get a look at the locking mechanism to find out whether the lock could be picked. Not that she herself knew anything about picking locks. She was, however, from Brooklyn, a place where necessity became the generator of resourcefulness to thrive in an environment that wasn't always conducive to doing so.

She was about to try again when she heard, "Regina, what are you doing?"

The sound of Eliana's voice made her jump back, nearly losing the tenuous grip she had on her balance at almost six months pregnant.

"I was… I was…"

She saw Eliana's waiting expression, the one that said, *I know exactly what you were doing.* Instead of cowering because she'd been busted, she leaned into her conviction that she needed to know what was behind that door if she was to protect her husband and their union.

"I was trying to get inside this room. I've caught your brother sneaking out of bed at night when he thinks I'm sleeping. Whatever is in there is taking him through it, and I want to know what this invisible enemy is."

Eliana's face softened, her bright blue eyes fading to a muted gray-blue as the happiness seemed to be leaking out of her.

"If you want to know what's in there, you're going to have to ask my brother."

Frustration, dark and ugly, began to grow inside her chest. Now more than ever, Regina understood she needed to know what was behind that locked door.

"Is this some royal version of snitches get stitches? If it is, it was juvenile back when I was a kid in Brooklyn, and it sure as hell is problematic now when I'm trying to help my husband."

"I know you are." Eliana moved closer to Regina, placing a compassionate hand on her shoulder. "You will never know how grateful I am to you for recognizing there is a problem and trying to figure out how to help. But this is something that belongs entirely to my brother. I will not violate his trust even if I think I'd be helping him by doing it. You must understand that, being a twin?"

God, did she. More times than not, she protected Reigna's trust with her complete loyalty at every turn. Knowing that in her head, however, didn't make her heart ache any less.

Accepting she wasn't going to get anything out of her sister-in-law, she resigned herself to the fact that she'd just have to address the matter with Aléx.

Aléx rushed into the palace, heading for his quarters. He'd left early this morning on what was supposed to be a two-day business trip. The separation anxiety and the need to be with his wife had set a fire under him, and he'd made sure to complete all his work so he could return home by nightfall.

As soon as he opened the door, he found her sitting in the family room on the comfy couch that had become her favorite spot to perch on as of late.

The flicker of light across her face told him she was watching television. If he knew his wife as well as he believed he was coming to, she was probably watching some kind of true crime or murder mystery.

He'd never know why she found those horrid things so addictive, and he didn't want to think about the implications of her ravenous appetite when it came to such shows. Instead, the only thing he could do was stand there and smile at the vision she made.

He walked into the room, making loud thumping steps so she was aware of him entering.

"Goodness, I've missed you, Treasure."

He sat down beside her and stole the kiss he'd been dreaming about all day. Her kiss was sweet and salty, probably remnants of the chocolate-drizzled popcorn she couldn't seem to get enough of. He wasn't sure if it was the taste of the treat or the taste of the treat on her that had him captivated. Whichever was true, Aléx would buy a lifetime supply of it if it meant he was privileged enough to experience it like this whenever he wanted.

She pulled away from him, her full cheeks and her slitted eyes nearly touching because of the satisfied smile on her face.

"It appears you did. Although I'm not sure why. It can't be the nightly trek I make you take to the freezer to get me butter pecan ice cream."

He stole another kiss. This time it was a quick peck, but it was still just as delicious.

"I'll have you know that I live to serve my queen in whatever capacity she deems fit. Those nightly treks, as you call them, bring me immense happiness."

His heart was alight with amusement and joy. Rich and bold, his ability to live in the moment became more and more corporeal as he connected to his wife.

He couldn't quite answer why that was. The truth was, he hadn't even attempted to consider it. He just knew that he liked himself when he was with her, and more and more, he was grateful she'd accepted his proposal. He shuddered to think what he might have become if she'd stuck to her original no.

"Just how, pray tell, do you plan on servicing your wife tonight, oh wise king?"

"Every possible way my depraved mind can think of."

He undressed her quickly, too hungry to take his time.

He burrowed his face in the crook of her thigh, loving the heady scent of her there. He needed inside her in the worst way. Before he allowed himself to take her, he would first make certain she was satisfied.

His lips kissed around her folds, waiting for her to spread her legs and make space for him. It didn't take long. He licked her seam, thrilled to find her arousal coating her skin and now his tongue. Too eager to please her, he continued to lap at her clit as he slipped one and then two fingers inside her. The way her muscles were rippling around his digits, he could tell she was right where he wanted her, so close to the edge that a soft wind would push her over the cliff.

"Come now, Treasure. Don't keep me waiting. Give me what I want."

She mewled so prettily it was almost his undoing. Later, he'd have to decipher why her acquiescence made his dick so hard. Presently, however, the only thing that mattered was watching her splinter at his command.

Regina would be beautiful in a burlap sack. But lying on the sofa with her legs spread and her glorious braids fanned out on the arm of the chair, she was the epitome of wanton need that had him ready to come in his pants like a schoolboy.

He gently lapped her sex, allowing her pleasure to ebb. He unzipped his pants, pulling them down just far enough that he could take his wife without causing damage to himself.

He coaxed her onto her knees and positioned himself behind her. Her bump was just large enough that him rutting against her in the missionary position wasn't comfortable for her any longer. Since then, he'd made sure to have her in every position that she could tolerate. This, with her head down and her ass in the air, had become their favorite.

"Brace yourself, Treasure."

She held on to the arm of the chair as he entered her from behind. It was as if her body were made for him. Her sex molded to the exact shape of his length to give him the perfect amount of friction against his sensitive skin. As a reward, he angled his hips to hit that spot she adored, and together they surrendered to this unrelenting need they couldn't seem to quench.

"Treasure," he huffed. "You feel like silk wrapped around me."

That garnered a needy moan from her, signaling that she was close to another climax. He sped up his pace. Having her come while he was buried inside her was only ever outmatched by when they came together. As if on cue, her body began to tighten as he stroked her hard and fast, racing to meet her at the finish line. When she clamped down on him as the first wave of her climax came, it was as if she were drawing his release out of him.

That first jet inside her was sheer bliss, pulling him into nirvana right here on earth. He stroked them both through their mutual orgasms, holding on to her as a lifeline in this sensual storm they'd created.

She was his and he was hers. He knew that as well as he knew his own name. What he didn't know was where this invisible thread that made him want to be with her every moment of every day had come from. He didn't understand what it was. There was only one thing he knew with absolute clarity concerning this matter.

He liked it.

He held her next to him, breathing in the calm that seemed to rise from her skin. Just being next to her settled every demon inside him. It especially settled those demons he wasn't completely free of.

He knew he should tell her what those demons were. He was ninety percent sure he would feel better if he did. Living like he was torn between two worlds, those of the living and the dead, made it impossible for him to settle completely in either space. Five years ago, he'd thought he'd deserved to be one of the walking dead, still alive but numb to anything that made life worth living.

Now that he had this woman in his arms, and she was growing their baby inside her, for the first time in five years, he felt his heart beating again. So what was holding him back? What was keeping him from opening up to her?

Fear. It was the only truthful answer.

What if she blames you the way you've been blaming yourself for years? What if she takes away the new warmth flowing through you whenever you see her or think about her? What if your confession sends you right back to the abyss you were trying so hard to climb out of? Or worse, would she think his inability to move beyond his past was connected to whatever feelings he possessed for Farah? Would telling her the truth make her feel like she was living in someone else's shadow yet again?

The mere thought of that last question made him wince. He could never knowingly put that kind of doubt in her head, not when he'd seen firsthand how such thoughts impacted her.

The questions ran through his mind on loop every time he thought about speaking his truth. As selfish as it was to keep things from her, the alternative, the risk, it was unthinkable.

Jasiri's warning about someone else telling her echoed through his head, and Aléx had to bite his lip to keep from saying, *impossible*. His sister and Jasiri were the only two people on his side who knew who Charlie was to him. His former head of security was the one who'd dug up the information and made Aléx aware that he was a father. Trusting the man with his secrets and his life, Aléx had sent him to collect Farah and Charlie and bring them home. He'd carried Aléx's secrets to his watery grave.

The only other people who knew were Farah's immediate family. They'd assisted her in keeping Charlie a secret from him. They'd gone as far as secreting her out of the country before Farah's pregnancy could be known or documented on Obsidian Island. They would never betray her by telling the world she'd given birth to the king's illegitimate child. Well, most of them wouldn't. There was one among them who was mercenary enough to completely disregard Farah's desires. But even this individual had to know Aléx would use his considerable power to make them regret that miscalculation for the rest of their life.

Comforted by his assessment of the chance of Regina finding out from someone other than him, he pulled her tighter into his embrace and welcomed the familiar sensation of her body snuggling into his. This woman was his lifeline, and he couldn't gamble with that, not for anyone or anything. Not even for her.

CHAPTER SEVENTEEN

REGINA STOOD BEFORE the mirror in awe. She'd had glam teams work their magic on her before, but this was next-level. She was seven months pregnant, and all her natural curves were deeper and more profound. From her pregnancy boobs, to the swell of her belly, to the deep curve of her hips, everything was on display.

She wasn't at all distressed by the changes in her body. Her pregnancy boobs were a thing of beauty, and Aléx hadn't been able to keep his hands off them. She'd gloried in his attention and her body's ability to both build a human and keep her husband's tongue wagging. Her voluptuousness notwithstanding, the idea of shoving all these goodies into a formal evening gown gave her pause.

She'd called her cousin Amara, who was one of LaQuan Smith's favorite clients. The famed designer from Brooklyn had talked to her for a few minutes and within a week had sent her sketches of dress ideas. She'd picked a bodice from one, a silhouette from another, and before she knew it, she'd had the final product hand-delivered by the designer himself.

As she stared at herself in the large antique mirror in her walk-in closet, she was amazed by that man's talents. He had managed to create an off-the-shoulder, sweetheart-bodice, short-sleeved gown that hugged her curves and made her look like one of the Greek muses, with a chiffon cape to boot. He'd also managed to make it out of some sort of magical material that was stretchy, but elegant, so it would still fit in the event her growing baby decided to add more inches to her already protruding waist.

The design was magnificent, but the bloodred color was very much giving sexy goddess. And she knew from experience that as soon as Aléx got her alone, he'd peel it off her like a second skin.

That thought warmed her until she thought about what was likely to happen the moment she'd undoubtedly fall into postcoital sleep. He'd sneak out of bed and walk down the hall and spend hours in that room.

Before, those visits were infrequent. They occurred enough that she was still concerned after she'd tried to sneak into the room herself without success. Now, it seemed the closer she got to delivery, the more his visits had increased. At this rate, with four weeks to go before her anticipated delivery, he'd probably move into that room instead of sleeping with her.

It was all so confusing. Aléx was the most attentive person she'd ever had in her life. He anticipated her needs before she even realized she wanted something.

Like the time he noticed her rubbing her back when she woke up in the morning. She'd hardly had time to realize the weight of the baby was starting to pull the muscles in her back. The next thing she knew, he was bringing her a C pillow and a belly brace.

Though she hadn't worked in her lab since they'd discovered she was pregnant, she did still go to her office to further develop her formulas and meet up with her marketing team. When she returned to the palace tired with aching feet, he'd be waiting on the sofa with a pillow at one end, patting his leg until she placed her feet in his lap.

For a man who hadn't done much manual labor in his life, he sure as hell knew how to rub a foot. Within minutes, the aching in her soles melted away, and she was relaxed enough to fall into a dead sleep.

Then there was the time her sister told him he had to fulfill her food cravings or it would mark the baby. In response, he'd had a mini-fridge and freezer moved into their bedroom so he could satisfy her butter pecan cravings more readily. She'd tried to tell him that was a Black wives' tale, all superstition and no fact. It hadn't mattered. He'd done it anyway, because she was giving him the greatest gift. The least he could do is make sure she had the ice cream the baby seemed to have an addiction to.

Goodness, he was so damn caring, and yet he still kept her at arm's length when it came to whatever was going on in his head. One moment, she'd think they were crossing that imaginary line he'd drawn between companionship, care and love. The next, he'd firmly shut the door on her, letting her know she would never truly be part of his inner circle.

Talk about emotional whiplash. Add to that her pregnancy hormones, and she was on an emotional roller coaster the likes of which even Vivian Green couldn't fathom.

"Your Majesty, it is time to don your crown."

Regina turned around to find Janice, a tall young woman with auburn hair that she kept pulled into a tight bun. She was one of the personal staff members Aléx had assigned her. She found Janice to be pleasant, courteous, and above all, punctual. So if she said it was time for her to get the diamond-encrusted headband secured to her head, Regina needed to sit at her vanity and have it placed now.

Aléx chose that moment to enter their bedchamber. He

was dressed in what she'd come to know as his king's uniform: a black tuxedo with a cape attached at his shoulders. The breast pocket of his jacket was adorned with military and royal insignias, and his red sash tied his regal look all together, making one breathtaking picture.

He carried a velvet pillow in his hands that held a full diamond crown with what looked like the largest, clearest rubies she'd ever seen in her life. When he stood beside her, she had to fight the instinct to run her fingers across it. Yes, she wanted to touch it, but it was so beautiful she couldn't bring herself to dull its brilliance with even a partial fingerprint.

She looked up at Aléx, trying to recognize the look on his face. His features were straight, but beneath the polished look, she could see his jaw ripple and his eyes brighten with hope.

Hope for what? She couldn't discern.

"This isn't the same crown you presented to me when you introduced me to your court."

"No." His voice was thick as if he were trying to fight the emotions simmering just beneath the surface from breaking through. "This is the crown made specifically for my mother's coronation. It would thrill me to no end if you'd agree to wear it tonight."

She was about to speak when she saw Janice's reflection in her mirror. What Regina had to say was for his ears only.

"Janice, would you please excuse the king and me?"

Janice gave a quick bow of her head before she disappeared, leaving no trace that her presence was ever in the room.

When Regina looked at the crown again, a lump formed in her throat. Forgotten was its physical beauty; she was too overwhelmed by its sentimental value to be concerned with that.

"You want me to wear this?"

"I do." He gifted her with his million-dollar kingly smile, and she wanted so desperately to get lost in it.

It would be so easy if she could just accept that Aléx couldn't love her. He'd told her that from the very beginning. But every time he did something thoughtful and caring for her, her stupid heart just wanted to dive headfirst in love with him.

"Shouldn't your sister wear it? She's Queen Carisse's daughter."

He placed the crown down on top of her vanity, then stood behind her, placing his hand firmly on her shoulders as he looked at her through the mirror.

"Do you not want to wear it?"

She closed her eyes, wishing it were that simple.

How do you tell the kind man who treats you like you are in fact a treasure that it hurts every time you let your guard down, when he moves closer to you, only for him to pull away each time?

Bluntly, like you do everything else.

Why her conscience was such an asshole she didn't know, but she was throwing it major internal side-eye right now. That didn't change the fact that it was right, however. She needed to be clear with Aléx. She needed to draw some boundaries.

"It's a beautiful crown, Aléx, and I'd be honored to wear it. It's just, I find it hard to believe you would share something so personal and sentimental with me when you won't even share with me what's going on with you."

His eyes widened, and she realized she'd sideswiped him with her question.

See? her conscience rang out in her head. *I told you blunt was the way to go.*

Ignoring it, she stood, forcing his hands to drop from her shoulders, and turned to face him.

"Regina—"

She held up her hand to stop him. If he started talking, she'd go stupid listening to that smooth-as-silk voice of his. Then he'd kiss her, and she'd lose full control of her faculties. It wasn't happening today.

"I'm worried about you, Aléx. You're barely sleeping, and you're sneaking out of our bed more frequently."

He raised a brow, confusion pulling his smooth skin into taut lines on his face.

"You noticed that?"

She swallowed, refusing to back down now, even if it made her sound pathetic.

"I always notice when you're gone. Don't you know that by now?" His mouth hung open, so she continued. "I feel safe and protected when I'm with you. Since that first night you held me in my bed after my fight with my sister, I never sleep as well as when I'm in your arms."

"Regina, I'm—"

"If you say 'I'm sorry,' I swear I will find your scepter and bop you on the head with it. I don't want your apologies. I want to help you through whatever the hell is going on with you."

She could see his constitution breaking, falling chip by chip. But just as quickly as he let the wall drop a little, he slapped spackle on it and started layering one emotional brick at a time right before her eyes.

"I ca-an't, Regina. I want to. I just can't."

She closed her eyes, trying to strengthen her legs to keep her upright in this moment. Refusing to let him ruin all the hard work her glam team had done on her makeup, she took a deep breath and sat back down in front of her mirror.

"You can. You just won't. It's your way of showing me you care about me, just not enough to share all of yourself with me. I guess I should've taken you at your word when you told me you'd never love me. Because if you did, you'd know how much watching you suffer would kill me, and you'd do anything to stop that pain for me."

He placed a hand on her shoulder, and she shook it off. She was honestly too tired to deal with this anymore.

"If you'll excuse me, I need to finish getting ready for the ball. I'll wear your mother's crown. So, you can go now."

Aléx snapped his head back as if she'd slapped him. As a king, he probably wasn't used to being dismissed. Well, he'd have to get used to it, because she was tired of him trampling over her heart. From now on, she'd stay in the place he'd given her. Companion and coparent and nothing more.

She watched him out of the side of her eye with his shoulders slightly bent like he had lost just a bit of his strength and a whole lot of his kingly luster.

There her stupid heart went again, wanting to call him back and hold him until her Aléx was back. That, however, was the problem. He wasn't ever *her* Aléx, and he never would be.

CHAPTER EIGHTEEN

ALÉX FOLLOWED REGINA'S form throughout the room. For someone who said she hated people, she certainly did have the ability to command an audience. She was stunning in her gown. With his mother's crown upon her head, she looked the part of a queen who knew her power.

It was just an act, however. That's all it could be if she didn't know how much he cared for her, how much he craved being in her presence.

His confession was on the tip of his tongue. He'd wanted so desperately to just let the truth slip into the air.

Then what stopped you?

He'd asked himself that every time he replayed the hurt in her eyes when she asked him to leave her alone. Every time, he came to the same conclusion. There were only two reactions he could imagine her having. The first was pity, the second, disgust. Either way, he couldn't stand the thought of her associating either of those emotions with him.

The alternative wasn't that much better. Watching her hurt and close herself off from him was cutting him into tiny pieces, and he didn't know if he'd be able to tape himself back together again.

"Things are not well between you and your queen, are they?"

He closed his eyes at the sound of Jasiri's voice. Of course he and his ever-observant mind would call the situation for what it was the moment he saw it.

"What did you do, Cousin?" Jasiri prompted.

Aléx turned narrowed eyes on Jasiri and found the man waiting for him expectantly.

"How do you know it's my fault?"

Jasiri didn't even try to hold the knowing chuckle in. "I know you too well, Cousin. Of course this is the result of something you did." Jasiri took a long gaze at him before he said, "Or more accurately, something you didn't do. You haven't told her, have you?"

Aléx used that moment as an opportunity to snatch a champagne flute from a passing tray and downed it in one swallow.

"You see that look in your eyes," Aléx countered. "The look that says, 'The poor little king. He's so pathetic with grief and loss that he can hardly function.' I refuse to be viewed by my wife in the same way."

He saw understanding cast a shadow on Jasiri's deep brown skin. He of all people should understand exactly what Aléx meant. When Aléx had received news that the ship had gone down on the border of Obsidian and Nyeusian waters, he'd called Jasiri when he couldn't reach his father and begged him to allow Obsidian naval ships to search inside Nyeusian waters.

He recalled how panic had pulled through him like a taut rope. He was wound so tightly in it, he could hardly think, and he'd lost all eloquence and poise.

Jasiri had heard the panic in Aléx's voice, and even though they hadn't spoken in years, he not only granted Aléx's request, he met Aléx on the water with Nyeusian ships and divers in tow to help with the search. He'd stood on Aléx's ship with him and had held him when he'd collapsed to his knees when his captain announced they'd discovered the bodies of Charlie and her mother.

"I don't want to be that man again. I don't want Regina to know how broken I am. I don't want her to know it was…"

He couldn't say the words. He couldn't make himself say them. Jasiri placed a strong hand on his shoulder, squeezing tightly enough to make him wince, intentionally dragging him out of the fog of grief that was trying to cloud his mind again.

"It wasn't your fault, Aléx. You told her not to travel because of the storm, and she insisted."

Aléx shook his head. "It doesn't matter that I told her not to travel that night. They were only on that ship because I'd demanded to see Charlie immediately or I would use all my power to make Farah's life a living hell. She knew I wasn't lying, so she risked the trip for fear of what I'd do if she didn't make it at the assigned time. No matter how you try to clean it up, I'm the reason they're dead."

Jasiri squeezed his shoulder again before he moved to Aléx's side. He looked out over the balcony they were standing on, watching the people milling about beneath them in the ballroom.

"Aléx, I tried to carry the fear and utter panic I had when my uncle was targeting Reigna's life. I wouldn't let her in, and I tried to make her a prisoner within the walls of the palace. The only thing trying to handle all that pain and fear by myself did was push my wife away until she chose to leave me over watching me devolve into rage and insanity."

Aléx snapped his head toward Jasiri, searching the man's face for any hint of an untruth. His sullen face and his ticking jaw were better than any lie detector in creation: Jasiri was telling the unvarnished truth.

"I didn't know she'd left you. I know she played a hand

in trapping Pili in America. I just never realized she was there because she'd left you."

Jasiri pursed his lips. "No one does. Not even my parents. It's not exactly something I wanted in a royal press release, if you know what I mean. I nearly lost everything that I loved. We didn't know it yet, but Reigna was pregnant at the time. If I hadn't gotten myself together, I could've missed out on watching her grow with our daughter. I could've missed how our love deepened once I had her in my arms again. If I hadn't found a way to be honest with myself and my wife, if I hadn't found the sense to listen to her instead of acting as if I had everything under control, I would've lost it all."

At that moment, Reigna looked up from the ballroom as if she'd felt her husband calling to her. She raised her eyes and gave him a warm, broad smile that seemed to make Jasiri stand taller.

"Open up to her, Aléx. Let her love heal you."

"Regina doesn't love me. We both agreed that bringing love into the equation was a bad idea."

Jasiri fell into a big belly laugh, no doubt at Aléx's expense. Frankly, it was beginning to get on his nerves.

"I'm sure that's some nonsense you came up with and Regina went along with."

Aléx shook his head like a recalcitrant child. "She doesn't love me, and I don't—"

Jasiri interrupted Aléx. "Don't even speak that lie into the ether. That woman loves you. She'd shower you with it if you let her believe she had a chance of you accepting it."

Jasiri pointed to where Regina was standing, talking to one of Aléx's ministers.

"You haven't taken your eyes off her for a single moment of the conversation we're having. That is not the behavior of a man who isn't obsessed with his wife."

"She's pregnant with my child, Jasiri. Of course I'm always concerned with her well-being."

Jasiri shook his head silently.

"Strange, then, that you were looking at her just as intently on your wedding day too. She wasn't pregnant then, was she?"

Jasiri knew she wasn't. Regina had more than likely shared with her sister that they'd unknowingly conceived on their wedding night.

Could the words his irritating cousin was speaking be true? Love? Is that what this impossible feeling was in his chest that made it hard for him to breathe every time he had to leave her? Is that why his body went up in flames any time he touched her, or she touched him? Is that why the thought of losing her and their child the way he had Charlie and her mother nearly paralyzed him with fear?

He took measured breaths, trying hard not to have a panic attack right there on the balcony. For one, it would be all over the news before the last guest left. Second, he wouldn't give Jasiri the satisfaction of gloating.

"Tell her, Aléx. She loves you. She'll understand. Telling her will make dealing with your loss better and will stop you drowning in your pain. Let her be your life raft and your anchor."

Jasiri slapped a hand on Aléx's back as Aléx watched his wife. He wanted to, he needed to, be with her. He'd just decided that he would tell her when he saw Katia whisper in Regina's ear. The two women disappeared through the south doors on the other side of the room from where Aléx and Jasiri were standing.

He didn't know what that was about, but he knew trouble when he saw it.

"I've got to get to her now."

* * *

"Katia, whatever this is about, I'm tired and really not in the mood."

The woman held her hands up in surrender as she stepped toward Regina, leaning down closer to her ear to speak. "One of the aides just asked after you. She was called away by another staffer as she was about to enter the ballroom."

Regina eyed her carefully, and Katia gave what appeared to be a genuine smile. "Listen, I know when I'm beat. I can't say I'm happy about it. But I'm also not stupid enough to do something to the queen that could land me in prison for the rest of my life."

That made Regina chuckle. Of all the things Katia had said, Regina believed self-preservation was the woman's first priority.

"Did you see which way they went?"

Katia led her to the foyer and pointed her in the direction of the kitchen. Regina turned around to get another glance at Katia. They'd probably never be friends. But she could respect a woman who could acknowledge her losses as well as her wins.

She nodded and walked toward the kitchen, finding it abuzz with activity. There were people zipping around everywhere until they noticed Regina's presence. At that moment, everyone stopped and bowed their heads.

"Please, don't let me stop you from your work. I was told one of the staffers was looking for me."

A young woman in her mid-twenties stepped out of the frenzied bustle in the kitchen and into the corridor. She dug in the pristine white apron that rested against her black uniform dress and pulled out an envelope that she then handed to Regina.

The envelope's heft and texture spoke of its quality. Her

name was scribbled on its front in what looked like perfect calligraphy.

Regina lifted her head to the aide with a pinched brow before she met slightly nervous eyes.

"Who left this for me?"

CHAPTER NINETEEN

ALÉX FINALLY MADE his way through the throng of people that had delayed him from getting to his wife. By the time he made it through the south doors, he saw Katia walking back toward the ballroom.

He stopped abruptly in front of her.

"What the hell have you done? Where is my wife?"

Katia's face twisted into confusion.

"She went to the kitchen to find a staffer who was looking for her. After that, I have no earthly idea."

"Katia." He ground out her name through his clenched jaw. "So help me God, if you've done anything to hurt her."

Katia's neck snapped back in shock as she glared at Aléx. "I'm pushy and I might go too far sometimes, but I'm not violent, Aléx. I wouldn't try to physically harm a pregnant woman."

Her eyes misted over as they moved from side to side in an anxious fashion. As if she were trying to tell him he should know better.

He put space between them, letting some of the tension bleed out of him. "I'm sorry, Katia. Please, go and enjoy the rest of the party."

When Katia was gone, he traced Regina's steps to the kitchen and back upstairs to their living quarters. He took the steps two at a time to get there. Considering the last thing they'd said to each other, her being out of his sight made him uneasy. He needed to fix things.

He called out for Regina once he made it inside their quarters. The rooms were silent, too silent. Fear ricocheted through him as all sorts of imagined scenarios ran through his head. He shook his head, trying to free himself from the dark thoughts that would paralyze him if he allowed them to.

And that's when he saw it: the soft light coming from that room at the end of the hall. To his horror, Charlie's room door was open. A shift in the air behind him made him aware he wasn't alone. He turned to find his sister standing there with worry written into the lines of her face.

"I swear I didn't think she would react this way, Aléx."

"React what way?"

"I didn't think she would leave when I…"

His mind filled in the blanks, coming to the only conclusion he could. "Eliana, you gave her the key?"

"She was hurting, and you refused to tell her the truth and stop her pain."

His sister had always pushed the boundaries of respectability, but never anything like this.

"It wasn't your place. It wasn't your truth to reveal."

"I'm sorry, Aléx. I was trying to help the both of you. I can't watch you hurt anymore, and I won't watch you hurt Regina in the process. Hate me, banish me if you must. I just couldn't stand by and watch you destroy the best thing that's ever happened to you. I was there when you lost it all before. I can never watch you go through that again."

He could see the hurt in his sister's watery gaze and her trembling lips. His pain had impacted so many people, and he'd selfishly only concerned himself with his own. He grabbed his sister in a hug. He'd deal with his anger later. Right now, he just needed her to feel the love he had for her. After sacrificing so much for him, that's the least she deserved.

"Go find her and bring her back where she belongs, Aléx."

He locked gazes with his sister and nodded.

"I promise I will."

"Your Majesty, this is the head of security. The queen is at the docks. She's on the ferry to Nyeusi. We're holding clearance until you get there."

"Is my helicopter ready?"

The docks were a thirty-minute drive from the palace. The helicopter would cut that down to ten minutes.

"The pilot has been notified and is making his way to the helipad. However, King Jasiri's helicopter is ready to take flight immediately. He says he's waiting for you."

Aléx ended the call and headed toward the car in the courtyard. Jasiri didn't say a word to him once he'd boarded. Instead, he instructed his pilot to take off. Before Aléx knew it, they were landing atop the roof of the ferry depot directly across from the docks.

He went to step off the helicopter, but he stopped. He grabbed Jasiri into a tight hug and yelled, "Thank you, Cousin," hoping he could hear Aléx among the whirring of the helicopter blades.

He jumped out of the helicopter and quickly made it to the docks. Just as Regina was about to walk inside to the seating area, he grabbed her arm and said, "Not like this. Please, don't go like this."

His grip on her arm was tight. She was about to pull away from him until she looked into his stricken face and saw his pale skin and his pinpoint pupils that were locked on to her.

He's scared. No, he's terrified.

She didn't understand this. She had expected concern, possibly anger that she'd dared to leave him, but not fear.

And then he spoke words that doused any anger she'd harbored.

"Not like this. Please, don't go like this."

He looked so unlike himself. He wore the same tailored clothes, but they appeared crumpled and disheveled, as if they were a signifier of the panic she saw covering him.

"Regina, I promise you, if you want to leave, I will have my pilot take you to Nyeusi first thing in the morning. But please, please don't leave me like this. I couldn't survive it if something…"

He let the rest of his words die off in the silence. Nonetheless, she was certain he'd intended to finish that sentence with the words, *happened to you*.

Puzzle pieces clicked into place as she read between the lines.

"They died on a boat, didn't they?"

He couldn't seem to speak. Instead, he gave a single nod as an answer. His breathing started coming fast.

"Please," he stammered. "Just don't—" Again he couldn't finish his sentence. He was almost frantic with fear and nervous energy. This man was truly afraid. Seeing him like this, it broke something in her. Suddenly she forgot how hurt and angry she was, and she found herself pulling him into her arms, holding him and rubbing his back in an attempt to get him to calm down before he started hyperventilating.

"I'm fine. The baby's fine. You don't need to be afraid. I'll get off the ferry."

He held her tighter. His body was literally shaking in her arms. This was so out of character for Aléx. He was always calm to the point he was almost stoic. Yes, he'd come out of his shell more as they'd spent more time together. Never, not one single time in the eight months of their marriage, had he ever come this undone in her presence.

He stood there holding her for a long time until he could get himself together, and then he took her hand and helped her onto the dock.

"I promise, I won't stop you if you truly want to leave. I just need you to give me a chance to explain before you make up your mind. I know I don't deserve it. But I'm not above begging for that grace."

There was a car waiting for them, and he helped her inside before he walked around to the driver's side and got in. The drive was silent, both too afraid to break the fragile truce that had her agreeing to return to the palace with him.

Truly, there was no other choice. He had looked as if he were going to explode with fright if she'd refused to get off the ferry. With how anxious he was, she truly believed he wouldn't have survived if she left on that boat before he'd had the chance to stop her.

He drove with one hand, keeping the other clasped around hers as though he were afraid she would float away if he weren't acting as her anchor.

From the time they exited the car, he took her hand again. He directed her down a path that would keep them away from the guests they'd left in the ballroom. It led directly to their private quarters.

She'd expected him to stop in the drawing room, but he didn't. He kept walking down the corridor until they were standing in front of that door that had changed everything in the blink of an eye.

He placed his thumb on the keypad, and the lock clicked loudly. He gave her hand a squeeze, as if to tell her to prepare herself, before he held the door open and let her walk in, following quickly behind her.

He grabbed the picture frame before he walked over to the rocker in the corner, motioning for her to sit.

Refusing to let her hand go, he used his foot to position the ottoman right in front of her so he could keep hold of her. It was as if he needed this connection, partly to remind himself she was still here, and partly because he was afraid of her slipping away.

"As the heir to the throne, there are so few choices you have about your life. Who I'd become, where I'd go to school, how my coronation would be planned, even my funeral. All these things were known to me from the moment I can remember being conscious about who my mother was and, by extension, who I would be."

She wanted to reach out to him, soothe the sadness in his voice. Yet she somehow knew if she interrupted him, he might not ever be able to tell her this story to its completion.

"The only thing my mother wouldn't allow to be chosen for me was my bride. Jasiri's father had won his fight against arranged marriages when he married Jasiri's mother. She thought that her son should have the same choice."

He looked up at her, giving her a weary smile before he continued.

"I met Farah and her sister my last year of my graduate program at university. The three of us were great friends and we became comfortable around each other. They were part of the aristocracy, so like me, they knew they had to be wary of what kinds of friends and connections they made, because there was always someone waiting in the shadows to take advantage.

"Of the two sisters, it was Farah who hated everything that had to do with life at court. Her sister, on the other hand, didn't share the same reticence. As time went on, I began to distance myself from her sister because it became clear that she didn't just have an affinity for court. She was angling for something greater, to be the next queen. As a result, my friendship with her sister faded. I thought that would mean losing Farah too, but our friendship deepened. We sort of just fell into this comfortable pattern that led to us dating seriously."

"I bet her sister didn't like that."

The slight curve of his lip confirmed her suspicions. Apparently, Regina and Reigna weren't the first set of sisters to upend this man's life.

"Two years into our romantic relationship, I proposed. It just made sense that we would marry. We grew up in the same world. We both preferred to be out of the limelight. We got on fabulously. But when I asked for her hand, she said no. Two days later, I went to find her to try to convince her to change her mind. Her sister told me she'd left the day before, and the family had no idea where she'd gone."

"Don't tell me her sister decided then was her chance to shoot her shot?"

He did that thing again where he silently mouthed her words to make sense of them. She loved that he did the work of applying basic context clues to understand her Brooklyn and her AAVE. It was often hilarious, but she loved it all the same.

"She did in fact 'shoot her shot,' as you say. She hasn't stopped shooting it since then, no matter how many times I tell her it will never happen."

It was time for her to puzzle the pieces together until his words solidified their meaning in her head.

"Katia is Farah's sister?"

He closed his eyes and let his head sink in emotional exhaustion.

"Tell me the rest."

He laced their fingers together, rubbing his thumb against her skin, causing electricity to flow through her. It tethered her to him, connecting them on more than a physical level. He was drawing strength from her.

"Less than a year later, my mother died, and I became king. Two years after that, my head of security walks into my office and tells me he has news. Apparently, when you become king, at least in the first few years of your reign, royal investigators search for threats to the monarchy, including but not limited to illegitimate children. Evidently, right around the time my mother died, Farah had a baby. My baby."

She could see the weight of those words bearing down on him, cutting through to his core. It made her squeeze his hand in return, a silent reminder she was here.

"I confronted Farah. Came down on her with the full weight of the crown. I demanded she bring my daughter to me, or I would take the child from her because she'd stolen the girl from me. She tried to explain that she'd kept Charlie a secret because she didn't want her to have to live as my bastard child at court. I reminded her that Charlie wouldn't have been illegitimate if Farah had married me like I'd proposed. She said she couldn't. A gilded cage was still a cage, and she didn't want to feel imprisoned for the rest of her life."

His eyes began to redden as he continued.

"I was so pissed with her. She'd stolen my daughter from me. Charlie was born three weeks before my mother died. She robbed my mother of knowing her grandchild. I gave her a week to return to Obsidian Island. If she missed the deadline, I would have an arrest warrant issued for her. She was on Nyeusi, with whom we have an extradition agreement. She knew I had the power to realize those threats, so she agreed."

The anger slid away, and sorrow crept in. She could see the ache of loss begin to eat at him, and she wanted so badly to comfort him, to tell him it was all right. But she couldn't. She couldn't ignore this thing that had been cutting him to the bone and taking more and more of him away from her and their baby.

"The day she was to leave, weather reports warned of a coming storm. As soon as I learned of it, I told her not to leave, that she could come after the storm without penalty. But she was so angry with me for forcing her hand that she wouldn't listen. She told me she'd already packed up her place, and she was leaving early enough that the storm shouldn't be an issue. They'd be here in an hour."

A single tear slid down his cheek as he looked at her, reaching for a lifeline to help him get through this last part. The worst part.

"The storm came early."

The impact of those words hit her square in the chest.

"They lost control of the vessel."

Again, another thump in the middle of her chest as the staccato of his cadence beat against her like a drum.

"The boat capsized, and they were lost at sea. Search teams from both Nyeusi and Obsidian Island implemented every rescue plan available. Soon, however, rescue turned into recovery. They were gone."

She reached out for him, pulling both his hands into hers and pressing her lips against them.

"Dear God, Aléx, I'm so sorry for your loss."

His head snapped up as his gaze landed on hers.

"My loss? You don't blame me?"

Regina was a very smart woman, there were few things in the world that she didn't understand or couldn't figure out easily if she dedicated her attention to them. This, however, had her stumped.

"Why on earth would I blame you? It was an accident."

He shook his head and stood up, pacing back and forth in front of her.

"Because of my selfishness, my need to reclaim what was mine, I led the three-year-old daughter I'd never met and her mother on a path that ultimately led to their deaths. This is my fault."

She sat back, trying to take him in, seriously trying to follow his logic, and she couldn't. She just couldn't. Too raw from all the emotions of the night, she just didn't have the stomach for any of what was happening. There was only one way she could handle this situation and him. She would shoot straight from the hip.

"That is bullshit, Aléx, and you know it. Are all kings this arrogant, or is there some sort of stupidity gene that runs in royal bloodlines? I swear, between you and Jasiri, I don't know who has it worse, me or my sister."

"I beg your finest pardon." He stopped dead in his tracks and looked directly at her.

"Listen, you and Jasiri spend a whole lot of time taking on the weight of the world and thinking that the women in your lives can't handle it. Everything is on you. News flash. You are a king, not a god. You have no more control over the weather than I do my bladder at night when your kid is tap-dancing on that organ like it's Savion Glover, Gregory Hines and Sammy Davis Jr. all wrapped into one."

He stood with his mouth hung open, and she figured he was either too shocked to speak or having some sort of brain aneurysm. Either way, she figured since she'd already pressed her luck this far, she might as well keep going.

"It was a tragedy, Aléx. There was nothing you could've done to save them."

She walked over to him, poking her finger in his chest in hopes the discomfort might bring him out of his apparent stupor, because he still hadn't responded to her.

"You had every right to demand Farah bring your daughter home. I don't care what her issues were with being at court. That did not give her the right to rob you of being a father. Her dying doesn't absolve her of that."

She put one hand on her hip and jabbed the air with her finger as she spoke. She was so damn pissed. This man, this kind and caring man had wallowed in pain for five years because of someone else's action.

"There is no one to blame for their deaths, Aléx. It was a terrible, terrible accident. But that's not what all this guilt is really about, because you know there is nothing you or anyone else, including Farah, could've done to stop this."

His shoulders stiffened as he asked, "What are you saying?"

"I'm saying you don't blame yourself for their deaths. You blame yourself because you can't find it in your heart to be angry with a dead woman, so you'd sacrifice your own soul to avoid the truth. You're mad as hell at Farah for keeping your daughter from you. Had she not died, I have no doubt you would've made her very aware of that fact."

She threw up her hands, hoping the gesture would help her message break through to him.

"Here's another news flash, Aléx. You have every right to lay that particular blame at Farah's feet for lying to you all those years."

He stood there just watching her, taking in her heaving chest as if he couldn't recognize her in this moment. That's because he hadn't had the opportunity to meet protective Regina. This was who'd threatened Jasiri, warning him not to hurt her sister or his ass was hers. And she didn't care that Farah was dead. She wasn't letting her slide after watching her husband suffer so much guilt that he couldn't sleep at night.

"You're out of line, Regina. What the hell do you expect me to do? Just forget them and move on with my life as if they never existed, never mattered? I'm grieving, Regina."

His pain reddened his tanned skin, making him look like he was burning from the inside out. He was in a hell of his own creation, one he had no clue how to leave.

"You're no longer grieving, Aléx. You're punishing yourself because you lived. You are allowing your past guilt to rob you of joy in the present. I would never ask you to forget them. They are part of you. The problem is, you're making them all of you, leaving no room for yourself, me, or this baby."

She grabbed his hand and laid it on her stomach, holding it there, hoping it would be enough to bring him in from the cold.

"I need you, and this baby needs you, and I'll be damned if we lose you because of your misplaced guilt. I love you too damn much for that. So, here's how this is going to go down."

She stepped around him, walking toward the door before she looked over her shoulder at him.

"I'm tired. I'm tired of holding back, and I'm tired of pretending that I don't love you. I have more than enough love to keep the three of us afloat while you dig your way out of this abyss. But I've got to know you are trying to free yourself of this. Now that I've said my piece, I'm going to put on some comfy fuzzy pajamas, eat some butter pecan ice cream, send off some emails to my team to firm up the launch of my hair care line, and take myself to that ridiculously big bed of ours and go to sleep. Do whatever you need to grab hold of the truth, and if I find you in bed with me tomorrow morning when I wake up, I'll know that you've chosen to live in joy with me rather than suffocate in guilt."

She turned, her shoulders drawn back as she waddled down the hall. The ball was in his court now. She'd laid everything on the line. He knew where she stood, and she knew she couldn't allow herself to watch Aléx be consumed by his guilt any longer. It would kill her. For her sake and their baby's sake, she had to force his hand. He had to make a choice. Settled in her conviction, she refused to acknowledge the twinge of worry that asked, *What if he doesn't choose you?*

She knew the answer. She'd hurt like hell. It was as simple as that.

CHAPTER TWENTY

ALÉX STOOD IN the graveyard as his eyes scanned the cold double headstone that read, "Farah & Charlie, Together in Eternity."

By rights, Charlie should have been laid to rest in the royal mausoleum. Though she would never have been able to rule because of legitimacy laws, her parentage meant she should have rested beneath the palace where all the monarchs and their children were interred.

When Farah's family requested they be buried together, Aléx had not been able to deny them. The thought of his daughter alone, without the one person she depended on her entire life, seemed unnecessarily cruel.

Since their burial five years ago, he'd not been able to visit this space. It was too strong a reminder of what he'd lost. It augmented his self-recrimination and made it impossible for him to function on the most basic levels. But today, he had to be here. For once in his life, the cost of his guilt was too high a price to pay.

"Farah and Charlie, I must apologize to you. I have allowed my remorse to twist your lives and your deaths into something ugly that neither of you deserved. You deserved to rest in peace and not have my pain poison your memories. You deserved loving and happy thoughts that would've tied your legacies to love instead of pain. I wronged you so terribly, and I hope that you can find some way to forgive me."

The wind whistled lightly through the air, and Aléx had to wonder if it was just nature, or the two souls he was talking to letting him know they could hear him.

"I too must find my way to forgiveness. I need to forgive myself for taking on the blame of your deaths." He turned his head to the left, looking specifically at Farah's name chiseled into the ornate concrete slab. "And Farah, I need to forgive you too. All these years, I blamed myself for your deaths so I wouldn't let my anger toward you rise. You stole the most precious thing in the world from me. You made a selfish decision without consulting me, and as a result, I never had the chance to meet my child. I couldn't admit that until a very blunt woman made me face that fact last night."

He could look back on Regina's words with muted amusement now. Last night, however, he hadn't found them the least bit funny. He was still too mangled by his guilt to see reality.

"I love her, Farah. In a way I never thought I'd be able to love a woman. She pulls out these gnarled old parts of me and buffs them to perfection until they are shiny and new. I've been so afraid to love her for fear of losing her and for fear of disrespecting your and Charlie's memories.

"It's been hard for me to see this, but she made me realize love doesn't have to be an either-or situation. It can be a both-and. I can mourn your loss and still be angry with you for what you did to me. I can hold the love I had for you and Charlie in my heart and still love Regina and the child we've created completely."

He kneeled, swiping his hand across the cold stone and smiling reverently at it.

"So I've decided that's exactly what I'm going to do."

Tears filled his eyes, painting the headstone in a shimmering cascade. He cried for the loss of their lives. He cried for the loss of his opportunity to know and love his daughter. And then he cried for the hurt he'd caused himself, but most of all, Regina. He cried until he was empty, and the only thing left inside him was hope. Hope for a tomorrow he'd never dreamed he could see.

He pulled his handkerchief from his inner jacket pocket and nodded to them, but more so, to himself.

"I'm going to honor the two of you by loving her boldly and honestly, and by being the best father I can to our baby. I'm finally going to let the two of you rest in peace."

A gentle breeze connected with his cheek as if a hand were cupping his face, acknowledging what he'd said and encouraging him to follow through.

Suddenly light with hope, he stood, bent into a bow to show his reverence, and then he turned toward the car. His wife and child were expecting him, and he'd be damned if he'd keep them waiting any longer.

She fought hard not to wake up. The moment she rose, she would have to face whether her husband chose his guilt or her and their baby and the life they were supposed to be building together.

Even with the blackout curtains drawn, she could tell the new day was upon her. She could also tell something else.

Her husband was not in the bed with her.

Refusing to hide, she pulled herself up and leaned her back against the massive headboard. Her eyes were still closed as she made a running list of the things she would have to do now.

Contact a divorce attorney.

She was married to a king. Could she even get a divorce? Charles and Di and Andrew and Fergie divorced. There had to be a way she could rectify this mistake. It was one thing for her to marry a man knowing he would never love her. It was something altogether different to know he couldn't or wouldn't love her because he'd rather hold on to crippling guilt than accept the love she wanted to give him.

Look for a place to live on Obsidian Island.

They might be splitting up, but she wasn't leaving. No matter how her heart hurt, she would never take their child from him. She wanted Aléx to be an active, present parent.

Staying on Obsidian Island would be hard. She knew that. She would miss every second she wasn't with that man. Aléx had somehow embedded himself into her bones, and freeing herself from his hold was not going to be easy. She'd have their baby. She'd also have her work and her lab. She'd stayed up much later than she intended trying to numb her mind with work. Her line, Obsidian Queen, was set to launch six months from her due date. Now she was transferring leadership to her assistant in preparation for her maternity leave. Aside from distracting her from her hurt and worry, hopefully the work she was putting in now would keep the launch on schedule. Apart from their child, her hair care line might be the only thing she had left to keep her going if things didn't work out.

Relief bled through her as she thought of her work. She'd made certain the entire deal she'd made with Aléx gave complete, irrevocable ownership to her. She'd spent most of her working life in a lab. The wheeling and dealing part of business just wasn't for her. But she'd picked up enough from watching her sister and their Devereaux cousins to know how to protect her assets and interests when it came to signing contracts.

Her forethought meant she could be independent here, something she'd come to treasure. She'd never regret working with her sister all these years. Having something of her own…it meant she was finally learning who she was. And deep down, Regina was strong. It would hurt, leaving this man she loved so desperately. Yet she had no regrets. She'd done all she could do. He'd made his choice, and now they would all have to live with it.

"Are you done making your list in your head? If you are, I've got your morning cup of orange tea and this godawful apricot jam you insist on putting on your toast."

She kept her eyes closed but couldn't stop the happy tugging at her mouth that demanded she let the biggest smile she'd ever shone cut loose.

"Don't knock it 'till you've tried it. Your kid is on this fruit kick that's got me in a chokehold."

She heard him settle the tray on the nearby nightstand before he crawled into bed beside her, pulling her into his arms until she became the little spoon to his big spoon.

"It was my intention to be here when you awoke."

He held her tighter, as if he were afraid she would slip through his fingers at the first opportunity.

"Then why weren't you?"

"Because I had to take some time alone to say goodbye. I went to their graves and paid my respects."

Her hands clasped around his, making her strength available to him if he needed it. She'd seen him at his most vulnerable last night, and her protective instincts, where he was concerned, made her want to fight the world on his behalf, even if that included him.

She held her breath as she waited for him to continue, knowing whatever words he spoke next would be the most consequential of her life.

"I told them that I loved them, that I would never forget them. I told them I had to live, that I wanted to live, so that I could love you and our child completely."

She let the breath she was holding escape through pursed lips, her lungs deflating like overextended balloons.

"I thought I could do this without loving you, Regina, and I was wrong."

He lay there with her, letting his words hang in the air, letting her soak them all up. Like a menthol balm to achy muscles, those words melted in her flesh, seeping deep into her soul.

"I should've known I was wrong when I woke up in my hotel room alone and I had to fight myself not to follow you back to America and drag you back home with me."

If he'd thought waking up without her had been difficult, he should've tried leaving. She'd had to force herself out of his hotel room because she'd known if she stayed, she'd never be able to walk away. Knowing he was suffering just as much gave her a perverse kind of joy. It was petty as hell. But at least she wasn't alone in her misery.

"I should've known it when I wanted to murder someone because I thought the woman who'd thoroughly ruined me was marrying Jasiri."

What she and her sister had seen as a harmless lie had such a serious impact. Aléx's confession was proof of that. She would forever regret the anguish he'd suffered as a result.

"If I could ignore all those things, I should've known how deeply I'd fallen for you when you collapsed in your lab." His arms tightened around her even more as his body tensed against hers. Even talking about this still affected him.

"The thought that you could be seriously hurt, that you might leave me…" He couldn't finish the sentence, but the hard and fast tempo of his heart against her back made her understand how that incident had terrified him. "And once we learned you were pregnant, it triggered all my fears about Charlie and her mother."

That surprised her. She turned in his arms to face him, a feat that wasn't exactly easy at eight months pregnant.

"What are you saying, Aléx?"

He cupped the side of her face, and she burrowed into it, loving his warmth, needing it to get her through whatever he was about to say.

"The reason I couldn't sleep at night wasn't because I was mourning them, Regina. I couldn't sleep because I kept having dreams that I would lose you and our child just like I had them."

"Aléx."

Her heart pained her, thinking of the agony he'd been fighting through alone.

"You couldn't have known, Treasure. I wouldn't have let you know. I was so determined to be the suffering hero of my own story. Talking to you felt like letting you down. I was afraid you'd either pity me or hate me. Either way, I couldn't tolerate you thinking of me in either sense. Not when I knew what it was like to be held in your esteem."

Her eyes watered, and her tears spilled onto her face. He immediately wiped them with his thumb, smiling down at her.

"Treasure, I will never hurt either of us like that again. Seeing you on that boat put things into perspective for me. I can't be without you. I don't deserve you, but I'm begging anyway. Please love me, and let me love you. If you do, I promise you will never regret granting me that grace."

She remained quiet for a second, trying to slow her racing heart so she could have a clear thought. This wasn't something she could rush into. Then she looked up into those electric eyes of his, and the noise was silenced in her head. This man was her home, her refuge. Now it was time for her to be those things to him.

"I've got two conditions."

"Name them." His words left no doubt he was eager to accept any terms she put forth to make them a reality again.

"You're so lucky I'm a good woman. Otherwise, I could take you for everything you're worth."

"And I'd gladly give it."

She didn't doubt it.

"First, we never keep things from each other again. Aléx, we've been so locked in our own heads, carrying around old hurts and pains and not being there for one another, and it almost ruined us. We only deal in truth from now on."

"Agreed."

Satisfied with his answer, she continued. "The second is, you've got to give me one of your incredible foot massages at least once a week after the baby is born. There is no way I can exist without them."

His laughter shook them, and before she knew it, she was joining him. The heavy tension they'd dragged around unnecessarily was laid by the wayside. They'd made it through the storm, and instead of tears, there were smiles and laughter.

"Your conditions are agreeable, Treasure. Shall we kiss to seal this accord?"

The baby chose that moment to kick, and because of the position they were lying in, Aléx felt the strength of it against his own torso. He placed his hand on her belly where he'd felt the kick and soothingly rubbed it until the little one calmed down.

"Dearest One. You mustn't kick your mother that way when I'm trying to secure our future. It's rude."

"That's rich coming from a man who told me I owed him a baby."

He didn't deny it. From the smug look on his face, he

didn't even have the decency to feel ashamed. Instead, he placed a kiss on her forehead before staring down into her eyes.

"I'm better now, thanks to you. Let me repay that favor ten thousandfold every day for the rest of our lives."

The amusement left his face, and she could see the intensity of his feelings in his eyes and the straight set of his jaw. She kissed him back, placing a hungry kiss on his mouth and moaning when he matched her press for press and stroke for stroke.

This new Aléx, the one who wore his feelings on his face, he was the man she wanted by her side. They'd gone through hell for him to emerge, but he was here, alive, and she was in his arms.

He broke away, leaving them both panting with chests heaving.

"Does that mean yes?" His words were thick with love, passion and need. He needed her to say yes.

"That means yes, ten thousandfold for the rest of our lives."

EPILOGUE

"LOOK AT AUNTIE'S BABY!"

Aléx watched as his sister-in-law fell in love with his daughter. He couldn't blame her. His Dearest One had been sublime perfection since she'd made her entrance into the world a few hours ago.

Aléx looked down at his wife in her hospital bed. He was in awe. She was the real hero of the day, laboring for hours and then bringing their daughter safely into the world. He laced her fingers in his and brought them to his lips, whispering "I love you" against them.

"All right, you two." Reigna's warning tone pulled their attention away from each other and onto her. "Y'all had better keep all that kissing to a minimum or you're going to be right back in here in nine to eleven months."

"You're a whole lie." Regina deadpanned. "Now that I know what contractions feel like, I'm gonna need a few years to recover before we even contemplate trying that again."

Before the two sisters dissolved into a fit of giggles, Aléx walked over to Reigna with his hands out and waited for her to place his sleeping daughter in his hands. Once he had her securely in his arms, the baby cooed as if she knew this would be one of two safest places for her from now until eternity.

Looking at his daughter, Aléx couldn't believe how far the four adults in the room had come in less than a year.

Regina's hair care line was primed for a successful launch in six months. The fear she'd had that her sister wouldn't understand disappeared when Reigna, outside of Aléx himself, had become Regina's biggest supporter. Her support had healed whatever hurt their past shared trauma had created, making the sisters closer than anyone could've imagined, even for twins.

He and Jasiri had mended their rift. Letting down his guard had meant Aléx had a trusted confidant to help him through his low spaces. It also meant he got to experience Jasiri's joy and exuberance for life firsthand. Aléx hadn't understood how much he'd missed experiencing Jasiri's bold and carefree personality until he'd let the man in again. Now that he'd found the strength to, he and Jasiri were closer than two brothers could ever be. He trusted that man with everything, including the precious little girl sleeping in his arms.

Aléx stood in front of Jasiri and handed him the newborn.

"King Jasiri, would you honor my daughter by giving her your blessing?"

Jasiri beamed with pride in much the same way he had when Aléx had blessed Jasiri's daughter four months ago.

"It would be my honor."

He motioned for Aléx to remove the Nyeusian standard from his nearby satchel. Draping it over the baby, he looked at Aléx and said, "Have the two of you decided on a name yet?"

Aléx nodded, his heart pinching inside his chest with bittersweet love.

"It is an Obsidian tradition that the heir bears the names of the kings or queens who came before."

Aléx glanced over at his wife, and she proudly said, "We decided to name her after two of the greatest queens in the Obsidian royal line. Nairobi Carisse."

"Regina," Aléx finished. "If we're going to name her

after the greatest Obsidian queens, then her mother's name must be included too."

Regina was shocked. Aléx hadn't discussed it with her because he knew she'd say no. In his eyes, there was no contest. She was the greatest queen Obsidian Island had ever seen. She'd given him back his life, loved him, and made him a father. To him, there were no greater feats accomplished in his royal bloodline.

Jasiri nodded, arranging the standard gently around the precious babe.

"Princess Nairobi Carisse Regina, daughter of Queen Regina, issue of the great King Aléxandros, standard bearer of the Obsidian royal line of succession, heir apparent, and crown princess of the Obsidian throne."

He slowly swiped a reverent thumb across the child's head before he spoke again.

"May you possess the wisdom of all your ancestors so that you will rule with forethought and foresight."

He flattened his hand on the babe's chest, and Aléx's shoulders sat a bit straighter and his chest a bit broader as he watched Jasiri continue with the ceremony.

"May your heart be filled with compassion and kindness, so that you will rule with grace and benevolence."

Jasiri lifted the open hand the princess had strewn across half her face.

"May your hands be as open and strong as your heart so that you may carry and comfort your people and your nation through the sorrows life will inevitably bring."

Nairobi gave a long stretch before she settled against Jasiri's chest again. Jasiri gently clasped her foot between his forefinger and thumb, and the princess was rewarded with an enamored smile on the neighbor king's face.

"May your feet be strong and sturdy, so that you may

stand as a beacon to your people in times of light and darkness."

Aléx watched Jasiri make eye contact with him, and he could've sworn he saw a hint of glass in the Nyeusian king's eyes. Could the big strong king be fighting back tears? He wouldn't have been the first man in the room today. Aléx had cried multiple times since the doctor had laid the new baby in his arms. And he didn't feel the least bit bad about it.

"To Princess Nairobi of the Obsidian royal line of succession, may your reign be long and may your legacy live on forever."

This time it was Aléx who motioned to the sisters, and they each joined Aléx in repeating after Jasiri in unison.

"May your reign be long, and may your legacy live on forever."

Aléx leaned down to his wife, placing a wisp of a kiss across her puffy lips. Joy filled him as he sat down on the edge of the bed and whispered in her ear, "May our love reign long, and may its legacy live on forever."

She returned his peck, her eyes slightly exhausted, no doubt from all the work she'd put in today. The strength of this woman never ceased to amaze him.

As she'd said, she'd had enough love to carry them to this place where elation washed away the darkness in his heart and left it full of light and possibility. She shouldn't have had to bear that alone, and he would make certain her reward would be a husband who would love her through joy and tribulation. He would love her to life and through life until he breathed his last breath, and then from the grave, he would continue to love her into eternity.

She placed a hand over Aléx's heart, and it beat stronger for her. She looked up into his eyes before she repeated, "May our love reign long, and may its legacy live on forever."

* * * * *

SNOWBOUND AND ROYALLY FORBIDDEN

MAYA BLAKE

MILLS & BOON

CHAPTER ONE

PRINCE VALENTI DOMENE OF CARTANA jumped down from the two-seater fighter jet with a litheness that widened the young pilot's eyes.

At times like these, it helped to be a prince of a powerful kingdom. Better yet if Azar Domene, your older brother, the king and commander in chief of the royal military, had several fleets of fighter jets at his disposal.

It had cut down the normal hours-long journey to a mere forty-five minutes, with airspaces cleared with one phone call.

He saluted the pilot and whirled around, the sight of the gleaming black sports car waiting for him twenty feet away, easing another layer of the angst riding him hard. This one was courtesy of his twin brother, Teo. Valenti would get a ton of back-chat and demands for favours, but for now, he was grateful for the expedited support. He slid behind the wheel, gunned the engine and floored the accelerator out of the military base north of the small Scandinavian country of Reykland.

Soaring fir trees flashed past in shades of green and red, but the autumnal beauty of one of the most beautiful places he'd ever visited barely impinged on his roiling senses.

All of this would be worth it if the recipient of this entire upheaval would appreciate the effort.

His lips flattened. The chances of that happening would be nil. Not after the way they'd clashed at their last meeting, when years of fondness and easy conversation had morphed into…something else. Something he was still at a loss to describe.

At a loss or…unwilling, even unnerved *to pin down?*

It didn't matter. Not if she was in danger.

Quelling the anxiety threatening to rise, he thumbed the voice-activated phone system. His deputy answered before the first ring finished.

'Status report,' Valenti barked.

'We've been here an hour, Your Highness. It's all safe and sound.'

Safe and sound.

How he hated that term. In his chilling experience, things tended to be safe and sound…until they weren't.

Safe and sound had turned into a harrowing nightmare in the blink of an eye seven years ago, shattering one family and introducing him to a dark world of anguish and bitterness he didn't need to look very deep to locate. It was the invisible cloak that yes, stole his joy, but also maintained his focus razor-sharp, ensuring that one devastating event *never* had the chance to repeat itself. *Ever.* Collateral damage was considered part of running a security outfit, but he refused to accept preventable failure.

And this was very much such a scenario.

'You're still at the club?' he asked, although he was merely confirming an answer he knew. The person they were watching was as intractable as a dog with a bone.

'Yes, sir.' An infinitesimal hesitation before, 'She…she's refusing to leave.'

With any other client being actively stalked, Valenti wouldn't even have to say the necessary words. *Remove her by force*. But he'd long ago drilled into his men that this particular client wasn't to be touched. Under any circumstances.

And yes, while it baffled him completely that he would go to such lengths with her, he hadn't been able to retract his extreme reaction to having anyone lay their hands on *her*.

His ward.

Lotte Lillegard.

A twenty-two-year-old walking nightmare and albatross around his neck for the last seven years. And for the next three years. But once she turned twenty-five, he could wash his hands of her. Because he would have fulfilled the promise he'd made. *Finally*.

The knife of guilt sliding between his ribs robbed him of breath, making him grit his jaw as he stomped harder on the accelerator, shooting past slower vehicles and changing lanes, willing time to pass just as fast.

Spotting the Asbjørg Bridge that would take him into Ljomi, Reykland's capital, a layer of tension eased. Not enough until he clapped eyes on her, confirmed for himself that she was fine. And even then, he knew a different, *original*, weight would resettle in its place.

'Do not take your eyes off her for one single moment, is that understood?'

'Of course, Your Highness,' came the brisk reassurance.

Valenti didn't feel guilt for reiterating the command. Overkill wasn't a word in his vocabulary. Not anymore. He'd failed to stress a dire situation once in his life, and he'd lost a good friend, one who, had she lived, could've changed the course of *his* life. Knowing the loss had crushed his own dreams was a guilty secret he couldn't shed. A secret that chased him into his nightmares. And yes, he knew it was also why dropping his guard where Lotte was concerned wasn't an option. He could and had learned to live with many things, but that wasn't one of them. Even if Lotte Lillegard tested his last nerve.

The combination of traffic-monitoring gadgets, and probably Azar greasing the way further for him, meant he wasn't stopped for speeding.

He stepped out of the sports car, kicked the door shut, and was inside the nightclub in under a minute.

One of his subordinates met him at the opening that led to the cavernous room where dozens of bodies writhed in tempo to the thumping music. Not his second in command because he was obeying Valenti's command.

'This way, Your Highness.'

The man, almost as tall as Valenti and even broader than him, muscled his way through the crowd to the back of the club. From the corner of his eye, Valenti saw the guard flick him a nervous glance before respectfully backing away. Revealing his quarry in all her glory.

For the briefest moment, his footstep faltered. Seeing her for the first time in three years, Valenti had hoped the unsettling elements that had churned between them then would've dissipated.

The clenching in his gut said otherwise.

It was a combination of fury—although he wasn't entirely sure what this fresh bout of fury stemmed from—shock, disquiet and…primal, soul-scorching—

No. He was not *going to dignify that insufferable hint of a forbidden sensation with a label.*

He'd received weekly reports from the security team in charge of her safety; he'd spoken to her older brother every few months—although with Gunnar Lillegard busy with his Doctors Without Borders duties, he too rarely saw his little sister; he ensured her apartment, food, clothing and education and the trio of staff to take care of her needs were all in place. *But* he, Valenti, hadn't set eyes on Lotte since her nineteenth birthday. And even then, for all of half a day. She'd turned up unannounced in San Maribet, stunning the hell out of him, after giving her security team the slip and earning five men immediate firing. And while he wasn't proud of himself for barely recognising the woman she'd seemingly turned into overnight—since most of their contact had been by phone or hurried text lately—he hadn't suppressed the visceral need to be rid of her. To listen to the hindbrain warning that keeping her around was a mistake. Her protests about being sent away had threatened to rattle him, until he assured himself he was doing the right thing. She was better off in Reykland—statistically one of the safest places on earth.

That hindbrain caution returned full force now, sending sheets of shock through his system as he stalked to a halt at the edge of the dance floor, his gaze riveted on the woman lost in the throes of music and dance without a care in the world.

The shoulder-length waves he remembered had grown out to almost waist-length, straightened tonight so they fell in iron-straight silky sheets that flew around her as she gyrated in sky-high heels.

The second observation crept far too close to that forbidden sensation he'd first experienced three years ago, and try as he did to smash it to oblivion, it continued to bloom within him.

The reality was that Lotte Lillegard had left every trace of girlhood behind; had bloomed into a stunningly attractive woman. Even more breathtakingly beautiful than—

Valenti shook his head to dispel the direction of his thoughts, stalking forward with a thin burst of satisfaction when bodies hastily fell away, giving him a clear path to the girl…*woman* who still hadn't noticed him.

Who according to his team, had dismissed the danger

she was in with a shrug and grimace. As if it was a pesky fly in an easily replaceable cocktail. The same way another threat had been dismissed, with lethal consequences almost a decade ago.

His stomach knotted as memories pushed harder. Of him dropping to his knees, gathering an unresponsive body in his arms...*swearing, pleading, praying*...to no avail.

Which was why he arrived next to her with a red haze of renewed fury rushing across his eyes. Why he closed his hand over her arm when she continued to remain oblivious to him. Grew angrier when he noticed just why she was so oblivious.

The phone in her hand, turned onto some live social media platform, dozens of hearts flowing up the screen as eager strangers rabidly followed her exploits.

'Excuse me!' She rounded on him, to her credit aiming a slender leg in a defensive posture he remembered teaching her eons ago. He blocked it easily, then steadied her as she stumbled on stiletto heels, her blue eyes widening in shock.

'V-Valenti?'

His belly clenched in weird reaction to his name on her lips, then noted why. Her voice had lost its high girlish pitch, had dropped several octaves into a huskiness that tunnelled deep, into dark, *forbidden* places it really shouldn't.

'What are you doing here?' she demanded.

Valenti didn't bother holding back his ire. 'I should be asking you that. What the hell do you think?' She opened her mouth to answer. He stopped her by sliding his gaze to the phone clutched in her hand. 'Turn that thing off. Now.'

Shock replaced the obstinacy he remembered well. And traces of wary censure he didn't. He ignored the flickers of unease the latter trailed over his nape, reminding himself he'd long passed caring about personal opinions. Duty, purpose and the strength of his oath were all that mattered. And he'd taken an oath to keep Lotte safe.

And yes, that included keeping her safe from *himself*, from those unacceptable thoughts that flashed through his mind during her unannounced visit to Cartana three years ago. *These thoughts circling the edges of control right now.*

'Why?' she demanded. 'And you still haven't answered me.'

He'd been called 'intense' many times by so many people, he'd lost count or care. He felt zero guilt for bringing that emotion to bear as he waited for her to comply.

She didn't. Instead, she brought the hand holding the phone to eye level, right in front of his chest, and flashed a smile so striking, so eerily similar to another smile embedded in searing memory, every last scrap of air left his lungs.

Mocking him with why he'd kept his distance from Lotte all this time…

'Sorry to cut this short, *elskurnar*, but I gotta go. Remember, be kind, love hard, live free. And don't party too hard without me!' She tossed a peace sign, then closing lushly lashed eyes, puckered her lips for three excruciating seconds before blowing a kiss at the camera.

A deep growl left Valenti's throat before he even realised it was building. He barely noticed the crowd take a collective wary step back, but he did note that the music had died down significantly, probably courtesy of one of his team. Enough to hear himself think.

'Are you happy now? Everyone is looking at us,' she hissed, a blush creeping into her cheeks as he dragged his bizarrely compelled gaze from her lips to her eyes.

He plucked the phone from her hand and slotted it into his pocket. Then he led her decisively towards the exit.

'What are you doing?'

'What does it look like?' he growled. 'We're leaving.'

'You may be, but I'm not.'

Valenti stopped abruptly. She stumbled into him, then grabbed his arm to steady herself. 'I'm not having a conversation with you in this place,' he said, seething, noting the various phone cameras aimed their way. Teo was going to have a field day with this.

'Then leave! You weren't invited here in the first place. I— What the hell!'

Valenti ignored the outraged screech as he tossed his wayward charge over his shoulder. Gritted his teeth when her wriggling dug his shoulder into her soft belly.

The clubbers who'd stopped to gawp he quickly dispatched with furious glares that had them scrambling.

Sixty seconds later, he had her ensconced—and bristling like a wet cat—in his front seat, his command for her to stay put, *or else*, seemingly working despite the ice-blue fire in her eyes.

Thank *Dios* for small mercies.

'You're supposed to be ten miles away, at finishing school. Why are you not?' he enquired coolly, grateful the strange roiling had settled down.

'Are you serious right now?' she scoffed, her glare drilling into the side of his face.

'You're an intelligent girl or so your college professor told me when we last spoke. What do you think?'

'I think if you cared about my education at all—even the useless part that for some reason requires me to go to finishing school like some mid-nineteenth-century non-feminist waif in desperate search for a husband—then you would know I graduated *three weeks ago*! Alone.'

A jolt of disquiet shook through him, one he didn't allow to show as he accelerated through the busy streets. A quick mental calculation provided the reason for the lapse. He was one week from the next monthly report on her activities. He'd only received the alert about tonight because his security had rightly deemed it an abnormal risk.

Still, it was…disconcerting that she would no longer be mandated to be locked away in some academic institution, as safe from harm as he could order her to be with his security team nearby to provide an extra layer of protection.

Even more disconcerted that she hadn't bothered to reach out and berate him for his absence. Did she…hate him?

And why did that chafe when he shouldn't care?

He smashed away the wavelet of discomfort. He was here to deal with a more perilous situation.

Pulling up to a red light, he slanted a glance at her and frowned when he saw the chagrin she was trying to hide. Replaying her response, he experienced another jolt.

'What do you mean alone?' he rasped.

Her nostrils quivered for a single second before she said, 'Do you need the definition?'

'I mean,' he forced through gritted teeth, 'when I spoke to your brother three weeks ago, he was still in Reykland. He said he would be home for another two weeks. I assumed he would be around to attend your graduation.'

A faint frown feathered across her brow. 'Do…do you speak to Gunnar often?' she muttered.

'At least once a month, *si*.' It was how he learned snippets of her life that didn't make it into his professional report. How he knew Lotte hadn't forgiven him for rejecting her in Cartana. And why, as much as the fractures were unfortunate, he didn't completely wish them gone. Because they kept a necessary distance between the Lotte who was no longer the carefree girl he once knew—and the woman she'd become—and the rigid guard he'd discovered he needed to keep around her.

Her gaze dropped to her folded hands, then quickly

switched to the window, blocking his view of her face. 'Well, he didn't attend. He was called away four days before I finished so...'

This time her delicate jaw clenched for several seconds before she visibly relaxed it. And kept looking out of the window. Ignoring him.

His own jaw started to clench, but then she turned, and he exhaled the absurd agitation rising in his chest.

He was here to take care of a problem. One yet unaddressed. 'Did you not think it would be useful to tell anyone you'd recently acquired a stalker?' The snarl in his voice he deemed appropriate. Necessary even. Just having to speak that infuriating and disturbing sentence riled him anew. But the gravity of the situation couldn't be underestimated. He'd done that once and lost a best friend, a vital ally and changed the trajectory of his life.

'Anyone? Or you specifically?' she taunted.

'You do not want to test me right now.'

No. He didn't feel an ounce of pity when she paled. When her fingers twisted faster in her lap as he approached the apartment building he'd personally vetted for security before installing her at the very top. Ostensibly away from the kind of attention she'd attracted and blithely ignored.

He was waiting when she finally faced him. 'How did you even find out about that?'

He arched a brow, the simmer rising to a boil.

She stared him down, misplaced fury making her bold. And reckless. 'And that's what it takes for you to jump on your royal jet to see your unwanted burden?'

'I didn't use my royal jet. I came by military jet to get me here faster,' he corrected crisply, then took satisfaction in her widening eyes and sharp intake of breath. 'And you're not deflecting this. Answer me, Lotte.'

Did he imagine her shiver at his use of her name? *Dios*,

was he hallucinating this whole inconvenient but dire situation? That explanation—an eagerly welcome one—would fit why he was noticing far too many aspects of his ward. Like how the streetlight intensified the glow of her skin. The elegant sweep of her neck. How well her hips fit into the bucket of his passenger seat.

He swung into a parking spot too fast, upsetting her balance. The side of her breast and hip imprinted on his arm before she righted herself. And that bizarre sensation from three years ago returned, making his fingers curl tighter around the wheel.

'Every social media personality with more than a handful of followers attracts trolls these days. It's not a big—'

Launching himself out of the car silenced her. Valenti utilised the time it took to round the hood to drag control back into his being.

To remind himself that feelings and emotion and pleas and considerations didn't matter. *Couldn't matter.*

He'd sworn an oath to a dying friend, an exceptional woman who'd given much more than he'd been able to give back. He would keep his oath come hell or high water.

He yanked her door open. 'Out.'

'Valenti—'

'We will discuss this properly indoors, and I would seriously suggest you come up with a better explanation for the oversight than *it happens to everyone so it's no big deal.*'

The moment she stepped out, lips pursed in displeasure, he wrapped his hand around her arm again. Not because he feared she would flee. Even his headstrong ward wasn't that foolhardy.

No, it went deeper than that, he knew. And as disturbing as it was to admit, keeping his hand on her, reassuring himself that she was safe and breathing next to him, seemed paramount to quell his agitation.

She kept her silence until they were in the lift. Then her blue eyes narrowed. 'You didn't answer me. How do you know?'

He slanted a look dry enough to burn tinder. 'Is that a serious question?'

'Doesn't the word *privacy* mean anything to you?'

'Does it to you? You share yourself with millions. I take an interest in whoever seems out of place. And when it comes to your safety, I won't compromise or apologise,' he returned with zero remorse.

Her mouth dropped open. 'You know I can have you arrested for that, don't you?'

'You'd be wasting your time. And mine. Or have you forgotten what we are to each other?'

Something flickered in her eyes, followed by a wave of pink in her cheeks before she turned her head sharply, directing her focus to the front doors of the lift. But while he couldn't immediately decipher that expression, that whisper returned, a little more persistent. A little more abhorrent. Because it was unthinkable. In this lifetime or the next.

Because he would be heaping dishonour on top of a multitude of failures and sins.

The doors opened to the trio of staff who covered Lotte's penthouse apartment.

Leif, the butler Valenti had hand-selected five years ago for his past military expertise, bowed when he saw him, followed swiftly by Ada, the housekeeper, and the young maid. 'Your Highness, I'm so sorry, we weren't aware you were coming. We would've been better prepared.'

Valenti caught Lotte's pursed lips before she walked past him into the living room.

'It was unscheduled,' he replied, then froze when he saw their unease. 'Something has happened. What is it?'

Leif exchanged a wary look with the housekeeper. 'It might be nothing—'

'Tell me,' Valenti insisted. 'Now.'

Leif exhaled. 'I think it's better if I show you, Your Highness.' His gaze darted to Lotte. 'And it would be better if you stayed here, miss—'

'Absolutely not. And I really wish everyone would stop treating me like I'm some fragile flower.' Whirling around, she headed where Valenti remembered was her bedroom.

His hand circled her arm for the second time, pulling her into his chest before she'd taken the second step.

'And I really wish you would stop manhandling me, *Your Highness.*'

His title from her lips was all fire and zero respect, which alarmingly ignited sensations he'd rather not experience. With her. 'Stop diving headlong into danger and I might consider it,' he replied. Then watched affront leach the colour from her cheeks for two seconds before it came flooding back. A delicate pink.

An *alluring*—

'How dare you! I have a right to go anywhere I please. This is my home.'

'Paid for by me,' he muttered in her ear. 'Or have you forgotten that too?'

A dash of hurt accompanied the fury this time, then naked pain as memories shadowed her eyes, darkening them from ice to cerulean blue.

Valenti bit back a curse as she yanked herself free. Things had gone from bad to worse, starting with the urgent text he'd received while in Cartana with Teo and Azar.

It had elevated the threat level of one of Lotte's followers on social media. Valenti knew a handful of pesky individuals always needed deeper scrutiny with any client seeking security, especially if that client had a substantial online presence.

Just as he'd known his ward's active social media presence would draw the inevitable trolls. His cyber experts had quickly identified the problematic ones, his team successfully neutralising any hint of a threat.

Except one had slipped through the net.

Because everything was *safe and sound…*until it wasn't.

He pushed back another wave of harrowing memories and captured her gaze, ensuring she didn't miss the severity of his command.

'You can come with me. But you do not move from my side. Agreed?'

Perhaps the gravity of the situation finally filtered in. Perhaps the memories had done their job of reminding her of their loss.

Either way, she jerked out a nod.

But Valenti didn't feel in any way appeased as he strode down the short hallway, her wrist held firmly in his hand. Her pulse fluttering beneath his thumb.

He yanked his mind back from dwelling on how soft her skin felt. How delicate and smooth. Because *Dios mio*, he had no business even *thinking* it.

Then he stopped thinking altogether when he saw the deeply disturbing scene splayed out before him.

Lotte sucked in a sharp breath, her face leaching of all colour as her hands flew to her mouth. 'Oh my God!'

Valenti pulled her closer, glad he hadn't let her come in here alone.

Spread out on her bed were over a dozen pieces of lingerie, each one pinned with a shiny red plastic heart. The kind usually tossed into a gift box.

The rage that hadn't dropped below a simmer since he received the text resurged, threatened to boil over.

He rounded on the men and women filling up the room behind him. 'How the hell did this happen? How did an intruder gain access to her room without anyone noticing?'

Staff and security team alike flinched at the lava-hot demand. Valenti throttled back the deep urge to fire everyone on the spot. But his attention was diverted when she took a step towards the bed.

'*Dios*, what did we agree, Lotte?'

'I just want to see—'

'*Absolutamente no!* You don't touch anything until the authorities have been through here.' His gaze clashed with the head of her security detail. The man pulled the phone from his pocket. Valenti switched his gaze to the housekeeper. 'Ada, one of my men will drive you to the nearest House of Domene boutique. It will be open for you. Get Lotte everything she needs for an extended stay away from this apartment.'

Ada bobbed a curtsy. 'Yes, Your Highness.' She hurried out, the young maid on her tail, as Lotte frowned.

'Wait, what are you doing? Valenti—'

He pressed his thumb firmer against her wrist, heard her sharp intake of breath and saw her swallow. His silent admonition only lasted ten seconds before she was glaring at him.

'We need to talk about this. You know that, don't you?'

He texted his twin with his request before sliding his phone back into his pocket, and met sparking blue eyes. Over her head, he saw Leif position himself in the doorway to her bathroom, a determined look on his face that made Valenti's gut clench tighter. Valenti sensed that whatever was in there, far more than what was on his ward's bed, was why the housekeeper hadn't wanted Lotte to come in here.

Returning his gaze to her, he leaned close once more, ignoring how the sweet fragrance of her scent sparked pockets of sensation within him. Sensations he wasn't going to examine.

'If you insist. But it won't be right now, *pequeña*. What you want or believe or disagree with doesn't matter anymore. You have a stalker, Lotte. One whose existence you've treated with astonishing disregard. And while you might rail and hiss that it offends your feminine sensibilities, know that in this moment, only what I say goes. Know that until I'm one hundred percent certain that you are safe, I won't relent or retreat. Know that until such time when we're free of each other, *you belong to me.*'

CHAPTER TWO

NO, NO, NO.

She wasn't going to go there. She absolutely was not going to—

You belong to me. You belong to me. You belong to—

Lotte took another step back, desperately keeping her outrage at the forefront and the horrifying...*elation* buried at the back of her mind. She couldn't be feeling this again. Wasn't the most humiliating half hour she'd experienced three years ago enough? While Valenti would never be labelled effusive with his feelings, she'd believed for years that he was fond of her. At least tolerated her. Until that moment in Cartana when he'd scoured her with those silver eyes, something deeply grave and earth-moving, changing his demeanour. And his attitude. Changing their dynamic forever.

So no, she couldn't *like* his hand on her. Not when he was running roughshod over her wishes. Not even if he seemed to have forgotten himself just now.

Because for one lousy minute, most likely in response to the horrible spectacle that had forever tarnished her well-loved bedroom, Prince Valenti Domene had lowered his titanium guard.

And he'd caressed her wrist.

She should be addressing this violation, the increasingly insistent and belligerent follower whose friendliness had crossed a line recently. Who she'd dismissed because deep down she'd trusted that Valenti, despite not wanting anything to do with her personally, had charged enough well-trained men—hell, a veritable small army and the last word in over-kill—with protecting her.

She should've been thinking of that.

Not the waves of heat and ice unravelling through her. Unravelling *her*.

She withstood the all-consuming sensation, let it bathe her from head to toe. She had learned painfully that it was the only way, because her self-preservation *would* kick in. Sure she would be a little hollowed out, clutching the frayed tatters of her composure. But there would be enough left to pick herself back up again.

She stepped forward when Leif and Valenti exchanged another look. 'What is it?' she snapped.

Valenti's jaw clenched. Then he turned to her and examined her for an age before he spoke. 'There is more. And no matter what you feel I don't believe it will benefit you to see further…unsavouriness. Will you stay here and let me?' he rasped.

That…disarmed her. Threatened to dismantle her out-rage. Because this less high-handed manner reminded her of the Valenti of old. The Valenti who didn't order icily and instead…engaged.

She tried to resummon fury, but while it arrived on cue, another sensation threatened its potency. She vividly remem-bered how it felt to be draped over his hard, powerful body. How her fingers had brushed over his tight backside as he marched her out of the nightclub. She cursed the blush she could feel racing into her cheeks. Cursed her fair skin for consistently betraying her where this man was concerned.

Slivers of that guilt blasted her for the feelings she could never completely contain around this man as she boldly met his gaze. Searched for mockery or rejection. She found none, but then neither was there further evidence that he was softening. Maybe this was merely a ploy to get her onside, but… did she really need to see what other horrors had been left in her bathroom? 'Fine, I'll stay here. But we're definitely discussing any other plans you're cooking up. Including where we're going and how long we're going to be away.'

His eyes narrowed. 'Why? Do you have a hot date to keep?'

She wanted to blurt *yes*, but that would be lying. Besides, he monitored every corner of her life. She'd known the deal when she turned eighteen and, erroneously believed she was free of him, only to be disavowed of that anticipation of bittersweet joy. Until she turned twenty-five, Valenti Domene held the key to her freedom. She'd tried seeking an ally in her brother, but Gunnar, after shamefacedly confessing he wasn't 'parent material' had urged her not to fight the guardianship, subtly reminding her of the power and might of the Domenes.

As if she could forget. Even now, she couldn't escape the granite perfection of his face. The high, proud cheekbones. The haughty nose.

The small nick across his right eyebrow that would forever distinguish him from his identical twin. But only if you were close enough to him to see it. Or if his twin weren't the starlit night sky to Valenti's fathomless black hole.

Yin and yang. Two sides of an endlessly complex, priceless whole. Except she'd never found Teo as soul-searingly fascinating and hauntingly perplexing as she found Valenti. Even from a young age.

'Lotte.'

The rumble of warning made her insides jolt. Made her gaze slide from his to the bed she would never be able to sleep in again. The bed she was sure Valenti would instruct Leif to remove and burn before sunrise.

Then she glanced at the faces of the people paid to handle her well-being. Those who took care of the practicalities while leaving her alone to wander the wilderness of her loneliness.

While they were devoted to her every material whim and plea, and on some level she knew they cared about her well-being, they wouldn't be here if Prince Valenti Domene wasn't paying their salaries.

Before abhorrent self-pity and claustrophobia of her gilded cage could suck her under, she shook her head. 'I have a life. One I'm not willing to have hijacked by anyone. So yes, I'll let the authorities do what they need to, but I also demand to know when I can return to my life.'

Even if that life left her increasingly only half fulfilled.

Even if that reality was—now that she didn't have to fill her head with useless information like polo tournament etiquette or how to rectify the social *faux pas* of offending a man by stating an opposing opinion—shining a far too bright light on how empty and lonely her life truly was, now she was helping other women realise their dreams.

She pushed those tendrils of desolation far away as his lips flattened for one second.

'Are you sure you want a timeline?'

Those tendrils morphed into apprehension. 'Why wouldn't I?'

'Very well. At the very least one month or six weeks. Perhaps longer.'

'You must be joking!' It was the second time she'd proclaimed him humorous. Maybe it was subliminal wishful thinking. A gut reaction yearning for a time long gone. Because the last time she'd seen him crack a smile or approach anywhere near playful had been…

Her insides twisted. Then those twists knotted hard until her chest burned with the torture.

The distinct sound of the lift's arrival galvanised movement from the security team. Silent commands were passed from Valenti to a handful of them. Nods of acknowledgment tumbled like falling dominoes.

Then he was ushering her out, a firm hand at the small of her back she was absolutely not going to think about.

'I'll be out in a moment,' he rasped then stepped back and shut her bedroom door, temporarily severing the electrifying connection of his presence.

Her breath shuddered out, the sensation of having the air restored making her chest heave.

Like always, he'd arrived with the deadly power of a midnight sonic boom, turned her inside out, and left long before the devastation of his presence shattered around her.

But she wasn't eighteen anymore, when she'd forced herself to label the feelings seething like hormonal explosions beneath her skin, ready to burst free if she so much as *thought* of him. Or nineteen, when she'd allowed those emotions to dominate her. To rob her so completely of common sense that she'd boarded a plane and presented herself in his beloved kingdom, hoping for some regard from the man who'd cared so deeply for her flesh and blood but it turned out, had been *pretending* a fondness for Lotte.

That reminder and the searing embarrassment it dragged along with it powered her feet and determination, and she watched with a weighty amount of glee as the guards jumped apart to let her through.

Just in time to greet the trio of policemen who walked in.

They were introducing themselves when Valenti joined her, his face set in even more icy resolution.

He crossed to the mantel where a small fire blazed in the hearth and positioned himself before it, arms crossed. Dominating the room with unmistakable authority.

Lotte wasn't surprised at all when the police fell over themselves to start taking notes.

With each revelation that yes, she'd received uncomfortable messages from a stranger, that yes, she'd ignored most of them and that, yes, her unwanted admirer had become increasingly aggressive, finding ways to overcome her attempts to block him, the more rigid with deadly tension Valenti grew.

Until the police were casting him more wary glances than they were her.

To the point she was almost relieved when he returned to her bedroom with the uniformed men.

Lotte should've stayed put in the living room as agreed, but dammit, this was about her. She was damned if she'd turn into some meek doll just to please Prince Valenti Domene.

'It's clear these pictures were taken by a drone outside her bedroom window,' Valenti's arctic fury cut through her thoughts.

Dear God! Pictures? Of her?

'We can only be thankful it's winter and her French windows were shut or who knows—'

'You think?' Valenti snarled, cutting off the policeman's useless speculation. 'How did this happen?'

'Unfortunately, drones aren't illegal,' one policeman said.

Before she could stop herself, she was rushing into the room, skirting Valenti's towering form to see the pictures they were examining.

All of her moving around in her bedroom.

'Lotte.' She ignored Valenti's clipped warning, snatched up the photos and quickly leafed through them. Thanking the heavens for small mercies that none were of her naked.

Still she felt violated enough to rapidly swallow the wave of nausea that rose.

She let him retrieve the pictures from her, a curse barking from him as he handed them over to the officers before marching her back out of the room.

'It's becoming clear that you've been left for far too long to your own devices,' he hissed as he led her down the hallway.

'How dare you?'

'Oh, you're about to find out. Trust me on that.'

She *hated* the dual outrage and the illicit thrill that went through her at that dark promise. The very unnerving thought that she was getting the attention she'd assured herself she didn't want from her guardian.

She'd already let herself down enough by revealing how alone and unwanted she'd felt when she'd had to attend her graduation on her own, the pitying looks she'd been subjected to since *everyone* knew who her guardian and benefactor was. The Great Valenti Domene of the Even Greater Kingdom of Cartana. Second son of the recently abdicated king. Making him a prince in his own right.

Gunnar had sent her a large bouquet of flowers with a note sending his regrets since he was on the other side of the world saving precious lives. And she hadn't had the heart to be overly upset, because she knew he was doing what he loved.

Valenti had sent nothing but stony silence. She'd known it. Expected it in fact after their awful last confrontation. And yet she'd spent half of that ceremony with an eye on the door, scouring the crowd, kicking herself for hoping he'd miraculously materialise. Apologise for turning up late. And if not crack a smile and congratulate her for sticking to the education she'd hated every second of every day—because she'd stupidly wanted to win his approval—then at least shake her hand. Brush a whisper of a kiss across her cheek. *Deign to look at her for a scant second, even invite her to play a game of chess, like he had when she was younger and desperately wanted to forget the fog of grief hovering over her.*

Lotte had hated the burning tears that wouldn't be wished away all through the ceremony and in the long hours after when she'd logged online and allowed her adoring fans to fawn over her. Hating Valenti Domene every bruising second.

She clung harder to that resentment now, her muscles unclenching as it took hold.

'Whatever rights you may think you have, it doesn't give you the authority to show up when it suits you and manhandle me however you please. We have laws here that explicitly prevent you from acting like a...'

One dark eyebrow arched when she stumbled to a halt. 'Like a...?'

'Like an overbearing jackass!'

His head tilted, his keen gaze not straying from her for a moment. 'Not the worst thing I've been called. But do go ahead. Call whoever you need to call.'

She held out her hand. 'Give me back my phone and I will.'

'Not happening. Your phone stays off until we get this situation under control.'

'What? You can't do that.'

'And yet I'm doing exactly that.' He turned and strolled out of the room, leaving her no choice but to chase after him like some pesky, unwanted pet.

He rasped instructions she was too enraged to hear at Leif as the police departed and he headed for the door, not bothering to look over his shoulder as he added, 'You should know, I'm not averse to carting you around like luggage if that's what it takes, but you probably won't like that. So come, Lotte. Now.'

She didn't bother pleading with Leif or the handful of guards strewn around the room and in the corridor. Every single one of them answered to Prince Valenti Domene. All he needed to do was lift a finger or that scarred eyebrow that somehow, *maddeningly*, made him hotter, and they'd jump to do his bidding.

She wasn't about to lower herself kicking and screaming like a toddler, no matter how frustrated she was. Besides, as much as she hated to admit it, those pictures had...perturbed her. It was one thing being trolled or harassed online. A post could be blocked, an app or email deleted.

That whoever it was had gone to the trouble to track her

down to her home, to capture intimate images of her while she was completely unaware…

She sucked in a breath. Pushed down the resurgence of nausea. Quietly admitted to herself that she wanted to get to the bottom of this. Soon. So she could return to her life.

What life?

She ignored the taunting voice.

It didn't matter that she'd started her social media platform mostly to alleviate her loneliness. With her parents and one sibling gone, the remaining sibling burying his grief in his missionary work and a smattering of snobby private school friends comprising her social circle, it'd initially felt almost desperate to seek friends online. But surprisingly, she'd found acceptance with mostly decent people who were happy for the connection. Perhaps even welcomed her input.

It'd grown into something she was proud of. *Something of value, dammit.*

She curled her hands into fists and hung on tight to that knowledge. Valenti Domene wasn't going to devalue all the work she'd done. She'd given him a chance for a better connection three years ago. He'd rejected it. She would fight him tooth and nail to keep this vital lifeline.

He called up the lift.

She notched her chin and sailed into it, head held high.

And when the door slid shut, she pinned him with her iciest stare. 'This is far from over. Believe that if you believe nothing else. And when it is over, I promise you, I'll be ecstatic never to set eyes on you again for as long as I live.'

Anger was the reason he was so unsettled.

Anger and regret. He was doing something about the wave of helplessness that had caught him unawares. Thankfully it hadn't made a reappearance after that one and only instance when he'd seen the pictures.

Valenti detested the invasiveness with every fibre of his being. It helped a little that the tech geniuses and hackers he paid millions to every year had promised they'd track down every pixel within twenty-four hours. It paid to challenge great people to greater heights. And yes, he'd feel every millisecond of the next day, but he was also confident he wouldn't have to live with it for long.

He was a master at compartmentalising. He'd needed to be. Long before the tragedy that had cemented his belief that emotional attachments were a distraction he couldn't afford, that duty and tangible goals like ensuring his family's safety were his destiny, he'd made the mistake of believing he could choose his destiny. Hell, he'd been well on his way. The dream he'd all but given up on—of being a surgeon— back within touching distance. A misjudgement, a tragedy had erased all of that, leaving him with no choice but to accept the line drawn for him, a destiny he couldn't shirk.

On those days where he strayed to within a whisker of internalising, which were rare, thank God, he envied his twin brother. Teo had given the two-finger salute at gravely muttered words like *duty* and *responsibility* and *sacrifice*.

His carefree twin had delved wholeheartedly into doing what pleased him with hedonistic zeal. And while Valenti suspected it had all been a front, he still experienced flashes of uncustomary awe for Teo's brazen rebellion. He'd thrived the way Valenti had once dreamed of thriving doing what he loved.

Instead he'd stepped up to the plate he didn't want, sworn allegiance far removed from the one he'd envisioned for himself as a growing boy.

He hadn't doubted that he would excel in any chosen field. Even the one handpicked by his father and the self-venerating council who'd expected the bewildered young king suddenly married and saddled with three sons birthed by two different women, to jump to their every demand.

And when Valenti had reconciled himself with his new destiny, it'd been a simple matter of wielding the field of security and surveillance to his will and ascending to the top of that particular mountain. Until he was simply the best in the world. Until he'd accrued more independent wealth than he could spend in several lifetimes.

But all that had come at a great cost. He'd wanted to become a surgeon. His father and kingdom had disagreed, pushed a different destiny on him. Too late, he'd realised that resentment left unresolved in his heart had long ago calcified. Fused into his being. Leaving him cold and numb to the outside world.

Most days he was perfectly content with it.

But when a crack appeared, and hints of emotion dripped through the fractures, like that brief time he'd believed his dream was salvageable because Helga, his unlikely friend, had made him believe?

Or now…

When he was reminded just *why* distance from Lotte was necessary?

Then he knew he needed to double down. He wasn't completely clueless. He recognised Lotte's emotional neediness. The hints of loneliness that clung. But he'd failed one sister by not saving her life. He was damned if he would permit this unnerving state to persist. Emotions like need and desire clouded judgement.

So he forced himself to take a breath. Then another.

Forced his body not to react to her presence or her scent. Even though both seemed hell-bent on infiltrating every corner of his psyche.

'Where are we?' She looked around his penthouse with curious, then wary eyes.

'This is my place.'

She rounded on him. 'You have an apartment in Ljomi?' It was a mixture of accusation and…hurt?

'Yes. Where do you think I stay when I'm here?'

'How the hell would I know? You drop in and leave when you feel like, never deigning to tell me beforehand about your comings and goings, but I assumed you…'

He stiffened when another flash of hurt crossed her face. 'What?'

'That you stayed with Gunnar. Or at a hotel.'

'Hotels aren't secure. And Gunnar lives in a one-bedroom apartment.'

She spun around, arms held out with unbridled sarcasm painted on her face. 'Of course, and only the very best for Prince Valenti will do, *jà*?'

'Yes,' he answered simply, without inflexion. 'I'd find actually wearing sackcloth and ashes a little overkill and highly uncomfortable.'

Her face fell and he wanted to kick his own ass. Not because he'd made her sad, but because he'd drawn their attention to the subject he'd sworn to stay clear of on this trip. The subject he'd found himself thinking about two minutes ago.

Helga Lillegard.

Her sister. Her *dead* sister.

His hand twitched at his side, the urge to plough his fingers through his hair in frustration biting chunks out of him. *Control.*

'I have money coming out of my ears, Lotte.' It was less of a boast and more of a fact he didn't see the need to be bashful about. 'You know this since you benefit immensely from it. Pretending otherwise is tedious. And at the very least I have a reputation to uphold.'

Why the hell was he explaining himself to her? Why did he care about wiping that wretched sadness from her face?

He shouldn't care one way or the other whether she was defiant and spirited instead of morose. His only responsibility was to ensure her safety, then return to his preferred role of guarding her from afar.

'Come, I'll show you around.'

She folded her arms, mutiny lining her slender body. 'Why? I won't be here long enough to need to know my way around. Once your security people find me another place nearby, I can be out of your hair.'

Valenti curbed another biting remark, along with the humourless smile tugging at his mouth. She was in for a shock if she believed he would trust anyone but him to keep her safe until her stalker was apprehended.

'Ada won't arrive for another hour or two. I need to make a few calls. If you don't want a tour, fine. The kitchen is through there when you're ready.'

She frowned. 'Why do I need the kitchen? I hope you're not expecting me to make a meal like a dutiful little maid?'

Valenti sucked in a slow breath and prayed for strength. 'The food is already here. I thought you might be hungry since you haven't eaten since lunch.'

'And you know this, how?'

This time he didn't stop himself pinching the bridge of his nose. 'Do us both a favour and accept that when I make a statement it's because I know what I'm talking about.'

Somehow the snarky laugh that barked out of her managed to tunnel straight into him, sparking more sensations he didn't welcome. 'That's very high and mighty of you, Your Highness. Pray tell, is that omniscience something you can gift to others at Christmas or are you hoarding it all to yourself?'

He dropped his hand, sauntered back to where she stood and caught the wariness that slowly crept into her face, making her eyes sparkle even more. 'Tell me if I'm wrong then.

Are you hungry or not, Lotte?' he pressed silkily, keeping his voice low and heavy.

Her nostrils fluttered delicately. Then her eyes fell from his, darting around the room. Her skittishness would've been endearing if he wasn't busy noticing how full her lips were. How the faintest dimple twitched in her cheek when she pursed that mouth.

'It could be…a wild guess…'

He wheeled away from her, despising the thoughts that wouldn't shut off. 'I don't have time for this, Lotte.' He prowled down one hallway, exhaling when he heard the click of her heels as she followed. 'Guest room is through there. My office is there.' He indicated with a wave of his hand. 'Do not disturb me when I'm in there.'

She muttered under her breath at that, and he had that strong desire to smile again. She hadn't lost the sharp wit and snark she'd secretly amused him with as a teenager. Valenti also admitted he missed it. Not enough to regret the chasm between them now, though. Breaching that chasm would be dangerous. *Emotionally unviable.*

'There's a gym, sauna and a library through there,' he continued, then entered the pristine kitchen. 'The executive chef brought up an assortment of food so you should have more than enough to satisfy you.'

'Are you sure? I could be a picky eater.'

His last nerve jumped, and he had the insane urge to sit her down and make her eat her words by hand-feeding her from the platter he knew very well contained all her favourite foods. 'Well then I suppose you'll have to make do with crackers and water until we get to our final destination.'

'Which is?'

'Not important for you to know.' He pivoted, at once eager to escape and reluctant to leave. He forced himself to do the former. 'And just so you know, the front door won't open without a personal code. And no one can get up here without my express authority.'

'Great. Is the treat-Lotte-like-a-prisoner session done yet? I'm getting worn-out here.'

He froze, glanced over his shoulder. The defiance was there, but in the arms she'd folded in outrage, he caught her defensiveness. Her lingering hurt. And frowned.

He was being overbearing. It was a fault Teo called him out on very often. It wasn't a trait he could shut off easily. Something moved from his chest into his throat as his gaze travelled over her once more. As he accepted that part of his gruffness was a defence mechanism.

Lotte Lillegard had turned into a woman when he wasn't looking. No. He exhaled harshly. Perhaps that wasn't the entire truth. Maybe he'd refused to look. Refused to accept it.

But there was no denying it now.

Her slender form curved in all the right places, the hip she'd cocked in irritation demanding a second, third, fourth look. Which he most certainly wasn't going to do. The previous hints of chubbiness in her face had long settled into beautiful angles of pert nose, strong delicate jaw and high cheekbones that made his fingers tingle once again.

And those legs.

Valenti halted his gaze from tracking them, then ruthlessly smashed the heat attempting to rise when she rocked from one foot to the other, changing her stance in a mesmeric slide of thighs.

No.

'I haven't treated you any differently to how I'd treat a client in the same situation,' he half lied. He wouldn't have jumped onto a fighter jet to halve the time he reached an ordinary client. His heart rate most certainly wouldn't have been strained to hit Mach one for any other client, no matter how needful or exclusive.

It's because she's Helga's sister.

True. But…that was another half lie.

Her impetuous visit to Cartana on her nineteenth birthday resurfaced. An inconvenience at the very least because he'd had duties requiring attention, but he'd still created a short space in his schedule to entertain his late friend's little sister. Perhaps let her beat him in a game of chess she liked so much.

Until he'd seen her.

Valenti suspected the shock of registering that Lotte wasn't a child anymore, that she'd blossomed into a stunning, sexy woman, had shattered his benevolent intentions. Had turned his plan on its head so he was ordering her out of his sight, berating her for giving her security the slip.

He shook his head briskly. Focused to find another flash of anguish crossing her face. He gritted his teeth.

'Well, in that case, this *client* wants to be left in peace. If it's not too much to ask?'

'Lotte…' He stopped when he caught her tiny flinch.

Enough. Very much unlike any client he'd dealt with, his every word and gesture seemed to make things worse.

And as he turned and walked away, Valenti also admitted a disconcerting truth.

Just like her womanly body triggered forbidden sensations, the sight of Lotte's distress rubbed him in several wrong ways.

CHAPTER THREE

LOTTE CALLED HIM many very bad names as she munched on her third sublime sushi roll. She wanted to hate herself for having even a crumb of an appetite right now, but it would be a waste of time. And dammit, as much as she wanted to deny it, he was right. She hadn't eaten since lunch, and she was starving.

Cutting off her nose to spite her face wasn't her thing. What would be the point?

But buried beneath the satisfying name calling was the well-deep pain of having her suspicions confirmed.

She meant nothing to Valenti Domene.

He'd rushed over here because she was neatly slotted into the pigeonhole of *client*. And as her brother, Gunnar, had pointed out the last time she'd protested about the whole guardian/ward situation, Prince Domene's oath to her dead sister was the reason she was trapped with the royal prince as her guardian until she turned twenty-five. She didn't even register as the most tenuous link of almost family, despite being legally his ward.

Even worse was that flash of bleakness when he'd referred to sackcloth and ashes. Valenti was still very much caught up in her dead sister's memory and the promise he'd made. He was visibly desolate every time her name came up. Knowing that raked over her already bruised feelings, which was enraging and confusing.

Her own grief rolling over her, she dropped the last bite of sushi onto the plate as her emotions overcame her. She was done attempting to coax even a crumb of humanity from Valenti Domene. She was done trying to elicit some of the cordiality she'd believed they'd shared when she was younger and a little perplexed but grateful for her new guardian, who also happened to be a real-life prince. When he would spend an hour or two doing something as simple as sharing space with her as she read in the library. Or letting her win at chess even though she knew he held near grandmaster status. He obviously didn't see her in any way but as an irritating inconvenience. Her jaw gritted as she forced down a glass of mineral water.

If he wanted to treat her like a client, then she would treat him like a glorified bodyguard. And at last when all this was over, she would break ties with him once and for all.

Feeling better after her meal and even a little grateful for knowing the penthouse's layout, she headed for the guest room. The last thing she wanted to do was to run into him.

Shutting the door behind her, she undressed and stepped into the shower. The water was heavenly, and she scrubbed herself from head to toe before shrugging into the fluffy robe hanging on the back of the bathroom door. Tying the belt, she grimaced when she realised that Valenti hadn't returned her phone. For half a second, she contemplated going to his study to demand it back.

But she suspected the outcome of that conversation, and she wasn't in the mood for it. But then neither was she going to cower away like an unwanted guest.

He may have taken her phone, but she had another way to circumvent that and achieve the necessary task she performed every night before bed.

Leaving the room, she tried to curb her itching need when she passed his study door. This desire to persistently engage with him was something she needed to get over quickly. Setting her lips, she entered the living room and picked up the remote.

A few clicks of the button and she'd accessed the internet and called up the page she was looking for. Relief pulsed through her when she saw the blank message box. Assured that nothing untoward had happened since the last check-in, she accessed five more, all with the same result. She would need to do another check-in in a day or two, but for now she could rest easy. She was about to click out of it when her senses leapt to life.

'What the hell do you think you're doing?'

She spun around, the remote dropping from tingling fingers. He'd shed his jacket at some point and his sleeves were rolled up, exposing brawny hair-dusted forearms. Against the pristine white shirt, his warm olive complexion made her mouth dry, then flood with a sensation she refused to accept was hunger.

She aimed her gaze over his left shoulder, not giving him the opportunity to see any unwanted emotion in her eyes.

'What does it look like? And before you jump down my throat, I was using an alias. I have several online personas.'

He muttered a curse under his breath, the brackets around his mouth tightening again, drawing unwilling attention to his strong throat and corded neck as he rounded the large sofa, pulling his phone out of his pocket. 'You will list every single one of them for me. Right now,' he breathed.

'Valenti, I don't—'

'I don't know how else to get through to you that this is not a joke.' He thrust the phone at her. 'Right now, Lotte.'

She snatched it out of his hand but didn't move to do as instructed. 'I will on one condition.' His lips parted. Knowing he was about to issue another directive, she rushed in, 'Promise me you won't delete them.'

His brows clenched. 'And why should I make such a promise?'

She swallowed hard, the temptation to tell him eating away at her, but she suppressed it. He didn't care about anything she did. Never had. To him she was an unwanted burden he couldn't wait to be rid of.

This part of her life was far too precious, far too private to be exposed to Valenti Domene's ridicule or indifference.

'Because they're harmless. And this can be as simple as me asking you not to do a thing and you deciding not to be a bastard about it.'

His eyes blazed silver fire at her, searing deep, attempting to see to the very heart of her. She held his stare, her heart slamming hard in her throat.

'You should know better than to think I would accommodate frivolous demands.'

She refused to let him land another sucker punch. She lifted her chin, resisting the urge to fold her arms defensively as she had before. *Then* he'd looked at her with something far too close to pity. Over her dead body would she let that happen again. 'I don't care what you think. This is what *I* want. Give me your word and I'll give you the names.'

Silence throbbed between them as his eyes drilled deeper. She wasn't afraid of what he would find within the little pockets of identity she'd created online. She'd gone to great lengths to ensure the messages would be indecipherable to anyone but her and their recipients. If she kept the true nature of those messages to herself, Valenti would not be any wiser.

'You have my word that as long as nothing poses a danger to you, they will be left alone.'

Relief unknotted her belly. She had to be satisfied with that.

Fingers flying, she typed out the aliases then handed back his phone.

Valenti eyed his screen, as if he could decipher the truth by just looking at the names. Then his eyes lifted to her, the frown still wedged between his dark brows. 'What the hell are you doing, Lotte?' he bit out.

She forced a shrug. 'Nothing you need to concern your-self about.'

His lips parted, but the knock on the door stopped what-ever he'd been about to say. 'We'll pick this up later. Ada has brought your things.'

Swallowing the nerves building in her at his rabid scru-tiny, she nodded.

Another beat passed before he strode to the door, typed in the code and pulled the door open.

Ada and two bodyguards entered carrying several large shopping bags. She followed Ada as she deposited them in the guest room, summoning a smile when the housekeeper turned to examine her.

'Are you okay, *elskan*?'

The woman who'd been more like a mother to her since her own mother passed raised her plump hands to cup Lotte's cheeks. She had to swallow the surge of reactionary tears. 'I'm fine, Ada. Thank you for doing this.' She indicated the bags.

'You know you don't need to thank me for anything. It's my pleasure.'

Lotte smiled. 'Thank you, anyway,' she said, summoning a tiny laugh that eased the concern in the housekeeper's eyes.

She started to pull out garments, laying them out in neat piles on the bed. 'I'm glad the Prince is here. He will sort everything out, you'll see.'

Lotte pursed her lips to stop herself from saying anything she would regret. At best she would be letting on that Val-enti affected her in ways that bewildered and angered her. At worst, she would be bad-mouthing the person Ada clearly idolised and who also signed her pay cheque.

Ada and Leif were dear to her. Despite being elderly and not having much in common with her, their presence had al-leviated her profound loneliness.

Lotte couldn't risk the livelihood of the two people who'd

been the most stable in her life since Helga died, with Gunnar more absent than present.

'I'll leave you to get ready,' Ada said when she was finished.

Swallowing the lump crowding her throat, she nodded, and Ada left. About to shut her bedroom door, she froze when Valenti appeared in the doorway.

'You have half an hour. Pack a suitcase and dress for the cold.'

Before she could ask again where they were going, he spun on his heel and stalked away.

His words echoed in her head as she picked out a variety of gorgeous sweaters, leggings and slacks, cashmere scarves, gloves and woolly hats from the pile. She couldn't quite throttle the pang of disappointment that pierced her when she guessed they wouldn't be going to Cartana.

At this time of the year, the Mediterranean kingdom she'd only so briefly been allowed to visit would be bathed in sunshine and balmy temperatures, no thick sweaters and wool scarves needed.

She chose a cashmere sweater in her favourite caramel colour, paired it with dark chocolate leggings, thick socks and a pair of tan boots, then wrapped a snowy white scarf twice around her neck.

Placing a pair of leather gloves on the side, she folded six interchangeable outfits into the small suitcase and tossed in the toiletries Ada had thoughtfully added. She reached for the handle, then stopped. She needed a moment to collect herself, to remind herself that all she was doing was using Valenti as a means to an end to her freedom. She would divorce her feelings from any interaction with him for as long as it took. Tightening her gut, she wrestled her composure into place and left the room.

He was pacing the living room, his phone glued to his ear. Contrary to every warning pep talk she'd given herself, her footstep faltered when she saw he'd changed too. His clothes were complementary to hers, except he looked like he'd stepped off the pages of a luxury magazine extolling the virtues of the great winter outdoors.

His turtleneck sweater was a rich, smoky grey paired with dark jeans and boots, and the dark grey coat he'd thrown over it only highlighted the silver in his eyes when he turned at her approach.

A few murmured words and he was hanging up, slotting his phone into his inner pocket before striding forward to take the case from her. Handing it off to one of his guards, he took her elbow.

She refused to admit she was tongue-tied at the jaw-dropping evidence of his rugged masculinity. Refused to admit the restless throbbing between her thighs, the puckering of her nipples and the wild tattoo of her heartbeat as she caught his scent.

She wasn't a virgin. She knew what her body was telling her.

Perhaps she was caught in that inconvenient hormonal conundrum of denying her body's needs for so long. Maybe when this was all over, she would go on a date, scratch an itch…

Distaste filled her mouth, and she shook her head to dislodge the thought. Most of her dates had ended in disappointment, which was why since that one encounter at university, she hadn't bothered to seriously date anyone. It was a waste of time and her time was precious. So no, she would be denying whatever her body was screaming at her. Just like his fleeting passages through her life, this nonsense sensation too would pass.

Thankful for the emergence of common sense, she stepped into the lift next to him. Was even confident enough to reach for the ground floor button. Only to gasp when Valenti caught her hand.

'We're not going downstairs,' he stated.

Eyes widening, she stared at him. Watched him punch the button for the roof. A handful of seconds later, the door slid open to reveal a sleek black helicopter crouched thirty feet away.

'Where exactly are we going, Valenti?' she demanded for the third...fourth time?

His gaze dropped to her and raked over her face for several beats before he answered. 'I have a cabin fifty miles from here. It's secluded. No one will find us. Unless we wish them to. It's where I mean to keep you safe until this inconvenience is over.'

No. No no no.

She stood frozen and he paced a few more steps before he realised she wasn't following. And predictably, when he turned around, his face was a mask of bridled impatience.

'Same offer applies, Lotte. Come willingly. Or be carried. Those are your two choices.'

Lotte sucked in a breath—an exercise she seemed to be doing quite poorly tonight—her face burning at the thought of Valenti tossing her over his shoulder again like a sack of grain.

Remember you're just his client. He would order every one of them about just like this. The reminder had the curious twin effects of bolstering and bruising as she started walking on even shakier legs towards the aircraft whose rotors were slowly spinning into life.

But Lotte couldn't stop the feeling that if she could've wished for anything at all in the world, she would've wished to *not* be secluded in a cabin with Valenti. Because she sensed her armour was about to be severely tested.

Still she took one step. Then another. Her senses screaming at her as she followed him to the open doors of the chopper.

CHAPTER FOUR

VALENTI WONDERED WHETHER she knew her own power.

That she above all people, even his family, had the power to command him with a word or a gesture. That in making that final promise with Helga's last breath, he'd placed himself entirely in Lotte's hands. Because he would slit his own throat before he allowed a single hair on her head to be harmed.

Which made her protestations and righteous anger almost...laughable.

Because along with the almost melodramatic heights of his vow came the equal, paradoxical determination and conviction that he would save her *despite* herself. So turning away from the naked plea in her eyes hadn't been as insurmountable as it'd first seemed.

He fixed his gaze on the snow-laden horizon, thankful he hadn't needed to act on his threat. Hadn't needed to test his resolve by having her in his arms. Unexpectedly though, her side of the helicopter had quietened. He frowned, wondering for a moment if he'd forgotten whether she was afraid of heights.

She didn't look panicked or distressed.

He welcomed the peace, a knot easing in his gut. He had little patience for melodramatics. He had enough of that from his mother who, apparently finding his frigid silences a challenge, had needled him since long before he had grown out of long shorts. Unfortunately, she hadn't grown out of that particular sport and even at thirty-six he had to frequently contend with her histrionics. Her need to drag everyone down to her level of unhappiness because, all these decades later, she was still desperately aggrieved about not being picked as queen of Cartana. Never mind that growing up, he'd had his own battles to overcome as one of the King's bastard sons, shunned by other snobbish aristocratic houses and his own father's royal council. That he and Teo hadn't even been allowed to live in Cartana or its *palacio* until much later in life. *After* he'd been found to have a use the council couldn't deny.

But Valenti had long shored up his foundations so that these days very little penetrated his armour.

So yes, he welcomed Lotte's silence.

What he didn't welcome was this need to keep glancing at her from the corner of his eye, to check for signs of distress. She shouldn't be unhappy. She should be frothing with gratitude that he was making such an effort to keep her safe.

Twenty minutes flew by and still she said nothing.

He shifted in his seat, frowning at his inability to stop checking on her. Their headphones had two-way communication. They were guaranteed the privacy of a closed cabin, with his two bodyguards up front with his pilot. Was this the longest time she'd gone without speaking? His mouth twisted at the thought.

Her gaze flicked to him then, irritation sparking her eyes. Valenti's stomach clenched, and his breath held as he braced for another episode of dramatics. But after a moment, she turned back to the window.

And for the first time in his life, he was served up the return experience of being given the silent treatment.

'You asked where we were going,' he offered gruffly.

She turned her head again, but her eyes no longer held

the spark. Then she had the audacity to shrug. To dismiss him once more.

Gritting his teeth would be too much reaction so he forced himself to relax into his seat, to cross one ankle over his knee. Again, her eyes flickered over him briefly before returning to the landscape.

'My cabin is in Syren.'

No reaction.

'We'll be there in another twenty minutes.'

Her gaze stayed on his for all of three seconds before she nodded.

Another four minutes passed before impatience drove him to tap his headphones. 'If you're worried about being overheard by anyone else, this channel is private.'

Her eyes widened then moved over his pilot and guards. 'There's nothing I want to say to you in private that I wouldn't say in front of them.'

His eyebrow quirked, openly mocking. 'Then I'm curious as to why you've gone mute.'

'You seem eager and determined to throw your weight around, ignoring what I want at every turn. So what's the point?'

He should've been pleased with that. He wanted her compliant, docile even, didn't he? *Yes.* So why was there an itch beneath his rib like he was pulling a resistant muscle?

He dismissed the thought, and angled his body so he could avail himself of her profile. 'And what exactly do you want besides being kept safe from unwanted attention?' The very mention of the danger she'd treated so blithely made anger roll through him once again. 'Isn't a secluded cabin with a roaring fire one of your favourite things?' he grated.

The moment the little nugget left his lips he wanted to take it back. But he shrugged it off. He was perfectly within his rights to learn every single thing about her. Her gaze turning fully on him also shouldn't have drawn such a pleased reaction. What the hell was wrong with him?

'You remember that?' she muttered, her gaze searching his far too keenly.

He sucked in a breath, already wishing back the silence he'd interrupted.

'It's the middle of the night. Using the cabin for this purpose was merely expedient,' he said briskly. 'Once we resolve this problem you can be back to whatever you get up to within hours. Besides, as I said before it's my duty to know everything.'

'Well, this particular duty belongs in the archives. I liked frozen cabins once upon a time, maybe when I still believed in Santa and leaving cookies by an open fire the night before Christmas. If I remember correctly, you have dozens of properties across the world. I could've been on my way to sun myself on a beach in the Bahamas. Or in a jungle paradise in Costa Rica. If you'd bothered to ask me, I would've chosen anywhere but a snow cabin in the middle of nowhere.'

It was clear evidence of what a dangerous road he tread when he immediately considered changing his plan, granting her wish. *No.* 'Nevertheless, that's where we're staying for the moment.'

A corner of her plump mouth twisted in half mockery, half resignation that pulled at the muscle in his chest again. 'Like I said, why do I even bother?'

For the rest of the journey, he was forced to ask himself the very same question. Unfortunately, the answer that came back to him was one that pulled at a very different muscle altogether.

The muscle of loss and guilt. Of promises made with blood on his hands and sorrow a permanent vice around his heart.

* * *

'You've got to be kidding me!'

Valenti stood, arms folded in the middle of the cabin's living room, listening as her feet thundered down the short hallway in the two-story structure before descending the stairs at a speed that made him wince and lock his knees so he wouldn't lunge for her if she stumbled.

'Problem?' he drawled.

'Of course there's a problem. There's only one bed. If you expect me to sleep on the floor or hang upside down like some bat, you've got another think coming.'

'While I would pay good money to see you indeed hang upside down, that's not what I had in mind.'

'Good because this is starting off like a horribly clichéd romance movie that is only destined to get worse.'

She stopped in her tracks, her face reddening as the words left her lips. Within his own body, he also experienced an unnerving reaction. 'You can rest easy as there's no possibility of that,' he said firmly to counter said sensation.

She blinked once then hastily stepped back. He didn't know whether it was in reaction to his words, or a residual counteract to whatever was charging the air between them.

'That's a relief because that was the farthest thing from my mind.'

He noted her eyes remained wide as she blinked again and then gestured around. 'So where exactly am I supposed to sleep?'

Dropping his arms he pointed to the wide sectional sofa that dissected the living area from the kitchen. 'That turns into a perfectly adequate sofa bed. You'll have more than enough room.'

Expecting another outburst, he saw something flicker in her eyes before she veiled them. Curbing the punch of curiosity, he shrugged off his coat. Walked away to hang it in the closet.

'Now that the question of bedding is settled, we need to go over a few ground rules.'

'Stop.'

He turned, eyes narrowing. But before he could speak, she took a step toward him, her gaze once again bold, and spirited. Valenti hated the loosening of clenched muscles that felt absurdly like relief because she was no longer freezing him out.

It was *so much* worse than she'd thought.

He was revered royalty. Second in line to the throne of Cartana. Surely, she hadn't been ludicrous in thinking the cabin he'd referred to would be more substantial than one, granted large, room with a well-stocked kitchen, a short corridor leading to a small office, and wooden stairs leading to the one and only bedroom and bathroom?

Hell, she could sprint from one end of the structure to the other in three seconds flat.

'This is… I can't…' She stopped, scrambled for her composure. 'Look, this isn't going to work.'

'Too bad,' he bit out with zero mercy.

Gritting her teeth, she prayed for calm and tried again. 'I will stay here, on one condition.'

He went very still, in the way that completely disarmed her, made her very much aware not just of the deadly predator he was but how much of a prey she was. How he could easily overwhelm her with just his silence.

She'd heard enough rumours of Valenti's background, and what Helga had divulged in the far too few occasions her sister had had time to spare from her busy life. Lotte knew he'd been in a special branch of the Cartana military, the part not spoken out loud in social gatherings. She knew that scar slashing his right eyebrow had come from being injured in one of those clandestine missions.

Furiously, she fought the urge to fidget. To show weakness. To remember with a sinking bleakness in her belly that Gunnar had told her Valenti had been drawn to Helga initially because of her brilliant medical acumen but also because of her sister's bold and fearless outlook on life, especially in helping those in need. That she'd used her platform as a renowned doctor to broadcast her outspoken stance on human rights issues, a stance that had drawn the attention of eager acolytes and benign institutions, but also, eventually, dangerous, heartless enemies.

Did it upset her that she'd had to learn all these things about her own sister from articles and online posts alongside conflicting and secondhand speculation about how she'd died? Yes. Helga had been far too busy to share the ins and outs of her life with her little sister. And after her death, her brother had found every excuse not to talk about the sister they'd both idolised, his grief too overwhelming. The result was that Lotte was still in the dark as to what really happened to rip her sister away. The few times she'd attempted to broach the subject with Valenti, he'd shut her down.

Lotte knew that in his eyes she didn't measure up to her illustrious sister. Wasn't that why his geniality had gradually cooled as she got older? Why for the last three years he'd all but pretended she didn't exist? Why he even now deemed her insignificant when she was standing two feet in front of him?

Lotte swallowed the building lump in her throat and ferociously blanked her expression as he responded.

'You'll probably be wasting your time and mine, but sure, let's hear it.'

She clenched her fist, utterly disarmed by the need to slap his face. She, who abhorred violence, promoted peace and kindness at the beginning and end of every post because it was the very opposite thing that'd wrenched her sister from her?

Shaking her head inwardly, she tried to regain her composure. To remember that speaking to Valenti in the same robotlike manner gained her more ground than throwing about emotional pleas and heated protests. Those he batted away like irritating nuisances.

'I'll stay in your cabin…for a reasonable amount of time to be discussed between us like rational adults, if you leave and let your security team take over my protection.'

For the longest time she held her breath as he studied her like a science project under a microscope. Then he slowly strode back to where she stood.

Paused long enough to give her a one-word response. 'No.'

By morning, Lotte was convinced she was on the brink of insanity.

Besides using the bathroom upstairs she'd had no choice but to remain in the living room, subjected to his overwhelming presence every second.

The only other room besides the open living and kitchen area was the tiny office that contained a desk and chair, and one wall filled with books.

At any other time she would have found this place absolutely darling.

Not today.

Valenti's point-blank refusal to leave her with his bodyguards unsettled her more than she was willing to admit. The possibility had dominated her mind when he'd eventually divulged their destination. Her every dread unfolding had her dragging her fingers through her hair, resisting the urge to pace the living room. Because on top of not knowing vital details about her sister's life, she also hadn't been able to verify if Helga and Valenti were an item. And the last thing she wanted—even though her mind and body had different ideas—was to have feelings for her sister's ex.

Are you sure?

She slammed down the taunting whisper. *Hard.*

'If you're in search of something to do, you can come over here and help.'

That her senses instantly jumped at his voice sent her spiralling faster.

He'd come down the stairs ten minutes ago, taken one tight-lipped look at her curled in the corner of the sofa she hadn't bothered to pull out into a proper bed, and sauntered past to the kitchen to start putting together their meal.

She eyed the front door, every bone in her body yearning to escape this situation. Accepting that she couldn't, *for now*, she joined him in the kitchen, sternly refusing to stare at the towering body clad in cargo pants and one of those thin insulated sweaters that cost a small fortune.

After a long glance, he nudged his chin at the fruit that needed cutting.

They worked in silence for all of a minute before the madness threatened again. 'How long could you expect this to take? You're supposed to be good at all of this.' She waved the knife and then stopped when she saw his pointed glance at it. 'I'm not going to attack you if that's what you're afraid of.'

One brow lifted. 'Not at all. But what *you* need to be worried about is what I'll do if you injure yourself.'

'What will you do? Put me over your knee and spank me?'

Oh sweet heaven.

She stopped breathing. Wished fervently with every atom of her being for the flames engulfing her face to devour her whole and leave her in a pile of ash at his feet.

They lapsed into silence, a state he was terrifyingly comfortable in all through breakfast and the rest of the long, snow-laden day.

Lotte was almost grateful when he bit out a terse goodnight just after sundown and climbed the stairs into his bedroom.

Bundled up on the sofa bed—which he'd pulled out and dressed in fresh sheets and blankets while she was brushing her teeth—she twisted. Turned. Then groaned her frustration. The temptation to demand her phone was strong. But adversely, she was thankful for its temporary absence. As much as she loved interacting with her followers, she would've found it a strain to remain upbeat. Especially in light of a threat she'd hoped, *prayed*, wasn't serious but had proved otherwise.

Unable to remain still, she jumped up, paced the living room, then desperate for further reprieve, she threw on her coat and faux fur–lined boots and stepped out of the front door.

The snow had stopped several hours ago, and the midnight sky was clear enough for the carpet of stars to twinkle brightly overhead. Stepping off the porch, welcoming the soothing crunch of fresh snow beneath her feet, she sucked in what felt like her first full breath since forever.

Only to yelp in alarm when a strong arm closed around her waist and lifted her clean off her feet.

'Wait! What are you doing?'

'I should be asking you the same question,' Valenti replied icily as he marched back towards the cabin. 'How far did you think you were going to get? Let me answer that for you. Not very far.'

Her mouth gaped. 'What? You think…?' She laughed at the absurd inference. 'I wasn't running away. Regardless of what you think of me I'm not stupid enough to cast myself into an icy tundra in the middle of the night.'

He set her down on the porch and glared icy bullets at her. 'Then why were you out there?'

'Because I can't sleep! The bed is lumpy, it creaks and… and there's an awful draft.' She sounded like a shrill petulant toddler. And in some ways that was what she was because it was the role he'd cast her in. So really none of this was her fault.

Come on, really? What next? You're going to blame him for how gorgeous and Insta-worthy he looked silhouetted against the snow? How strong and virile with his piercing silver eyes and lock of inky black hair falling over his brow?

She cringed at the mocking voice as she marched back into the cabin. Refused to turn when she heard him shut and bolt the door. Refused to witness the pity or irritation at her tantrum.

Until the distinctive creak spun her around.

'Wh-what are you doing?' she stammered, something distinctly hot and disturbing stirring in her middle as she watched him slide into the place she'd been only ten minutes ago.

'Solving another problem for you. I'll take the sofa. You take my bed.'

Her jaw dropped as she stood frozen, unable to take her eyes off him.

'It's the middle of the night, Lotte. Take my bed. Or don't.' He reached out and flicked off the lamp next to the bed, plunging the room into semi darkness. His body's outline *right there* sent shivers through her. Keeping her immobile for far too long watching the steady unperturbed rise and fall of his chest.

Eventually registering that it was decidedly creepy just standing there staring at him, she stumbled away and on shaky legs, climbed the stairs. Sensation rapidly resembling anticipation sizzled through her blood as she approached his bedroom.

In the doorway she stopped, swallowed at the sight of the

rumpled bed, the image of Valenti sprawled between the dark sheets sending fresh waves of heat through her. Telling herself she hadn't asked for this bed but would happily take it in recompense for Valenti's misconception of her, she shed her outer clothes, leaving only her nightshirt, and crawled between the sheets.

It was mildly infuriating to welcome the deep comfort of Valenti's bed. To sigh with almost embarrassing contentment as the residual warmth he'd left behind engulfed her. As she took a deep breath of his incredible smell and shamelessly burrowed into the nearest pillow.

If she'd hoped the change of bed would calm her restless mind, she was wrong. Her body sinuously stretched from one comfortable position to the other, a different madness taking over. One that teased her with blush-inducing flashes. Of Valenti. In bed with her. Not a single combative word between them.

Instead hot, seductive words that made her writhe faster, moan longingly and…

And blink awake with the gasping breathlessness of being caught in the middle of a wet dream. One she chose not to fight, her face flaming brighter as she slid her hand between her legs and stole a defiantly selfish moment for herself.

She came downstairs the next morning fighting her unsettling mood while admitting to herself that giving in to that moment of weakness hadn't been the wisest decision because it was occupying far too much of her thoughts.

The sight of the sofa bed neatly put away and Valenti already setting out their breakfast only added to her disgruntlement.

But it was the idea of another day filled with sombre, brooding silence that finally made her set down her orange juice with a sharp click. Which immediately earned her a narrow-eyed glare.

'I would like my phone back,' she said.

He stilled. 'What's the point? There's no reception out here.'

'Why don't we both accept that this is a failed experiment and be done with it?'

Thunder rolled across his brows. 'A failed experiment?'

'*Jà*. You made a promise, I get that. But don't you think it's better to throw in the towel than to make things worse?'

'It doesn't work that way.'

'Pray tell, how does it work? How many wards have you successfully managed to fit into your very busy life?' she asked, ignoring the barbs of jealousy darting like destructive fireworks through her system.

'You're my first. Most definitely my last.' Something forbidding and intensely intriguing pulsed in his voice, making her emotions roil that much faster.

'Because I'm the worst burden you ever imagined you would be asked to carry?' she pushed with a compulsion she couldn't fight.

A spark, not quite so harrowing but intense nevertheless, lit his eyes. 'Not quite.'

She sucked in an audible breath, dragged both hands through her hair. 'I'm hanging on by a thread here, Your Highness.'

The smallest quirk of a self-deprecating smile twitched across his face before his brooding expression settled in once more.

'What was that about?' She waved a hand over that expression.

For several beats he didn't respond. Then, 'You think you know what frustration is, *litla*?'

Litla. Little one. The sound of his deep, gruff voice

wrapped around that endearment sent shafts of heat through her body. 'Don't call me that.'

'Why not?'

'Because it suggests a fondness that we both know is a lie.'

His nostrils flared. 'It's interesting you're protesting about threads, yet you keep pulling at mine,' he rasped.

The shrug she attempted seemed to require monumental effort. 'It should bother you only if it's one of two things.' She flicked a finger out. 'One, that it's untrue.' Then another finger. 'Or even the merest hint of it aggravates you greatly.'

Slowly he leaned forward, unapologetically into her space. His silver eyes were bullets, aimed with deadly accuracy for her most vulnerable spots.

'Consider a third option.'

'Which is?' Dammit, why did her voice quiver like a leaf in a hurricane? And why the hell couldn't she stop the searing need to lean in just as boldly as he had, breathe him in until he filled every corner of her being?

'That I couldn't walk away from you, even if I tried.'

The pulse intensified, turned into a mesmerising drumbeat that fused with her heartbeat. Fast. Slow. Fast. Setting more fireworks along the way through her bloodstream. Robbing her of breath. Making him the only thing she could see. Smell. *Yearn to taste.*

'And do you want to? Be honest.'

His hand shot out, making her gasp as he curled one long finger beneath her chin to ensure her gaze remained pinned on his. For the longest time he examined her face like a specimen he was endlessly fascinated with. And just when she thought she'd burst out of her skin with all the sensations flooding her, he spoke. 'Let's be clear about one thing. I will never lie to you.' Still holding her captive, he thumbed the skin beneath her lower lip, a place Lotte would've bet a great deal of money wasn't erogenous.

And yet here she was, experiencing definite, unrelenting arousal in the form of her nipples pebbling, her sex plumping and a supremely carnal moan building, building, building at the back of her throat.

It was proof of her rash yearning that she came within a whisker of believing him. 'Oh come on. You wear me like an unwanted cloak you can't wait to cast off. I'm giving you permission to shed me once and for all.'

'It's not up to me—'

'Of course it is,' she interrupted because she couldn't bear to hear it. Just as it bruised her to admit what she said next. 'Gunnar doesn't give a damn one way or another. Which begs the question. Why are you putting us both through this torment?'

He speared her an openly derisive look. 'It's a torment to live a life of luxury being waited on hand and foot?'

'It is when it comes with the baggage of guilt and martyrdom you wear like badges of honour.'

In the deathly silence that followed his face lost layers of colour, his chest rising and falling as fury boiled around him. 'What did you just say to me?'

Since she'd already pulled the pin, she might as well throw the grenade. 'Would you even be here if it wasn't for Helga?'

'Lotte.' Her name was an icy warning.

'I'll answer it for you. No, you wouldn't. And somehow, I've been swept into a remorse crusade I never asked for.'

His chest expanded, quiet deadly fury wafting off him. He grasped her arms and propelled her one step back into the cabin wall. 'Watch yourself, *litla*.'

She laughed and the acid of it scoured her throat. 'There you go proving my point. I'm twenty-two years old, Valenti. Your continuing to treat me like a child is pathetic and insulting. She was my sister! And you know the absolute worst thing? In all these years nobody has bothered to tell me what happened. Gunnar clams up when I ask him or quickly finds somewhere else to be. And you? I only so much as hint at her memory and you turn into the Hulk. Did either of you bother to check what your silence means for those who weren't there? That what our imagination conjures up might be worse than the actual thing?'

His lips twisted, his features haunted. 'Nothing you ever imagine can be worse.'

'Well pardon me if I don't take your word for it. If I'm fed up to the gills of being fobbed off by dismissive selfishness disguised as well-meaning concern.'

Shock and fury warred on his chiselled face. 'You think a blow-by-blow recounting will make you feel better?'

'Feel better? No. Offer some sort of closure? Yes.' Her voice lost a little volume partly due to her building grief and because she was exhausted from being left behind, being left out in the cold. 'She was my hero. She meant something to me too.'

He prowled to the window, and against the silhouette of white, his giant frame filled every corner of her vision. Her world. Again she was struck by the harsh reality that soon she would not have this. That the next time Valenti walked away from her would be the last time she set eyes on him.

Fresh desolate sadness filled her, but she held it under wraps when he started to speak in deep, rumbling tones entirely devoid of inflection as he scraped his fingers through his hair. 'I wouldn't wish that on anyone.'

'I know. Neither would I.'

He didn't acknowledge that. She touched his shoulder, felt his muscle twitch beneath her finger. 'Valenti…'

'Stop. Enough.'

'No, you stop. I'm not going to let you keep pushing me away. I know this is the last place you want to be. But since you're too stubborn to do things my way, you'll have to suffer the consequences of my presence and everything that entails.'

'*Dios mio.* You're fucking impossible,' he muttered under his breath.

Somehow, hearing him swear made him a little bit human. A tiny bit flawed and more approachable. 'I'll take that as a compliment. Maybe.'

He turned fully to face her, and her breath strangled in her throat. 'To answer your questions, no. I do not want to be anywhere else,' he rasped hoarsely.

CHAPTER FIVE

HER PULSE HITCHED. Now such an annoyingly frequent oc-
currence, it had become the norm in his presence.

She wanted to dissect that, *endlessly*, but she wasn't sure
how she could handle it if he dismissed it. So this time she
would save herself the trouble, move on to more important
things.

What's more important than this.

She ignored that just as she ignored the continued racing
of her heart when he led her to the sofa, pressed her into a
seat and perched opposite, cupping her face with one hand.
She needed every scrap of strength to pull back from the
finger exploring her lower lip. From the shadows and light
dancing through his eyes as he stared at her with a ferocity
she wanted to embrace with every fibre of her being.

And when she managed it, she watched his hand drop
back between his spread knees, much slower than she'd expected. As if he too was reluctant to break the connection.

No. She absolutely needed to stop ascribing sensations
and emotions to him that weren't present. Wishful thinking
would be her downfall if she wasn't careful.

Consciously clearing her throat, she opened her mouth,
to say what she wasn't exactly sure. Something, *anything* to
dilute the thick need prowling through her blood.

'Truce?' he bit out. From his demeanour, it seemed the
last thing he wanted. And yet.

She started to shake her head because of his confusing expressions, but when his eyes narrowed, she hurried to speak. 'I'm not refusing the offer. I'm just curious. A truce from what exactly?'

The barest hint of a smile appeared before it was swallowed beneath his ferocity. 'Perhaps it's more of a reprieve than a truce. From continuously rubbing each other the wrong way?'

It was the last thing she expected. Probably the last thing a man with his power and position would offer. Why that sent warmth and apprehension through her, she couldn't quite put her finger on. But she accepted that the release from always being on edge would make this process so much easier. So she nodded.

'Say the words, Lotte. Just so we understand one another.'

'Do you want to spit shake as well to seal the deal?' she half joked, but when his eyes dropped to her hands braced on her thighs, her breath snagged yet again. The possibility of another touch, another stroke of his fingers over her skin made her breath stop completely.

'Fine. Truce agreed. So what does this actually entail? Do we agree on a set time where we stay out of each other's way?'

His eyes narrowed to silver slits. 'Is that what you want?'

No. The vigour of the word almost hurt. She took a half beat so she wouldn't appear too eager. Then forced a shrug. 'Not necessarily. But I would like to not be cooped up in here every day until you deem it fit for me to stray three feet from the door without rugby tackling me into the snow.'

'You make me sound like a cross between an ogre and a tyrant. Or what did you call me? The Hulk?'

Her lips curved into a smile independent of her will, and she was close enough to hear his sharp intake of breath as his gaze dropped to her mouth.

Slowly, the tension eroded her smile and his fleeting humour. She had time to miss that ephemeral light moment before he spoke.

'Very well. A trip outside once a day if the weather permits.'

She nodded readily, half torn between relief and curious disappointment.

'And just so we're clear, that venture outside includes me.'

The swift disappearance of disappointment made it glaringly obvious that this response was what she'd hoped for. That for all her protestations she hadn't truly wanted to be free of him. The revelation was at once stomach-hollowing and depressing.

It didn't stop the next impossible thought that followed. She'd won a small but significant skirmish. Perhaps she could take on a bigger battle.

The hands on her thighs grew damp as anxiety pinched at her nerves. 'I have a stipulation of my own then if we're tossing them about.'

He stiffened. Her palms grew damper. She rubbed them over her leggings then stopped when his eyes dropped there.

Seriously, this conversation should be taking place with the width of the room between them just so his every move wouldn't be so damn distracting. But her body refused to obey the suggestion.

'*Si*?' he rasped tightly as if he suspected her motives.

In a way he was right. She was skirting the vault clearly labelled 'keep out. Or else.' 'One question a day, during the walk. That's my condition.'

His withdrawal was instant, his remote yet compelling expression an unscalable cliff face. Lotte held her breath and waited, fully expecting a cold dismissive refusal.

'And these questions I assume aren't going to be as benign as curiosity about my favourite colour?' he mocked.

'No, I already assumed it would be as black as your default mood?' she tossed back.

That twitch returned and disappeared just as quickly. 'You're so brazen playing with fire, *litla*,' he mused, almost abstractedly. Except his eyes maintained that dangerous warning to keep her wits about her.

She waved at the frozen wind howling against the window. 'A little fire doesn't hurt. At the very least, it'll help keep me warm out there.' And because she couldn't suffer the suspense one more second, she continued, 'Deal or no deal?'

It wasn't until his hand closed over hers that she realised she'd held hers out.

And just like that slow drift of his thumb over her lips, he took his time wrapping her small hand within his, his gaze never straying from hers as his fingers gripped firm. Then firmer. Until she felt her pulse drumming between their heated flesh, completely drowning out the moment he answered. 'Deal.'

'Why is this taking so long? This weasel had the nerve to scatter his DNA and digital footprint all over her bedroom. So why has he managed to evade you for almost a week?' Valenti snarled into his satellite phone.

A throb of uncomfortable silence pulsed through the still air of his cabin office. Then his most experienced operative cleared his throat. 'The two locations we pinged turned out to be dead ends. We're doing everything we can to find him, Your Highness.'

Por el amor de dios. 'Do better!'

He ended the call with barely restrained patience. Then surged to his feet to prowl to the window.

The sun was almost up but it'd been white outside for several hours now. Not that it mattered to him one way or the other. He'd barely slept more than a half-hour stretch last night after Lotte headed upstairs to bed and he locked himself in his office.

What he was suffering from was more than cabin fever.

He snorted under his breath. It was a different sort of fever entirely. The kind that seemed to push him into making curiously unwise decisions. Like touching the softest skin he'd ever felt in his life. Then compounding that forbidden temptation with striking deals he had no business making. Willingly agreeing because his *ward*, a woman *fourteen years younger*, stared up at him with those…breathtaking eyes? The plea to divulge information they both found painful, and him agreeing?

Eyes that reflected every emotion she was experiencing?

Was that all it really took? Or was it something else? Something even more disturbing. *Dios*, he could feel that emotional landmine he'd been avoiding inching ever closer. And it was imperative he stop it. Before he failed someone else.

He was almost relieved when his phone buzzed. He sensed who it might be before he swiped it off his desk.

Everything okay?

He gritted his teeth and his fingers tightened around his phone. For a brief time back in his teens, he'd mourned the sudden loss of the emotional connection he'd had with his twin.

In the trying years in the army and the different, harrowing path he'd had to take by decree of his father, the King, followed by the hell of loss and tragedy, he'd been secretly grateful to nature, the cosmos or whatever entity existed out there that he'd been given the tools to spare his brother the turbulent oceans that ran beneath his pretended calm.

Except recently, that connection had begun to regain

strength, breaking through his resistance once again. It'd started recently at Azar's wedding, slowly, sensing a twinge of Teo's anxiety here, a spark of his frustrated resentment there. Then a flurry of elation when Teo had pulled his disappearing act and ended up on Morocco with Sabeen, his creative director and soon-to-be wife.

After that it'd tapered off for a while and Valenti had been ambivalent about it. On the one hand he was pleased for his twin, but he'd been grateful for the reprieve of being bombarded by hints of Teo's bliss.

You know I'm going to keep asking until you answer, right? That or you stop bombarding me with these...interesting feelings.

Valenti squeezed his eyes shut. The last thing he needed was his well-meaning but incorrigible twin brother digging beneath the surface of emotions Valenti seemed unable to stop broadcasting.

Because not even one could be allowed to escape the forbidden darkness.

Because he couldn't possibly find his *ward* insanely breathtaking enough to want to—

No.

He exhaled a harsh breath and punched in a swift response.

Nothing to worry about. Just dealing with persistent irritants.

He wasn't surprised at all when his phone trilled to life almost immediately the text was sent.

'*Qué deseas?*' he demanded tersely.

'Nice try, brother. We might do things differently, but if you don't know I'm a stickler for details, then we're not twins. So spit it out. What's going on with your ward? I'm assuming you're still in Reykland?'

'Yes. And nothing is going on with her. Nothing that's not under control, anyway.'

His twin's laughter grated his last nerve. 'You forget I can feel you lying to me?'

'We both know *that's* the lie. The connection doesn't work that way.' He sighed. Right now, he wished it would return to being defunct. 'Seriously. Leave it alone, *hermano*.'

'Val?' The humour had left Teo's voice.

Valenti waited, silent.

'If you need me, you only need to ask. You know that, right?'

He exhaled. Relieved and touched in equal measure. '*Sí*, I know.'

'Good. Now, I'd be grateful if you'd wrap things up there so I can have you back here pretending to be interested in your duties as my best man and giving me crap about security,' his twin griped good-humouredly.

Valenti felt a flash of brief elation that wasn't a direct result of Teo's own brimming emotions. He was happy for his twin and for Azar. Against all their expectations, his brothers had found deserving partners, achieving the envious feat of putting their miserable pasts behind them.

Sure, it would make his job of protecting his ever-expanding family that much more of a challenge, but it was a sacrifice he'd dedicated his life to. One he'd proved repeatedly that he excelled at. Yes, it hadn't been the dream he'd set out for himself. He'd tried, and failed, to change that. Life, he'd discovered was all about harrowing disappointment and disillusion. Duty and sacrifice were solid goals that left him little time to dwell on the gaping chasms in his own life.

Chasms he'd found himself wanting to fill with— 'I'll be there,' he rasped into the phone just to distract himself from horrifying betraying thoughts of...*seducing his ward*. Then hearing the sounds of stirring one floor above him, he grasped that too. 'I have to go.'

He didn't wait for his brother's response, his feet propelling him to the door even before he'd fully hung up and tossed the phone in his drawer.

But just as he'd dealt with his failure to protect Helga and the guilt that had weighed him down ever since, he would handle this unexpected challenge too.

Lotte was halfway down the stairs when he reached the living room.

Her nightshirt reached mid-thigh but might as well have been a skimpy negligée because, with the combination of sleep-tousled hair, sleepy eyes and tentative smile that combined innocence with sexiness, Valenti couldn't drag his eyes from her or stop the furious cascade of forbidden lust through his veins if it was the single necessary thing needed to keep living.

'*Buenos días,*' he muttered, then wondered why the hell he kept speaking to her in Cartanian.

She paused at the last but one step, bringing her face closer to his eye line. Closer to his avid gaze that insisted on roaming her face unceasingly.

Her lips parted on a soft sigh. '*Góðan daginn,*' she murmured.

'Did you sleep well?'

'*Já,*' she said, then her mouth twisted, immediately drawing his gaze to her plump lips. 'As well as can be expected.'

Lips he'd touched, then spent the night dreaming about. Lips he'd wanted to taste with a need and fervency he knew and accepted came from the ocean of forbidden reasons why he couldn't. He was *years older* than her, and yet...wasn't the taboo often the greatest of lures?

And here in this secluded cabin that he'd insisted they

come to, when she'd rightly pointed out that they could've gone anywhere else in the world with guaranteed safety but with ample room to avoid each other—an ideal, much more prudent course of action—he'd placed himself directly in the path of that allure.

It's not too late. You can do something about—

She stepped forward that last step and tilted her face up to his and Valenti's thought dissolved to nothing.

'Coffee?' she muttered huskily, even as her own gaze roamed over him, before coming back to meet his eyes.

He nodded, a jerky thing of little substance that somehow saved him from appearing like a dazed schoolboy. Forcing his body to move, he took one step back, then pivoted towards the kitchen. Ignoring the frantic urge to look over his shoulder, watch her follow him. Going to the sophisticated coffee maker he'd installed when he'd had the cabin decked out, he pushed the requisite buttons, bracing his hands on the counter and willing sense and reason back into his brain as he waited for the beverage to percolate.

And yes, he told himself he remembered just how she liked it because it was his duty to pay attention to the minutest detail.

Because not doing so risks lives. Sometimes fatally.

Like with Helga.

Helga, whom he'd protected on assignment eight years ago, and on seeing her exceptional talent as a doctor had divulged his most secret, abandoned wish of becoming a surgeon, then spent hours and days discussing her favourite subject. Helga, who, like her younger sister three years ago, had suddenly appeared in Cartana, offering friendship while daring him to reach for his dream, with her help. She'd selflessly offered her eye-wateringly exclusive services to his father, the king, with a view to advocating on Valenti's behalf, even though he'd protested, proud and determined to stick to his new destiny, but secretly welcomed her advocacy.

Helga, who'd died a mere handful of months later before she could complete her self-imposed task. All because he'd dropped the ball on her protection.

The icy, bracing showers of guilt and regret shaved off the layers of unwelcome sensations, so that he could turn and hand her the coffee with his emotions back under tight control where he preferred them.

Whatever she saw in his face made her eyes widen, then the light dulled.

Valenti told himself he didn't care. All he had to do was get through today. Then tomorrow. If the progress he sought hadn't been made by then, someone would need to have serious answers for him.

'Do you want breakfast before or after your outing?' he asked briskly.

Her fingers wrapped tight around her mug and her lips pursed before she answered, 'After, thanks.'

He nodded, turned to fix himself another espresso. At this rate, his blood would turn to pure caffeine before the day was over. But at least he'd have an excuse for his angstiness if his twin persisted in his curiosity.

He grimaced at the pathetic line of his thoughts.

'You don't have to come if you don't want to, you know? All of this can still be reconsidered.' She waved her hand between them.

A sharp spark lit his insides. 'Excuse me?'

'That sour look on your face just now? I'd much rather not have to deal with another day of it, thanks.'

'Not every thought in my head is about you,' he replied, a little more gratingly than he'd intended. Because most of them had been since he'd walked into that nightclub... *Dios*, was it only a couple of nights ago?

'Then what are you thinking about?' she blurted, then blushed to the roots of her hair.

Valenti bit his tongue to keep from commenting on how utterly adorable she looked nonplussed and ruffled. But that would be widening a door he most definitely needed to kick shut.

He tossed his espresso back and set the tiny cup down none too gently. 'Drink your coffee, *litla*. We leave in fifteen minutes.'

Lotte was glad she hadn't chickened out. For a moment while she layered on warm clothes so she wouldn't freeze on their walk, she'd toyed with calling the whole thing off.

Not least because spending a second night in his bed hadn't been any easier than the first. And because those torrid dreams had returned, raunchier, *needier* than before, making a mockery of the woefully scant sexual experiences she'd indulged in a couple of years back. The kind she'd believed then were the height of all there was to know about sex but now suspected were mere shadows of the real thing. Of what could possibly lie in store for her.

That thought had dug furrows through her until she'd woken up with her every sense heightened. A state that had intensified on seeing him standing there, like a grumpy, sexy god, staring up at her as she'd descended the stairs.

She could honestly say she hadn't been in her right mind when she'd demanded to know what he was thinking because he'd effectively scrambled most of her brain.

Which probably accounted for the wildly absurd question she'd just asked him.

A full three minutes ago to frigid, gritted-jawed silence.

'Are you going to answer me?' she demanded, then cringed when her voice emerged shaky. And dear God, needy.

As needy as the 'Why did you agree to be my guardian?' question she'd just spilled.

But she refused to take it back. She wished it was entirely because of the guardian/ward parameters of their relationship. Or even the freedom she craved to take charge of her own destiny. A freedom he'd point-blank refused to hand over on her eighteenth birthday, stating categorically that the twenty-five age limit was his and Helga's wish. The money she would've happily walked away from, but not so much her sister's wish. But beneath all that, she knew her need to be free stemmed from something she wasn't sure she fully wanted to contemplate. Something like freedom to meet Valenti Domene toe-to-toe. As an equal.

As absurd and laughable as that was because he was miles more sophisticated, a *prince* and second in line to the throne, she couldn't fully dismiss it. Nor did she want to...

So she held her breath while her heart hammered at the marble-like profile she glimpsed from the corner of her eye as they powered up one shallow peak and another. And another. In silence.

Until... 'Technically I agreed to you asking a question, not that I would answer. And certainly not to answer with an essay instead of a yes or no.'

Hurt and anger spread through her body, lighting a fire that predictably warmed her up. 'That's cheating and you know it. More fool me for believing you were honourable.'

He stiffened and a tic throbbed at his temple. And his gaze didn't once leave the snow-bordered path or the white fir trees surrounding them.

They reached a small clearing before he deigned to slant a sardonic glance at her. And when he answered his voice was calmly level, if derisive. 'The fault is yours for failing to work out the small print, *litla*.'

'That's bullshit. And don't call me that.'

He opened his mouth, but she veered away from him, a strange ache in her chest. It struck her hard that she'd hoped this would be the start of her chiselling away his reserve, to finding some sort of connection with him because, contrary to her every stern pep talk, she hadn't written him off.

She had believed last night that he would be leaving the door open, and she had spent the night admitting to herself that despite all her assertions, she wasn't quite ready to relinquish the ephemeral feeling of having Valenti Domene as her guardian. Her brother, whilst he loved her in his own abstract way, had little in common with her. Gunnar was nearer in age to Helga and they'd been close, sharing a deep love of medicine. That had left Lotte on the outside long before Helga had died. Then Gunnar was so consumed with his grief and his career as a *Médecins Sans Frontières* doctor that half of the time, he forgot she existed.

The story of her life. She was everyone's second, third or fourth afterthought. Never first.

Her feet crunched ice underfoot as she fought the urge to break into a run. That would be giving too much away. But she did quicken her steps, her path blurred by the stupid tears burning her eyes.

'Lotte, stop!'

'Fuck off!'

She had no idea where she was going and right this moment, she didn't care. So when strong, powerful arms wrapped around her waist and swept her off her feet, she screamed.

'*Qué demonios*, watch where you're going!'

She strained to free herself from the bonds of his arms. 'Get your hands off me!'

'So you can go ahead and break your stupid beautiful neck?'

'Valenti—'

'Stop. Look,' he growled in her ear.

Fighting the decadent shiver washing through her with his warm breath on her lobe and the arms locked tight around her, she swallowed. Focused on her surroundings. And gasped.

A mere ten feet ahead, the snow-covered ground fell away at a steep angle, with occasional rocks breaking through the white landscape. At the pace she'd been travelling, she would've surely tumbled down into the ravine, breaking a bone or several, possibly her neck.

'Oh God.' Her hushed exclamation wasn't just for the narrowly avoided accident. It was also chagrin that he seemed to be saving her from a series of reckless mishaps.

No wonder he didn't want to be around her. Tears brimmed faster and she wanted to kick herself one more time for yet another weakness.

'Let me go, please,' she said in a more subdued tone.

He didn't comply. Of course he didn't.

Between one breath, and the next, he swung her into his arms, striding back down the path.

He didn't stop until they were back at the cabin, where he set her down in the middle of the living room, hands propped on his lean hips, and those molten eyes glaring holy hell at her. Much like the night he believed she was running away.

Lotte held up her hand. 'Before you have a go at me, I take full responsibility for that. Granted I was annoyed with you, but I should've been looking where I was going.'

If she had hoped her pre-emptive apology would defuse the situation, she was very much mistaken. He shrugged off his coat and tossed it aside with barely restrained fury, his eyes never leaving hers.

'Apology not accepted,' he seethed. 'Allowing your anger or dissatisfaction with me to lead you into danger is completely unacceptable. I could be scraping you off the side of a mountain by now.'

'Oh come on!' She took off her own outer garments, rolling her eyes as she hung them up. 'That's a little melodramatic, don't you think?'

A dark rumble of thunder rolled out of his throat. 'Melodrama is more your language. Maybe I should learn to speak it.'

She rolled her eyes again. 'What next, a spanking to teach me a lesson?'

His eyes flared. 'Now there's an idea.'

She barely had a chance to react to that before he was reaching for her.

'What are—Oh my God, don't even think—argggh!'

The sharp sting on her backside, a direct result of being tossed over Valenti's bent knees was as shocking as it was... *hot*.

'How dare you!'

Her screech was more to cover up what was happening in her body than anything else. Because, *sweet heaven*, as the stings subsided as quickly as they'd arisen, the follow-up righteous outrage that should demand he explain and apologize for treating her like a child, swiftly died.

Because the sensations rampaging through her were not even remotely childlike. The mind-blowing, intensely arousing sensation left behind a trail of fire that heated her up far more than her anger and hurt had. That dragged liquid heat between her thighs and a fierce blush to her face the moment he released her.

Thick silence filled the room, punctuated by their loud breathing. She couldn't bring herself to look at him, to risk him seeing just how intensely, *carnally* his spanking had affected her.

Dear God, could this get any worse? Could she really be turned on by such an act? But deeply compelled, she couldn't stop herself from pushing back the curtain of hair blocking her view. Watching in fascination as his eyes squeezed shut and his fingers speared in his hair repeatedly.

And then his eyes flew open to reveal smouldering fire aimed at her. 'Come here,' he ordered with a voice so guttural it was barely audible.

She moved almost independent of thought and will, with an even deeper, bewildering fascination, this time at herself. At her willingness to be so compliant with this man.

His knees parted, making room for her. Room she breathlessly accepted.

And it was as she slotted herself into the place she yearned to be that she registered the fine tremors rippling through him.

A few more beats before the enormity of *why* settled even deeper. Valenti witnessing one sister perish was bad enough. But even the outside possibility of witnessing two…

He surged to his feet, but before she could stop herself, she raised her hands and placed them on his chest. A deeper trembling unravelled through him, and his eyes drifted shut for another beat or two before they opened, fierce, perhaps even a little unhinged, to hook into hers.

'*Perdóname*,' he rasped.

'Apology not accepted,' she echoed his response. 'Unless you accept mine.'

A low bark of laughter escaped him as he shook his head once. 'You drive me to the fucking edge,' he hissed, then his jaw clenched tight.

'Too soon,' she teased, but that died away because the charge between them, rather than dispersing, grew, spun around them like an unstoppable vortex. A black hole pulling them into intensely alien territory.

'Promise me you won't ever do something like that again,' he pressed with hot, ragged insistence.

Her hand scrambled up, curled on his shoulders, her breath coming in gasps as she felt him tremble again. 'I promise.'

Her ready promise made his eyes narrow for several moments. Moments during which she found herself swaying even closer, his aura gripping her tight, craving that warmth and care she'd missed so very much for what felt like all of her life.

For just one moment, she wanted to experience the heady knowledge that she was the single most important being in his existence. Even if it was a delusion she would need to wake up from eventually.

'I'm sorry,' she whispered against his lips.

For one long moment, he remained silent, their positions frozen. Then the icy drips of reality started to invade the warmth.

It would never go beyond this.

She was once again on the brink of humiliating herself before this man. Her stupid crush refused to die. A sound burst from her throat, wounded, chagrined and much to her horror, a little lost. A lost little lamb no one wanted, destined to be always left out in the cold.

Angry with herself for the pathetic self-pity, and yes, with him for making her needy when she'd been imperfectly lonely on her own, comfortably self-deluding, she lurched back, eager to get away from him.

He made that sound again. Pained. Frustrated. Intensely annoyed. *Ravenous.*

Strong, firm hands halted her retreat. Then reversed it. Pulling her into his body with the same urgency he'd returned them to the cabin with.

'Right to the fucking edge,' he growled against her mouth, before he slammed it on hers.

CHAPTER SIX

OF COURSE.

It was disarmingly predictable that a kiss from the man she'd futilely crushed on for more years than she cared to admit should be earth-shattering.

Had she not been in the process of having her mind and body smelted by the great Valenti Domene, Lotte would have been deeply resentful.

She *would* be. At some point in the distant future, she was absolutely certain.

For now though…

She moaned deep, almost worshipfully, her breath held as her lips parted in response to the demanding sweep of his tongue. To the tease and delivery that confirmed that yes, whatever she'd experienced before had been a pathetic, pale imitation that wasn't worth the fleeting thought.

This was a proper kiss.

This was what a real man's hands felt like moving over her body, applying the right amount of pressure to mould and direct. To caress and pleasure.

His tongue dominated her mouth, boldly stroked hers until her knees gave way. She moaned again as he grappled her closer still, plastering her chest to his, then his fingers speared her hair, a gruff sound tearing from deep within him.

In the next moment he pulled her down onto the thick rug,

their bodies barely separating as he stretched out on top of her without breaking the kiss.

He kissed her like a man possessed. One driven to the edge. *By her.*

That heady, powerful thought had barely lit through her brain long enough to be celebrated before he was jerking away, cursing beneath his breath as he launched himself off her. Returning to his favourite position of staring out the window. Leaving her cold, dazed.

Lost and rejected.

But slowly, thankfully, that self-righteous anger made a welcome appearance. 'When are you going to admit that this isn't working?'

He stiffened and even from her position on the floor, she knew his face was set in granite.

'Or is this some sort of self-flagellation process I'm not privy to?'

His breath hissed out and he spun to face her. 'Perhaps we both deserve a little penitence for what just happened.'

She swallowed at the bitterly recriminatory tone. 'I beg to differ. And I'd thank you to leave me out of your self-imposed Greek tragedy.'

His jaw worked for several beats. 'You know this shouldn't have happened. It was wrong.'

'Why? Because you made an agreement that no one bothered to ask if I was on board with?'

'You were a child,' he said.

'I was hardly a toddler, Valenti. My opinion should've counted. But even if I'm inclined to let that slide, I'm a woman now. And I'm sorry but I won't be joining in your martyrdom at the expense of my freedom.'

'*Eres increíble,*' he muttered under his breath.

Her laughter was easy, throaty. If only it didn't burn so mercilessly on its way out. 'Am I? Why? Because I don't share your views that I'm anathema to you because of a connection you put in place?'

Fury lit his eyes, no doubt at her gumption. Her inability to kowtow to him as many across the world, clients, acolytes and minions alike, frothed at the mouth to do.

'Go on then, tell me all the ways you're a woman,' he invited silkily.

She couldn't bear to tell him the most important or the most vulnerable things dear to her heart. The idea born and fuelled in part by her sister's example of helping those in the greatest need. So she went for shock and awe. And yes, something guaranteed to shatter his illusion of her once and for all.

Still lying on the floor where he left her because somehow rising felt weakening, she examined her fingers unnecessarily for several strung-out moments before she sighed and said, 'I touched myself when I was in your bed last night.'

A strangled sound rumbled from his throat. The muscles in his arms bunched visibly as he grappled for control. That control strained as he prowled back to crouch next to her, his eyes burning coals drilling holes into her.

Leaning in close until they were sharing the same air, he rasped, 'The next words out of that delectable mouth better not be that you were thinking of another man while you were in my bed,' he breathed.

She shuddered at the primitive fury in his voice, the thrill of dancing so close to the edge of his volcano. 'And what if I did? I'm not a nun and it's not forbidden.'

He breathed in slowly. 'You're playing a very dangerous game, Lotte.'

'If you want it to end it's very simple. Leave. You're very good at doing that anyway. Aren't you?'

His eyes flicked between hers. Digging. Probing.

She bit back the exposing sob that rose to her throat when he slowly rose again and stepped back.

'Goading me for a reaction isn't going to work out for you, *cariña*.'

'Are you sure, *elskan*?' she tossed back. 'I do so love a challenge. And you've shown me that you're not averse to playing dirty by finding a loophole not to answer my questions. So you see, two can play that game.'

He smiled a purely predatory smile. 'And have you thought about the consequences of those actions, or do you merely exist in the moment? Unable to grasp the big picture?'

She shook her head. Right in this moment the big picture was too depressing to contemplate. Any picture where he didn't feature, even abstractly, commanded a swell of sadness so profound she wanted to curl into herself and beat her fists against the ground. But she was damned if she would let him see her crumble.

'You say *consequences* like it's a bad thing. Some consequences are born through soul-changing adventure.'

His whole body froze and between one nanosecond and another his expression turned cold and austere. 'And others shatter joy and wreck lives forever.'

The bleak devastation in his voice shrivelled every last ounce of defiance in her. She was barely holding herself up when with one last arctic glance, he stalked away. She was still there repositioned on her backside and hugging her knees when she heard him open and shut the front door.

For a full hour, she remained alone in the cabin. She had no idea where he went but when he returned his mood was no better improved.

It became clear that lunch would be a chillingly silent affair when he icily and blatantly ignored her after setting a bowl of her favourite *kjotsupa* in front of her. The hearty lamb stew was tasty, but she barely took a few bites before she lost her appetite completely.

Setting down her cutlery, she cleared her throat. 'Are you going to tell me what you meant?'

Grave silver eyes clashed with hers. 'You know very well what I meant.'

'If you're talking about Helga, I would—'

'Is there anything else that has shattered your life beyond not having a phone within easy reach so you can revel in false praise from faceless strangers?' he mocked icily.

She forced a smile to hide the wounds of his words. 'You want me to appreciate and respect you instead of my devotees, Valenti? Here's a tip. Stop playing at being a guardian from afar. Show me the role means something to you besides writing a cheque once a year or sending a trinket on my birthday. Those I can have with a click of my fingers from my raft of admirers.'

She tossed that last one in just to gauge his reaction. Predictably, his nostrils flared. The high of getting a reaction from him barely lasted. Valenti might be possessive and proprietary over her—for reasons she desperately wished were angled more in her favour instead of her dead sister's memory—but until he did something about it, it truly meant nothing.

'All of this over questions I don't feel inclined to answer?' he derided.

But she saw through that haughty scoffing.

She'd rattled him, somehow. She would go as far as to surmise that nothing had gone as he'd predicted since they'd boarded his helicopter.

And perhaps that was her solution. To keep him destabilised. Long enough…

For what, exactly? A slither of apprehension wormed its way through her bravado. Did she have what it took to knock him off his foundation long enough for him to throw in the towel? Either accept her for something other than a burden or…let her go?

She had to. She refused to live in limbo for another three years.

'If that's what it takes. The better question is, what are you afraid of? Who will know the answers to these questions besides you and me?' she challenged.

Charged silence pounded through the small space. Lotte wanted to believe she'd won the small battle when after a string of seconds with his jaw clenched tight, he threw down the napkin he'd swiped across his lips and rose to take their plates to the kitchen before resting one lean hip against the counter, arms folded.

His gaze snagged hers after that.

'Your sister loved Gunnar, just as she loved you,' he said abruptly, the words torn from deep within him. 'But as the eldest she had a duty to ensure she wasn't blinded by that love when it came to your welfare. She knew Gunnar's strengths and weaknesses. It didn't include being responsible for a challenging teenager on top of pursuing a fledgling medical career.'

She set down the water glass she'd been toying with, drawing her legs up to her chest and wrapping her arms around them. If he saw that as a defence mechanism, so be it.

Since his reappearance in her life, he'd seen her at her worst.

He would be gone again soon enough, anyway. But if nothing else, she'd managed to pierce Valenti Domene's seemingly impenetrable armour. Sure, it wouldn't keep her warm at night, but it was a win she would treasure nevertheless.

'But why you when you clearly didn't want the job?'

His eyes narrowed. 'You persist in believing wants and needs were relevant in my decision. They weren't,' he stated bluntly. 'Your sister died before an alternative could be found besides your brother. And her last wish was that you be taken care of. I just happened to be the person she expressed that wish to.'

She drew in a shaky breath. There it was. The stark truth. She'd been pushed on him in a moment of great trauma and turmoil. And she'd become the burden he couldn't shed.

'Let me go,' she whispered low, almost inaudibly because more than even the wish her sister had had no business foisting on him, the shadows in his eyes when she spoke of Helga drew claws over her heart. And yes, it was very unnerving to realise those shadows bothered her more than she wanted to admit. Because she couldn't shake the unsettling feeling that the need to see Prince Valenti Domene free of those shadows was derived from a well much deeper than a mere schoolgirl crush.

She felt more than saw him approach, her eyes downcast on her knees. But she smelled him when he crouched before her. His gaze sizzled away the layers of her composure, until compelled, she raised her head. Met the implacable expression he wanted her to witness.

'No. I will not.'

It was so final it struck deep in her soul.

She was grappling with why that didn't completely shatter her when he continued.

'Even if I wanted to break the promise I made, I won't.'

'Why not?' Her throat was thick, her voice hoarse, her eyes unable to move from the mesmerising silver of his.

'Because you're yet to prove to me that you don't need a guardian. And no, sparking pure fire at me with those eyes isn't going to make your case.'

Hypnosis receded, replaced by a thrill-tinged anger. 'If you think I'm going to hang on your every word just to prove some sort of point to you, you're seriously—'

'I believe it's my turn now,' he interrupted firmly.

She frowned. 'To do what?'

'To have a question answered.'

'That wasn't part of the agreement.'

'It is now. You faltered on our very first outing. So I'm renegotiating our agreement.'

She plucked at the sleeve of her cashmere sweater, trying and failing to find a way to wriggle out of the corner she'd been backed into. Eventually she exhaled. 'Fine, ask your question.'

'How is showing off how to wear a shirt three different ways useful to anyone?' he mused drily.

It was unexpected. And the scoffing tone hurt more than she wanted to admit. 'You think I'm a waste of space?'

His mouth tightened, his raised eyebrow clearly held tones of 'You said it, not me.'

Her mouth twisted, her hurt deepening. 'Come on, at least have the balls to own it.'

'Watch your mouth,' he growled.

Her arms unshackled, her bare feet hit the floor as she glared harder at him. 'Or what? You think what I do is useless? Try being a single mother on minimum wage trying to improve herself by working her way through night school. She's striving to land her dream job but only has two outfits to wear before her first pay cheque. She sees my video and asks me to show her how many ways she can wear the two decent shirts that she owns so her colleagues don't think she's dirt poor.

'What I do may seem inconsequential to you but when she tells me I gave her a single ounce more confidence than she possessed the day before, that *nonsense* of helping her find a bit of dignity and pride is worth its weight in gold. Here's another one for you to toss into your arrogant pipe. I may not be the world's greatest chef and yes, you hired me a cook who makes my meals, but if I can show a college student how to make a simple meal so they don't exist on cereal or noodles every day or, shock-horror, starve because they don't have a clue how to cook a basic but nutritious meal on a budget, then don't you think it's worth it?'

Several heartbeats after her long, rambling breathless diatribe, he pointed out, 'I don't smoke a pipe.'

She surged from the table, throwing up her hands with a muted scream. 'You're an incorrigible mongoose bear kraken snake!'

A sensation bubbled in Valenti's gut, then erupted through his throat. A second later, it registered that he was...*laughing*.

Her face froze for a second and her eyes continued to blaze in a glare before she too dissolved into laughter.

The sound was far too lovely for his ears and that peculiar place in his chest. 'Did you just pluck real and mythical creatures out of thin air as insults?' He attempted to sound stern and somewhat vaguely succeeded.

She shrugged, the wide sleeve slipping off her shoulder to reveal flawless skin. 'Maybe. But now I feel sorry for all of them because compared to you, they're sweet and harmless.'

His eyebrows went up. 'Even krakens?'

She shrugged again. Slowly the laughter died.

Valenti had to mentally shake his head to remember the point he'd been trying to make a few minutes ago. The point conclusively trounced by her explanation, another corner of his chest replaced by a sensation eerily close to surprise. And respect. 'So a few people benefit from what you do. Doesn't take away the fact that it's not worth putting yourself in danger.'

'I didn't put myself in danger. Don't you get it? Social media isn't responsible. Freaks aren't just limited to online. They operate in real life too. Besides, this isn't my first—' She grimaced, cursing under her breath, but it was too late.

Shock and cold fury swept through him. 'Go on, don't hold back from telling me this psycho isn't the first person to hassle you,' he said, teeth gritted.

Her lashes swept down. A second later, he was cupping her chin, raising her gaze to the deep scrutiny of his. 'Answer me, Lotte.'

'There was a guy…at university.'

The coarse curse that left him turned the air black.

Her pert nose wrinkled. 'You're about to lose it again, aren't you?'

'Is the sky outside blue?'

She licked her lips, and he felt as if she'd licked every erogenous zone on his body, which was damn inconvenient when he was livid enough to start world-ending blazes. 'Who was he?'

'It doesn't—'

'It matters. And if you know what's good for you, you'll quit stalling and give me the information I'm asking for. Starting with his name.' He barely took a breath before he snapped. 'Now, Lotte.'

'Hans Wilden,' she volunteered with an equal snap.

He rose to his feet slowly. Against his will. Because he wanted to keep exploring her warm silky skin. Reassure himself she was okay. Because far from the calm, unremarkable morning he'd been hoping for after last night's turbulence, all they seemed to have achieved was more upheaval.

Starting with that tumble she'd nearly taken.

A residual shiver shook through him, the moment when she'd careened towards that rocky decline replaying starkly through his brain.

But he bunched that traitorous hand, marched into his office and returned with his satellite phone. His call was answered on the first ring. 'Yes, sir?'

'Hans Wilden. Recent graduate of Reykland University. Age?' he asked her.

'Same as me. I think.'

'Find out everything you can about him. And more importantly, find out where he is at this exact moment and keep him under surveillance until I say otherwise.'

'Yes, sir.'

He swung away from her, stalked to the window.

For a full minute he stared unseeing out at the half-frozen landscape. His thoughts ran helter-skelter, and yet he knew the exact moment she approached and stopped behind him. His skin jumped with the need to snatch her close, plaster that svelte, alluring, *forbidden* body to his.

'At the risk of repeating myself yet again, my job is to keep you safe. Yours is to help me achieve that goal. Which part of that do you not understand?'

'The part where you tell me whether it's guilt driving you. Or something else.'

The words were whispered. But they roared through him like a two-ton cannon.

Myriad expressions flitted over his face after her stark demand.

Lotte held her breath, *willed* him to speak his truth, and end this torture once and for all. But apparently, the fact-seeking was at an end. By royal decree.

Because, without answering or glancing her way, Valenti left the living room.

Then surprisingly reappeared an hour later, face still set in stone. 'We agreed to one question. We've strayed far from that. My leeway-giving is at an end.' Those terse words preceded him into the kitchen where he started to pull pots and pans from cupboards.

Less than twenty minutes later, the scent of roasting meat and vegetables filled the air. Her growling stomach reminded her that they'd both barely touched their last meal.

Feeling churlish for not helping, Lotte finally staggered upright from the sofa she'd fallen into after his departure, felt his sharp gaze when she swayed on her feet, then he returned to dishing out their food when she managed to steady herself.

In silence, she laid out cutlery and silverware, just as he brought two heaping plates to the table and pulled out a chair.

'Sit,' he instructed gruffly. 'And this time, we will both eat something. I don't want you weakened or falling ill from not eating enough,' he groused, his hard gaze daring her to argue.

She told herself she was too depleted to baulk at the order.

She sat, picked up her fork and tasted the hearty stew, then swore not to inflate his ego by groaning at how good it was. But she managed a mumbled 'thank you' as she demolished the bowl of food.

She was finishing the last bite when she looked up to see his gaze locked on hers. 'What?'

'Wilden's whereabouts are accounted for. He's been in Australia since he finished university. He's also engaged to marry.'

Why that sharpened his gaze on her face and probed for a long moment, she refused to question, instead settling for a shrug. 'Told you he was harmless.'

His eyes turned molten. 'No man who's met and interacted with you for more than a minute can be termed harmless.'

Something delightful but deeply apprehensive snagged deep in her heart. And she wasn't sure she could conjure up a better description of what this man made her feel. 'What's that supposed to mean?'

'You leave a distinct impression. One that lasts a considerable time.'

She was searching his face, breath held, when he jerked to his feet, sweeping up their empty plates.

Lotte stood too, feeling too jittery to remain still. 'Let me. You cooked, it's only right that I clean up.'

For a tense moment, he stilled. Then he nodded brusquely. 'I'll be in my office,' he said. Then walked away.

Left to her own devices with no phone and far too many thoughts, Lotte explored every corner of the cabin Valenti wasn't occupying. To her surprise, she uncovered a small shelf of books tucked into the hallway cupboard. Then was further stunned when she discovered it held some of her favourites.

Plucking one, she returned to the living room, pulled a blanket over her lower body and forced herself into the characters' lives, growing increasingly vexed when the process proved frustratingly strenuous.

She wasn't entirely sure when she nodded off. But when she jerked awake, Valenti was sitting in the armchair adjacent to her, the book she'd been reading in his hand. Recalling the raunchy paragraphs she'd skimmed just before she nodded off, heat flowed into her face.

'My library is fully stocked, if you want more reading material,' he said, setting the book aside.

Her eyes widened. She'd expected a return to the chilly standoff between them. Not a reversion to the brooding and aloof man she was used to. Lotte wasn't sure which she preferred.

'Thanks,' she returned just as evenly as she could manage. 'But I would like my phone back,' she added.

The flash of his earlier chill showed through, then his austere demeanour slotted back into place. 'You can have it, but you know there's no internet service here so what's the point?'

'That's not entirely true, is it? How else are you working in your office and making calls without a connection?'

A mirthless smile quirked the corner of his lips. 'You're suggesting I hand over valuable resources so you can stay abreast of how many followers you've gained in the last two days?'

'Not at all. But I would like to make use of *my* valuable resources and make proper use of my surroundings.'

His steady gaze hummed across her senses. 'Explain.'

'Content filming, Valenti. Heard of that?'

Another twitch of his lips. Without answering, he rose fluidly to his feet, disappeared towards his office and returned a minute later. 'Will this work?'

This happened to be a gleaming state-of-the-art camera, the kind she'd only admired from afar because it cost tens of thousands of dollars. Money better expended usefully elsewhere.

Straightening, she started to reach for it. He pulled it back at the last moment, a gleam in his eyes that set her pulse racing. 'You may use it on one condition.'

Her spirit plummeted. 'Of course you have conditions,' she snapped. She raised her hand, intending to wave him away. But curiosity overcame her will and she curled her hand into a loose fist. 'What conditions?'

'I would like to see you at work.'

Her lips parted in a soft gasp. Once again, he'd succeeded in pulling the rug from under her. 'Why?' she blurted, wariness and a more curious sensation tunnelling through her.

'You insist I've misunderstood you. I'd like to set those misconceptions straight.'

CHAPTER SEVEN

'INSIDE OR OUT?' he pressed when her muteness persisted.

Lotte, still fighting a blush and the heady acceptance of his olive branch, shot her gaze to the window. 'Outside, please.'

Even before his brusque nod and the narrowing of his eyes, she knew what was coming.

'And yes, I'll do my best to prevent any mishaps,' she said, then because she couldn't help herself, she added, tongue firmly in cheek, 'as long as you do your part to avoid fomenting my temper.'

The tightness around his mouth eased a touch. 'I would prefer a blanket pledge to be on your best behaviour.'

She made a show of glancing around, then throwing out her arms. 'I don't see stables around. You must be losing your touch of turning your wishes into horses, Your Highness.'

And for the briefest nanosecond, Lotte could've sworn she saw amusement glint in his eyes, before he turned to glance out the window.

'It'll be dark soon. You can have your shoot in the morning.'

Disappointment dashed through her, but anticipation levelled it out soon enough. And to her surprise they spent what amounted to a skirmish-free evening where she managed to read a few more chapters of her book, while Valenti brooded in the armchair, a sleek-looking laptop commanding the entirety of his attention, while also managing to make her acutely aware that he was cataloguing every breath she took.

It was almost a relief to head up to bed shortly after nine p.m. and fall into a dreamless sleep after a curious hour of wondering why she didn't feel inclined or defiant about tending to the need simmering in her pelvis.

Whatever the cause, she was glad to be free of the thought when she was showered, dressed and downstairs by seven.

To find Valenti also fully dressed, the sofa bed tucked away.

He held out a cup of steaming coffee which she accepted, fighting self-consciousness when his steady gaze seared over her, lingering on her face. 'Sleep well?'

Remembering the hour of tossing and turning, her face heated. 'As well as can be expected,' she muttered, then blew on the hot liquid, her belly clenching when his gaze immediately zeroed in on the motion. It took every crumb of composure to take a small sip and swallow, before forcing her body to turn away from him. To appear nonchalant as she looked out the window to the white and green landscape.

'Any ideas on where you'd like to start?'

She grimaced inwardly, knowing her answer would make her seem flaky, but then she shrugged. Pretending she was something she wasn't would only end up shaming herself and denting her integrity. And didn't she promise herself she was done attempting to contort herself to fit his expectations? 'Inspiration will come when it comes. I won't force it.' She paused, expecting his judgement when the silence stretched. 'I'm sure you think it's silly?' she asked, after blowing and sipping her coffee, and earning herself another sizzling scrutiny.

'You forget I have a twin who conjures magical creations out of thin air. I'm not unfamiliar with people who fly by the seat of their pants,' he said evenly.

'But you don't approve?' she pressed, wanting to know his thoughts despite all her frothy pep talks.

He breached the gap between them in two large steps, and for an age, he stared down at her with those brooding silver eyes. Assessing. Digging. 'I will never be an advocate for unbridled chaos but I'm learning that controlled chaos has a certain…appeal.'

Why her breath snagged so hard in her throat she was extremely reluctant to examine. Mostly because she freely admitted she was terrified of what the results would be. Especially when Valenti bracketed that answer with a hand raised slowly to her face, his hard knuckles brushing her cheeks almost experimentally, cataloguing the expulsion of her breath for another long moment before he stepped back.

'Finish your coffee, *litla*. The morning's wasting.'

She studiously avoided staring after him as he went into the living area, needing the few minutes to get herself under control after the lightest of touches had sparked an inferno.

Outside, the cold, crisp air did nothing to alleviate the heat building inside her.

Or was it the blistering awareness of him as he talked her through how to best utilise the camera? All she knew was that she was breathing far too much of his rousing scent, was far too keen on the dexterity of his strong hands and the thrum of his rumbling voice. Hell, even his long-legged stride and the crunch of his boots on snow made her insides somersault.

Lotte took the opposite path to the one they'd taken yesterday, glad she needed to concentrate on the rocky terrain. Just as she was almost glad when she spotted Valenti's bodyguards, dressed in mostly white winter gear to blend in with the landscape. It was a timely reminder of his stratospheric status and importance.

Thankfully, she was rewarded mere minutes later with a spectacular vista of a mirror-smooth lake, rimmed by soaring snow-capped fir trees.

She lost herself in capturing the beauty of the place and

filming herself without giving away her location, her heart flipping over at Valenti's nod of approval. But while it was bolstering to dive back into work, she knew her footage lacked depth. She was about to call it a day when she spotted a shoot of familiar green she hadn't seen in a long time.

She rushed to investigate, then held out the camera to Valenti. 'Do you mind filming?'

He took the camera, flicking the setting before he aimed it at her.

'And for those who need it, here's your tip for the day. Ice baths with a twist of mugwort.' She winked into the camera and held up the small bush of the healing plant. 'I know, it's horrifically unsexy, but my grandmother swore by it and after a few scraped knees and bruises, I can attest to the fact that it does wonders for quick healing. And yes, you can thank me later.' She smiled wide then taking a deep breath, signed off with her usual slogan. 'Be bold. Be brave. Reach for what you want. Remember I'm here for you, always.'

It was stupid to fight a blush when he slowly lowered the camera but kept his gaze pinned on her, the assessing look filling his eyes once more.

'You're making recommendations normally reserved for combat training personnel and athletes,' he observed when they started back down the hill to the cabin, his silver eyes probing and watchful.

Her breath strangled. 'So? Healing is healing, no?'

A brisk nod, but his eyes didn't leave her face. 'Have you used it yourself?'

Her eyes widened. 'You think I need it?' She strove for flippant and missed by a wide mile.

'There better not be another secret in your recent past you're withholding,' he warned, his voice a rumbling storm.

Anxiety knitted her insides because it just so happened, she was. She barely managed to stop herself from biting her lip in her agitation, choosing instead to divert attention. 'A woman is allowed some secrets, you know. And at the risk of sounding like a broken record, my life isn't an open book to you. And even if it was, you've missed several chapters.'

His eyes narrowed as they climbed the steps onto the cabin porch, she feared he'd see right through her ruse. 'Have I? Enlighten me then,' he invited silkily.

'You seem to want to control every corner of my life, but did you even bother to check my bank account? I haven't needed your money to live on since I was nineteen years old.'

He froze, surprise a sharp flint in his eyes. 'What?'

A punch of pride preceded her answer. 'I'm independently well off, Valenti. I don't have your billions, but I'm very capable of surviving on my own. The only reason I'm here in this cabin at all is because you won't let me go. Or am I mistaken in recalling that part of the guardianship means I have to get your express permission to go anywhere on earth?'

Shock reeled across his face, followed swiftly by intransigent rejection. 'Not quite. The agreement is that I have ample warning so your security can be arranged. As long as we're both clear on that abiding fact, there's nothing else to discuss is there?'

'Who's incredible now?' she threw at him, remembering his seething observation yesterday.

That eerily brooding calm settled over him once more. 'Do you want to keep filming or not?' he bit out.

She looked from his face to his camera and back again. 'Not,' she snapped. She started to walk away, then wheeled back. 'Would it hurt you to congratulate me for my achievements? For a modicum of recognition? Or does it stick in your gut that I'm not as useless as you think?' A scoffing laugh barked out before she could stop it. 'At this point I'm thinking you'd be more impressed if I said I had a sugar daddy on the side than admit that I'm capable of looking after myself.'

The roll of fury across his face was so visceral, so intense she took a hasty step back, scrambling into the doorway of the cabin. He kept coming, seeming to grow to twice his size, his aura filling every corner of her senses until he was the only thing she could see. 'For your sake I suggest you keep that suggestion strictly fictional and quickly discarded.'

'Oh yeah? And why is that?' she taunted, while a part of her brain shrieked at her for her return to recklessness. A mode she was fully intent on blaming on him.

'Lotte—'

'Because it infuriates you for me to have something you didn't provide?' she cut through his warning tone. 'Do you get off that much on having me beholden to you?'

He reached for her, one hand closing over her nape to drag her close. 'I am many things, but a power-hungry megalomaniac isn't one.'

Recklessness intensified, rushing through her veins like the sweetest narcotic. 'Then tell me, what are you, truly?' she challenged harder. 'Say it, Valenti. Why are you being intransigent about this? Why does my every move fascinate you so much.'

His nostrils quivered. 'No.' The word pulsed with warning.

'Then I'll say it for you. Because *you* want to be my sugar daddy.'

Unholy fire blazed through his eyes. '*Dios mío!* Stop,' he breathed.

She clamped her lips shut, but her eyes spoke volumes. And he saw everything. Saw and cursed some more before snatching her into his arms and marching into the cabin.

Taking the stairs two at a time he was in his bedroom in under ten seconds.

Only then did he set her down, one leg kicking the door shut. She planted herself in the middle of the room while he remained at the door, but his presence filled every corner of the space.

With anyone else, Lotte would probably have been frightened but not with Valenti. It stuck in her craw to admit he was probably the safest person for her to be around physically. That his iron control—and probably the way he could so easily dismiss her—meant he would never harm her.

But she wanted to test that control.

Wasn't that truly what she'd been doing since she looked up and saw him in that nightclub?

'You've found a hot little button you're enjoying pushing. *Brava*,' he growled. 'But before this goes any further you need to be very sure it's what you want,' he added. Succinctly. His eyes never leaving her face.

More than anything.

She was glad her mouth remained clamped, sealing the fervent, exposing response inside. Because apparently he wasn't done.

'Be sure you're not mistaking your little rebellion for something else.'

She raised her chin. 'Something like what?' she challenged, a small kernel of alarm inside her threatening to expand because he wasn't far from the truth. She feared this chemical reaction would lead to a startling conclusion.

'Like an inconvenient attachment that might not be altogether wise.'

That stung. Again because it strayed far too close to a truth she didn't want to admit. 'If that's your clever way of hinting that I'm in some way infatuated with you, you can kill that thought. I liked kissing you. And I want to…do more. Does it really need to be more than that?'

His eyes narrowed to molten slits. Then he prowled towards her with miles more swagger and finesse than she would ever manage. Three feet away he paused. She wanted to believe it was to safeguard against temptation to reach for her. But she knew otherwise. Valenti had more control in his little finger than she did in her entire existence.

He exhibited that by lazily resting his hands on his lean hips, watching her with the indolent regard of a predator completely confident in the vanquishing of its prey.

'If you're absolutely sure this is what you want, that this will remain here in this place strictly between us...then come here, Lotte. Let me deal with that insatiable need for rebellion.' His voice was low, mesmeric. Thickening that narcotic in her blood, making her dizzy with it.

That dizziness swayed her towards him. One step. Another. Until a mere half foot separated them.

'Undress me,' he instructed next.

Oh God. She couldn't help her swallow. The shudder that surged up her body lingered in the hands she raised hesitantly to his chest. A little terrified of the rage of emotions consuming her, she kept her gaze on the buttons of his outer jacket as she slid her hands beneath the lapels.

'No. Look at me,' he rasped huskily.

Raising lids that felt far too heavy, she met his mercurial gaze. Shadow and light. Fire and ice. A heavy, solemn watchfulness trained with singular focus on her, a specimen beneath his microscope.

Lotte discovered she didn't mind it, at all.

She'd wanted to be seen. Accepted. Even now when she felt more naked than she'd ever felt in her life. But curiously, any urge to hide had fled.

Her gaze fully fastened on his, she slid her hands beneath his lapels, the warmth of his rich wool-covered skin making her breath emerge faster as she tugged the coat off him. The long-sleeved polo neck moulded to his skin was next.

Hunger lent power to her as she took the hem between her fingers and started to lift. She only reached halfway before he helped, reefing it over his head and discarding it. Baring her gaze to the honed gladiator's torso, the mouth-watering ridges of packed muscle and hair-roughened chest that announced him as fully, completely masculine. A specimen *she* wanted to explore to her heart's content.

That chest expanded with a rough inhale when the tips of her fingers whispered over his skin in awed exploration, pausing at the puckered skin on his shoulder, a clear mark of his dangerous profession, possibly a connection to the harrowing incident that connected their lives.

She couldn't bring herself to ask then. So she moved on.

Her lips parted, the better to breathe him in. To fill every corner of her senses so there would be room for nothing else.

Like the whispered query as to how she would deal with what came next when they left this room. Like how that sizeable addendum he'd spelled out as to exactly what this was left a bubble of desolation within her.

Her fingers coasted lower, over the rough outline of his belt, and the even thicker outline of his cock, straining behind his fly. With that same hypnotic compulsion, her gaze dropped.

She swallowed. He was big. Almost intimidatingly so. What if—

His finger curling beneath her chin redirected her gaze up.

'Too damn slow,' he rasped, his tone full of hungry gravel.

With his other hand he knocked her fingers out of the way. Then the whip of his belt sliding free whistled through the room, sending further shivers racing through her. Somehow, being deprived of watching him complete the undressing heightened every last sizzling nerve. Or perhaps it was the slow morphing of the shadows and ice to pure fire and hunger that held her in thrall.

Whatever it was, she couldn't look away from him as he propelled her back into the wall and commanded her to 'Stay.'

Then Valenti proceeded to undress her at his infuriating leisure, entirely contrary to his own demand.

Lotte felt every stitch teased off her body, every maddening, shiver-inducing pause as he inhaled sharply, his own fingers lingering over her clavicle. Her inner arms and wrists. The upper slopes of her breasts. The outer curve of her hips.

But with each caress, she realised he was gauging her reaction. Studying her gasps and moans the way he observed every private and public interaction.

Seeking signs of a change of heart? Or taking ownership of every crumb of her pleasure?

She gasped when without warning, he dropped into a crouch before her. Insistent fingers hooked into her lace panties, and with his eyes still on her face, Valenti slowly drew them down and away.

Only then did he conduct a thorough inspection of her body, leaving her even more exposed and naked than before.

She'd wanted to be seen. Now there was nowhere to hide. Inside or out.

'So maddeningly breathtaking,' he muttered, almost to himself. 'Is this what you wanted, *querida*? Incite that beautiful chaos so I end up at your feet?' he demanded thickly, while showing zero signs of subservience.

In any other being, she would've been truly puzzled as to how he could be on his knees and still command so much power and presence.

In Valenti Domene it came as naturally as the royal blood running through his veins. She imagined that even shackled and blindfolded, he would still command armies.

'Only if that's where you want to be.'

For some reason, her hushed response made his nostrils flare, his eyes darkening and pupils dilating.

'Alas, it seems as if I have very little choice,' he stated with that customary solemnity that made her heart lurch.

Before she could dig into what that meant, he was lifting her leg. Tossing it over his shoulder in an utterly masterful move that bared her sex to his intense gaze.

'*Dios mío*. Very little choice, indeed,' he said throatily. Then fused his mouth to her slick flesh, tasting and devouring while she cried out in sublime unparalleled pleasure.

Every bone in Lotte's body melted as her fingers dug through his lush hair, gripping tight as he spun sorcery around her senses. 'Oh… God!'

He eased the pressure, teasing mercilessly with his tongue so she remained dancing on the edge as he rasped, 'You like that?'

'*Ja!* Please, more,' she pleaded. 'I want… I want…' Despite the very carnal act, she couldn't quite articulate her need, her face flaming as he shamelessly explored her.

'You'll get what you deserve, *mi preciosa*,' he promised darkly.

Another minute was all he required to crack her wide open, to push her over the edge so she could drop straight into unrivalled bliss. Lotte was wrapped tight in her climax when he rose, her pliant body draped over one shoulder as he headed to the bed and tossed her onto it.

The sublime drug of her release was nowhere near dissipated when he plucked a condom from the bedside drawer and catching both her hands in his, urged her to draw it over his engorged cock.

Her senses reawakened to eager life as she watched his head drop back, a starkly sexy grimace catch on his face as she moved her hands over him.

'Enough, *litla norn*,' he bit out on her third stroke.

A saucy smile curved her lips, delight still dancing within her. 'I'm a little witch? Does that make you a sorcerer?' she mused.

Dragging her exploring hands above her head, Valenti

braced himself above her, then took her tempting lips in another kiss, his obvious hunger feeding hers. When the need for air drove them apart, he kissed his way to her throat, then bit her earlobe. At her gasp, he laughed, low and deep.

'A sorcerer? I thought I was your sugar daddy?' he whispered gutturally.

Her louder gasp ended in a scream when he surged inside her without warning, filling her so completely, Lotte feared she would never be whole without him again.

Valenti's possession was unreserved and impenitent, his mastery complete.

'Have I achieved the impossible and rendered you speechless?' he taunted thickly as he dragged his tongue across one peaked nipple, then wrapped his lips around the aching bud, drawing another gasping cry from her.

Her defiance had withered away beneath the onslaught of incoherent pleasure, her only response as he increased the tempo of his thrusts, to scream her pleasure as she tumbled into bliss once more.

It would've been easy to place blame at her feet for his current predicament. But Valenti was used to standing tall and firm in the face of accountability.

So yes, he was equally, if not fully responsible for this. He'd clearly seen the red line stamped with the 'do not cross' sign. And he'd arrogantly and wilfully stepped over it.

Accepted, his reward, this *feast* of pleasure he'd thought would be commonplace but was turning out to be breathtakingly transformative, would rank as mostly worth it.

Mostly.

Regret would come, strong and hard, later.

But no army, earthly or celestial, could've dragged him from her in this moment. She was Aphrodite and all the sirens of myth made flesh. And he... *Dios*, he was just a man. Pushed to the brink by an intoxicating mix of defiance, helplessness, innocence and sass, yes. But still, just a red-blooded man.

Her nails digging into his shoulders shoved him back into the transcendental moment.

Her slick sex tightening around him gave him the answer to his risqué teasing. The same one he'd felt when she'd said those words. He had indulged in his share of kinks. None had struck a filthy vein of desire quite like her innocent lips spouting sugar daddies.

Valenti was certain in some dark corner of the cosmos deities amused themselves with this predicament he was grappling with. What they didn't know was that they wouldn't be laughing for long.

He was a master at problem-solving, after all.

All he needed to do, as he'd intended when he'd brought them into this room, was to work this madness out of his system. One night, perhaps two. That was all he needed.

It was clear Lotte was crying out for attention. And *sì*, he took the blame for some of that too. Had calculated that with her safety in place, a young woman like her needed little else. Clearly he'd been wrong. She'd needed answers long denied her. Closure he'd neglected to give. And physical attention too.

So he would give her the attention she so desperately sought. Wholeheartedly. Relentlessly. Until they both got their fill.

And when his men met his ultimatum and located her elusive stalker, he would remove himself from her life, as was the wisest plan.

Three years would pass in the blink of an eye.

Then he would *finally* be free of duty and oath.

Completely satisfied with that plan, Valenti deepened his focus on the magnificent creature beneath him. The woman who fired up his blood like he'd never known. A conundrum he was sure he was well on his way to eviscerating.

'Come for me one more time,' he commanded thickly.

He wanted her spent. Wanted her mercilessly slavish to pleasure so he could revel in this unholy gift he'd claimed for them both. But yes, he also wanted her mindless so *he* could analyse his alien behaviour. So he could slot reason back into place.

Because Valenti Domene, the careful strategist had fled the building in the face of her persistent demands and emotional challenges. And *santo cielo*, he needed reprieve.

'I… I can't…' she gasped, even as her hips rolled, chasing his, her unfettered and enthusiastic response tearing chunks through his reason.

'You can and you will. Now, *preciosa*.'

'Oh…oh!'

He watched her head thrash on his pillow, her scent and pleasure easily fracturing the last snatches of his control.

'Valenti!'

His name tumbling from her lips finally broke him. With a roar torn from a soul-deep place he barely recognised, he joined her in the most sublime shattering, letting go and feeling his lack of control soaring wild and free for the first time in what felt like a lifetime.

For mindless minutes, he wasn't weighed down with guilt. Or duty. Or expectations of toeing the royal line. Staying in the box his father had placed him in *for the sake of the family*.

He could pretend, in this blinding white space where nothing existed but rapture, that he hadn't broken several promises and dived headlong into the forbidden territory.

But…even as the tingles drained away, even as her soft gasps continued to echo through his room like the most beautiful strains of his favourite piano concerto, Valenti was being dragged back down to earth and to reality.

To the deeply disquieting thing he'd done.

He'd slept with Helga's baby sister.

His ward.

'As much as it feels great to be in this position, I can feel the weight of your regret pressing down on me. And it's not a comfortable one, Your Highness.'

A different shock shuttled through him at the soft, solemn words.

She had an ability very few people had—to disarm him with a handful of words. And as he was discovering, most of them were sharpened with truth-poisoned arrows that relentlessly landed with bull's-eye accuracy.

CHAPTER EIGHT

VALENTI SHIFTED HIS weight onto his elbows and looked down into her deep blue eyes. Sex-drugged, beautiful and turning increasingly wary.

He needed to move, put some much-needed distance between a bad decision destined to worsen if he remained where he was.

Yet, he couldn't move. Or look away.

So he saw exactly when wariness morphed into hurt. And the chafing he had experienced on the helicopter and so many times since expanded in his chest. He knew it was even more imperative that he rise, leave the bed, draw a definitive line under this catastrophe. But the longer he looked into her eyes, the more impossible that decision grew.

With a growl torn from deep inside him, he rolled sideways, his arms dragging her against his body, almost of their own volition. He was merely caught in the throes, he decided. Hindsight was a bitch with infuriating twenty-twenty vision, yes, but the world hadn't quite ended. Yet.

Besides, where the hell was he going to go?

Locking himself in his office was as futile as taking a walk outside. He would need to return to her, eventually. Until this nuisance was taken care of, straying far and leaving her vulnerable was unacceptable.

Is that what you're telling yourself?

He clenched his teeth against the mocking voice as his

breath caught when the hand splayed on his chest hesitantly slid up to the side of his neck. Then higher to cup his jaw. He kissed the inside of her wrist before he could stop himself, revelled in her shaky breath.

'How's that working out for you?' At his frown, her mouth curved in a sultry smile, though her eyes remained wary.

'What?'

'Shifting the weight sideways?' she clarified.

Bewildered laughter barked out of him. *'Dios mío*, do you ever stop?'

Her smile lost a layer of brilliance. 'I'd rather see what's coming than be caught unawares. Tell me you're not plotting ways to tell me you regret what just happened.'

The statement was softly spoken but still packed a punch of challenge.

A significant part of him was disarmed with admiration for her courage. Very few women in his past liaisons, if any, would be bold enough to risk jeopardising their position this soon after sex. They would be simpering and escalating their seduction techniques to entice him into longevity.

But she was not just anyone. *She was his ward.* Wasn't that what made this so catastrophic?

Basta!

He ought to see the bright side of this. She was making it easier for him. She already knew this was a mistake and was pre-empting a way to mitigate the disaster for both of them. Why not meet her halfway, put the barriers back in place? Go back to the way things were a week ago?

He hated the way his chest tightened, and his gut clenched at the very thought. It was just the aggravation of having to remain another couple of days in this charged atmosphere they'd existed in so far.

The voice returned to taunt him. Valenti pushed it far away in favour of a better solution to this dilemma.

Surely it was better to extend that truce to the bedroom as well? Keeping Lotte content enough in the cabin would ease his own peace of mind.

He had time, he decided, his senses easing a fraction as her fingers continued to caress his neck. And when the rest of his body followed into that curiously sated state, he allowed the reasoning to take root.

That state screeched to a disgruntled halt when she abruptly moved away, rising to sit on the side of the bed.

'Where the hell do you think you're going?'

She shot him a glance over her shoulder, her eyes a fraction darker. 'Making this easier for you. Isn't that what you want? Some distance?' she muttered.

Unease whistled through him at how accurately she read him. 'I would be exceedingly grateful if you would stop assuming you know what I want,' he replied anyway because no, he wasn't one to admit dismay easily.

Her snort was as unladylike as it was adorable. And he found himself moving once more, pulled by an invisible string that propelled him to her. Sliding his arm around her waist before she could rise, he caged her between his thighs, pulled her back to his front, stifling a groan at the feel of her soft, silky, endlessly enticing skin against him. He'd never fallen prey to any form of addiction, but in this moment, he got why it was a thing to be feared.

Triumph whistled through him as she settled against him, her head coming to rest on his shoulder. But she only stayed for a moment before she started to strain against him.

'Stay.' The prompt was torn from somewhere unnervingly needy inside him.

She startled at the growled command, her eyes once more finding his. 'Why should I?'

He could've gone for the lascivious truth, which was that contrary to what he'd believed, even hoped, he was nowhere done with her as his keenly stirring body was screaming at him.

Instead, he found himself stating a far more exposing alternative. 'Because it's snowing heavily outside, and the forecast is for more of the same for the next twenty-four hours. So your next walk is out of the question.' He leaned closer, caught her lobe between his teeth and was rewarded with a sexy little whimper. 'You get to ask your next question in the comfort of this bed. After I've made us some breakfast.'

She shifted, the better to search his face, but in the process wriggling her delectable ass against his growing erection that had him catching another groan before it slipped free. 'Really?'

He nodded. Then, with his wandering hands sliding up to cup her succulent breasts, he dragged his teeth down the smooth line of her neck. 'Perhaps not in that exact order.'

'What do you mean?' she asked breathlessly.

'I will give you three guesses, *querida*,' he said.

With an entirely too arousing moan, she twisted in his arms and slid hers around his neck.

Two days. Forty-eight short hours to get this malaise out of his system.

Then he could get back to his perfected cycle of duty, responsibility and ensuring that permanent stone of guilt lodged in his chest would never be experienced by anyone he held dear.

Her insistence on helping with breakfast earned Lotte a narrow-eyed, growly Valenti, whose breath caught when she giggled and danced out of his reach only to stumble as her legs threatened to give way on rising from the bed.

'*Calma*,' he rasped as he caught her. 'There's no need to be up. You need to rest.'

'All I've done since we got here is rest,' she protested.

That earned her an openly sceptical raised eyebrow, his silver eyes deriding. 'My memory begs to differ.'

She couldn't help her smile turning full bloom. 'Performing mental gymnastics with you is not as challenging as you think. Quite the opposite in fact.'

'I'm glad to see you thrive on it, whilst giving me grey hairs.'

'You mean more grey hairs? I'm sure I can find a few if I search hard enough,' she teased, flicking her fingers through the inky black wavy strands that showed not a single grey.

His growl intensified as he reached for her. She darted out of the room, only to remember she was buck naked. But when she turned, he was filling the whole doorway, hands on hips, an open dare in his face.

She knew returning to the room would mean her not leaving at all, so she shrugged again and sprinted down the stairs.

He followed a handful of seconds later, wearing only his jeans. And it was her turn to have her breath strangle in her lungs as she stumbled backwards towards the kitchen.

'Two can play at that game, *querida*. Remember that,' he advised as he walked past her, trailing his fingers across her collarbone before his hand dropped to cup one breast in an openly hungry caress that made her rethink her decision to start tussling with a maestro.

Thankfully, he took mercy, plucked an apron from a nearby hook and slung it over her head, securing it primly at her waist. Then with a brisk smack of her bottom that had her yelping in delight, he went to the fridge and started pulling out ingredients.

They ate, not at the small dining table, but in front of a roaring fire, with Lotte planted firmly in his lap as he fed her bites from their overflowing plates.

She fought against the swell of contentment that insisted

this was the happiest moment in her life. That, as impossible as it was, she wanted time to stop this very instant so she could savour it for as long as possible before the loneliness that dogged her life inevitably took over once more.

She knew she should be thankful for the stark reminder of what he'd said to her in the bedroom before he'd taken thorough possession of her. This tryst would only be accommodated under his remote cabin roof; the moment they returned to the outside world, he would revert to the near stranger and strict guardian role he preferred.

This was simply a moment in time.

But not even the impending weight of it could dispel the need to obey when he stopped her from rising after their breakfast to take the dishes to the kitchen, instead coaxing her to lay her head against his chest as he wrapped one arm around her back and the other over her hip, his thumbs gliding seductively over her skin, easing her into a deep comfort and serenity she'd never known.

For the first time in her life, Lotte felt no inclination to fill the silence, to challenge this man who had ruled her life from afar for so long.

And when drowsiness overcame her, she didn't protest when he rose with her in his arms and climbed the stairs, smiling when he tugged the apron from around her before tossing it away.

'Are you sore?' he rasped as he kissed his way up her shoulder and jaw to the corner of her mouth.

Lotte wanted to be sophisticated and worldly, but Valenti's possession was very much evident in the tangible ache of her inner muscles. Biting her lip, she nodded, unable to stop the heat suffusing her face. 'A little,' she confessed.

The bite of disappointment across his expression pulled at her heart, and she almost protested when he slid into the space beside her and gathered her up in his arms. 'Sleep then,' he encouraged roughly. 'Or I won't be held responsible for succumbing to my little witch.'

Just a silly little fantasy, she reminded herself sternly.

Still, she slid her arm around his waist, and when he firmly drew up her leg to drape over his thick thighs, she didn't complain. She merely sighed and let sleep take her.

She woke three hours later, alone, her heart hammering with alarm for vital seconds with the dismaying thought that she'd dreamed everything. But the indentation in the pillow and the discarded clothes verified what had happened.

She'd had sex with Valenti. Her guardian. And whilst that illicit thrill of the forbidden stole through her, Lotte admitted to herself that she didn't want it to be over. Not when they left the cabin.

Could she…

Her thoughts stumbled to a halt when Valenti filled the doorway.

He wore a black robe loosely tied around his waist and his silver eyes zeroed in on her with a fierceness that made her heart lurch. 'You're up.'

She nodded, her heart still racing as he prowled over, angled her head and slanted his mouth over hers. For long endless minutes he dominated her every sense, dragging out a helpless moan when he finally pulled away and perched on the side of the bed.

'Any news?' she attempted, even though she was secretly content to live in oblivion just a little longer.

His lips tightened for a moment before he shook his head. 'He is proving elusive,' he replied tautly, then his expression hardened into a mask so ruthlessly determined she was glad she wasn't on the receiving end of his pursuit. 'But not for long.'

Catching her shiver at that, his expression eased a fraction and he held out his hand. 'Come.'

'Where?'

The corner of his mouth twitched. 'Shower first, then whatever you want,' he offered huskily.

What she wanted, most of all was to dive into his arms, but a shower was a close second. Especially when they entered the bathroom and he immediately shrugged off his robe. Her senses leaping at the sight of his magnificent form, she could barely concentrate enough to walk into the large cubicle he filled the moment he entered.

Lotte wanted to hate him for being mildly amused at her awkwardness, but he mitigated that too when he lazily squirted soap into his hands, rubbed them together, then proceeded to wash her from head to toe.

The moans she tried to stifle earlier ripped free, then seemingly set loose, they relentlessly poured from her as his expert hands wreaked magic over her skin. At her silent demand to return the favour, he nodded, his gaze devouring her every move as she attempted to reciprocate, faltering embarrassingly when she reached his groin.

But, seeing her effect on him, Lotte grew bolder, wrapping her hand around his sizeable girth and stroking a scant few times before with an animal snarl and nostrils flaring, he captured her hands.

'*Dios*. Enough.'

At her soft protest, his eyes narrowed. 'Do you feel rested enough to take me again?'

Heat rushing faster up her face, she bit her lip and nodded.

Valenti stepped out for a minute, then returned, condom in hand. Silently handed it to her.

She eagerly tore it free, her hands shaking.

The second she sheathed him, he growled, 'Turn around.' Strong hands captured hers, lifted them high above her head to pin on the shower wall. 'Stay,' he ordered.

It was the third time he'd issued that command in this

cabin, and her senses now responded with an eagerness she couldn't deny. When one thick thigh slotted between hers to widen her stance, every nerve in her body shivered in excitement.

Then he was breaching her entrance, surging hard and so deliciously powerfully inside her that she cried out in delight.

'You are so beautiful, *mi amante*. So magnificently tight. *Fuck*, you wreck me.'

Robbed of breath and sense, she could only squeeze her eyes shut, sob her desire as he took her to the very edge of the world. His thick groans triggered her release, pleasure unbelievably more intense than before rocking her very foundations, rendering her boneless once more as he roared his release, then scooped her up in his arms.

Once again, the need to speak became unnecessary, their movements languid as he dried her gently and they went to the bedroom. She dressed in a soft grey lounge set, he in a dark T-shirt and pair of joggers minus underwear that almost made her swallow her tongue when her gaze became riveted to the muscled V-cut of his pelvis.

'If you want to leave this room and make a stab at having a normal day, you'll stop looking at me like that,' he advised with a wicked gleam in his silver eyes.

Her face, once again tomato red, drew husky laughter from him. She revelled in the sound she hadn't heard before and somehow doubted she would once they left this place.

The reminder snagged at her euphoria, dimming it after they'd gone downstairs to his office, and she'd ensconced herself with a book in the armchair beneath the window across from his desk. She willed herself not to stare as he slipped into dual roles of prince and security expert, easily switching between Cartanian, English and French with consummate ease.

Astonishingly, after ten minutes, the dark hypnotic drone

of his voice settled her racing heart, allowing her to delve deeper into her book.

Only to look up a short while later to find him staring at her. What he held in his hand was what drew her attention.

The camera he'd presented her with yesterday. The one they'd used to shoot content she'd totally forgotten about after their return.

She set the book aside, glad for the chance to do something else besides gawp at him. Glancing outside, she saw that the snow wasn't falling as ferociously as before. 'I think it's a good time to grab some pictures from the porch, maybe shoot a short video before the weather worsens again.'

To her surprise, he shook his head. 'Not just yet. Maybe later.'

Her eyes widened. 'Why not?'

For a tight stretch he remained silent, but a peculiar expression darted across his face. Then he bit out, 'You still look... well sated. I'm reluctant to share that with anyone else. I'll have to insist on being the only one who sees you like this.'

Her whole body flamed this time, especially when he pinned her with a stare so ravenous she lost the rhythm of her breathing. Then she turned even more frazzled when he picked up the camera. 'May I?' he asked.

Her head moved almost of its own volition even though she wasn't entirely sure what she was agreeing to.

He rose fluidly to his feet, and rounded his desk to perch on the edge. Forcing herself not to drool at his raw masculinity, *to just breathe dammit*, she watched his arm rise, the lens aimed at her.

'What are you doing?' she muttered as he clicked rapidly.

He stopped to flick through the photos he'd taken, his gaze glinting with dark appreciation. 'These are not for public consumption,' he said firmly, a far too possessive note in his voice that sent further fireworks through her bloodstream.

Rapt, she watched him raise the camera once more, prowling close with each half a dozen or so images he captured, until he dropped into a crouch before her.

Lotte knew she was exposing far more than was wise as she stared into the black lens, but she couldn't seem to gather the strength to reinforce her armour. Her attention sharpened on him when he took several up close, then muttered under his breath in Cartanian.

'What did you say?' she asked far too breathlessly.

He exhaled heavily, then shook his head. 'Never mind.'

She let it go, understanding the undercurrent of sentiments charging between them. 'Let's go make lunch. I'll film my segment after that.'

He nodded. Setting the camera aside, he braced his hands on the arms of her chair, bent low until his mouth brushed her ear. 'Then I put the rightful look back on your face.'

Lunch was a simple but sumptuous meal of prime beef sandwich and salad, washed down with a small glass of fruity Chianti.

Once they'd polished that off, she fetched the camera, and they stepped onto the snow-laden porch. The brisk air was refreshing. Lotte, stingingly aware as Valenti leaned against the wooden wall watching, extolled the virtues of her surroundings, then ended with her usual affirmation. After taking a few shots of the landscape, they returned indoors.

She watched him place the camera on the nearby shelf. Then as he was heading back to her, she cleared her throat and asked the question that, through a combination of outright denial, active dissuasion and consideration for others' grief, she'd waited a decade to be answered.

'What happened the day my sister died?'

He froze, the cold, stony façade she knew far too well sliding into place between one breath and the next. But in the split second before it descended and slammed into place, she caught a glimpse of desolation so bleak, it shredded her insides.

'Why do you want to put yourself through that, *litla*?' he asked an eternity later.

She exhaled shakily. 'Why does anyone search for answers to painful questions? To seek enlightenment and sometimes, to search for closure.'

He hadn't taken a visible breath since she posed her question, and he remained statue still at her answer. 'A third option is to let the past be. Not to rake over painful ground.' A ripple travelled through his set jaw when he finally moved, approached where she'd perched on the sofa, and crouched before her, determination to deny blazing through his eyes. 'Don't do this to yourself, Lotte. Your sister is gone—'

'I'm well aware of that,' she interjected firmly, a shroud of sadness and loss wrapping around her heart. For the sister she'd known far too fleetingly and in an almost absentee manner, even though Helga had stepped into the role of parent after theirs had perished in an avalanche when Lotte was only nine. 'And I disagree that ignorance is bliss in this case. It's far from it. And since Gunnar refuses to talk about it and you're the only other one who knows the true facts…' She trailed to a stop when his face set tighter, his whole body bristling with repudiation.

She held her breath, expecting him to stalk away to the window or even to his office. Hurt and disappointment tore through when he rose from his crouch, but to her surprise, he took the seat beside her, his focus pinned to the flames dancing in the hearth as he rested his elbows on his knees.

He exhaled, but his tension only continued to build. 'You know my father is unwell, *si*?'

She nodded.

'His health condition wasn't as serious back then, but I

think he knew she was a skilled surgeon to keep around.' A smile ghosted over his mouth but dissolved under solemn memory. 'We became friends. And when my father learned she was heading into dangerous territory for a humanitarian assignment, he asked me to accompany her, ensure her safety.' His jaw clenched. 'Sending a leading surgeon into a volatile zone, regardless of the reasoning behind it was never a good starting point. No matter the assurances anyone could provide,' he stated with a harsh edge to his voice.

Lotte nodded but remained silent. She'd clipped and kept every article she could find about her famous big sister, the ultra-talented cardiothoracic residents who broke all boundaries and put Reykland on the map. She'd been the envy of thousands in her field and several more grateful patients worldwide who'd benefited from her ingenuity.

'Why did she insist? I'm assuming she's the one who insisted on going?'

Valenti sent her a wry look before returning his gaze to the fire. 'Because intransigence runs in the family,' he delivered coolly, despite the raging storm beneath his tone. 'I was left in no doubt that whether I was on board or not, she would do as she pleased.'

A sharper austerity masked his face and to her surprise, he turned away for several seconds before he exhaled again. Had she not witnessed it, Lotte wouldn't have believed Prince Valenti Domene would ever need a moment to collect himself.

'How did you two meet in the first place?' she prodded in a hushed tone, partly because she didn't want her forthrightness to halt the flow of information he seemed staggeringly inclined to grant her. Partly because she would've been wholly insensitive to ignore the gravity of the subject matter.

One even her brother point-blank refused to discuss. Leaving her no choice but to push for it with Valenti.

'We first met in Cartana when she visited as part of a

medical delegation invited by my father, I suspect because he was showing early signs of the condition he has now.'

She'd never met the old King or even Azar, Valenti's older brother and the new King, his determination to keep her apart from her true family an act that still upset her more than she was willing to admit. It was partly why she'd presented herself at the Palacio Domene on her nineteenth birthday, only to be turned away in callous rejection.

She'd thought she'd learned her lesson then. Apparently not, because here she was prying open subjects that should be left alone.

But she was my sister, she insisted to herself. *I have the right.*

She refocused when he nodded abruptly. 'We discovered recently that he's been battling heart disease but chose to keep that to himself.'

'How bad it is?' she whispered.

Another tightening of his features. 'Bad,' he bit out without elaborating.

She chose not to press. Not when her insides still churned at the original subject.

Helga would be the same age as Valenti. Had the old King been attempting a matchmaking? In her weak moments, Lotte had trawled the internet for news of Valenti. Had seen the kind of women the Prince dated with stomach-churning dismay she would admit to no one.

Although his liaisons weren't numerous like his playboy twin brother, Valenti more than held his own on the dating scene. Stunning, sophisticated women like her sister, all with reams of accomplishments and accolades to their names. Each one had felt like a tiny taunt to Lotte, a reminder of her youth, inexperience and nihility.

The vice clenched tighter around her chest when she admitted Valenti and Helga were a perfect match. That they would most likely be together now if—

'So your father was the one who asked you to guard her?' she asked, interrupting her own frantic thoughts.

Another ghost of a smile. 'He more or less told me to drop everything to ensure Helga and her group were kept safe.'

Lotte's eyes widened at the clear bite of bitterness in his voice. Had he not wanted to?

As if he heard her, Valenti speared her with a pithy look. 'It didn't matter what I desired. What the King wanted the King got.'

'What does that mean?'

He started, as if surprised he'd veered off the subject with his telling remark. Then his lips tightened while silence reigned.

'You said you were friends…were you lovers, too?' she blurted when it became clear her other question wouldn't be answered.

His eyes narrowed on her, dark and piercing. More than a little chiding. Whether it was because he felt she had no right to ask that or that it shouldn't have featured in his retelling—true enough, even though she hadn't been able to stop herself from knowing—she couldn't tell. But she waited, breath held as he took his sweet time to answer.

'No.'

Lotte hated herself for the heady relief that swelled through her heart. And the need to prod at that scab. 'Why not?'

He inhaled sharply, his eyes narrowing in cold irritation. But beneath it she spotted another emotion she couldn't decipher. 'Does it matter?'

Yes. She ignored her screaming senses and settled for a shrug. 'You cared for her. Enough to…' *Spend endless years closed up in an emotional fortress no one else can touch because you're pining after her and possible could-have-beens.*

Enough to reject anyone who remotely reminds you of her.
Enough to reject me.

She didn't have the grit to pose those exposing statements, so she clamped her lips shut. Waited.

'Yes, I cared for her. Her safety was my priority. And there are a dozen things I should have done differently to ensure her safety. I let her talk me out of each one.'

Her heart lurched wildly at the black desolation in his voice.

'Why? Pardon my scepticism but you don't seem like the type to be talked into or out of anything you decide. I mean, Exhibit A…' She waved an expressive hand around the room, then at herself. 'We're here because you wouldn't be swayed into any other alternative. No matter how much I tried.' *Or did he find her easy to control because she wasn't Helga?*

Her heart lurched and canted disconsolately as tension whitened his lips.

'Some lessons are learned too late. Oftentimes with harrowing consequences.'

Unbidden, she reached out a hand. 'Valenti—' Then pulled it back sharply when he jerked away from her. Rejecting her once more.

Dear God, when was she going to learn?

She fisted her hand in her lap, curling her hurt tighter so it wouldn't bloom into larger life, humiliating her more than she was already.

An expression flashed through his eyes as he glanced at her, perhaps a hint of regret. But it was gone a moment later, smothered by bleak disregard.

'Finish it, please,' she rasped. She didn't regret the question but neither did she want to dwell in the distress churning through her or the devastation of loss he was doing a poor job of hiding. If she'd needed proof of what her sister meant to Valenti, it was now undeniable.

And no, she didn't want to contemplate whether it was a forever thing and if so, how she would cope with that knowledge. How it would factor, *if at all*. That was a conundrum for another day. And perhaps if she managed to rake through every crumb of this subject to find the closure she insisted she needed, she might find it didn't factor at all.

The mocking voice taunting her to *dream on* she firmly pushed to the back of her mind, just as she ignored her dismay as he opened his mouth.

'The country wasn't known for being unsafe. There'd been a spate of kidnappings and random violence in the area, but it'd died down a few years before Helga's group decided to go. Travellers were warned to be cautious but not prohibited from visiting. That was all she needed to insist the hospital give its approval. And she was right, for the most part. For the better part of the mission, it was incident free.' His fists bunched for a handful of seconds before he reasserted control. 'Until the last night.

'We were headed to the airport when she got the call that one of the patients she'd treated had taken a turn for the worse. I sent the rest of her group and most of my security team ahead and returned to the hospital with her.'

Lotte's throat tightened, her mouth dry as her heart dropped to her toes.

'It happened fast.' A harsh, arid laugh punched out of him. 'The irony was that she was putting on the bullet-proof vest I insisted she wear when the first shot came at us.'

Lotte's gaze darted to his shoulder. To the puckered mark she'd suspected was a bullet wound but had hesitated to ask about.

'It went through me and hit her,' he answered her silent question. Then eyes as turbulent as a lightning storm met hers. 'She knew instantly that it was fatal, and she didn't waste time. She wanted to spell out her wishes for you before she…'

'Wh-what did she say?' she whispered.

Eyes gone haggard lingered on her, but Lotte suspected he wasn't really seeing her. That he was firmly in the past with a ghost that very much ruled his present.

'She regretted she wouldn't be around to see you grow up. Regretted that she hadn't spent more time with you. But above all she wanted to ensure you were taken care of. She requested I be your guardian, and I vowed to honour it.'

Her head bowed at the finality of it all, hot tears spilling down her cheeks. Her breath hiccupped when she felt the firm grasp of his hand on her shoulder. 'I wish I'd known her better too. Then maybe she would've realised something.' The words were barely audible, but he heard them.

His hand slid to her chin, raising it so she met his eyes. 'What?'

'That I may not have known her as well as I wanted but she was my hero. And that while I appreciate her making you promise, I would've been strong enough to survive without it.'

His grip tightened infinitesimally, his eyes narrowing. 'Does it really chafe that much to have me in your corner, *litla*?' he rumbled, a trace of something that sounded like mild upset in his voice.

She swallowed, unwilling to admit what she truly felt. That she wanted so much more than for him to see her as his weak, helpless *litla*. But as much as she tried to keep the emotion suppressed, it bubbled free. 'Not if it means you seeing me as you do.'

The words ricocheted around the room, both of them breathing hard as their gazes pierced into one another.

'I think the last twenty-four hours has proven conclusively that that is not the case.'

Despite her face flaming at the reminder of their incandescent lust, she kept his gaze. 'Has it?' she challenged softly. 'What changes when we leave here?' she asked boldly.

His eyes continued to drill holes in her even as his expression shuttered. As his solemn stillness slid back into place. 'Lotte…'

'Exactly,' she echoed softly, then pulled back. That he let her go to prowl back to the window said everything she wanted to know. Or perhaps, didn't.

She rose, bunching her fingers into fists when they twitched. 'Thank you for telling me. I know it wasn't easy for you.'

He didn't turn around or acknowledge the words. But his shoulders moved as he inhaled. Exhaled.

She hated the emotions that had nothing do with her sister or the memories she'd unearthed storming within her.

Snatching the camera, she walked calmly up the stairs, absolutely not admitting she was fleeing the horrific realisation that her emotions were very much on the line where Valenti Domene was concerned. And if anything, she was getting more entrenched in a place she didn't want to be.

CHAPTER NINE

THERE WAS A reason Valenti much preferred to live a life free of excessive emotion. A reason the grounding routine of unwavering duty to family and the Cartana throne was all he accommodated these days.

His brothers knew and accepted—mostly without complaint—the tight boundaries of what affection he could express. The crown gratefully accepted his allegiance to serve and protect with everything he had.

No one expected more from him and didn't dare to ask because what he'd provided far exceeded anyone's highest level of excellence.

So sitting in his office, feeling like he was wearing his every nerve inside out while his usually sedated heart beat overtime was highly inconvenient and most infuriating.

For the life of him, Valenti couldn't find the off switch and with each moment that passed without locating it, his senses roared his distress until he wanted to flip his desk upside down just to experience something other than the chaos rioting inside him.

He blamed her. He blamed himself.

He invited this…this *fiasco*. Welcomed it with open arms when usually a cold, hard no had seen any curiosity killed dead, and those who dared broach it seen off with their tail between their legs. Hell, even his father and brothers had only received an abbreviated version just the once and never since.

Hours had passed since she thanked him for exposing his greatest regret and failure to daylight and scrutiny. Since she shed tears then told him she wished he hadn't bothered to look out for her. Since she'd retreated upstairs.

Valenti expected she would regroup soon enough to lay blame where it rightly deserved to be. At his feet.

Even now, the roaring dimmed intermittently so he could listen out for her. Almost willing her to return to challenge and rile him. To scream at him for not protecting the sister she'd loved.

Is that the only reason you want her back in your presence?

He gritted his teeth and stabbed at his keyboard. There were clients clamouring for his attention. Even a message from his father via the old King's personal aide, seeking an update on the situation. The last line enquiring when Valenti would return to Cartana drew a fresh vein of bitterness.

He'd meticulously arranged it so he would never be personally needed in any situation except where his father and brothers were concerned. He'd rigorously trained every operative in his organisation, selected only the best of the best so he remained emotionally aloof and objective.

With each day, month and year of success, his father had heaped praises on his head for choosing family above all else. Entirely oblivious or not caring that the hole that remained in his heart from never fully realising his true desires had never come within a whisker of being filled.

Did the old man even realise that Valenti had often wondered, especially recently since his father took a steep decline, if he *had* been a doctor, if he hadn't been split-focused between looking forward with duty and looking back on his dreams, whether he could have found a solution where others had failed?

Si, an arrogant thought, perhaps, but he was a Domene.

Conceit flowed through his veins faster than blood. And just as he knew his own name and the depth of his talent and dedication, he knew he would've excelled as a surgeon too, had he been free to choose.

He surged to his feet, the roiling having achieved its purpose and driven him partly mad. When the view of pristine snow mocked him, he growled.

Enough. It'd stopped snowing and—

The noise from upstairs jerked his head up. He was moving towards the door before he'd clocked the movement of his feet.

She was at the top of the stairs when he emerged. Her hair was tousled, her face soft and drowsy. Valenti searched her features for signs of further distress and tears. Then her eyes for the blame he fully expected. He found none but the constriction in his chest didn't ease.

'*Halló*,' she muttered, and he wondered if she realised she'd spoken in her language.

'Are you okay?' he responded in the same tongue.

She hesitated for a moment, then nodded. '*Jà.*'

It wasn't relief pouring through him. He was merely doing what needed to be done with the circumstances they were faced with. He was practical if nothing else, after all, wasn't he? He held out his hand. '*Komdu.*'

Again she hesitated, then slowly made her way down, her eyes searching his. 'Is the truce still in place?' she asked when she reached the final step. 'Because I'm not in the mood for anything else.'

'Indeed it is. And we can suspend the question-and-answer part of it too if you wish.'

Distress flashed in her eyes gone too quickly for him to decipher what exactly she found objectionable. Then she was nodding, her gaze drifting past his to the window. 'I noticed it's stopped snowing.'

He nodded. 'Which is why I have a surprise you might find to your liking,' he said, the idea flashing into being, then solidifying when he didn't fight it.

Her eyes snapped back to his, brightening in a way that made air trap in his lungs. 'Really?'

'*Sí*. We'll head out after lunch. Okay?'

'Sure.'

He'd found the need to constantly feed her disconcerting at first, then like everything else with her in this unsettling atmosphere they hadn't been able to avoid, he'd given in.

The need hammered through him as he took her hand in his. Her easy acquiescence rattled. Not *him* personally. He just wished her a little more…animated. He took a minute longer than necessary rummaging through the fridge, then throwing a question at her.

That rattling he was sure was dramatic simply because they'd been under this roof for too long intensified when he turned to find her examining him like he was a newly discovered species she couldn't quite work out. 'Lotte?'

She jumped. '*Jà?*'

'I asked you a question. Is pasta okay?' he bit out, attempting to keep his unnerved state under his waning control.

She nodded abruptly. 'Of course. Yes. I was…'

He waited for her to finish. But her plump lips merely pursed before she looked away.

Greatly vexed by the return of the discordant roar that replaced the rattle, he quickly put together their meal and set it down on the table.

Moderately appeased when she polished off the meal, he frowned when she started walking out. 'I'll be ready in ten minutes,' she threw over her shoulder, then paused as if to ask a question before changing her mind.

No, he didn't like this turn of events.

Because this sombre version of Lotte? It wasn't to his liking. At all.

Sombre and stoic were *his* remit, after all.

Which was why he found himself peeling back another layer of himself and taking her to a place he'd never shown anyone else. Suspecting it might raise even more questions. And discovering he would withstand them...if it brought Lotte contentment and peace.

Lotte looked around her, awed at the sight of the deep blue water-filled fissure they'd tracked about a mile from the cabin. The fissure fed a larger fjord at some point, which she guessed was where they were heading.

Valenti hadn't divulged their final destination, but he'd answered her questions about their surroundings. They were still on private land—which he owned for as far as the eye could see.

Her gaze drifted to the rucksack he carried, curious as to its contents but she bit her tongue. She'd had enough upheaval today. Time to give her emotions respite from turbulence. So she asked innocuous questions about geography and topology, until the magical sight dried her words and stopped in her tracks. 'Is that...?'

He stopped next to her, his eyes on her face. 'A hot spring leading to a fjord? Yes.'

There were several such springs in Reykland, but few were this private, this stunning and perfect. The last of the setting sun against the snow dappled the still water in faint golden light, the wisps of steam rising from the naturally hot spring pool surrounded by boulders, mesmeric.

Lotte dragged her gaze from one breathtaking view to the other, of Valenti and the possibility that he'd brought her here to show her something special. To...lift her mood?

She swallowed, suddenly overcome with the very emotions she was fleeing from. Surrendering to the pull of the small body of water she moved towards it, felt him follow. The air grew sultrier with every step and by the time she was a few feet from the lip of the spring, a pang was lighting through her. 'I would've brought my swimsuit if I'd—'

Valenti moved, drawing out an item from his rucksack. 'I took the liberty of anticipating that need,' he said.

Her eyes widened. One of the three bikinis she'd packed on a wild whim dangled from his fingers. That awe warring with her surging emotions, she took it from him. Then glanced around. She may have taken more bold steps these past few days than she had in her entire life, but she wasn't quite ready to step into exhibitionist mode.

'There's no one around. I've made quite sure of that,' Valenti said, a tight edge in his voice that said he'd driven that command home quite thoroughly.

Her fingers tightening around her bikini, gulping when Valenti set the rucksack down and started to unzip his insulated coat. Next, he tugged off his sweater and the T-shirt he wore underneath. At the sight of his bare, hard-packed chest, her fingers convulsed around the scrap of Lycra.

Then her face flamed when he raised an eyebrow at her avid stare at his fingers on his belt. She busied herself taking off her things. Realising she had to completely undress before slipping on her bikini, she flushed.

Valenti of course, had stripped completely naked, his expression showing not a single ounce of self-consciousness. Lotte reminded herself of what had happened this morning and yesterday. How he'd seemed enthralled with her body. The confidence boost helped, warming her fingers and galvanising her into shedding her clothes faster.

And when that same expression returned, spikier, lustier than before, she fought to contain the thrill of it. The warm air coming off the hot spring duelling with the cooler air at her back, making her nipples pucker as she slotted the bikini top into place.

Valenti was waiting, half submerged in the water when she was finished. Silently, he held out his hand. She took it. And stepped into pure heaven.

The sensation of the water, like warm silk, enveloped her from neck to toe when she went in deeper.

'Oh my God, it feels incredible,' she whispered.

'Hmm.' Valenti didn't let go of her right away but drew her deeper into the pool. 'There's a natural ledge right here. Come.'

She trailed him, watched him perch on the submerged ledge, then her heart missing several beats, let him tug her closer and position her in front of him before drawing her down between his spread thighs.

With their height difference, Valenti's upper chest and shoulders were above the waterline, while she was gloriously submerged up to her neck.

For several minutes, they remained in peaceful silence, the tension slowly draining away. Or it could've been the melting sensation of the naturally heated water permeating her whole being. Whatever it was, she found herself relaxing into the solid column of Valenti's body, a small but deep sigh escaping her when his arms came around her and his lips brushed over the shell of her ear.

Ever-present need pounded through her, but Lotte curiously realised that right in this moment, she preferred to have his arms around her, all the problems held at bay. For as long as she could.

Even the faintest twinge of the lost opportunity to capture this magic place on camera came and went with very little regret.

'I suppose you wish you'd brought the camera?' he rasped, uncannily reading her mind.

She shook her head. 'No, I don't. Some things are worth keeping sacrosanct. This place is one of them.'

'Hmm,' he hummed again but with a deeper octave that made her tilt her head to glance up at him, but she couldn't quite decipher the emotions moving through his eyes, only the ferocity of it.

Her heartbeat revving, she dragged her gaze away, striving for composure and asking the first question she could think of. 'Why did you buy this place?'

Even in the dwindling light, she saw his eyes shadow. A shaft of now familiar dejection spasmed across his face, right before he broke her stare to settle his gaze on the water.

'I needed to get away from everything after the incident. My father…' He grimaced with a head shake. 'He was determined to find ways to "cure" my…what did you call it? My self-imposed Greek tragedy of guilt? Which in his book mostly meant getting back on the horse immediately.' He paused for a heavy beat. 'But I realised it was better for everyone if I removed myself from circulation and civilisation for a while. I was angry, you see. And also it felt especially cruel to see a life that held so much potential cut short. Harder still when…' His lips thinned, physically stopping his words.

'When what?' she pushed gently.

Hard emotion twitched across his face, followed by harsher laughter. 'When that life was similar to what mine could've been.'

'I don't…understand.'

A tic flitted across his jaw, his tension so heightened she expected to see smoke smouldering out of him. 'My ambition before I entered the army was to go into medicine.'

She inhaled sharply. 'You wanted to be a doctor?'

He nodded once. Gravely.

'Who…what happened?'

His lip twisted sardonically. 'A combination of good fortune and bad timing working against me.'

'I don't understand,' she repeated, completely lost. She'd thought she knew everything there was to find readily online about Prince Valenti Domene. And she'd discovered that having information readily available to devour about a certain subject led to a kind of obsession. Nowhere had she learned of Valenti's ambition for medicine. Not when he'd been so wildly successful at the profession he currently held.

And yet, looking at him now, she could easily see him in a white coat, stalking down the pristine corridors of the world's most revered medical institutions, leaving interns and colleagues at once terrified of him and sighing with jealousy over his brilliance.

His chest rose and fell in a heavy exhale. 'My father decreed that all young men should serve a term in the military before they turned twenty-one. The good fortune was that Teo and I were able to build a better relationship with Azar where things had been fraught before through no fault of our own. I think that was my father's ultimate plan. The bad timing was that it shattered my plans for medical school.'

She shook her head. 'Why would it if the service was one term?'

A brief self-deprecating smile without humour withered away beneath the weight of recollection. 'I turned out to be too good at certain…skills in the army. Skills my father and his palace councillors decided would be better honed and utilized to serve the kingdom.'

Mild shock shivered through her. 'So you didn't choose to become a security expert rather than a doctor? Your career was chosen for you?'

A heavy beat passed. 'No I did not. And yes. I was charged with protecting my family and the kingdom. A noble calling as was impressed on me. And generally risk-free…until it wasn't.'

'And then you had to watch Helga—' She winced when a wave of bleakness swept over his face. Had they been in the cabin, Lotte was sure this was the moment he'd have shoved his hands into his pockets and prowled across the room.

'She was extremely passionate about her career. We would talk for hours about the wonders of medicine. She reawakened my dreams and desires to be a surgeon. So much so… I toyed with rejecting my duty. She was adamant that I pursue it. Hell, she even threatened to take it up with my father. But after her death, after I failed to save her…' He shook his head.

'You thought you would fail at reaching for your dream too?' she rasped.

The tight clench of his jaw said everything.

'Valenti—'

'Save your pity,' he bit out, a flash of formidable power in his eyes. 'It's quite unnecessary. When I'm not being tested by my defiant ward, I find I quite enjoy my position in life. I've made a success of the hand I was dealt.'

She knew his reminder of his guardianship was deliberate. A distancing mechanism. But her insides withered all the same, even as her heart ached for everything he'd lost.

'Well for what it's worth, I don't pity you. I'm just…'

Heartbroken for you.

Wisely, she kept those words to herself, almost relieved when he continued to speak.

'As to your initial question, I came here because I also had a new responsibility, one I was determined not to shirk.'

She glanced up sharply and got pinned by his gaze. 'You mean me?'

He nodded. 'I bought this place because it allowed me to do both.'

Lotte looked around them, seeing the place with new eyes.

Sympathetic eyes. Touched, even. 'You came here to heal...' she whispered.

'And to be near you,' he finished, then jerked a chin at the opposite horizon from the cabin. 'Twenty-three miles that way was your boarding school. That first year, I checked on you twice a week every semester, not because you were in danger. Just because... I thought that was what she would've wanted.' His mouth twisted. 'I was forced to make a sizeable donation to the headmaster for the privilege since it wasn't strictly permitted.'

She gasped as something heavy and intensely soul-shaking moved through her. Lotte felt like she couldn't breathe through the force of it. Through this new lens he was focusing on a subject she'd believed she'd known—and loathed—for years.

To learn the depths of his guardianship... 'Valenti...'

His nostrils flared, probably in rejection of the shaken awe in her voice. She didn't much care. She'd revealed so very much of her emotions to him these endless and exposing days. What was one more?

Especially when that *one more* was a revelation that set all her beliefs, challenges and accusations on their head?

He hadn't entirely forgotten her like she'd alleged. He'd had the chance to go anywhere in the world to heal. Chosen to perform his guardianship from afar from the onset, an easy feat with a man of his wealth and stature. And while he'd done that later, when duty and family had no doubt reclaimed him, he'd chosen this place with her in mind. A decision that couldn't have been easy, with the very earth and sky reminders of the ordeal he'd just been through.

And yet he'd done it.

The pure, almost sacrosanct emotion amplified, consuming her, changing her from the inside out. It awed and terrified in equal measure. And because she had no outlet for it other than through the man directly responsible for it, she spun in the water, bracing her knees on either side of his thighs as she cupped his magnificent jaw in her hands. As she looked into eyes shadowed with memories and ghosts she yearned to help him free but might never succeed.

The thought threatened to rip sobs from her very soul, so she hurried to speak, to distract her heart from the weighty reasons why easing Valenti Domene's pain was so imperative for her. Why this man who'd let her believe she was an afterthought should be her first thought.

But maybe she now, after these trying and revealing days spent under his roof, had some inkling why he'd been avoiding her. Maybe it wasn't because he didn't care. Maybe it was because like everything in his grand life, guilt had assumed unreasonable proportions. If that was the case, wasn't it right that she do her part to alleviate it?

'You are—'

'No. Lotte…' It was part gruff warning, part perplexed.

'Shh,' she whispered. 'Let me speak,' she insisted. Then, taking her risk with the heart pounding its way to exposure on her very sleeve, she leaned in and pressed her mouth against his. 'Thank you,' she whispered against his mouth. 'Thank you.' A kiss to the corner of his mouth made him stiffen. '*Takk fyrir.*'

'Lotte.' A gravel sighing of her name, right before his hands tightened on her waist. On her next pass over his lips, he captured her in a firm lunge. A frantic swipe of his tongue, and upon granting entry, a feverish kiss that set her whole body alight. But just as quickly, he pulled back, silver eyes searching hers. 'You shouldn't be thanking me,' he rejected roughly. 'You should be condemning me for the most grievous failing—'

She stopped him with the simple act of sealing her lips

to his once more, only stopping when a layer of tension left his body. 'You've done enough self-condemning, I think.'

His lips thinned and he remained silent, but the hard, implacable look in his eyes said her words had made little, perhaps no, impact at all. He held firm to the conviction that he could've saved Helga.

Lotte's heart sank a little, but she took solace in him not pushing her away as he would've a handful of days ago. Took solace in reminding herself that even drip-fed water could crack stone...eventually.

She would...*could* be that balm...

And that perhaps like her sister, she would be better off seizing her chance, instead of waiting around for it to fall in her lap.

That empowering thought in her mind, she kissed him once more. Bold. Open-mouthed. Relentless. And when they needed to come up for air, she strung kisses from his mouth to his hard jaw, then to his ear. And like he'd done with her before, she paused and said what she needed to. 'Until now, this place is associated with a deeply harrowing experience. Let me give you different reasons to remember it by?'

He stiffened for a moment, but she kept on peppering kisses, his warm skin as addictive as the need to offer reprieve from the weight he carried.

'I do not need—'

'I beg to differ,' she interjected. 'I'd go as far as to say it's essential.'

Searingly aware of the hard bulge pressed between her thighs, Lotte rolled her hips, gloried in the hiss that shot from his lips. Then she went one better. She reached up with one hand, tugged the strings of her bikini free and felt it fall away from her breasts.

His hands clamped hard on her hips, holding her in place

against his thickening erection. *'Dios mío, me vuelves loco, preciosa.'*

Those were the last words they exchanged for a long time. Long after they'd driven each other to soul-shaking climax once, then again, they were gifted with the most sublime aurora. Purples, blues and greens curtained the sky above their heads, drawing a curiously tearful lump to her throat.

Lotte, aware that she was letting the moments get far too close to her heart, attempted to pull herself together, only to gasp again when she looked down to find Valenti's intense gaze unabashedly fixed on her, his nostrils flaring wide.

'You're beautiful.'

Simple words she'd heard many times.

Yet she experienced the greatest fracture in her armour. And long after he'd wrapped her in a blanket and carried her all the way back to the cabin, his face set in new lines of sombre contemplation, Lotte was beginning to think Prince Valenti Domene had, with those two words, breached her defences permanently.

'Is there something you want to tell me?'

Lotte hinged upright in the armchair and frowned at the deep, quietly furious and perhaps even disappointed voice. Blinking she glanced across the room, forcing her brain to track. But after a long night of lovemaking with Valenti, she'd fallen into heavy sleep upstairs, only to wake when she missed his presence beside her. She'd come down, wolfed down the large breakfast he'd made, then promptly fallen asleep again in the armchair in his office.

Moving now, she flushed at her deliciously protesting muscles, a little dismayed that she'd displayed just how inexperienced she was by falling asleep while he looked so vibrant and rampantly male.

Even if highly vexed. 'Like what?' she drawled, nonchalant even as her heart began thumping for the reason she suspected he'd uncovered.

He held up his sleek tablet. 'I have your latest security report.'

She played for time. 'And?'

His baleful stare said he knew what she was doing. 'After drawing my attention to it I've had a deeper look. You claim to be independently wealthy, which is true enough. But more than half of your earnings is immediately parcelled out to secret accounts in two dozen different countries. What the hell is going on? And before you think to evade or challenge me, know that I can have that information too within the day. You think I don't respect your privacy? Evidently that wasn't the case since your safety was my priority over the contents of your bank account. But that can all change,' he finished with implacable warning.

Perhaps it was some newfound confidence from this precarious circumstance and connection they'd formed. Perhaps it was as basic as sharing her body with him and seeing her effect on him that strengthened the core that seemed so shaky before. He'd accepted compromises whereas as recently as her nineteenth birthday, he'd coldly dismissed her from his presence—a memory that still stung if she was honest.

Whatever it was steeled her spine and lifted her chin, pride pulsing through her. Being overwrought at how Valenti would perceive her deeper goals didn't hold such sway over her anymore. *She* was proud of herself and the work she was doing. 'I started a secret network that helps victims, mostly women in…precarious, often abusive positions.'

He stiffened, several emotions streaming through his eyes before they went ablaze as he leaned forward to rest his palms flat on his desk. 'You what?' he breathed.

'You heard me perfectly well. You can growl and rage at me—'

'I'm not raging.' He paused, jaw clenched, and exhaled audibly. 'You must know that kind of help, however well-meant, brings risk, especially from those abusers?' His voice was low, deep. Curiously shaken.

'I know. That's why I use an encryption system.'

'How did you come by this system?' he asked, his brow a giant thundercloud. 'And how many people know about it?'

She told him about the college roommate who'd written the software for her. 'I trust her. She's the reason I started it in the first place. Her home life wasn't ideal. There was abuse and neglect and fear and...' She shook her head. 'I know what I'm doing and I'm very careful, Valenti.'

He dragged his fingers through his hair, but a layer of tension left his shoulders. 'My people will vet the system thoroughly. And you'll give me the list of everyone you've helped, past and present.'

'If you're about to suggest I stop, the answer is a hard no,' she warned.

His nostrils flared but the look in his eyes was no longer the curious mix of fury and concern. It had morphed into surprise and...respect. Her heart lurched, a lump rising thick and fast to block her throat.

'Come here,' he rasped, still in that peculiar voice.

Chin angled in irritation, she shook her head. 'No. You come here.'

Mouth twitching, he rounded his desk and approached. When he reached her, she pushed him into her armchair, making room for herself between his muscled thighs, a place she was discovering she liked a little too much. His hands braced her lower thighs, then with his gaze pinned on hers, slowly worked their way up her hips to cage her waist.

Electricity zapped between them, hot and powerful. But as always, it was overlaid with intense watchfulness. As if he saw into her very soul.

'I'm not mad, *litla*. Far from it. I'm proud of you,' he stated with thick gravity. 'You will have no opposition from me, once I've established what you're doing is safe,' he added with unyielding firmness.

Shock and surprise dragged a sound from her throat, a hybrid sob-laugh that made his mouth twitch before the sombre expression resumed. 'I thought I'd have to pull out my bigger guns to win this battle,' she teased, then her smile slowly dissolved as his face grew increasingly taut and bleak. 'But if there's no problem, why do you look like your worst dream has come true?'

CHAPTER TEN

HE'D DROPPED THE BALL.

Again.

He'd done the necessary and ensured her day-to-day physical safety with prime bodyguards and fully vetted staff, then retreated without digging deeper. He hadn't factored in her personal or emotional fulfilment or that she might be surrounded by people but yet lonely, which was ironic since he knew that state very well indeed.

Valenti had taken the report on her activities, seen no major red flags, and satisfied himself that she was fine. He'd retreated, stunned by his illicit feelings after her visit to Cartana three years ago, and insulated himself from everything else but her physical safety. And even that had proved lacking…

The horror of failure washed a tsunami of ice through his veins.

'Valenti…'

'I failed you,' he rasped through a throat lined with sharp rocks.

'What? No!'

He released her, jerking back and away as she stumbled to her feet. Touching her, revelling in her achievements, that smile, felt wrong. Undeserved. This too was another emotion he knew well. He'd been stifling the hard truth of it since that first stolen touch, the illicit kiss. That first thrust into her delightful body—

No.

He felt her draw near and clenched his gut, knowing there was no excuse this time. It was time to draw a line under this madness.

He faced her, to find her arms crossed, the beautifully sleep-tousled female who'd seemed sexily confused moments ago, gone.

'Fine. If you believe that you've failed me, then do something about it.'

He raised his eyebrows, unwilling to admit he was perhaps a little apprehensive of the determination on her face. Which should've been laughable for someone with his experience and the types of operations he'd undertaken in the army. And yet… 'What?' he bit out, half relishing the challenge.

'Take me with you when you leave.'

He stiffened, then shook his head.

Clean break. You opened yourself up to friendship, to dreams, and look how it ended. Never again. And especially not with Helga's sister!

Anything else was asking for tormenting temptation and trouble. 'You need more than I can give beyond security and protection, Lotte.' Why the hell did that drive a knife through his ribs?

'Excuse me?' she snapped.

'I'm not well-equipped to provide emotional support. Nor do I wish to.'

Her nostrils fluttered. Her eyes shadowed. But, *santo cielo*, watching her chin rise, to stare him down was something.

'I'm not asking to come hang around you at the palace like some emotional groupie or uber-royalty simp. I've been thinking of what I want to do with my degree. Pick any country, and I'll find people who need help. I already have a long list of charities I want to visit. And I'm assuming you don't plan to stay in this cabin forever? That you hoped the stalker would've been apprehended by now and we would've left already?'

'Correct,' he agreed, his tone deadly.

'Then let's leave anyway. You can make things up to me while going about your own business and assuring yourself I'm fine. Win win win.'

'Or I could grant your other wish, seclude you on my island in the Caribbean or aboard my yacht in South Africa? You can get all the sun you want?'

Where it's one thousand per cent safe.

She waved a dismissive hand, and his insides churned with a peculiar mix of aggravation and anticipation. 'Your window of opportunity has passed on that one I'm afraid. This is my one and only proposal.' She looked around her, taking in the armchair, the bookshelves Ada had apparently stocked with the kind of books Lotte liked without his knowledge. Because deep down, he'd hoped to one day show her this place? To completely go insane and reveal secrets he'd kept buried deep, like he had at the hot springs yesterday?

He shook himself, to dispel the deeply unsettling emotions roiling through him. 'Taking you with me is out of the question,' he delivered with as much as ice as he could summon. Which wasn't very much when recalling what they'd done, how generously she'd given herself to him, threatened to melt his every resolve.

Every nerve ending tightened when she slowly approached, her eyes brazen on his. 'Then consider yourself warned. I'm not going to stay meek and mild and wait for you to grace me with your presence. You forced me to come here, but I no longer hold it against you, because you've also helped liberate me. Helped me find closure. But if you insist on standing in my way, I will fight you. With everything I've got.'

He felt her raw power wash over him, weakening his knees while charging him in ways he would've denied were emotional if his life depended on it. He opened his mouth, to say what, he wasn't exactly sure.

The distinct buzzing behind him froze them both.

Lotte watched his head jerk up, a frown marring his forehead before he was rounding the desk to snatch up the satellite phone.

It took moments to recognise the emotion flowering within her. To realise she wasn't ready for whatever was coming before she stumbled closer, her feet barely making a sound as she approached his desk.

'When did this happen?' Valenti snapped into the phone.

When she gripped the sides of his desk, his eyes flicked to her and stayed. If he saw the frantic question in hers, he chose not to answer.

'And he's being brought back here? Are you sure?' Several beats passed. 'Good work,' he said, then hung up.

Lotte's heart lurched and she sagged against the hard wood. With relief, she insisted. Not dejection. Not fear that he was about to leave. 'I... It's over?'

For several seconds, Valenti's gaze remained on the phone in his hand, then he looked up. '*Sí*. He's been apprehended in Holland. Bert Keglar. Does that name mean anything to you?'

She shook her head. 'No. Should it?'

A flash of relief washed over his face. 'He's being brought back here to face charges. It could happen as quickly as the next seventy-two hours.'

A pulse of silence passed, then because she'd been so bold minutes ago, and absolutely didn't want the pathetic weakness to return, she grasped the bull by the horns. 'So I'm free?'

Another dance of shadow and light over his face before he exhaled. 'Not quite yet, *litla*.'

Again she told herself the heady sensation pounding within her was affront. Anger, even. Not giddiness. Not exultation at the idea that Valenti wasn't in a hurry to wash his hands of her. Because *that* would be truly pathetic.

So she folded her arms once more and glared at him. 'What then?'

He cupped her nape, his thumb caressing back and forth on her jaw in a motion she suspected he didn't even realise he was performing.

'We will go on this magical tour of yours if you wish. But *you* heed *my* warning. I'm not making the mistake of dropping my guard until he's behind bars.'

Two things happened in quick succession once he summoned the helicopter.

His walls went back up the moment they stepped aboard. It was as sudden and as jarring as having a door slammed in her face. And she realised that Valenti intended to keep to his word about their sexual liaison ending once they left the cabin.

Which immediately birthed the second, stark realisation.

She missed the charged intimacy of the cabin. Would give anything to turn the aircraft around and return there.

And so she found herself in the same position as the outbound journey—consumed by her thoughts. Only this time they weren't thoughts of how much she hated Valenti Domene and his imposition in her life.

It was how much of herself she'd given to him in that cabin. And the sinking feeling that she'd committed the grave blunder of giving her guardian her heart.

A heart he showed every sign of rejecting.

Lotte deeply despised how hard it was to imitate his de-

tachment, then she hated him for making her crave that in-
human desire in the first place.

So yes, she was very much in her thoughts, sitting in the
Royal Class Executive Lounge in Ljomi Airport as Valenti
and his super elite guards pored over the half dozen destina-
tions she'd chosen. Her request for more visits to her charities had been taken 'under advisement'. And really, since she
considered six a win, and she secretly planned to make the
other trips by herself—something she looked forward to, she
insisted to herself, as a means of passing what she suspected
would be a trying time after Valenti reached his capacity and
walked away from her—she let him get on with it.

Still, her senses jerked into wild life when she saw him
striding towards her. Stopping before her, his keen eyes
probed her for several seconds.

'You still want to do this?' he rasped.

She wished she could say no, end this right here and now.
But even the tiniest idea of it contracted the vice around her
heart. She nodded. 'Yes, I do.' She matched deed to words
by rising and holding out her hand. 'And I'd appreciate you
returning my phone now too, thanks.'

The reluctance she sensed in him increased, a flash of unease darting across his face. After several beats, he reached
into his jacket pocket and drew out her phone.

As her fingers closed around it, flickers of anxiety danced
through her.

Helping people from afar was one thing. Being face-to-
face with them, seeing their challenges was another. And
as much as she wanted to deny it, she had little experience
providing direct support.

What if—

'Lotte? What's wrong?' he asked, his voice a rumble of
moving gravel.

She shook herself free of negative thoughts.

If Valenti Domene had made a huge success of a career he hadn't chosen for himself, surely she could take the first step in striking a meaningful path in her life?

And yes, it was ironic to be taking comfort and strength from the very man she suspected would devastate her with his complete rejection in the very near future. But until that happened...

She raised her chin. 'Nothing. Where are we headed first?'

By the time they landed in the tiny, jewelled haven of Turks and Caicos ten hours later, her mood and nerves were frazzled.

They were whisked away in a fleet of armoured SUVs to a breathtaking villa at the tail end of Grace Bay bordered by powdery white sand and sparkling turquoise waters. A property that Valenti's twenty-strong security team immediately began patrolling.

'This is a bit much, isn't it?' she snapped, raising her hand to massage the throbbing ache at her temple.

It'd started a short hour into their flight when Valenti barely touched the meal they were served, seemingly interested in staring sombrely and contemplatively at her, as if willing her to take a certain course of action, like perhaps blurting that she'd changed her mind. That she would prefer to return to Reykland.

Answering that look with a taunting one of her own for near on an hour had birthed the headache. Valenti stalking away to the conference room with his team had only worsened her headache and nerves.

She summoned a smile for the housekeeper whose name she'd shamefully not retained due to her preoccupation with following Valenti's imposing figure as he promptly, and without further words, made himself scarce.

Lotte didn't see him for the rest of the day, although she

very much felt his oversight in the long hours that followed via a staff member dancing in attendance at the beach with sunscreen and a message from Valenti not to get herself sunburnt. In the lavish feast of her favourite meals at dinnertime even though he'd made his excuses, leaving her to dine alone.

And in the dressing room full of clothes suitable for the tropics she discovered he'd had Ada pack for her.

Of course, the place where she felt his haunting absence most was in her vast bed in one of the most dreamy and luxurious bedrooms she'd seen in real life. Lotte almost resented the beatific sounds and scents of the night outside her open window, taunting her with myriad scenarios of how this night could've been magical.

If only—

No. She would absolutely not do it to herself.

Instead, she rose just past dawn when she accepted sleep was impossible, and sitting cross-legged against the sea of pillows, opened her laptop and went to work.

She was showered, dressed in a House of Domene jumpsuit that made her feel like a million dollars, and biting her inner cheek with nerves when the head of the charity was allowed through the gates of the villa.

Beside her, a silently brooding Valenti—who'd unsurprisingly made an appearance the moment his security alerted him of her visitor—fixed his gaze on the approaching taxi. She'd given up attempting to take shorter breaths so she wouldn't greedily inhale the scent of his body she'd missed more than she knew was good for her. Nor could she stop her heart lurching wildly when he took an almost imperceptible step closer when the middle-aged woman alighted from the taxi.

The woman's eyes widened a touch on seeing Valenti, then her gaze swung back to Lotte, her hand extending. 'Miss Lillegard? I'm Abigail Pierre. I can't tell you how pleasantly surprised I was to get your email yesterday. And how much I've been looking forward to meeting our anonymous bene-factor.' Her warm smile shaved off a few layers of Lotte's nerves and she felt her own lips curving in greeting. 'I had no idea you were this young.'

Lotte felt Valenti stiffen even harder. 'We think it's best Lotte's personal details aren't disseminated all over the in-ternet. I trust you'll keep whatever you learn to yourself, Mrs Pierre?'

The woman startled and Lotte glared at him, to zero ef-fect. Hell, he didn't even bother to spare her a glance, so busy was he drilling his will into the charity head.

'O-of course,' Abigail stuttered. 'You can count on my discretion.'

With one darker glare at the man she found infuriating and captivating in equal measure, Lotte pivoted away from him, widening her smile as she gestured towards the living room. 'I thought we could have coffee?' She glanced sharply over her shoulder when she felt Valenti's aura crowd her. '*Einn, takk,*' she added to him.

His eyes narrowed, understanding her '*alone, thanks*' wasn't up for debate. 'Lotte—'

'I insist.'

A muscle ticked in his jaw, but after a long moment he nodded. 'I will be out on the terrace.' *Watching*, he added silently.

She led Abigail into the living room where coffee, fruit and pastries had been laid out, taking the time to compose herself as she poured two cups.

The older woman smiled her thanks, then glanced at the French doors. 'Your man is very protective of you. It's lovely to see.'

Lotte's heart squeezed so viciously she barely managed to suppress a gasp. 'He's not...' She paused, the very act of confirming the wretched truth making her throat ache. 'He has his reasons,' she amended.

Abigail's gaze rested pensively on her for several seconds before she shrewdly nodded, sipped her coffee, then opened the messenger bag she'd brought with her.

She took out a small file and handed it to Lotte.

'This is a list of everyone you've helped since you started supporting us last year. And this is a spreadsheet of everything we plan to do for the next five years if we remain the recipient of your generosity. As you'll see there are several outreach programs to neighbouring islands that don't have an established charity yet. Also our network is growing day by day so...'

Even though her focus remained on Abigail's verbal report, a sense of awe swept over her as she perused the document, a grounding she'd never experienced before settling deep. She hadn't come seeking selfish validation, but *this* was tangible evidence that she wasn't a waste of space.

That she'd made a difference.

'Oh...my dear, are you okay?'

Lotte startled a little as Abigail's hand covered hers, and she realised to her surprise that she was blinking back tears.

'Yes.' She swallowed and plastered another smile on her face, determined to get herself together. 'I'm perfectly fine.'

And she was, she reiterated to herself long after she'd given the charity head her promise for further financial support and agreed to become a patron. And promised, now that she had a better sense of the sheer scale of need, to use her platform to garner more support.

Abigail had thanked her profusely and left. She'd returned to the living room to find Valenti waiting for her.

Intense silver eyes tracked her face, lingering no doubt on her slightly blotchy eyes. About to turn away from the far too keen inspection, she froze when he said, 'Your sister would be proud.'

She gasped and started to face him again. Lotte suspected her yearning for more very much poured off her in waves. For one electric moment, she thought, *hoped*, the blaze that lit his eyes echoed her hunger.

But it winked out with shocking ease before his walls slammed firmly back in place, and Valenti calmly walked away without a backward glance.

It set the tone for Costa Rica. Then Brazil. South Africa. Switzerland.

The only difference during the six-week tour was the magnificence of the Domene-owned residences and the many changing faces of the staff who bent over to accommodate her every wish, as per the orders of their boss, who haunted her presence without once relenting on his vow to not touch her. Or engage with her longer than the perfunctory greeting or dismissal.

And more fool her, but Lotte's heart continued to hope with each interaction, then squeeze with anguish as he became her shadow, staying no more than three feet away when she met with the tiny but mighty charities dedicated to helping those in dire need of escaping harrowing circumstances.

He didn't hesitate to fire questions at each group she met, meticulously shoring up any gaps in her own concerns. It would have been perfect. If not for the austere guilt etched into his face that he didn't bother to hide.

Valenti had taken his emotion-free stance, and he intended to stick to it. At first it frustrated and saddened her. Then the conviction that he was using it as a real but effective crutch turned those emotions into anger.

'I can speak for myself thank you,' she interrupted when he began firing questions at the Moldovan charity head.

Perhaps it was the unyielding awareness that this was their

final stop. That their time together was running out like sand in an hourglass.

Or perhaps it was the growing confidence and fulfilling acceptance that she'd indeed found her goal.

Whatever. His head snapped in her direction.

Whatever he saw in her expression widened his eyes a fraction before he jerked a nod far too regal to be called true acquiescence.

And whatever it was bubbled up all the way back to the presidential suite of the hotel he'd rented in Chisinau.

'Something bothering you?' he drawled when she all but leapt from the lift the moment the doors opened, almost trotting in her haste to get away from him. Because, it turned out, she *did* have a ceiling when it came to withstanding Valenti's rejection. To witnessing his blatant self-flagellation.

And she was ready to blow when she whirled on him at his question. 'Do you really need to ask me that?' she seethed.

'Evidently I do.'

She started to rip free with every roiling emotion inside her, but the words locked in her throat. Because a great part of her questioned the futility of it.

'What do you care what anyone thinks, least of all inconsequential me?'

His statue-still form didn't alter, nor did he rush to correct her assertion, much to her chagrin.

She sighed. 'I'm tired, Valenti. I'm going to lie down.' To compose herself before he dropped the news that he was done with her once and for all.

Her legs felt lead-heavy when she turned away, only to freeze when he moved, closing the gap between them. Her breath lodged in her throat, anticipation firing through her. But he only drew out his phone, and glanced down at it before pinning her with his gaze.

'You only have two hours to rest, I'm afraid.'

'Why? What's the rush?'

He flashed another glance at his phone before returning it to his pocket. 'It seems my twin is determined to follow Azar's footsteps and hurtle down the aisle with no regard for how it inconveniences everyone else.'

The rumble of discontent was half-hearted at best, his expression more mildly vexed than angry.

The little Lotte had seen of Teo and the reams she'd read about him online pointed to a joie de vivre, a polar opposite of Valenti. Although she had the strong suspicion that it was all an act. That Teo Domene's near hedonistic outlook on life hid a deeper character that rivalled his brother's.

'Or he knows what he wants and is willing to bend time and space itself to achieve it,' she murmured, not without a flash of jealousy and longing.

His gaze sharpened on her face, and she wondered if she'd given herself away. If all the longing she'd felt reading books with heroes who did the exact same thing Teo Domene was doing—destroying every single obstacle in his way in order to bind himself to the woman he adored—had bled through.

And perhaps it was that little she-devil on her shoulder that whispered at her to keep her chin up. To meet his gaze boldly as she added, 'Haven't you ever felt that way about anything?'

There was barely an infinitesimal hesitation before he answered. 'No.'

The fist around her heart tightened at the resounding denial, but something in his face held her breath. Or perhaps it was his lips moving, muttering a follow-up she couldn't quite catch. 'What did you say?'

He stared at her with ferocious fixation. Then to her chagrin, he shook his head. 'It doesn't matter.'

'It matters, Valenti. Everything matters in the end.'

A flash of perplexity. A faint flare of his nostrils. Then

he was striding to where she stood. 'My brother weds in two weeks. As his best man I need to return to Cartana, and I'm not ready to let you out of my sight. You wanted to visit Cartana. I'm giving it to you. So yes or no?'

Of course he would couch it like that. Remind her that this wasn't a benign, wholly cordial and social invitation, but Valenti Domene wanting to maintain surveillance on his ward. Force her to recall, with much stomach churning, how her previous visit had gone.

And wasn't it a pity then, that because she was so desperate not to lose this connection between them no matter how much strife it seemed attached to, that she would reply with the only response her heart and mind and body and soul would permit her. 'Yes.'

But I'll find a way to break this dependence. I have to.

And if he'd heard the silent vow and narrowed his eyes because of it, she told herself she didn't care. Her very survival dictated that she find a way.

CHAPTER ELEVEN

'VALENTI, THE CITY is as splendid as you left it many weeks ago. I would be grateful if you paid attention to what my fiancée's saying to you?'

Valenti turned from the third-floor window and faced the lavish living room in the Palacio Domene where the umpteenth wedding meeting was being held. He ignored his twin and summoned a smile for his soon-to-be sister-in-law. '*Perdóname*,' he offered. 'You were saying?'

Sabeen's wide smile was indulgent, then it grew pensive. 'Perhaps we should pick this up another time—'

'Absolutely not,' Teo interjected, reaching for her hand and dropping a lingering kiss on the back of it. 'We've worked around Valenti for long enough.' His twin shot him an exasperated glare. 'If you haven't noticed, the world indeed revolves around my love, so do me a favour and pay attention?'

He gave a brisk nod. 'We've discussed the schedule. My suit is a perfect fit, and my speech will be ready as promised. What else is there?'

'We noticed you brought a plus one,' Teo said.

He stiffened. 'I didn't realise that would be a problem considering your guest list is well over eleven hundred. A logistical nightmare if you care to know, but that too is well in hand.'

'It's not a problem,' Sabeen hastened to say, her eyes locking on Teo's before returning to Valenti. 'But I...we wondered whether you…she would be willing to be in the official wedding party?'

'What my love is saying is that she'd hate to put anyone's pretty nose out of joint. So what's it to be?'

His gaze flicked back to the window, towards his home in the Residence, one of the dozen cottages he and Teo preferred to stay in instead of the Palacio Domene. When he and Teo had got over being excluded from royal life as children and young adults, they'd been grateful for the separate residence. For one thing, it'd taken them out of the chaos and dysfunction of witnessing their mother play out her dramatic displeasure at not being the queen their father had chosen after discovering he'd got two women separately pregnant within weeks of each other.

King Alfonse had chosen to marry his eldest's child's mother, leaving the woman who'd borne him twins feeling endlessly aggrieved and bitter.

These days, Valenti was thankful for having his own space to brood in peace, out of the view of inquisitive palace eyes.

To ponder what the hell was happening to him. Ponder why his every waking thought seemed to circle around Lotte Lillegard. Indeed, to wonder what the very big deal would be if he—

'You forgot one thing,' his brother's voice came from behind him.

Valenti turned, surprise jolting through him when he realised he'd pivoted towards the window again, his focus on the villa's miniature turret he could just about make out. Was Lotte resting? Was she bored? Angry? Or wearing that sombre and bruised look that punched a hole in his chest whenever he saw it because he was fairly sure he'd been the one to put it there. That his emotion-free choices weren't reaping the sound outcomes he'd envisaged. That—

'This is the part where you ask me what.'

Stifling a growl, he ruthlessly stifled a twinge of jealousy and sharpened his focus on his twin. Noted the absence of shadows in his brother's eyes, replaced by a deep contentment that drew a sharper awareness to the yawning chasms he inhabited. 'What?' he echoed less gruffly.

His twin's happiness was undeniable. And Valenti would honour that if it was the last thing he did. Especially after the suffering his brother had endured.

'You haven't given me an update on the stag party to end all parties. You do know it's only a matter of days, right?'

Biting back another growl, he glanced around, ready to plead out of this social nightmare. Only to discover that they were alone, Sabeen and her assistants having departed while he was preoccupied.

'If you're looking for Sabeen to save you, she left to ask Lotte herself if she wanted to be in the bridal party.' At Valenti's stiffening, his twin laughed. 'Yeah, you dropped the ball on that one. And my beautiful wife doesn't mess around when she wants something.'

'She's not your wife yet,' he pointed out dryly.

'Oh yes, she is,' Teo parried with quiet, resounding certainty. 'She's already mine in every way that counts. The wedding is just a formality and an excuse for a party. Now about the stag party...'

He was happy for his twin.

And that chasm? It was merely the grounding signpost signalling he needed not to recross lines he'd painstakingly redrawn. Because while he could handle physical landmines all day long, he saw no dishonour in backing away from emotional ones. Even if doing so took every last ounce of willpower he possessed.

Even if doing so felt like he was ripping his own chest out.

If King Azar's declaration of love to his wife on international TV had earned them most romantic meme of the decade, then Teo Domene and Sabeen El-Maleh's wedding of the decade deserved its laurels.

Three hours past the fateful, breathtaking event and Lotte was still pinching herself at the fairy tale dream of it all. It'd started with Sabeen arriving at Valenti's Residence to ask her to be part of her bridal party, an invitation Lotte had been delighted to accept, partly because it'd added to the business of working furiously from morning till mid-afternoon on her charity work, then posting on her social media platforms until late evenings before throwing herself into physical activities like swimming or working out in Valenti's basement gym. It filled up her time. It exhausted her so she could fall asleep the moment her head touched the pillow.

It didn't stop her dreaming of Valenti, but it was a small mercy.

She blew out a breath now, her damp palm sliding over her thighs then glanced down anxiously to see whether she'd marred the cowl-necked, blush-pink silk dress, with its delicate gold and saffron piping—Sabeen's beloved late grandmother's favourite colours. It fitted her like a dream, a testament to Sabeen's talent. The last thing Lotte wanted was to ruin it.

But her shakiness wouldn't subside. Glancing around to ensure she was alone, she plucked her phone from the tiny matching crystal-studded clutch, and activated the social media site, her breath catching all over again at the post.

Three-point-seven million likes. And counting.

Her eyes flicked to the photo of herself at last night's rehearsal dinner. She'd respected Teo and Sabeen's privacy and hadn't divulged the occasion or venue.

Breath strangled, her gaze landed on the left corner, and the reason the post had gone viral.

She'd thought she was alone. Apparently not. She'd unwittingly captured Valenti just out of direct shot, his reflection caught in a mirror.

A reflection of him staring at her with unmissable hunger. Lotte had stopped reading the comments when it'd surged into the thousands, but the general tone swung between deep green envy and avid followers thirsting over him and asking if he was her new love.

Her new love.

Her heart lurched wildly each time the phrase reeled through her brain, a recurrence which had gathered serious momentum in the last few hours.

A phrase her heart had accepted as its abiding truth.

Valenti was her new love. Her old love. Her eternal love. She loved him stern or half smiling, broken and guilt-ridden, remote and breathtaking.

'Lotte.'

The deep, sombre voice made her jump, her thoughts making her flush with anxiety when she turned to face him. Faced the decision she'd made in the cathedral while watching another Domene claim his woman.

She wanted to be claimed by this intensely magnetic man wearing his House of Domene wedding tuxedo that elevated his beguiling good looks to stratospheric levels. Who'd honoured her sister and kept his word to look after a near stranger even though he'd been grieving and suffering his own shattered dreams. Who'd left women slack-jawed and starry-eyed up and down the aisle when he'd stood next to his twin. Heavy residues of those sensations pranced through her now as she faced him.

'Yes? Did you want me?'

His eyes darkened, then blazed in that way she so yearned for. But far too soon, the barricades descended.

'I'm required to dance with every member of the bridal party, I'm told. It's your turn.'

Her heart pinched hard, but she summoned a smile. 'Let's do it then.'

If he clocked her false gaiety, he didn't comment on it, merely held out his hand and waited for her to come to him. To place her hand in his, touch him for the first time *in weeks*, and confirm to her thrilled dismay that the galvanised magic he wrought within her hadn't waned one iota.

Breath lodged firmly in her throat, she followed him onto the dance floor. Quivered from head to toe when he pulled her close and began to sway with suave ease that should've been surprising considering his eternal sombreness, but somehow wasn't because he was Prince Valenti, the man who could click his fingers and have his every wish delivered.

Lotte wanted one of his wishes to be her. And…perhaps she knew the path forward to achieving that goal?

'You look breathtaking.'

Shock jolted through her, her gaze flying up to meet his. From the gruff delivery, she wondered if he hadn't meant to say that. Just as he hadn't meant to be caught looking at her like that in the photo?

Nerves consuming her, she licked her lips. 'Thank you.' Another minute passed, then she cleared her throat. 'Umm, there's something you should know…or more like, see?'

One dark eyebrow arched, the flashes of reserve building in his eyes even as he seemed to step closer, his warm body imprinting against hers, his scent invading every corner of her being.

This was her chance. She couldn't blow it.

'*Sì?*' he prompted at her prolonged silence.

'I…posted a picture today without realising…you were in it. Until it was too late.'

He stiffened momentarily, then continued gliding her across the floor, his eyes fixed on her face, gauging her every emotion. 'I don't recall taking a photo with you. So I fail to see how this is problematic,' he drawled in the end, effortlessly unbothered.

It struck her then that she was perhaps reading too much into it. That as virile, rampantly male as Valenti was, he would see nothing wrong with looking at a woman the way he did in that picture. That with his vast worldly experience, he would shrug it off. *Because she meant nothing to him.*

Her stomach dipped in dismay. Her smile felt brittle as spun glass. 'Fine.'

She fixed her gaze over his shoulder, willing the song to end, willing whatever machinations gleamed in his eyes as he continued staring fiercely at her not to manifest.

'But clearly you're fretting about it, so perhaps I should see this picture,' he stated unexpectedly, just as the last strains of the music echoed in the grand ballroom. 'Come.' He held out his hand again.

'Don't you have to dance with other women?'

His gaze remained on her, that drilling intensity building. 'No, I saved the last dance for you.'

Lotte told herself she really hated him for the ease with which he controlled the rollercoaster of her emotions. It didn't stop her from taking his hand again, walking him back to the terrace where she'd left her clutch.

Hands shaking, she fished out her phone. Displayed the picture.

Watched his nostrils flare and his jaw ripple. His eyes widened slightly when he saw the millions of views.

Thin-lipped, he raised his head and held out the phone. 'Is there a reason you've waited this long to show it to me? Or why you didn't delete it in the first place?' he enquired, his voice silk wrapped in a scimitar.

'I didn't see it myself until a short while ago.' She pulled a shrug out of her dwindling composure bag. 'Deleting it now will only fan the flames.'

'There are no flames to fan,' he said in an octave so low and deep, she stepped closer to hear him.

Her heart dropped, but she refused to be cowed. 'Are you sure?'

Livid eyes lit on her face. 'Be very careful what you say next, Lotte.'

Her heart dipped lower. 'Why? You've built a monument of self-pity to yourself and fortified it with a self-righteous fortress.' She shook her head. 'I'm thinking I'm wasting my time attempting to get through to you.'

'Melodramatics aren't quite necessary, Lotte.'

'Oh, screw you, Valenti,' she hissed. 'I will have my say. You won't get to throw me out this time before I have.'

His head jerked back, a haughty motion primed to remind her of his status and power. 'I'm your guardian. I know what's best for you. Don't blow what we did out of proportion.' His eyes flicked to the phone, disdain flickering over his breathtaking features. 'It's borderline infatuation based on heightened emotion and enforced proximity and I daresay a level of childish defiance on your part. I'm saving you embarrassment and undue distress in the long run.'

'God, what is it about this place that makes you repeatedly reject me?' she muttered, despair clawing her soul.

He frowned. 'What?'

She shook her head. 'You should finish the job you started last time I was here, step over here and pat me on the head, maybe ruffle my hair while you're at it. Because I'm a simple child who needs placating, aren't I? Who played at being grown up but isn't quite up to your standard of sophistication? Or is it something else? You're too busy being a martyr? Is that what I'm dealing with here?'

Silver eyes narrowed. 'Watch it, *litla*.'

Misery and fury mixed into a lethal cocktail. 'You've lost

the right to call me that. And why should I watch it? Aren't we speaking plainly?'

'Plain speaking, sure. But impertinence will get you—'

'What? Another spanking?'

Electrified silence thrummed between them after that terribly unwise question. She wouldn't have believed he could get any more rigid, but it happened right before her eyes.

Had she not known better, she would've toyed with the idea that Valenti didn't want to move for fear of what would happen. Hell, *she* didn't want to move. Because the way her heart was hammering, the reminder of everything that had happened after he spanked her, blazed like the showiest Times Square billboard through her mind.

After an eternity, he finally moved, stalking closer.

She tilted her head to meet his gaze and almost wished she hadn't. His eyes were mercury lakes, intent on swallowing her whole.

'You're drawing ever closer to one of those fires I warned you about.'

'Am I? Then I think I'll go for broke, shall I? Since you've been painstakingly avoiding me, you won't know that I've been busy this past week. Amongst other things, I had my lawyer look at the terms of the guardianship.'

Displeasure marched like angry little soldiers across his face. 'You have a lawyer?' he said icily.

'Oh yes, I've learned to take many pages from your book, approach things clinically. As you probably know, and it came as a pleasant surprise to me, it states on page eleven of the guardianship contract that I have options. I guess, I should thank you for not making the whole thing entirely draconian and in your favour.' She pinned on a bright smile, one that didn't sway him a bit if the darkening of his features was a clue.

'Options?' he bit out.

'Hmm. Specifically, one way to free myself of this whole guardian-ward melodrama is if I simply…get married.'

She looked back into the grand ballroom, not bothering to keep the wistful expression off her face. She wanted him to see it, to know deep in his soul how his rejection hurt. 'Good old-fashioned marriage,' she mused with a fake smile. 'Once again to the rescue.'

He exhaled harshly, came within a whisker of losing control. But being the great Prince Valenti Domene, he recalibrated with infuriating ease, his face smoothing out as if the infinitesimal faltering hadn't happened.

But the bleak fury on his face, and the hand snapping out to grip her hip told a different story.

'If this is a joke it isn't funny at all—'

'Who says it's a joke? Do you know how many marriage proposals I receive on a daily basis? Especially since I went super viral?'

His Adam's apple moved, his expression tight with dire warning. 'It also says you need my approval for any such marriage to take place.'

'Approval yes, but it doesn't say it has to be written.' She shrugged. 'So really, who's to say I don't have my dear old guardian's wholehearted blessing when I hop on a plane to Vegas and find an Elvis impersonator to do the deed, then present you with a fait accompli?'

'I'd advise you not to waste your time trying. You won't get anywhere near a wedding chapel. Not while I still draw breath.'

'Be careful about daring me, Valenti. I might just cut off my nose to spite your rejection.'

'Lotte—'

She pushed away from him, not bothered by who saw them.

People could draw whatever conclusions they wanted. Besides, weren't weddings the very place for a little melodrama? 'I'm done dancing around you. There's a platter of shrimp calling my name. Or is it the vintage champagne? Either one is preferable to staying here with you.'

She turned and strutted back into the ballroom, past the dance floor, putting a little extra sway into her hips because, God, he infuriated her and saddened her and treated her heart like it was a disposable toy, and she was damned if she would continue to hope that something...*anything* broke through to him.

It never would, she realised.

She was too late. While he'd been locked in duty and purpose and mourning his one failure and shattered dreams, Valenti Domene's heart had calcified into stone. Nothing and no one would get through. Not with empathy. Or laughter.

Or...love.

The no-holds-barred undying kind she'd bent over to re-label as anything else. Crush. Frustration. Defiance. Good, old-fashioned sublime sex. It had all eventually led to one truth. She loved her guardian more than life itself.

While he felt...nothing.

So she would rather go live a half life somewhere else than break herself on the jagged cliffs of his rejection.

The old King was sitting at a table close by, and Lotte wasn't entirely sure what made her look over at him. But when she met the silver eyes he'd passed to his sons, and caught a gleam of approval in his gaze, she nearly sobbed.

She bobbed an abbreviated curtsy—she still didn't know how to execute a perfect one—then immediately changed course, striking for the imposing doors that led to an alcove.

The thought of food made her stomach heave, especially that shrimp she'd loftily mentioned. But the bottle of vintage Krug nestling in a nearby silver ice bucket virtually screamed her name.

She snatched it on her way out the door, taking a huge gulp

straight from the bottle the moment she stepped onto another terrace with wide stone steps winding down opposite sides onto the landscaped grass. She took the left set, rushed to the bottom then immediately spat out the champagne.

Her period was still two weeks past a no-show. At first she'd thought it was the stress of everything she'd lived through the past two months. But in the last week, she'd started to wonder. To hope.

If she was carrying Valenti's child…

The sob finally tore free as she discarded the bottle on the last step.

Kicking her heels away, she stepped onto the lush grass and sucked in a deep breath that didn't quite hit the bottom, leaving her still breathless.

Breathless with heartache. Breathless with misery.

She wanted to scream at fate for the relentless barrage of desolation, but it stuck in her lungs. Because if she was being truthful with herself, she regretted very little of what had happened between her and Valenti.

Including the very daunting, heart-rending truth that she'd fallen in love with him. Heart and soul. Body and spirit and everything in between.

She loved him. She loved him. She loved him.

And he felt nothing.

Hot tears welled in her eyes as she kept walking, a little grateful when the sounds of partying fell away. As much as she was happy for Teo and Sabeen, their barefaced bliss pulverised her shattered heart.

All she needed was a little time alone to regroup.

Time healed all wounds, including a traumatised heart, right?

She would fill her days and nights with the fulfilling work she'd started. Throw herself into it until she was too exhausted to feel, never mind think about Valenti Domene.

And perhaps this was as good a time as any to start. While Valenti was busy with the only family he would ever care about.

Decision firming, she brushed her tears away and straightened her shoulders as she approached the front doors leading out of the *palacio*.

Several footmen stood on hand, and one turned to her. 'May I be of assistance, Miss Lillegard?'

About to request a ride to Valenti's Residence, she spotted Valenti's sports car. 'Can I have the keys to Prince Valenti's car, please?' she asked, breath held because it wasn't above reason for Valenti to instruct them not to allow her anywhere near his car. Or any vehicle for that matter without an armed guard.

'Of course, right away, miss.' He sprinted away, then returned seconds later with the sleek little fob.

Lotte greedily grasped the little spark of rebellion as she pressed the fob, and the door slid up. It was short-lived however when she slid into the dark, luxurious interior and was immediately engulfed in Valenti's hazelnut and spice scent.

She gave herself a vulnerable little moment to breathe him in, perhaps for the last time, to run her fingers over the steering wheel, imagining him doing the same.

Then gunning the throaty engine, she headed for the Residence.

Ten minutes was all it took to snatch her passport and pack the barest essentials. Whatever else she needed she would get once she reached wherever the first flight out of Cartana took her.

Changing into a pair of jeans and a top and slipping her feet into sneakers took another minute. She held her breath all the way back down the stairs, only to belly-flip when the butler appeared.

Lotte saw his eyes flick to the small case in her hand and

over her outfit, but his years of experience prevented him from showing any emotion.

'May I be of assistance with anything, Miss Lillegard?' he asked evenly.

Summoning a bright smile, she shook her head. 'No thank you, I'm fine. You can go back to…whatever you were doing.'

He didn't. He followed her to the door and as his throat cleared diplomatically, probably to politely enquire what she was doing or where she was going when the wedding was still in full swing, she pre-empted it with another smile. 'Thanks for everything, Soto. And there's no need to disturb Prince Valenti.'

He nodded, but she felt his keen regard as she forced herself to walk calmly to the car. Heart in her throat, she drove at a sedate pace to the *palacio*'s main gates.

The security guard was a little less circumspect. He peered into the car, then at her. 'Miss Lillegard, you don't have your security with you?'

'I'm just going for a quick drive. No need to disturb the Prince.'

His respectful smile didn't budge. 'I'm afraid I must call his aide. I won't be a moment.'

She prayed to all the gods in Valhalla for the aide's phone to be busy, and when the guard strolled back two minutes later, uneasy frustration stamped over his face, she exhaled slowly.

Lotte waved at the line of cars queuing behind her. 'I'm keeping everyone waiting. Let me through, please,' she said firmly.

With clear reluctance, he opened the gates.

The taste of freedom wasn't as sweet as she'd imagined, but she suppressed the wave of desolation that swept through her. Took her time to pull over, dig out a tissue to mop tears that wouldn't stop falling, before programming the GPS in the direction of the airport.

Three streets away, she eased to a stop at another traffic light just as her phone started ringing. Her heart jumped into her throat, then plummeted. While she knew it could only be one person, Lotte was well aware Valenti's only reason for contacting her would be to throw more of his authority about.

To keep her living under the weight of his guilt.

So she ignored it, then startled violently when horns blared around her.

Quickly dashing away fresh tears, she'd just stepped on the gas when a mighty jolt knocked her forward.

No. *No, no, no!*

Slamming on the brakes, it took her a minute to realise she hadn't hit the vehicle in front. That the driver behind had rammed into *her.*

Relief warred with alarm as she carefully stepped out, her heart dropping when she saw the damage. The back of Valenti's supercar was mangled, the taillights shattered and the sleek bumper now crumpled. She didn't need genius status to know the cost of repairs would be astronomical.

'Oh God. I'm so sorry. I wasn't watching where I was going.'

Rearing back at the too-close voice, she looked up into dark brown eyes. The guy was tall and wiry, young, maybe a year or two older than her.

His clear distress cut through her own as he looked closer at the damage and grimaced. 'Damn, I really did a number on that, didn't I? It's not going to be cheap.'

'Do you have insurance?' she asked hopefully.

More horns blared, drivers irritated at the growing logjam.

'Yes, I do—' He flinched when another horn blasted. 'Look, can we get off this busy street? Then we can exchange details?'

Lotte hesitated, her urgency to get out of Cartana, as far

away as possible from Valenti, returning full force. But she couldn't walk away from an accident. Even with a car she'd taken without express consent.

Staring longingly in the direction of the airport, she sucked in a breath. 'Yes, but we have to be quick. I have a plane to catch.' *And soul-flaying heartache to start managing.*

He nodded, pointing to the nearest side street. 'I'll follow you there. We'll be done in no time.'

As she slid behind the wheel, her eyes fell on her phone, and she saw several more missed calls. For a hopeless, broken moment, she wanted to snatch it up and hit Dial, hear Valenti's voice one last time, even if it was so he could command her to do the last thing she wanted. She gripped the steering wheel hard and blinked back another swell of tears until the yearning passed.

Then, cringing at the sound of grating metal when she stepped on the gas, she took the turn into the quiet, leafy residential side street. The area looked affluent, the houses set back from the street.

Turning off the ignition, Lotte stepped out. Then frowned at the man.

Had he been wearing a cap before? She shook her head, brushing aside her confusion. She really needed to get out of here. Get herself under control before she lost it entirely.

'Hey, are you okay?' he asked when he reached her, stepping far too close again. 'I'm not sure if I apologised before—'

She waved him away. 'I'm fine. Can we get on with it please?'

'Yes, but…you're crying. Are you hurt? I'd hate it if I—'

'It's fine,' she cut across him again. Then blinked when a flash of ice went through his eyes.

A moment later he was nodding, his gaze rueful. 'Here.' He held out a pristine, folded handkerchief. 'I hate seeing a woman distressed.' Then he held up a pen and a scrap of paper. 'I'll write down my details.'

'Thanks.' Lotte took the hanky just to move things along, then cringing for blubbering in front of a complete stranger, she pressed it to her nose.

The sweet, sickly scent assailed her, confusing her for several seconds before she jolted in comprehension.

Oh God.

Her gaze flew to the man, who was tucking the paper and pen back into his pocket. His hand shot out as her heart lurched, pressing the handkerchief firmly over her nose and mouth, his titanium grip on her nape holding her captive, keeping her scream muted as she struggled.

Oh God. Oh God Oh God.

'That's it, aisling, breathe it in. Let me take all your troubles away,' he whispered hoarsely.

Lotte's last thought as she felt her knees sag and her vision blurring rapidly, was that she wished she'd answered Valenti's call.

Heard his deep, sombre, magnificent voice one last time.

CHAPTER TWELVE

VALENTI WASN'T SURE who he was more furious with, Lotte for tossing out hypotheticals he'd rightly said he would see happen over his dead body—because, *sí*, he would be damned if he stood by and watched another man place a ring on her finger, even if it was an imaginary, convenient one to get herself away from Valenti—or himself, for the terror holding him hostage, clogging words he'd wanted to roar at her deep in his throat.

Admitted, they were terrifying words. Exposing words. Words that would flay decades of calcification off his heart and soul and leave him vulnerable. To great and moving feelings.

Haven't you been vulnerable all this time?

He swallowed against the bracing voice, the image of her face, free of subterfuge or guile, filled with hurt *he'd* caused, making his next breath rumble out like a faulty engine.

What the hell was he doing?

She was his ward, yes. But she was also a strong, capable woman—as he'd been privileged to witness these past few weeks. Besides, he'd stepped over the line weeks ago. And as he'd consoled himself with predicting, the world didn't stop. Hell, if anything, it—and she—had revealed a glory of possibilities. If he was brave enough to reach for it.

True, the picture she'd shown him on the terrace had shaken him to his core. But he'd also seen the hope in her eyes. Seen her pain when he'd dismissed her feelings as infatuation.

And if he was still inclined to hide behind the potential scandal of admitting he felt something for his ward, theirs wouldn't be an original story. Hell, his family had scandals coming out of their ears, and he should know. In his line of work, he'd become privy to more shenanigans than anyone deserved foisted on them in one lifetime.

So stop making excuses and act!

'This is where I kissed my wife for the first time. Do me a favour and don't ruin the memory for me with any sombre, stoic bullshit, today of all days, would you?' Teo said with a firm slap to his shoulder.

'What are you talking about?' he hedged, even as he turned around, his gaze scouring the ballroom for Lotte.

'You weren't exactly subtle in your little skirmish with your ward. On the contrary, it looked quite dramatic.'

'Have you seen her?' he asked sharply when another sweep didn't reveal her.

'She left the ballroom about ten minutes ago. And for God's sake, answer that buzzing. I would've thought you of all people would be more diligent about that sort of—what?' he demanded sharply.

Valenti wasn't paying attention. Because the chill sweeping through him at the number of alerts he'd missed on his phone was the last thing he wanted to be feeling right now. In his experience it didn't portent anything good. Coupled that with Lotte's disappearing act—

His heart staggered sickeningly as the phone buzzed to life in his hands. 'Soto. What is it?'

The first few words from his butler propelled him into movement.

'For God's sake, what is it?' Teo demanded, all traces of humour wiped from his face.

'It's Lotte,' he bit out.

'What about her?' the sharper query came from Azar, who'd stepped onto the terrace, that same sixth sense that bound them all unsurprisingly summoning him. In some abstract part of his brain Valenti admonished himself starkly to stop this scene from unfolding a third time.

'She's taken my Temerario,' he threw over his shoulder as he raced down the terrace steps.

Teo cursed under his breath as he followed. 'And?'

Valenti didn't answer. He couldn't. The knot of fear in his gut was expanding, spreading ice through his veins.

'*Hermano*, wait!' Teo grabbed his arm. 'Talk to me.'

Valenti paused even as his heart thundered wildly. 'She had a suitcase with her.' Repercussions raked over his skin like lethal blades. *Dios*, had he ever imagined he knew torment? Because it was nothing compared to this reality. 'I think she's leaving me. And… I'm not ready to let her go. Because I think she's it for me. Is that enough?' he almost snarled at his twin.

Teo's frown eased right before it strengthened. 'That's not all,' he said.

Valenti's fingers tightened around his phone, and he forced air into his lungs. Still the ice expanded. 'The car's GPS has stopped off the highway. In the middle of some random street.'

Azar's frown didn't ease his anxiety. 'Could she be stopping for something? Gas, maybe?'

Valenti scoffed at the absurd question. Even if he wasn't royalty, he would have enough minions to ensure he or anyone else who drove his car didn't stop to pump their own gas. 'I don't have time to answer your questions,' he spat, just as Sabeen appeared at the top of the steps. The prospect of further delays made a growl rise from his throat. 'Your wife wants you, Teo. Go.'

He stalked away, fully aware that his brothers had ignored him, were following hard on his heels.

'Valenti?' Teo called out.

Teeth clenched, he shook his head. 'Seriously, not now, Teo.'

His twin caught up to him. 'You will find her, and you will bring her back. Then you'll lock her down by any means possible. *Sí*?'

The charged imploration further terrified Valenti. Because he wanted every single one to be true. 'My security team will keep in touch. You'll know everything they know in five minutes.'

'*Gracias*.'

'Valenti,' Azar's voice brooked no argument.

He stopped despite every sinew straining to race away. '*Yes?*'

Eyes eerily similar to his examined him with the same intensity he knew lived in his eyes. It was the Domene way. 'She means something?'

His breath shuddered out, the truth permanently altering him forever. 'She means everything.' He may only have accepted that recently, but deep inside he knew Lotte Lillegard had held a powerful place in his heart for a long time.

Dios santo, let him be given the chance to repair the damage he'd done.

'Then do whatever it takes to bring her back. You're not allowed another misfortune. Do you hear me?' the King demanded.

A rock wedged in his throat. With a brusque nod he finally gave into the urge and raced to the *palacio* doors.

The King's own fastest supercar waited with the driver's door open and the engine running. Behind it, three cars filled with Cartanian's black-clad personal army.

But even as he dove into the car and stomped his foot on

the gas, he knew that not even the world's most efficient army could do a single thing if the woman he loved had been harmed. But Valenti knew one simple thing to be true.

If he lost Lotte, he would also lose the will to live.

'Hello, beautiful. You're awake. Good.'

Lotte forced her eyes open, then blinked to better see in the dark surroundings. She was in the back seat of a car, and it was dark outside.

The vicious headache throbbing at her temples made her swallow a moan.

Memory filtered in as she attempted to move and felt a sharp pain at her wrists. The row with Valenti. Fleeing the *palacio*. The crash…

Bleary-eyed she glanced down. Her breath stopped.

Dear God, she was tied up?

'You've given me quite the runaround,' her captor said, twisting in the front seat to peer down at her. 'No worries. I relished the challenge.'

She sucked in a breath which threatened to turn into a sob. No, she was absolutely not crying over this situation. 'Y-you're sh-sh-posed to be in jail.' She stifled another moan. He'd given her something, maybe drugs that slurred her speech?

His grin would've been almost charming if it wasn't borderline unhinged. 'It helps when you happen to be the favourite grandson of a judge,' he said.

She squeezed her eyes shut, gathering herself. 'What a-are you planning to do with me?'

His eyes darkened. 'Are you going to live up to the promises you made?'

'Wh-what promises?'

'Be bold. Be brave. Reach for what you want. Remember I'm here for you, always.'

Her signature words, repeated back to her in his mildly sinister voice sent chilled shockwaves through her. She didn't think it was wise to point out that she'd said that to millions of her followers.

'And what is it you want exactly?' she asked as evenly as she could manage, considering the heart hammering itself into extinction against her ribs.

Disappointment reflected in his face. 'Did the flowers and the notes not clue you in? I'm in love with you. We're meant to be together.' He tapped the laptop on the passenger seat. 'And once we get you ready, there's a celebrant waiting online to marry us.' Another demonic smile displayed perfect white teeth.

A hysterical laugh tore from her throat before she could stop it.

Wasn't it just *marvellous* that she would throw the loophole of freedom through marriage in Valenti's face only for her to land herself in this situation? Could she have scripted this demented set of circumstances any better if she'd tried?

'Don't laugh at me,' came the growled warning.

She shook her head frantically. 'I'm not. I'm laughing at myself.'

His anger didn't abate. 'I still see nothing funny about us being together. If you hadn't made me chase you around the globe, rescued you from him...' He leaned over and lowered his face to hers. 'I don't know what the hell you saw in him. He's twice your age. Is it the royalty thing?'

She pursed her lips so nothing would fall out and compound her already dire situation. Had she been free to, she would have told him that no, Valenti's status had nothing to do with how she felt for him. She would love him no matter what. His very act of staying penitent for what was ultimately an unfortunate set of circumstances, while harrowing and formidable for having such a stranglehold on him, revealed

an honour and loyalty that touched her. The wide river of feeling that spoke to his humanity that made her love him. And
yes, her frustration that she couldn't overcome it was breaking her heart into even smaller pieces right in this moment.

'Because my great-grandmother was third cousin to the
last king of Reykland by marriage if that helps?' Her captor
peered hopefully at her, triggering another hysterical bubble.

She swallowed it just in time. 'How long was I unconsc…
asleep?'

'Five hours,' he snapped grumpily, then shrugged. 'I mis-
judged the dosage, but you're awake now. We can get on—'

'May I have some water? I—I have a headache.'

Annoyance flashed over his face again, then he looked
out his window. Following his gaze, fear filled her when she
saw the shack. 'I have to go inside. I can't bring you in, just
yet. It has to be right. Will you wait here. Behave yourself?'

At her hurried nod, he opened his door, and went into
the shack.

Alone, she sucked in another breath, tried to think ra-
tionally. Five hours. More than enough time for Valenti to
know she was missing. Her spirits plummeted. Because she
knew it would be yet another reason to confirm he was right
to write her off.

Maybe this was what was required for him to wash his
hands of her completely? To absolve himself of all responsibility?

Lotte swallowed down the lump of self-pity and looked
around.

The back doors were on child lock when she tried the
handle, but he hadn't locked the front. Dragging herself upright, she half sobbed in thanks that he hadn't tied her legs.

Without a second thought, she threw herself into the gap
between the seats, relief surging when the door opened at
her push. She shoved it further and dove through it, yelp-

ing when she landed roughly on her hip. Ignoring the stab of agony, she clambered up and raced from the car and the dwelling that didn't look much more than a hunter's shack.

Terror tore through her at the angry bellow behind her. She didn't look back.

The road leading away from the shack was dark and unpaved. Rocks dug into her bare feet as she fled, blind in the inky darkness.

All too soon she heard pounding footsteps.

The sob she'd tried to stem finally broke through, tears blurring her vision. Angrily she blinked them away. She wouldn't let him catch her.

She wouldn't. She wouldn't.

Her frantic thought screeched to a halt as headlights flared to life, in front of her.

She screamed.

Then the world turned upside down.

In the agonising seconds it took for his brain to connect with his feet, Valenti sat behind the wheel of his SUV, frozen in terror.

After roaming the Cartanian countryside for six hours, the sight of Lotte barefoot, running for her life, was almost too much to assimilate.

Perhaps she was a beautiful ghost come to haunt him.

Her scream tore him from his stupor. Just in time for him to watch her tumble head over heels, landing in a heap six feet from the front of his bumper.

Por favor, Dios. Por favor. Por favor.

He was reciting, pleading with the Almighty as he almost tore the door off its hinges to get to her, peripherally registering his team wrestling down the man who should've been behind bars, awaiting trial for stalking the woman Valenti loved. The man some corrupt judge had set free on bail in the middle of the night ten days ago and managed to keep secret from the authorities through a series of fraudulent paperwork. A criminal and judge Valenti swore to destroy if it was the last thing he did.

He stumbled to where Lotte lay winded, her chest rising and falling with gulping sobs until it stilled when her eyes landed on him.

More tears filled her eyes. She blinked them away, but fresh ones surged.

'Valenti?' she whispered.

His hands shook frantically as he reached for her, cutting the ropes binding her wrists. '*Sí*, it's me, *litla*.' He barely recognised his own voice. Barely recognised the man he'd been before that race to Reykland weeks ago. The man who'd been filled with guilt and duty and so much self-righteous bitterness he could perform three dozen TED Talks on it and not run out of subject matter.

And all for what? So he could remain on that lofty perch of sanctimonious hubris? Where everyone could point to his life-long sacrifice as a beacon of piety to be followed? While he remained silent and anguished and deeply alone?

'Are you hurt?' he asked uselessly. Because of course she was hurt. Physically, no doubt. But definitely emotionally. Because hadn't he also made everyone around him suffer, if only by making them feel inferior to his mighty self-sacrifice?

Even his mother had learned to pick her moments around him very carefully after he'd returned home after Helga's death, not wanting to be seen to be vilifying Cartana's superhero in case she angered the palace and had her privileges revoked.

He'd secretly welcomed and celebrated that position, silently said nothing as the majority of her vitriol was redirected to his twin.

Oh yes, he had a lot to be ashamed about.

But most of the reparations were owed to the beautiful creature lying on her back in the dirt at his feet. His heart. His precious soul.

'N-nothing that won't heal, eventually. I hope,' she said, her voice shaken. Soft. Warm despite everything she'd been through. 'You came for me.'

A thick, pain-filled rumble swelled in his chest. 'Too late. Far too late, *litla.*'

She started to shake her head, then winced. The rumble tore free. Charging him into scooping her up carefully. Oh so carefully. His whole body wracked in tremors as he strode to his SUV.

A bodyguard hurried to throw the back door open.

Valenti climbed in and tucked her into his lap, his senses screaming when he saw the gashes and grazes on her beautiful skin.

'Take us to the hospital. Now,' he barked at the driver. To the head of his security who stood at the window, he snarled, 'Him you take to the palace dungeon. Keglar will face Cartanian justice. Is that understood?'

The car was moving before his man executed his salute.

His Adam's apple bobbed convulsively as he stared back down at her. With a groan torn from his soul, he buried his face in her hair. 'Forgive me. *Por favor.* Forgive me.'

Her fingers curled around his nape, dug in, holding him. Always holding him closer than he deserved. 'There's no need—'

'No, there's every need,' he insisted. 'I minimised everything you said, everything you felt because...' He paused, the weight of it too much to handle. 'For the first time in my life, I met a challenge I couldn't overcome. This thing...this beautiful thing you shoved in front of me and forced me to acknowledge. It terrified me when it shouldn't have. It was why I reacted the way I did when you came here three years ago. Why I've been running since.'

Her head slowly lifted. 'What are you saying, Valenti?'

'What you said at the palace…at the cabin, it was all true. I have been hiding behind my guilt and my tragedy and my bitterness. It was…safer that way.' A mirthless smile twitched his lips. 'I will move mountains so you never find out, but I can attest that people will leave you alone when they believe you live permanently in a state of pious sorrow and miserable self-sacrifice.'

She was shaking her head. 'But no more? Please, Valenti, no more. Helga would've hated for you to live your life like that in her name.'

'I know. A week and a half with you in a cabin brought more colour and bliss into my life than the previous three decades, Lotte.' He buried his face in her shoulder once more, breathing her in simply because she was life. A life he'd almost thrown away.

'Do you…do you still want to be left alone?' A sheen of tears filmed her eyes again. 'Because I can't bear to hope for…anything if you—'

'I need you, *litla*,' he confessed in a raw rasp, shaking his head at the sheer simplicity of it now he knew. Now he recognised that no alternative would do. 'To keep me living. To keep me sane. To remind me of the beauty in the world.'

The motorcade screamed into the courtyard of the private state-of-the-art royal hospital and relief poured through him. But when he went to step out, she stopped him.

'I can't go in, Valenti. Not until you tell me…not until I know.'

He stared into her beautiful blue eyes and swallowed. 'No more hesitation, Lotte. No more hiding. I love you. So very much. I'm yours.' A breath shuddered out of her. 'As arrogant as it sounds, I've been yours since Helga implored me to keep you safe. I intended to keep that promise long after you'd turned twenty-five. But now I intend to keep you as my wife. My lover. The mother of my children. If you'll have me?' He leaned in close and brushed the tip of her nose with his. 'I should also add that I will set you free if you wish it, but you will never be free of me. So really, it's in your best interest to—'

Soft, lean fingers brushed over his mouth, stopping his words. 'I believe you. Even the arrogant part. Which is why it helps that I love you too.' More tears spilled from her eyes, and he brushed them away the better to see the emotions surging free. 'You will never need to set me free, Valenti. I'm right where I want to be. With you. Loving you. Forever.'

The surge took hold of him then too, and everything and everyone, including the team of doctors who waited impatiently beyond the doors, faded away. '*Dios mío*. I love you, Lotte.'

Her throat moved. 'I'm so glad you're mine, Valenti. I hoped and prayed...'

He anointed her gift of love with a kiss drawn deep from his soul, the place he now recognised had been feeding him the sacred emotion all along. And when they came up for air, he braced his forehead against hers. 'We have to go inside now, *mi amor*. I have to make sure you're well.'

She looked from him to the hovering team, a small, breathtaking smile curving her lips. 'I'll come inside only because I know you won't rest until I do. But I have a feeling we'll leave here with a little more than we've bargained for, Prince Valenti.'

True enough, once her cuts and bruises had been thoroughly tended to and her blood tests came back with no adverse effects, Lotte took his hand. Valenti's breath caught at the near-celestial happiness in her eyes.

'Is there anything else, doctor?' she asked without taking her eyes off him.

The petite female doctor looked up from her notes, her professional demeanour slipping into a wide smile.

'Oh yes. Your Highness, Miss Lillegard, please allow me to be the first to congratulate you both. You're going to be parents.'

Valenti was on his knees, attempting to withstand the unrelenting waves of happiness drowning him when his brothers and their wives walked in.

Still dumbfounded, he allowed Lotte, the love of his life and the mother of his unborn child, to give them the news.

He kept swallowing, his eyes riveted on her, only her, as his brothers clasped his shoulders and enthusiastically gave their own congratulations.

'I feel like a toast about wild oats and mommy issues is called for right about now,' Teo muttered.

'No, *hermano*. It isn't. It really, truly is not,' Azar groaned.

They all broke into laughter.

And as Valenti finally rose to gather his heart into his arms, he knew the life of suffering and guilt was behind him.

Only love existed in his future with Lotte.

* * * * *

MILLS & BOON ®

Coming next month

GREEK BOSS TO HATE
Michelle Smart

Footsteps approached.

Draco dragged a breath in through his nose, inhaling the soft scent of her perfume, and braced himself before turning to face her.

'You've tidied up,' Athena said brightly, as if nothing had happened, as if she hadn't just cruelly insulted his mother and he hadn't cruelly rammed some home truths down her throat.

'Someone had to.'

She shrugged. 'Not much point in keeping it tidy or unpacking. I'll be out of here soon.'

His mind unwittingly zipped to her bedroom. If he'd had to imagine it, he'd have pictured it like a witch's coven, not the soft, feminine, spotlessly clean room that it was. 'Not for another two months.'

'You'll have sacked me by then.'

'No.' He drilled his stare into her. 'That is not going to happen. You are going to spend the next two months tied to my side. By the time you're released from the contract, you'll be as sick of me as I am of you. Now, drink your coffee. We need to get going—we've got a long day of work to do.'

Continue reading

GREEK BOSS TO HATE
Michelle Smart

Available next month
millsandboon.co.uk

COMING SOON!

We really hope you enjoyed reading this book.
If you're looking for more romance
be sure to head to the shops when
new books are available on

Thursday 18th December

To see which titles are coming soon, please visit
millsandboon.co.uk/nextmonth

MILLS & BOON

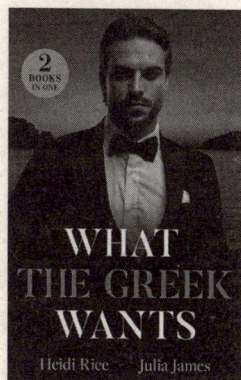

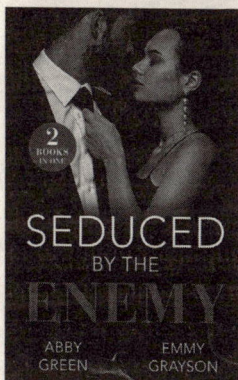

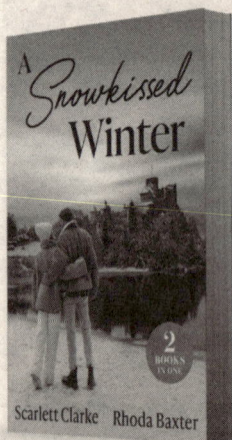

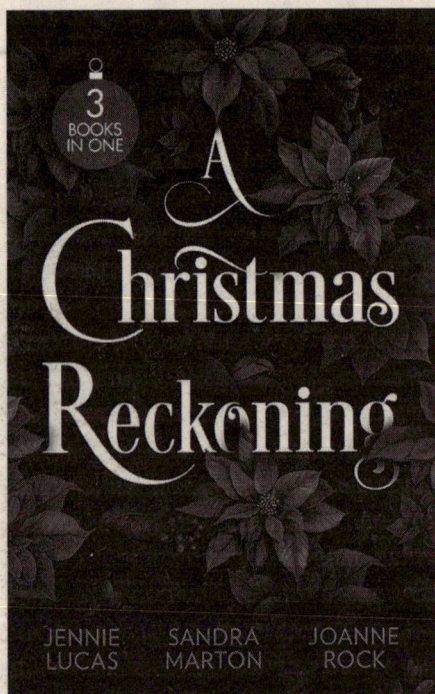

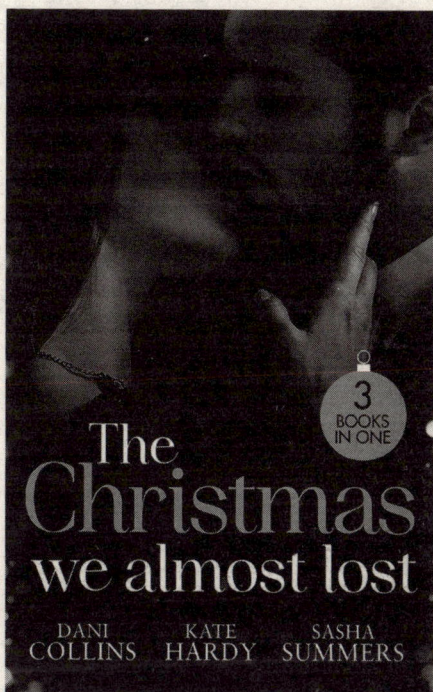

LET'S TALK

Romance

For exclusive extracts, competitions and special offers, find us online:

[f] MillsandBoon

[X] @MillsandBoon

[O] @MillsandBoonUK

[♪] @MillsandBoonUK

Get in touch on 01413 063 232

For all the latest titles coming soon, visit
millsandboon.co.uk/nextmonth